D0271584

THE THIEF-TAKER

Also by Janet Gleeson

Non-fiction

The Arcanum

The Moneymaker

Fiction

The Grenadillo Box

The Serpent in the Garden

JANET GLEESON

BANTAM PRESS

LONDON · TORONTO · SYDNEY · AUCKLAND · JOHANNESBURG

TRANSWORLD PUBLISHERS
61–63 Uxbridge Road, London W5 5SA
a division of The Random House Group Ltd

RANDOM HOUSE AUSTRALIA (PTY) LTD
20 Alfred Street, Milsons Point, Sydney,
New South Wales 2061, Australia

RANDOM HOUSE NEW ZEALAND LTD
18 Poland Road, Glenfield, Auckland 10, New Zealand

RANDOM HOUSE SOUTH AFRICA (PTY) LTD
Endulini, 5a Jubilee Road, Parktown 2193, South Africa

Published 2004 by Bantam Press
a division of Transworld Publishers

A catalogue record for this book is available from the British Library.
ISBN 0593 052609

Typeset in 11/12½pt Goudy by
Falcon Oast Graphic Art Ltd.

Printed in Great Britain by
Clays Ltd, Bungay, Suffolk

1 3 5 7 9 10 8 6 4 2

Papers used by Transworld Publishers are natural, recyclable products made from wood grown in sustainable forests. The manufacturing processes conform to the environmental regulations of the country of origin.

For Paul.

Chapter One

AGNES MEADOWES FIRST SAW THE GIRL ONE MONDAY MORNING, huddled in a doorway in Foster Lane. She was no more than twelve or thirteen; her feet were bare, her hair lank, and apart from a bright-crimson shawl wrapped about her head, her costume was ragged and colourless with dirt.

But there was nothing remarkable about the sight of a beggar loitering in the streets of London in 1750. And in any case, Agnes had more important matters on her mind. As cook for the Blanchards of Foster Lane, her mind was occupied with ragout, and where to find the best green angelica for Mrs Tooley the housekeeper's syllabub, and how much Rose and Doris, her kitchen maid and scullery maid, would get done while she was out.

Despite all this, Agnes found her attention drawn by the girl, who was sitting as still as stone, her bony knees pressed up to her pinched face, her eyes fixed on the Blanchards' doorway. The shawl reminded Agnes of the one her husband had given her on their wedding day, and she shivered involuntarily at the recollection. Agnes rarely succumbed to fancy, but something about the girl, sitting alone surveying the street, struck a chord. She felt a moment of sympathy, mingled with suspicion.

But a few minutes later she had reached the market and was busy battling through the throng and making herself heard above the crowd. She stepped over rotting offal and cabbage leaves to prod breasts of pheasant and partridge. She sniffed oysters and herrings and asked the price of oranges, shouting her requirements over strident cries of 'New mackerel!', 'White turnips and fine carrots, ho!' and 'Fine China oranges and fresh juicy lemons!' She watched a juggler with blackened teeth catching knives in his mouth, then sampled a corner of gingerbread so spicy tears welled in her eyes. And the street child slipped from her thoughts.

Within the hour, Agnes had arranged deliveries with half a dozen tradesmen whose goods she could not carry, and jotted every item and its price in her notebook for Mrs Tooley's accounts. In her basket she had stowed, with the utmost care, sweet oranges, Jordan almonds, two dozen pullet eggs, a pickled salmon, half a pound of angelica, the same of glacé cherries. As she retraced her steps, the market's chaos receded, but her mind whirled with all there was to do. At the very least, Rose should have skinned and jointed the hare, plucked and drawn the pheasant, and (provided Philip had not distracted her unduly) begun to grind the sugar for Mrs Tooley's desserts.

Agnes turned from Cheapside into Foster Lane and approached the railings that lined the steps to her basement kitchen. Once again, she was wrenched from her musings. The girl was exactly where she had been earlier. Unaware of Agnes observing her, she had her eyes fixed on the first-floor windows of the Blanchards' silver workshop.

Suddenly, she seemed to sense Agnes's presence, and turned and caught her gaze. Lank tresses of hair emerging from the shawl partially covered her face. Behind them, Agnes detected a pair of eyes that were curiously disturbing: upturned and slanted, the whites very white, the pupils large and dark. Instinct told Agnes that the girl was up to no good. She showed every sign of being a cutpurse or some rogue's accomplice. Agnes would be well advised to keep clear of her. But the girl's limbs were thin as rope, her toes were blacker than crows and she was plainly in need of nourishment – and since Agnes regarded nourishment as a matter of the utmost importance, this disturbed her. Moreover, Agnes had a child of her own, a boy by the name of Peter, whom owing to her position as cook she saw infrequently. This filthy scrawny girl was some years older than her own boy, but she brought Peter to her thoughts.

Agnes was thinking of her son when the door behind the girl opened and a maidservant with a broom darted out. 'Get away with you, vermin!' she bellowed, thrusting the broom as if it were a sword. 'Don't think you'll get anything by begging.'

The broom whacked the girl in the small of her back. She fell forward, then scrambled to her feet. 'I didn't mean no harm,' she squawked, rubbing her back. 'I wasn't doing nothing wrong.'

'You was dirtying my step,' said the maid, still waving her broom, 'and Gawd knows what more besides. So scram, unless you want another feel of the hard end of this.'

'All right, I'm going,' said the girl, raising her hands and sidling away.

'Good riddance.' The maid gave the step a brisk once-over before retreating and slamming the door.

Agnes understood the maid's concerns. She was no more in the habit of defending beggars than dancing a jig, but something in the girl's demeanour, coupled with her own thoughts, impelled her forward. 'One moment, if you please,' she said, hurriedly coming up and rolling three farthings from her purse onto her palm.

'What?' said the girl, then spying the coins in Agnes's hand she added more politely, 'I ain't done *you* no harm.'

'Did someone ask you to wait?'

The girl looked from Agnes's hand to her face. 'No.'

'Then what are you doing?'

The girl said nothing, but Agnes noticed her eyes scouring the street. Holding her purse in one hand, she tentatively stretched forward the other, offering the coins to the girl on the flat of her palm, as if she were feeding a horse that might bite. The girl snatched them away, scratching Agnes's palm slightly in her haste. 'My pa's coming,' she muttered.

'But you have been here some time. Where is he? Has he employment in the vicinity?' Agnes waved towards the Blanchards' grand shop window, which glittered behind stout iron bars with a choice display of silver salvers, dishes, cups and candlesticks.

'He does business around here.'

Agnes's curiosity was roused. Still clutching her purse, she took an orange from her basket and lifted it to her face to sniff it, regarding the girl from behind the curve of the fruit. 'What manner of business?'

The girl gazed at the orange, then glanced over her shoulder. 'He fetches things for people.'

The description sounded most ominous. Agnes paused. What foolhardy impulse had possessed her to engage such a person in conversation and give her coins? The girl must think her soft in the head. At best, she had shown her that sitting in doorways was a feasible means of making a living. At worst, the girl might even now be signalling to her father to creep up and rob her.

The girl was still peering down the street when Agnes observed a sharpening in her expression. Turning apprehensively to follow her gaze, she observed a cluster of foppish gentlemen watching a pair of ladies descend from a carriage. Beyond them, the figure of a man clad in a long dun-coloured coat and tricorn hat could just be glimpsed. Agnes looked back at the girl, then pointed at the lurking figure. 'Is that your father?'

No sooner had she uttered these words than she felt a grab of surprising swiftness and force. The orange and purse were whisked from her grasp. 'Wait!' she spluttered as the girl ran off, away from the man who had distracted Agnes. But it was already too late. She had rounded the corner and gone.

'Trouble, Mrs Meadowes? Want me to chase after her?' called John, the first footman, loudly from the top step of the Blanchard residence. With powdered hair, dressed in his blue and gold livery and buckled shoes, he stood to attention, waiting to accompany Nicholas Blanchard, who always took a stroll to the coffee house at this hour of the morning. A flash in John's eye and a small tick at the corner of his mouth betrayed his amusement at the events he had just witnessed. As a rule, Agnes found John agreeable. He was sharp-witted, discreet and generally respectful, and not prone to lewdness – unlike certain others she could mention. But she disliked being the subject of mirth, especially when the servant in question was a footman. She prayed that John had not seen the girl take her purse, and thanked heaven that she had been robbed after rather than before her trip to market. The purse had only had a shilling and sixpence in it, but to Agnes this seemed small consolation for the damage to her pride.

She bustled towards the steps, shooting him a reproachful glance. 'Thank you, John,' she said with what dignity she could muster. 'I am in no need of assistance. I was about to give her the fruit, in any case.'

John nodded slowly, his eyes still gleaming. ''Course you was, Mrs Meadowes. By the by, would it cheer you to know the post boy just brought a letter for you? I left it with Mrs Tooley.' He tapped the side of his nose as if sharing a secret. 'Sender's from Twickenham. Who's that, then? Rare you get correspondence, ain't it?'

Agnes felt her stomach pitch. Twickenham was where her son Peter boarded with a certain Mrs Catchpole, who rarely troubled to write. Heaven forbid some misfortune had befallen him.

At that moment, Nicholas Blanchard appeared on the threshold twirling a silver-topped cane. 'Ready, John,' he declared. As he spoke, he observed that his first footman was engaged in conversation with his cook. A sudden alteration to the angle of his bushy eyebrows and a tightening of his jaw betrayed his disapproval of this state of affairs. He was poised to pass some remark, but Agnes had no wish to add to her humiliation. She dropped a curtsey, eyes lowered, then, clutching her basket of provisions like a shield, she scuttled down the basement steps.

*

The kitchen, which was Agnes's domain, had an uneven flagged floor and was lit by three high-set sash windows that were regularly scoured with vinegar and water to keep them clear. An open iron range with bread ovens and warming cupboards threw out such scorching heat that anyone approaching it turned redder than cayenne pepper. In a capacious dresser, the tools of Agnes's trade – pots and dishes, utensils and cutlery – were neatly stored. In front stood a long deal table, its surface pitted and scarred by ancient food stains and years of chopping.

Agnes carefully set down her provisions upon this table, next to a dish of jointed hare. She gazed distractedly around the kitchen, then enquired, 'Where might Mrs Tooley be?'

'Having a lie down – she's been taken strange,' said Rose, the kitchen maid, a slender yet buxom, attractive brown-haired girl, emerging from the larder bearing a large cod by the gills. 'She's got one of her distempers coming.'

Doris, the scullery maid, looked up from the bucket of potatoes she was peeling. 'She don't wish to be disturbed,' she added slowly, as if finding the words cost her considerable effort. 'Not 'less it's urgent.'

Rose slapped down the fish impatiently at the far end of the table. 'And she said to tell you to finish off the dessert. Only the orange cream – there's a jar of plums left out, and the apple pie from yesterday will do.'

Agnes suppressed a sigh; it did not do to reveal disgruntlement to those beneath her, in case it encouraged them to do the same. 'Did she say anything about a letter?'

Doris raised her plump face and tried to puff away a stiff carrot-coloured lock, without success. 'Don't recall. Did she, Rose?' she asked, shaking her head as a question mark of peel fell into her bucket.

'Only that she'd keep it safe till after your duties was finished,' replied Rose. 'She said you wouldn't have a moment before.'

Agnes had grown accustomed to ignoring her private

concerns in order to maintain the harmony of the household. She told herself firmly there was no reason to suppose anything was wrong. The letter might contain nothing more ominous than a list of what Mrs Catchpole wanted for Peter the next time Agnes visited. She walked to the side of the dresser. Hanging on a hook was a slate, with the menu chalked upon it in her own hand:

First course: almond soup, white fricassée, boiled cod.
Second course: chicken patties, jugged hare, roast venison, oyster loaves, mushrooms, cauliflower pickle.
Dessert: apple tart, orange cream, plums in syrup.

Under normal circumstances, Mrs Tooley should have taken care of the dessert, while Agnes should have done the rest, with the help of Rose and Doris. But at sixty-two years of age, Mrs Tooley's health was growing fragile and she was prone to sudden contagions. When she took a turn for the worse, it was her habit to wash her head with salt, vinegar and a spoonful of brandy, and lie in her darkened bedchamber, sipping an infusion of aniseed and opium until she fell into a deep sleep.

Mrs Tooley's condition invariably improved, but that might not be for several hours. In the meantime, Agnes would have to perform her culinary duties. Not that the task of making dessert was beyond her. Depositing the slate on the table, Agnes opened the middle drawer of the kitchen table and extracted a plump volume of handwritten recipes, bound in crimson cloth.

She had begun to compile this important record five years ago, when she first came to the Blanchards' house as undercook to the French chef. The household was one of middling size and means, with less than a dozen servants, but the family aspired to meals that could rival those in grander houses. Agnes had been a competent cook, having run a modest house for her husband, and although she had not had the least knowledge of foreign ways or sauces, she had known enough to comprehend that French cooking was greatly superior to traditional fare. Being ambitious and eager to secure her future for her son's sake, she had observed, questioned and deciphered all the chef deigned tell her in his heavily accented English, and had listed everything here. Now Agnes flicked through the pages of her recipe book with the ease of someone who recognizes the contents of every page. Written in her meticulous hand, it began with soups, continued with fish, progressed to roasting and boiling and then branched into all manner of fancy fricandos, ragouts, pies, puddings and desserts.

A year ago, after a barrage of angry shouting in the butler's parlour, the French chef had been dismissed. No one knew precisely why until Mr Matthews the butler, after a glass too many, let it slip. A missing half-barrel of port had led him to discover a significant discrepancy between the stock in the cellar and the accounts from the vintner. Agnes and Mrs Tooley – who was jittery as a sparrow at the slightest alteration or upset – had been obliged to make do until a replacement could be found.

But instead of the mayhem Mrs Tooley had feared, the chef's dismissal had caused the kitchen to run more smoothly. Pigeon pies, forced calves' heads and tongues roasted the French way were discovered to be all well within Agnes's capabilities. And while Agnes was satisfied with a salary of forty pounds a year, a replacement French chef would demand twice that sum. A lengthy conference had been held between Mr Matthews, Mrs Tooley and Lydia Blanchard. Agnes had been promoted permanently to the post of household cook. A new kitchen maid, Rose, had been engaged to assist her. And Mrs Tooley, assuming she was well, turned her hand to making dessert.

Agnes knew almost every recipe from the first two courses by heart, but thought it wise to glance again at the page for orange cream, so as to make it precisely as Mrs Tooley would wish. She glanced at the appropriate page, reassuring herself of the simplicity of the additional task. Then her attention returned to the dish of hare. To be properly tender it would need a good two hours' simmering. She told Doris to bring her the stone jug. 'Is this seasoned yet?' she enquired of Rose.

The girl was haphazard when it came to crucial matters such as pepper, salt and mace.

'Lord, no, Mrs M.,' said Rose unashamedly. 'It slipped my thoughts.'

Rose, Agnes noticed, had a purplish bruise on her cheek, and her eyes looked feverishly bright. But these oddities did not concern her as much as her manner of working. Rose ought to have grated more sugar – Agnes was certain there was not enough in the bowl. The girl was now slicing the cod into uneven steaks. 'Not too thick with those,' she said sternly. 'Try and keep them the same size. And mind you butter the dish well so they don't stick. And wash your hands after, or you'll taint anything else you touch.'

Rose raised an eyebrow in the direction of the butler's pantry, where Philip the second footman was standing at the lead-lined sink, cleaning knives. 'You've no need to tell me that, Mrs Meadowes,' she said pertly. 'It's not as if I haven't done it before.'

Nettled by this insubordination and Philip's winking reply, Agnes felt herself flush. She shot Rose a look before turning to the hare. She seasoned it, set it in the jug with herbs, bacon, a blade of mace, an onion stuck with cloves, two wineglasses of port, a tablespoonful of currant jelly and a covering of thin broth, and put it on the heat. Then she moved on to the orange cream. Being fastidious in culinary matters – why estimate and run the risk of being wrong, when you might measure and always be exact? – she began by taking out her balance and weighing the sugar which Rose had ground. As she had suspected, it was a fraction short.

'What delights you knocking up for us today then, Mrs M.?' asked Philip, peering over her shoulder. Something tasty. Make an extra serving for me, will you?'

Agnes disliked the feel of Philip's breath on her neck, but was chiefly preoccupied by her irritation with Rose. She sidestepped away from him, pushed the bowl towards Rose and, managing to keep the tremor from her voice, requested that she grate two ounces more sugar. Rose, with a sullen look that

Agnes affected not to notice, stamped off to the larder to fetch the sugarloaf.

Agnes watched her go with a measure of disquiet. Rose's deficiencies were becoming difficult to ignore; she ought to upbraid her more than she did. She ought to find out how she came by that bruise. She was not slow to tick Doris off when she found her work wanting. Why then was Rose a different matter?

She knew the unpalatable answer to this question perfectly well, although she disliked admitting it to herself. Six months had passed since an episode so branded upon Agnes's memory that she still had not erased it. She had gone to the larder to fetch a brace of partridge, but had discovered instead something shockingly unexpected. There was Rose, head thrown back, eyes half closed, skirts and petticoats rucked up, moaning and groaning in ecstasy, between a round of Cheshire cheese and a hogshead of molasses. There was Philip, breeches undone, buttocks bare, pressed against her. Both had been entirely unconscious of Agnes's presence. Overwhelmed, scalded by embarrassment, Agnes had not known what to do. Should she have coughed, or shouted, or dropped something? Should she have thrown a bucket of water over them? Instead, she had tiptoed away before they noticed her and brooded for hours over how to reprimand them. Eventually, having reached no decision, she had said nothing at all.

Ever since that encounter, she had found reprimanding Rose impossible. Agnes knew now that she should chastise the girl for her cheek, yet the memory of the larder still lingered and she found herself unable to do so.

Chapter Two

THAT SAME MONDAY, HARRY DRAKE ROSE IN HIS DANK CELLAR home, which nestled between a grain store and a ship's chandler, close to Pickle Herring Quay. He was alone. Elsie, his daughter, had risen before dawn to attend to his business and would not return for several hours. Later in the day, he would call on her to ensure all was well and she was doing as he ordered.

Without troubling to wash or shave, Harry Drake dressed himself in his finest: a dun cloth coat with pewter buttons, snatched from the back of an open carriage; buckskin breeches, lifted from the bedchamber of a cove who had taken so much port he never stirred a muscle; and a linen shirt, yanked from a washing line in Fetter Lane. He squinted in a shard of looking glass at his swarthy face, with its droopy eyes and crooked nose, then took up a broken tortoiseshell comb, raked his stringy hair flattish and secured it with a frayed ribbon. Telling himself he now looked quite the gentleman, he secreted in various pockets about his person a gold pocket watch, a silver snuff box, and a notebook containing details of amorous rendezvous between an eminent baron and a lady who was not his wife. This done, he gave a final admiring glance at his reflection before emerging from his lair and clambering up a flight of rotten stairs.

On the wharf, Harry stood and looked about him. The light on the river was yellowish and the tide was high – choppy brown water lapped over the wharf in parts. Over his head, gulls wheeled and cried and dipped, gusted by the wind. Harry Drake sniffed the air and felt a drop or two of rain sting his cheek. There was a storm coming. He smiled to himself, then thrusting his hands in his pockets he prowled away and disappeared into the city streets.

By the time the bells of St Dunstan's pealed five and the sun sank behind the rooftops of Blackfriars, Harry Drake's business was, by and large, satisfactorily concluded. In place of the valuables, his pockets now contained two gold sovereigns and two silver shillings. His earlier prediction of an impending storm had been correct: the quickening wind flogged his back. But the storm had not yet properly arrived, and nor had the dark hour for which he waited. Until then, he decided to pass the time pleasurably. First, he required food; a meat pudding and gravy was what he fancied. And afterwards, perhaps a sating of a different kind – a visit to Dolly's in Cheapside. With this pleasurable timetable settled in his mind, Harry Drake headed homeward.

It was twilight by the time he descended the steep stairs with careful footsteps, so that the rotten wood did not creak and betray his presence. He opened the door in a slow, furtive manner, like a man who wishes to see what lies within before he is observed. There was no window in the cellar. The only light was afforded by the stubs of three tallow candles ranged on a wooden board in the middle of a circular table. Through the smoky glow it was just possible to make out the figure of his daughter, Elsie, with her crimson woollen shawl wrapped about her shoulders. She was sitting by the hearth with a broken wicker basket at her side. The opening door caused a gust within, which caused the candles to flicker and Elsie to flinch and look round. Seeing her father's skulking shadow at the entrance, she nodded mutely and returned to her occupation.

She was building the fire, as she always did at this hour, whatever the season, for warmth never penetrated here. Piece by piece she picked out morsels of coal and wood from her basket, wiped them to remove the worst of the mud, then stacked them in the fireplace as delicately as if she were constructing a house of cards. When the mound was high enough, she ignited it by means of a splint lit from one of the candles, then puffed until her head was dizzy and the first hesitant flames began to lick through the black pyre.

While Elsie was thus occupied, Harry Drake took up a horsehair blanket from his bed and wrapped it about him for warmth. He watched his daughter's painstaking efforts, his temper mounting as his belly growled. The minute the flames took hold, Elsie sat back on her heels. 'Leave off that! I want food – now,' ordered Harry. He thrust a shilling towards her. 'Go to the chophouse. Get me a mutton pudding and a quart of ale. Straight back, no dawdling mind, 'less you want a leathering.' Elsie nodded wordlessly, took the coin and scurried off.

Ten minutes later she was back, jug in one hand, steaming pudding in the other. She banged them on the table and clattered about to find crockery and a spoon. Harry filled his tankard and gulped down the ale, then wiped the spoon on his shirtsleeve and plunged it into the heart of the pudding. A cascade of suet pastry, fat, gristly meat and gravy oozed over the plate. Salivating with anticipation, Harry heaped his spoon high and crammed its dripping contents into his mouth. He chewed, gulped, drank and refilled his mouth several times more before his eye strayed from his dish to his daughter. She had resumed her position squatting by the fire. 'Where's your dish, girl?' he said. 'Fetch it quick, or you'll go hungry.'

Elsie scrambled to her feet. She took a pewter saucer and a chipped stoneware mug down from the mantel shelf and tendered them hesitantly to her father. She watched unblinking while he pared off a sliver of pudding and congealed gravy, spooned it onto her saucer, half filled her mug with ale and thrust both towards her. He was sitting on the only chair in the place, so she perched on an upturned coal bucket to eat.

'So,' said Harry Drake presently, when there was no morsel left of the pudding. 'See anything today?'

Elsie shrugged. 'Nothing different. I was there by six. Shop opened at seven-thirty by one of the apprentices. The two journeymen was there soon after. The gentleman from next door came round eight.'

Harry Drake nodded, but then his brows knitted. 'When I happened by, I caught sight of you talking with someone, then running off. What was that about?'

'Nothing much.'

'I'll be the judge of that.'

Elsie thought of Agnes, of the pie she had bought with her coins, and of the purse still secreted in her pocket and the snatched orange she had eaten, rind, pips and all. She opened her eyes earnestly. 'Wasn't no lady. Only a servant going at me for sitting on her step.'

'Not a servant of the Blanchards?'

'No, Pa. I ain't careless. Nor stupid neither.'

Harry picked at his teeth with the point of his pocket knife. 'My business there will be done this night. Tomorrow get back to the river. We are low on fuel. And see what else you can find.'

Elsie nodded, holding the palms of her hands out to the fire to warm them. The flames were the same colour as the orange. Her mind was still distracted by the memory of it.

Chapter Three

GENERATIONS OF BLANCHARDS HAD LIVED AND WORKED IN Foster Lane. The grandly appointed shop had once been London's most fashionable silversmith, and the family house next door had been equally sumptuously adorned, for the Blanchards had always viewed themselves as being a cut above the craftsmen of other trades. At dinner, they ate off silver plate, with a dozen of the best beeswax candles burning in a pair of Corinthian-columned candelabra. This was no extravagance, claimed Nicholas Blanchard, the senior member of the family: a well-appointed dining table was not merely pleasurable, but canny business practice. Customers might be invited to dine. Nothing rivalled serving a perfectly roasted duck on a great oval platter, or a pyramid of syllabubs in trumpet vases, or pickles in scallop shells, to spur commissions.

Theodore Blanchard, Nicholas's only son, felt less certain of the need for display. A year ago, after much prevarication, Nicholas had handed him the running of the business. But when Theodore had looked over the accounts and order books, he had found that the seemingly thriving enterprise was far from being as profitable as his father had painted it. Trade in small silver was dire. With one notable exception – a gargantuan wine-cooler – no special commissions had been placed for months. Theodore had racked his brain to comprehend why business had dwindled, and what steps he might take to turn things round. He had instigated economies: limited his entertaining; ordered his wife Lydia, mistress of the household, to reduce the household expenditure and instruct the housekeeper to be prudent.

But when Nicholas got a whiff of these thrifty measures, he refused to comply. He questioned his son's pessimistic view of the accounts. If Blanchard's was less prosperous than hitherto, it could only be due to Theodore's inexperience and inefficiency. Perhaps Theodore would prefer his father to resume control. Meanwhile, whether there were three or thirty at table, he would see his tureens and platters set out, he would be reminded of what he had created.

On that particular late-January evening, there were no guests at the Blanchards' dark mahogany dining table; the family were dining alone. Theodore Blanchard took his seat between Nicholas and Lydia, while John the footman removed the domed lid of the tureen by its acorn finial, and ladled out the almond soup. Theodore's appetite was always formidable, and today was no exception. He slurped a spoonful, savouring the creamy sweetness, noting that Mrs Meadowes had expertly prevented the soup from curdling and had seasoned it to perfection with a mélange of nutmeg, pepper, bay and mace. Then he turned to his father. 'I wonder, sir, whether you have given further thought to our conversation a week ago?'

Nicholas Blanchard's gaunt, heavily lined face regarded his son. 'What was its subject?'

'Moving our business to a more fashionable part of the city,' said Theodore. 'As I made clear to you before, one reason our custom has dwindled is that the city has spread westward. Other craftsmen have begun to decamp. There are now several highly prosperous workshops in Soho.'

'And good luck to them,' replied Nicholas. 'Let them stay there – for rest assured, *I* shall not follow. Since time immemorial the craft has been centred on this very spot. Why should I want to move?'

He continued in the same vein as he had last week and the week before that, and on every other occasion that Theodore had proposed alteration of any kind. Ever since the Blanchards had arrived in this country, they had resided and worked in Foster Lane. The street lay at the heart of the profession that had established the family's fortune. Theodore had only to turn his head to the window to see that here stood the great Goldsmith's Hall; in the streets around – Cheapside, Gutter Lane, Carey Lane and Wood Street – craftsmen in gold and silver worked and prospered, as they had throughout the centuries.

Theodore gulped, jowls quivering, and discounted every word. 'That is all very well, Father, but nothing stays the same indefinitely. Fashions change, cities alter. The name of Blanchard is not held so high as it once was. If we do not acknowledge as much, and search for a remedy, our business will founder and land us bankrupt in the Fleet. It is my solid belief that trade would be greatly expanded if we considered moving west to one of the newer environs. Cavendish Square or St Martin's Lane, perhaps.'

Nicholas shook his head. 'What would be the purpose of decamping? So that each day hours are wasted in travelling to and from the hall for pieces to be stamped? So that we lose sight of our rivals and they gain the advantage on us?'

'We have received few sizeable commissions in the past months,' countered Theodore.

Unmoved, Nicholas fixed his steel-grey eyes on his son. 'What of Sir Bartholomew Grey's wine-cooler? The most valuable object we have ever made!'

'Yes sir, but that is the exception – and at the present time, in my opinion, it is unlikely to be repeated,' protested Theodore.

'How many other silversmiths can boast such a commission?' Nicholas dropped his knife and fork on his fish plate with a clatter, waving to John to remove it. 'I have said all I wish to on this matter, Theodore. You know my opinion. It is founded on thirty years' experience. Ignore it at your peril and do not expect it to change.'

Outside the wind had picked up and steady rain had begun to fall. Theodore could hear the wind flogging monotonously against the windows, rattling the sashes in their frames. He sat morosely, shoulders slumped. The footmen cleared away the dishes from the first course and replaced them with clean ones. Mr Matthews replenished the glasses with burgundy. Theodore tried to make conversation with his wife and consume a portion of jugged hare (usually one of his favourites) with a spoonful of cauliflower pickle. But either the hare was too rich or his appetite had been soured by his father's intransigence. And Lydia was not in a communicative mood. After replying to his enquiries after their children, she fell silent and offered no further conversation. He too was unable to think of anything more to say.

Theodore looked at his plate, at the parade of glittering silver dishes on the table and the haunch of venison congealing in a pool of gravy on the side table. He had been ravenous when he sat down, but the almond soup had disagreed with him. Now the very sight of so much food turned his stomach.

Chapter Four

THAT NIGHT, AS HARRY DRAKE HAD PREDICTED, A GALE BEGAN to blow. Such was its gusting intensity that the lanterns hanging outside the doorways of Foster Lane were all extinguished. A watchman was paid by various craftsmen to patrol the street and deter any villainy, but at two in the morning, reasoning that no villain would venture out, he ceded to the inclement conditions and decided to pass the rest of the night in his bed.

When the city bells chimed half past two, the moon was obscured by a cover of cloud. Thus no one saw Harry Drake step out of Dolly's whorehouse in Cheapside, where he had spent half a sovereign most enjoyably, and creep towards the shadows of Foster Lane. Along the way he darted into a passage and collected a cart, borrowed for the evening from a rag-dealing acquaintance. The cart was empty and easy to push, although the tempest hampered his pace. Some minutes later, Harry Drake reached the Blanchards' premises, where he had observed Elsie running off the day before. He left the cart stationed nearby, and huddled in a doorway opposite, his eyes fixed on the Blanchards' shop and his heart thumping in his chest. The wind eddied down the street, moaning like a dying man. But Harry Drake did not allow this thought to distract him. He was rapt in contemplation, recalling the information he had gleaned from his daughter, which conveniently supplemented what he had learned elsewhere.

There were three apprentices who slept in the basement of the shop, each of whom had a four-hour stint to watch the premises. The watches started at eight, twelve and four o'clock. The apprentice on duty was usually to be found sitting in the first-floor showroom, keeping guard over the most highly prized pieces of silver, including the one object for which Harry had come. He looked up at the three large windows that pierced the first-floor frontage. In one he discerned a yellowish dancing glow of candlelight and an indistinct form. This, Harry assumed, must be the apprentice keeping watch, seated in a chair. There were two hours to go until his colleague came to relieve him. What was he waiting for?

Harry Drake took a strip of black cloth from his pocket and wrapped it like a bandage over his nose and mouth, tying it behind his head so that only the slits of his eyes were visible. From another pocket he extracted a length of rope, which he wrapped several times about his fist. Then he dipped into his trouser band and brought out a long-bladed knife. Clutching this tightly, he stepped out from his cover.

On one side of the Blanchards' doorway lay a wide, bay-fronted shop window, but it was a narrower sash window at street level on the other side to which Harry Drake turned his attentions. He inserted the blade of his knife between the upper and lower sections of the frame. It was an easy matter to jiggle the blade and give it a swift twist so that the catch sprang back. Harry pushed up the sash, then, returning his knife to his pocket, took out a file. Having made quick work of a pair of iron bars, he flung his long legs over the sill and slid inside the Blanchards' downstairs showroom. It was so dark inside that even the silver objects were virtually invisible, but this did not unduly concern him. On other nights a pocketful of snuffboxes, ink stands or candlesticks might have held some interest for him, but tonight was different: these were not the prizes for which he had come.

For a moment, Harry Drake sat on the floor in the pitch

darkness to catch his breath and listen. Tension prickled in his spine. He began to unwind the rope from around his knuckles. If the apprentice upstairs had heard his entry there would be the sound of footsteps on creaking boards, and he would be ready. But save for the complaining groans of the gale, he detected no sound.

Harry Drake removed his hobnail boots and, holding them in one hand, inched forward silently. When he reached the corridor by the front door he put down his boots, then groped his way along the hallway. He slowly mounted the stairs, setting his feet as close as he could to the wall so that not a squeak should betray his presence. If the apprentice heard him he might wake the others, and then all would be lost and Harry would have to run for it. But Harry Drake was soundless as a mole and gave the apprentice no warning of his approach. At the top he paused. There were four doors leading off to the left and right of the landing, but he spied the tell-tale thread of candlelight beneath only one of them. He inched open the door. This was the most perilous moment. He must creep up on the apprentice and silence him before the boy had time to cry out.

The apprentice was seated on a chair before the dying embers of the fire. A burned-down candle stub flickered on a table beside him. Harry Drake squinted nervously at the boy's head, wondering how to approach. An instant later, a broad grin stretched across his face – wider than he had given all day. The apprentice's head had lolled forward limply; there could be no mistaking, he had fallen asleep on the watch. He could not have made the task any easier if he had tried.

Harry Drake did not dither for an instant. With the stealth of a pirate, in three strides he had gathered a turn of his rope about each fist and positioned himself directly behind the unsuspecting apprentice. He seized the crown of the boy's head and yanked it back so that his neck would be elongated for one swift twist of the rope.

Harry Drake expected a quick gurgle and a struggle. He did not anticipate the sight that confronted him. The apprentice's lips sagged open and his tongue protruded from the dark hole of his mouth, swollen and dark. His eyes were wide open and bulbous, as though something had surprised him. Something *had* surprised him. He was not sleeping. He was dead already, throat cut from ear to ear so deep that his windpipe was severed and his head hung on by no more than a few sinews.

Harry Drake was as astonished as the murdered apprentice must have been. He released his grip on the apprentice's head, but the sudden movement caused a new torrent of blood to spurt over the floor, as dark and thick as gravy. He was reminded of the pudding he had eaten earlier that night, and though he was not easily upset, his intestines writhed at the thought of it.

A moment later, these feelings were replaced by a different variety of agitation. If some other interloper had killed the man he had come to murder and rob, had his prize also been snatched before he got here? He moved away from the corpse, stepping over the pool of blood that was oozing wider as he watched. He picked up the candle stub from the table and held it aloft, anxiously surveying the silverware displayed about the room. His eyes flickered over all manner of chandeliers, dishes, tureens and ewers, only halting when they alighted on a hefty sideboard by the door. Alighted, rather, on what stood upon the sideboard: a massive oval vessel, over three feet long and two feet wide, as big as the copper basin his mother had used for boiling her washing. Only this was not a washing copper.

The object of Harry's attention was made of silver, adorned with mermaids, dolphins, tritons and a pair of stampeding horses dragging a naked Neptune from the foamy waves. It was Sir Bartholomew's wine-cooler; the most valuable item ever made in the Blanchard workshop; the largest piece of silver seen in the city of London for many a month; the prize that Harry Drake had come to steal.

He unbuttoned his coat and took from his inside pocket a length of sack cloth, which he laid over the wine-cooler, then tucked under each scalloped leg in turn, sighing pleasurably at the weight. The wine-cooler would take some lifting. It was as heavy, he reckoned, as Nelly the whore, who had clung about his waist earlier that night. Putting his hands under the cloth, he grasped the receptacle around Neptune's torso and a mermaid's breast, and, careless of whether or not the staircase creaked, hurried downstairs to the hallway. Having recovered his boots, he unbolted the door and opened it. Then, as brazenly as if he were Sir Bartholomew Grey himself, he picked up the wine-cooler once more and went out into the stormy street.

Chapter Five

LATER THAT SAME INCLEMENT NIGHT, ROSE FRANCIS EMERGED surreptitiously from the Blanchards' kitchen door into the darkness of Foster Lane. The gale still blew, but for several minutes her mind was so taken up with thoughts of the step she had just taken and the rendezvous ahead that she paid little attention to the wind or her surroundings. It was only when she reached Cheapside that the storm began to bother her. Her cloak billowed about, the lanterns on the shop frontages were all extinguished, sign boards swayed eerily in the wind, and clouds gusting across the moon made the street grow disconcertingly dark in the blink of an eye.

It was then, too, that she noticed the sound of footsteps a short distance behind her. Leather soles on cobbled streets, following the same route she had taken. There was no mistaking their unsettling presence.

She hesitated for an instant, clutching her valise and lantern, uncertain whether to turn and look or pretend she had heard nothing and proceed. Perhaps by some misfortune it was the watchman, whom she had hoped to avoid. The bells of St Paul's had recently chimed three. On this bitter night, at such an hour, she had expected to find the streets deserted. Had there been a links boy in the vicinity she might have hired his services. But, perhaps on account of the wildness of the night, there was none to be had. She was quite alone, apart from the person behind.

Unable to quell her curiosity, Rose turned to peer over her shoulder, holding her lamp aloft so the feeble light might pierce the gloom. As if to help, just then the clouds cleared and silver moonlight fell across the street. Some twenty yards behind, in the shadow of St Paul's, she thought she glimpsed a shape. She was unsure whether it was a man or a woman, but the figure seemed to be of large to middling build, and dressed in a cloak that flapped about like hers. It was not the watchman – the figure carried no lamp or torch of his own. But just at that moment, another cloud scudded over the moon and the figure melted into the dark. Thus her sighting was a fleeting estimation only. She had no real notion of who followed her.

Rose was, as a rule, immune from fears and fancy. She knew these streets, having spent the past year working as a kitchen maid to the Blanchards. She knew where she was headed – to a rendezvous in Southwark. And, being conscious of the perils of London streets at night, she had armed herself before setting out on her excursion. In her right pocket, tucked next to her purse, was a small pocket pistol with a silver-mounted handle.

When she had taken this weapon and stowed it in her pocket, she had felt excitement at her nerve, and not a glimmer of fear. Now, faced with a presence behind, she had a presentiment of danger that the pistol did nothing to dispel. Who was it? Please God let it not be one of the other servants from the house come chasing after her to bring her back. Surely that was not possible. When she had risen, the two other maids who shared her attic room had been sleeping peacefully in their beds. She had crept down the passage and back stairs, avoiding the basement corridor where the other servants slept. No one was up. No one could have observed her. No one knew her plan. Several hours would pass before any of them rose and began to question where she was.

And what would happen then? Mrs Tooley might be

summoned from her bed, work herself into a state and have to retire again. At the thought of the housekeeper sniffing her salts and flapping about in scrawny faced disgruntlement, Rose couldn't help smiling. Then a vision of Agnes flitted into her mind. She imagined the cook stirring her sauce or mixing her fricassée, growing a little pinker than usual with the heat from the fire. Agnes had always maintained her distance, requiring only that Rose perform her duties satisfactorily. But when Rose had been negligent, Agnes had hardly ever chastised her. Once or twice Rose had asked herself why this was, and grown remorseful for her lapses. More often, she misbehaved expressly to provoke Agnes. She had never properly succeeded, and recently this had spurred her on to worse behaviour. She had recounted her misdeeds afterwards with Philip and John, who disapproved, while delighting in the accounts. One of these days she would lose her post, Doris had droned. All of them were too dull-witted to see why she took such risks and was careless of Agnes's and Mrs Tooley's good opinion – she was leaving.

The footsteps distracted her. The persistent tread was still there. Was it her imagination or were the steps getting closer? Not wishing to turn again, Rose increased her pace, gripping the handle of her bag and her lantern, so that the leather bit into her palm and the light wavered about. What should she do? How should she throw him off? A few yards on, the foosteps still present and her anxiety mounting, an idea came to her. She could make a detour and head for the river. At any hour there were certain to be people about, and whatever the intentions of the person trailing her, he could pose no further threat.

Invigorated with new purpose, she directed her steps down Distaff Lane, a thoroughfare of overhanging clapperboard houses, all the while gathering speed, so that soon she was practically running. After several minutes, lungs aching, she stopped again and listened. There was no sound. She believed, in that instant, that her scheme had worked and she had lost her pursuer. But then the silence was interrupted; she heard the footsteps again, the tread seeming heavier and closer now than ever.

Rose Francis transferred her bag to the same hand as the lantern and, thrusting her free hand in her pocket, took out the pistol. With fingers that seemed oddly weak she flicked off the catch, then, turning abruptly right, slowed her pace. She felt cold perspiration gather on her face. She would confuse her pursuer into passing her. When he did so she would reveal her weapon, and, if necessary, she would use it.

But her pursuer failed to oblige. As if sensing a trap, he hung obstinately back in the overhang of a doorway. Rose edged forwards, the pistol gripped in her shuddering hand. She caught a glimpse of him lingering on the corner. Without pausing, she mustered all her energy and dashed in the opposite direction, into the first alley that she saw. She zigzagged wildly through the labyrinthine passages and streets leading to the river. But whichever way she chose, her pursuer seemed to anticipate. Every turn she made, there, inexorably, was his shadow.

The cobbles gave way to mud and Rose's costume hampered her. The wind was still fierce and the folds of her skirt and cloak tangled between her legs. From behind she still heard the thud of footsteps. Out of the corner of her eye she thought she saw a cloak and dark hat. Should she simply turn, aim and fire her pistol? Reason told her she should, but by now the instinct for flight had taken possession of her. She was unable to halt or do anything but clutch her possessions and continue running.

When she emerged breathlessly at Three Cranes Wharf, the clocks of St Mary Magdalene and St Austin's began to sound the hour with competing resonance. An oyster moon illuminated the river, and the wharfs and warehouses bordering its banks. The tide was low, and she could see the hulks of barges grounded on the muddy foreshore, lying strangely angled, but grey and flat as if drawn on an engraving.

Rose's eyes darted in every direction, searching for someone to assist her. There were fewer people than she expected. Nevertheless, she consoled herself, at least she was no longer entirely alone. A bald-headed man was slumped comatose in a doorway clutching a gin bottle to his breast. Another man wearing a greatcoat was stooped outside a warehouse, tying a barrel to a winch. Beyond, two figures sat hunched over a brazier, although whether these were male or female Rose could not tell. None of them appeared to notice her as she emerged from the alley at breakneck speed.

In the hope that the figures by the brazier might be watchmen, Rose cried out to them, but they seemed not to hear, remaining motionless and making no reply. She glanced back at the man with the barrel, only to see him disappearing into the warehouse. Directly in front of her were steps leading down to the foreshore. She sidestepped to the right, intending to head for the figures by the brazier.

Just then the winch with the barrel on it creaked and its chains rattled loudly. The sound pitched Rose into a panic and she let go of her lantern and bag, which dropped over the edge of the wharf. She heard them land with a heavy thud. Half crying, she hurried down the steps to recover them. She placed her foot tentatively on the soft mud of the foreshore, then lurched as her boots sank into the mud. She lost her footing and felt herself tumble forwards.

For a few seconds she lay sprawled there. Then, slowly, she gathered her senses and lifted her head. She glanced up, expecting to see her pursuer bearing down on her. But apart from the drunk, the wharf was now deserted.

Rose stumbled to her knees and then to her feet. She stood there in her sodden, ruined skirt, peering into the gloom, whirling around to check in every direction. It seemed that the person following her had vanished.

Her pulse began to subside and her breath came more evenly, but although the danger had apparently passed, remnants of terror lingered. Suppose he was still waiting in an alley, biding his time before making his attack? She thought for a moment. Her rendezvous was on the south side of the river, which meant crossing the bridge, a distance of half a mile from where she now stood. The tide being low, it would be possible to reach the bridge by keeping to the mud flats. This would be safer than returning to the streets, where her pursuer might be waiting for her.

Rose felt her courage return. She retrieved her belongings and picked her way over the mudflats in the direction of the bridge. A dark-cloaked figure emerged from an alley down which she had run and, clinging to the shadows, followed.

Chapter Six

THE NAME OF THE YOUNG APPRENTICE SO CALLOUSLY MURDERED that night was Noah Prout. At four o'clock, another of the Blanchards' three apprentices went to relieve his unfortunate colleague of his watch. On discovering the corpse and the great expanse of blood surrounding it, and observing that Sir Bartholomew Grey's precious wine-cooler was gone, he had hurried to raise the alarm. He roused his fellow apprentice, then charged next door and banged repeatedly on the Blanchards' kitchen door until his fist was raw and bleeding.

It was a good ten minutes before Mr Matthews arrived in his nightgown and nightcap to see what all the fuss was about. The butler's senses had been addled by sleep and several inches of port drained from the decanter, but the sudden blast of wind and debris that gusted in his face when he opened the door sobered him as effectively as a bucket of water to the head.

It took him a minute or two to decipher the apprentice's jumbled account of a nearly decapitated apprentice and missing wine-cooler. Mr Matthews then acted with the decisiveness that fifty years of service had taught him. The news was grave indeed, he declared. Grave enough to warrant rousing Theodore Blanchard from his bed.

Leaving the apprentice ashen and shivering in his parlour, Mr Matthews ascended to Theodore's room. He knocked discreetly on the door, then, hearing no response save raucous snoring, entered quietly so as not to disturb Lydia, who slept in the adjacent room.

Theodore was lying with his blankets tucked up round his chin and his nightcap over one nostril. The pointed tip of the hat puffed up and down with each great snore Theodore emitted. Mr Matthews had to give him several firm shakes before, with much incoherent groaning, he could be roused.

Eventually he sat up in bed. Pale and sombre, he listened to the news, then sat in silence for some minutes. He removed his nightcap and twisted it in his hands, then scratched his stubbly head, all the while saying nothing, asking no questions. Mr Matthews half wondered if his master had properly understood the news, and whether he should relate it all again.

Presently Theodore spoke. 'We are ruined,' he said firmly. 'That wine-cooler was the most valuable object ever made by this company. There can be no avoiding the fact – we are ruined.'

If he was taken aback by this admission, Mr Matthews did not reveal it by so much as a twitch. 'Surely not, sir,' he said, in the tone of formal deference he found best in a crisis. 'What would you have me do about the corpse?'

'Leave me in peace a minute, won't you?' said Theodore sharply. 'Don't expect me to think about that when such a catastrophe has taken place. Whatever am I to tell my father, and Sir Bartholomew? The wine-cooler has been stolen the very night before it was due to be delivered.'

Some time passed before Theodore recovered himself sufficiently to collect his thoughts and give practical instructions. The constable and magistrate were to be immediately apprised of what had happened. Theodore would break the news to his father himself in the morning, at breakfast. He expressly forbade that the tragedy be discussed below stairs until that time. 'And since you and I are the only ones who know, I rely upon your discretion, Matthews.'

'You may rest assured upon it, sir,' said Mr Matthews with a small bow.

Then, with Mr Matthews's help, Theodore dressed swiftly and went next door to view the scene of the crime with his own disbelieving eyes.

Chapter Seven

AS A RULE, AGNES MEADOWES SLEPT DREAMLESSLY, OR AT LEAST any dreams she had were forgotten by the time she awoke. But the night of Rose Francis's disappearance was different. The storm had disturbed her. She had passed an unsettled night, and when she woke next morning she was burdened by an unfamiliar sense of foreboding. Her bolster felt damp and her eyes were unusually swollen. The detail of the dream that had disturbed her was indistinct in her recollection, but she knew that it had caused her to weep.

Sitting up in bed, she caught sight of the letter that she had finally managed to extricate from the pocket of the ailing Mrs Tooley the previous evening. In a flash she understood: reading the letter before retiring had preyed on her mind and caused her nightmares. She plucked it from her night table and glanced at it again.

Twickenham, January 1750

Dear Mrs Meadowes,

I should have wrote to you sooner, but since your last visit a terrible nervous fever brought on after I was caught out in a shower has afflicted me so that I have not left my bed. The physician despaired of me when the fever and faintings were at their height. My sister Barbara has assisted me in caring for your boy, Peter, who has escaped the contagion and enjoys the best of health and spirits.

Now I am out of danger, but my head is still bad and I must convalesce until I am properly well again. Peter needs more than I can give him at the present moment. I cannot wait till your next visit two weeks hence. For the time being Barbara tends him, but she must return to her own family next Saturday. After that you must find somewhere else.

Yours most sincerely and truly,
Maud Catchpole.

Rereading the letter both relieved and disturbed Agnes anew. She thanked God Peter was well, and yet Mrs Catchpole's demand placed her in an undeniable quandary. Where would she find another person to tend Peter at such short notice? She was permitted only one free Sunday a month and that was not due for another fortnight. She would have to persuade Mrs Tooley to allow her an extra day off. If the housekeeper was feeling frail it was unlikely to be an easy task.

Agnes reminded herself that there was nothing to be gained from dwelling on her personal disturbances. Her duties awaited and should not be ignored. She would tackle Mrs Tooley as soon as an opportune moment arose. After all, there were five days until Saturday.

Agnes rose as usual at seven. She splashed and scoured herself with a flannel soused in icy water, and donned her everyday garb: a pair of brown woollen stockings, a chemise, a petticoat, a worn grey skirt and bodice, a freshly laundered apron. With the exception of the apron, most of these items had once belonged to Lydia Blanchard, who had passed them on to her maid, Patsy. But Patsy, being rather larger than Lydia, was obliged to alter her clothes to fit; those she could not let out or down were passed to Agnes or one of the other servants.

Being almost the same size as Lydia, Agnes had not needed to make adjustments. The costume nicely outlined her narrow waist and the fullness of her body above and beneath, but of these attractions Agnes was unconscious. It was several years since she had taken more than the most cursory interest in her appearance. Today was no exception. She arranged her thick dark hair in a bun and topped it with a cap. A glance at her reflection revealed a change in her tranquil features. Her amber eyes were shadowed with purple, her cheeks were drawn: the effect of her unsettled night and her worries over Peter. Agnes looked away, telling herself the matter would soon be resolved. Without further delay, she left her bedroom and briskly made her way along the narrow passage that led to the kitchen.

The sight she discovered thrust all other worries from her thoughts. By now the range should have been burning steadily, yet smoke and yellow flames belched from the grate, a sure sign it had not been lit long. The black kettle that should have been boiling for early-morning tea was barely tepid. There was no sign of the trays that should have been set out ready to take the tea upstairs, nor had the butter been patted or the preserves and jellies been put out in preparation for upstairs breakfast. And upon the hub of Agnes's realm – the kitchen table – stood a final outrage: not the crockery that should have been laid ready for the servants' breakfast, but a pair of muddy boots.

If the owner of the boots was for the time being unknown (though Agnes had her suspicions), there was no doubt as to the person responsible for the undone chores. Rose Francis should have been up and busy over an hour ago, but was conspicuously absent. Agnes stood for a moment, brooding. Today, she determined, she would not shirk her responsibilities. Rose's laxity was too blatant to ignore. It was as if the girl were challenging her. Today she would rise to that challenge and banish all thoughts of the larder. She would take Rose to task and stand over her all day if necessary.

Agnes searched for Rose in the yard, the scullery, and, steeling herself, in the larder. Finding no sign of her in any of these places, she headed towards the butler's pantry. She was startled by the sight of Philip emerging from it. Philip was the same height as John, but he was broader about the shoulder and stronger in the thigh. He had fine chiselled features, a wide full-lipped mouth, and a flash in his olive-green eyes that showed he knew he was handsome. Today, Agnes remarked, those eyes were bleary and bloodshot, and his complexion was unusually pale. He was brandishing the hog's bristle brush he used for cleaning boots, and reeked of sweat and stale beer.

'Morning, Mrs Meadowes,' he mumbled with a barely disguised yawn. 'Looking for something?'

'Have I *you* to thank for these?' Agnes enquired, waving at the muddy boots, which were still standing boldly in the middle of her table.

'Someone else must've left 'em. It weren't me,' said Philip, without a glimmer of contrition. He yawned again, more loudly and unapologetically, and whisked the boots back to the pantry, where they should by rights have been stored in the first place.

Agnes's brow puckered at the sight of several large flakes of mud on the table. She swept the dirt into her hand, followed Philip to the pantry and brushed her palms together, depositing the mud on the bench beside him with a briskness that conveyed controlled displeasure. 'Who then, pray?' she asked in a chilly but clear tone.

Philip was just moving a cloak and muffler that were lying on the butler's table to one side. At the sound of her voice, he winced and drew back. 'Not so loud. I ain't deaf. How should I know? Ain't you got more to worry you'n that?'

Agnes tilted her head, compressing her lips to a tight bud. 'Such as?' she said no more quietly than before. 'You mean Rose, I presume? Where's she got to?'

'Shh,' said Philip, sliding a smooth wooden tree into each boot before beginning to scrub at them. 'Her whereabouts are naught to do with me.' He glanced up and jerked his head towards the kitchen. 'Why don't you give me a rest and ask Patsy? There she is.'

'Ask me what?' said Patsy, Lydia's maid, looking from one to the other as she burst in from the pantry with a tea tray. She froze for an instant, her mouth downturned. She was dressed in a pale-blue woollen robe of Lydia's and looked quite the lady. She put down the tray and smoothed a lace ruffle on her sleeve. 'I suppose it's Rose. Everything's got behind on account of her. I'm not one to complain, but how am I supposed to do my work as well as hers? I oughtn't prepare Mrs Blanchard's tray, only take it up.'

'I'm sorry,' said Agnes, feeling responsible for Rose's failings. She had been as remiss as Rose, in her way. 'I can't think what's come over her.'

Patsy shrugged petulantly. 'Whatever her excuse, she's the cause of more trouble than anyone. I'd say she deserves a proper scolding. Anyway, I can't stop. Mrs Blanchard will be growing flustered with wondering where I am. I shall have to explain why her tea is delayed.' She shot a meaningful look at Agnes before scurrying off up the back staircase.

Agnes returned slowly to the butler's pantry, where Philip was still lolling at the lead-lined sink, pretending to burnish the boots with his brush. 'So where is she?' Agnes pressed, with uncharacteristic insistence.

Philip looked stubborn. 'I told you before, I don't know.'

'Are you certain you do not?' Her cheeks began to burn. A vision of Philip with his breeches round his ankles and his muscular buttocks flexed barged into her skull. She forced it away, looking over her shoulder to make sure they were alone. 'Forgive me for asking,' she said in a lower tone, 'but was she with you last night?'

'No,' said Philip, also speaking more softly. 'Between you and me, I passed the evening at the Blue Cockerel in Lombard Street. But don't say nothing to Mr Matthews about it or he'll cuff me. And hand on heart, after the night I passed there I wouldn't 'ave heard her if she'd been in bed beside me.'

Agnes was tempted to say he knew as well as she did that nocturnal sorties were strictly forbidden during the week and she saw no reason to keep his outing from Mr Matthews. But she swallowed and looked away, saying nothing. Embarrassment, coupled with respect for the hierarchy of the household, held her back. As cook she was one of the upper servants, but as a male servant Philip was beyond her jurisdiction. In any case, she was not surprised at Philip's reluctance to speculate on Rose's whereabouts. Nor did she believe his denial. Just because he had gone to the Blue Cockerel did not mean Rose had not accompanied him. Doubtless the pair of them had over-indulged last night and he wanted to protect her from trouble.

Agnes stalked back to the kitchen, took a stick of cinnamon from a tin on the dresser and bit down on it. Her fingers were smutted black – polish from the boots, perhaps – which did nothing to improve her humour. Her agitated musings were abruptly interrupted by a shuffling and clanking behind her. Doris, the flame-haired scullery maid, shuffled slowly through the kitchen with a bucket in one hand, a mop trailing in the other.

'About time, Doris,' Agnes greeted her sharply. 'You are an hour late with that. What has happened to Rose? Is she indisposed? If so, you ought to have told me; if not, you must fetch her at once.'

Doris's simple face flushed. 'Sorry, Mrs Meadowes,' she mumbled. 'I never heard a squeak from her all night, but then I always sleep sound. And it being dark and all, I never noticed nothing when I got up. But Nancy says Rose were never in her bed this morning. And since she ain't here it can only mean she's gone.' Doris spoke without stumbling – with what for her was unusual fluency and speed.

Agnes regarded her aghast. 'Gone?'

'Aye. Her bed were empty. Nancy thought she'd come down ahead of her and left her deliberately to sleep on. The pair of them had a great falling-out yesterday, and it came to blows. But Rose ain't here, as you see. It was Philip what said she must 'ave gone off. Last night he saw Mr Matthews lock up, and just now when he went to the coal store, the kitchen door was open.'

'Lucky we wasn't all murdered in our beds,' added Philip drily.

Agnes remembered the bruise on Rose's cheek. Nancy and Rose often squabbled, but she had never paid much attention to them. Ought she to have discovered what had happened and forced the pair of them to make peace? Was this disruption her fault? 'What was the fight about?' she enquired.

'Dunno, Mrs Meadowes,' said Doris. 'But the screeching was something terrible.'

'Both of them was sweet on me,' said Philip jovially. 'I was no doubt what caused it.'

Agnes shot a reproachful look towards the butler's pantry, where behind the door Philip's profile was half visible. He was scrubbing with exaggerated concentration at the sullied hem of a cloak. 'I thought you said you knew nothing of her whereabouts.'

'She fought over me – that don't mean she told me where she was going.'

Without troubling to reply to this, Agnes turned back to Doris. 'You might have had the gumption to call me earlier.'

Doris swallowed and blinked, looking down at her puffy hands. A limp strand of hair emerged from her badly pinned cap and plastered itself to her glistening forehead. She began picking at the hem of her apron with nails that were not as clean as they might have been. 'I didn't know what to do, ma'am. Nancy said to leave you and Mrs Tooley or we'd be in trouble. She said get on as best we could till you came.'

'Nancy is only the housemaid,' said Agnes darkly. 'She's no right to give orders.'

'Ain't that a bit harsh, Mrs Meadowes?' called Philip from the pantry. Then to Doris, 'Never mind her, beauty. I'll look out for you.'

Doris's chin trembled and her cheeks flushed the same colour as her hair. 'Pardon me, Mrs Meadowes. It was only after I'd scrubbed the floor and scoured the pots that John came down and told me he didn't know where anyone was, and if I didn't set to making the fire I'd catch it for knowing what had happened and doing nothing about it.'

Agnes steadied herself and forced a smile. She was fuming because she knew Philip was right. 'Yes, yes,' she said. 'I see you've done your best, though if you had let me know she had gone it would have been better. Even so, Nancy will have to help later on.'

'You'll be lucky,' muttered Philip, emerging from the butler's pantry with the boots between the pincer of his forefinger and thumb and the cloak draped over his arm. He blew a kiss towards Doris.

'That's enough from you, Philip,' snapped Agnes, forgetting hierarchy for once.

He responded with a good-humoured wink, and went off up the back stairs whistling.

Doris, who sorely wished Philip had winked at her, and treasured his compliments like gold, curtseyed and contrived to follow him. Agnes suppressed her annoyance and gently began to prod the fire. Philip's buttering was only so he would get his own way, an extra favour here, a perk there. But what right had he to butter any woman after what he'd got up to with Rose in the larder? Philip's quips and compliments always vexed Agnes; it never failed to astonish her that every other female in the household held him in awe. Her thoughts turned back to Rose. The girl going off had come as a shock; nevertheless, thinking about it now, in her heart of hearts she was not entirely surprised.

Rose had come to work for the Blanchards a year ago. Her previous position, so she claimed, had been in the London mansion of a Lord, where there was a staff of thirty, including half a dozen grooms, four carriages, a steward and five servants just for the nursery. She had never mentioned what had made her exchange this grand establishment for such a modest one as Foster Lane, nor had Agnes asked. Nevertheless, observing Rose's character, Agnes had occasionally wondered whether a man had been the cause of her leaving. And now that she had run off, Agnes's opinion had not changed. Most likely a man had lured Rose away with a promise of some kind.

The only question in Agnes's mind regarded that man's identity and his real intentions. Her own experiences of men had left her with a pessimistic view of them. Her father had been a physician of substance, a stern widower who had been possessive of his only child and had hardly permitted her to mingle with other girls of her station, let alone respond to potential suitors. He had died leaving her with enough to live on independently, but Agnes had craved companionship and had hurried into marriage with one of her father's patients, a well-to-do draper. Not until after their nuptials did she discover that her husband's ailments and misadventures were caused mainly by his fondness for brandy. Or that when he returned from a night in the tavern, his affable nature changed and he grew careless with his fists.

On the sixth anniversary of their marriage, by which time her husband had ruined his business and spent nearly all Agnes's inheritance, fate intervened in their unhappy partnership. Her husband had eaten his supper, then left her to pass the evening in the Golden Magpie. At the stroke of midnight he had inadvertently been shoved in the ribs by an over-friendly barmaid. He had stumbled and tripped over a log basket and fallen plumb into the hearth, where his heart had been impaled on a cast-iron fire dog.

Agnes had been relieved to be rid of him, but had been left almost penniless, bruised, and with Peter to care for. She had risen to the challenge of supporting herself and her child by pursuing her culinary inclinations. Cooking had always been a solace, never more so than now. Having achieved the elevated status of cook, she had formed the unusual opinion that relations with men were no substitute for an independent life. Provided she did her duty, she could be sure of a roof over her head, a warm bed, and that she would never again be woken and punched senseless in the middle of the night.

Rose had yet to be taught this lesson. But Agnes believed there was no doubt she would learn it, and little doubt either that any promise a man had made to Rose would not be all it appeared. Perhaps, thought Agnes with mingled apprehension and hope, Rose would be back in a day or two.

Chapter Eight

AT EIGHT-THIRTY – HALF AN HOUR LATE – NANCY THE HOUSE-maid tapped on the door to Nicholas Blanchard's bedchamber and bade him good morning. She was carrying a scuttleful of coal with some kindling scattered on the top. Having deposited her bucket by the hearth, she moved to the window, aware as she did so that Nicholas Blanchard watched her closely, like a cat observing a moth.

His bedchamber overlooked the narrow street, with two large sash windows, a carved wooden chimneypiece and an elaborate stuccoed ceiling. Thirty years earlier, when Nicholas had succeeded his father and had a wife to warm his nights, the room had been hung with damask silk wall-covering and fringed curtains. Since then the silk had faded and grown discoloured by damp, and his wife had died, leaving him to seek his warmth elsewhere.

Nancy drew back the curtains gingerly, for the heavy fabric had rotted in the sun and threatened to disintegrate in her hands. As she always did, Nancy rubbed a roundel in the mist on the window-pane to survey the sky. 'Not bad today, sir. Frosty but bright,' she said, holding her stomach in tight.

Nicholas grunted a reply, whereupon Nancy returned to the hearth and set to riddling the embers before laying a new fire.

When she had the flames burning at a steady crackle she turned to glance over her shoulder at her master. Nicholas caught the look and, as he often did at this hour, threw back the bedcovers and called her over. Nancy unpinned her cap and went wordlessly towards him, feeling faint and a little queasy, for she too had passed an unsettled night.

It was all over in a matter of minutes. Having removed her boots and loosened her bodice she lay stiffly beside him. He pulled up his nightshirt, rolling on top of her as he pinched her breasts with a bony hand. She tried not to wince, for they were much more tender than usual. She felt his bristly chin scratch her cheek; he smelled different from Philip – of tobacco and pomade and claret, rather than sweat and ale. A minute later he had drawn himself in and was pumping up and down. Nancy lay there silently, surveying the ceiling with its cupids and nymphs embracing one another, trying to breathe in shallow breaths to quell the nausea rising in her belly. Usually she felt grateful to Nicholas for singling her out as the recipient for his favours. She had saved most of the money he paid, and the sum now amounted to almost ten pounds. But her predicament was now changed.

Should she confess to Nicholas that she was carrying his child? Suppose he denied responsibility and dismissed her? What would it be like to be swooped up by one of those nymphs and spend all day suspended in the air, with no chores to carry out and no child growing inside or Nicholas to please? What could she do to make Philip kinder? She closed her eyes and imagined a world of white clouds and flowers and music. An instant later, Nicholas shuddered and finished.

He rolled away from her to scrabble under his pillow for the purse in which he always kept a few coins. He picked out a silver shilling and stuffed it in the top of her bodice. Then, unusually, he stuffed a further sixpence into her hand. 'Leave me now. You are late – don't think I hadn't remarked it. Make up for the time lost or there'll be trouble with Mrs Tooley. And you needn't expect me to take your part.' He said this in a matter-of-fact tone, not unkindly. Then he patted her arm in an almost fatherly manner.

'Thank you, sir,' she said, opening her palm and examining the extra coin. ''Course I won't dally.' Already she was feeling better for sitting up. Once out of Nicholas's bed, she retrieved the coin from her corset and put it, with the sixpence, carefully in her pocket. She straightened the bedclothes, then walked to the looking glass to quickly refasten her clothes. The face that looked back at her was thin and narrow, with neat small features and hair that was glossy and smooth, the colour of polished oak. Nancy tidied her bun, then pinned her cap back on top of it. Her pale-grey eyes shone unnaturally bright this morning, and the stubble on Nicholas's chin had given her cheeks a pink glow that improved her palid complexion. She turned her head sideways to examine a long red scratch on the side of her neck. She shivered, remembering the stridently screeched accusations Rose had made, then adjusted her collar, thankful that Nicholas had not noticed it.

The clock struck the quarter-hour as Nancy opened the cupboard by Nicholas's bed and removed the half-filled chamber pot. The stench might have sickened some, but Nancy concealed any flicker of revulsion. She placed a duster over the rim and, with a careful curtsey, left the room.

At nine, Mr Matthews knocked on Nicholas's door and swept in, bearing a tray of early-morning tea. He plumped the pillows so that Nicholas could sit comfortably while he drank it. He set Nicholas's dressing gown of crimson brocade, matching hat and embroidered slippers to warm before the fire, which thanks to Nancy's ministrations was now giving out a steady heat. Then, reopening the door leading to the back stairs, he descended as far as the crook in the stairs, where he halted and bellowed down, 'Oi there, Philip! What are you waiting for? Hot water for the master. At the double, if you'd be so kind.'

Mr Matthews was a few years older than Nicholas, having been in the Blanchards' employ for the past five decades. He had started out at the age of fifteen as a lanky-limbed under-footman when Nicholas's father was alive. In those days he had mounted the stairs three at a time – and more often than not got his ears cuffed on account of it. Since then his back had grown stooped, but he had acquired the carriage and dignity of experience. He never ascended stairs at anything but a stately rate, and even then journeys up and down had him puffing. He returned now to Nicholas's room with a pair of polished shoes in one hand and a well-brushed suit draped across his arm, feeling breathless and warmer than was comfortable. Trying to conceal his exhaustion – last night's upset had drained him – he made his way to Nicholas's dressing room and arranged the belongings carefully in his press cupboard, among his other jackets and breeches and boots.

While he waited for the water to arrive, he took out a leather razor strop and passed the time sharpening the blade he would employ to shave his master. He had performed this task almost every morning for twenty years, and took considerable pride in the steadiness of his hand and the fact that in all that time he had hardly caused a scratch on Nicholas Blanchard's complexion.

This morning, however, the butler was not himself. Nicholas Blanchard had yet to learn of what had happened next door, and Mr Matthews was apprehensive on account of it. The moment Theodore broke the news an outburst would be sure to follow, and in such a mood Nicholas had a habit of making his servants equally miserable. Mr Matthews was further troubled by Theodore's reaction to the news of the murder and robbery. If the business was on the brink of ruin, what would happen to the stipend he had been promised to keep him in his old age? Was he also to be ruined?

He was conscious, too, that the matter of Rose Francis's disappearance ought to be mentioned. Nicholas relied upon him to supplement Lydia's reports of what went on below stairs. But here, too, Mr Matthews was torn. Rose's disappearance would irk Nicholas, and he would doubtless blame it on Agnes Meadowes. He had always regarded her as inferior to the French chef she had replaced. Mr Matthews detested incurring Nicholas's wrath, but neither did he wish to cast Agnes in a bad light. He recalled the quarrelsome and erratic Monsieur and shuddered. In all his years he had known no cook more reliable than Agnes. At this stage of his life a tranquil existence was what he craved above all else. Far better, he thought, if he kept quiet on the subject of Rose. Lydia could raise it at breakfast, when Nicholas would be distracted by the news of the wine-cooler's loss.

A good ten minutes passed before Philip arrived, carrying a steaming pail. Nicholas Blanchard had finished his second cup of tea and was growing restless. By then Mr Matthews's arm ached from sharpening the razor, and his head throbbed from his various anxieties.

Mr Matthews glared at Philip. 'Took your time, didn't you?' he hissed.

'Fire wasn't lit, was it, sir? It took twice as long,' whispered Philip.

'I'll give you twice as long,' muttered the butler, jerking his head towards the washstand. 'That's what comes of having a trollop for a kitchen maid.'

'You said anything to him about that?' said Philip, quiet but undaunted.

'No,' replied Mr Matthews in a whisper. 'I'm waiting for the moment.' Then in a louder, more formal voice that Nicholas Blanchard could hear if he chose to listen, 'Pour it in the bowl, if you please, Philip. And mind you don't splash the floor. The master don't like his feet getting wet.'

When Philip had gone, Nicholas rose from his bed, stepped into his warmed slippers and allowed Matthews to ease him into the sleeves of his silk dressing gown. Lowering himself into a comfortable armchair before the fire, he stretched back his head so that Matthews might shave him and anoint him with powder and pomade, but not so far that he could not glimpse his reflection in the looking glass.

His face was large and angular, dominated by hollow cheeks and a long nose with hairy nostrils that flared outwards when he was riled. His head was a carpet of dark grey stubble, almost a week having passed since Matthews last shaved it so that his wigs would sit comfortably. At the lower limit of his forehead luxuriant brows formed an almost uninterrupted line, overshadowing his eyes. There was scarcely a trace of grey in them; when his wig was on, he often thought, he could pass for a man ten years younger.

Being tired and more preoccupied than usual, Mr Matthews lacked his customary steadiness and the razor caught under Nicholas's nose. The nick was painless, thanks to the sharpness of the blade, but a pearl of blood beaded up on Nicholas's smooth skin. Nicholas saw rather than felt it, but that did not stop him bellowing at the butler, calling him a clumsy oaf. Mr Matthews murmured an apology, and with a trembling hand anointed the wound.

Chapter Nine

ON THE STROKE OF TEN, STILL ATTIRED IN DRESSING GOWN, CAP and slippers, Nicholas Blanchard descended to the morning room to take his breakfast. Philip was waiting to open the door for him; John was bustling about with a tea kettle by the sideboard. When his master appeared he put the pot down, drew out a chair at the head of the table and helped Nicholas to sit down. Nicholas's paper – the *Morning Post* – and two letters had already been arranged in a neat pile beside his place.

Lydia was already seated at the table, nibbling a piece of toast. She acknowledged Nicholas's entry by half rising and giving him a jerking curtsey, the expression in her grey eyes grave and distant. Nicholas nodded unsmilingly and muttered an inaudible reply, upon which Lydia returned to her seat and her toast.

Lydia rarely found her father-in-law easy. Today she could see from the brusque manner of his entry that his temper was up. There was a small red mark under his nose and she wondered if it was this, or the news of Rose Francis's departure, that had caused it.

Lydia had learned of Rose's disappearance from Patsy, and while her maid had dressed Lydia's hair and anointed her face with powder, positioning a beauty spot on her left cheek, they had pondered what reasons the girl might have had to leave. Patsy had reminded Lydia that Rose had been in the habit of wandering about upstairs, where as far as anyone knew she had no business to be.

'You recall the letter Nancy found?' Patsy had said.

Lydia had nodded uncomfortably. 'Were there other occasions?' she'd sharply enquired.

Patsy's eyes had narrowed. 'I believe so. Mr Matthews caught her on the stairs leading to the best bedrooms only yesterday. And she caused a dispute with Nancy. The pair of them went for each other like dogs – John had to pull them apart.'

'Dear God!' Lydia had said, eyes clouded with concern and concentration. 'What was the reason for the altercation? Why ever did Mrs Tooley not tell me?'

'It only took place in the afternoon, ma'am. No doubt she will tell you more when you see her this morning. Among the obscenities it was not easy to make out what they said. I believe it may have had something to do with the letter. Certainly the word "thief" was used.'

Lydia had shuddered. The dispute and the girl being upstairs when she had no business to be had an ominous ring. Why might she have strayed? She had concluded that Nicholas might very well lie at the root of it. Nancy, she knew, already shared his bed. Was Rose another of his amours? On more than one occasion Nicholas's affairs had upset the smooth running of the house; several girls had fallen with child and had to be dismissed. Perhaps Rose – being a pretty bold girl, the kind that Nicholas preferred – had fallen prey to his predations, found herself with child and run off in distress. Or perhaps the argument with Nancy had been some form of jealous spat and Nancy had bullied her into leaving. What else, wondered Lydia, might have caused Rose's forays upstairs, her argument with Nancy and her sudden departure?

Just then, Patsy, who was prone to being heavy-handed on occasion, had tugged too tightly on the laces of her corset.

Lydia had pulled away, told Patsy to have a care and tried to dismiss Rose from her thoughts. But as Patsy was flattening her collar, smoothing her skirts and fastening the buttons on her shoes, Lydia could not help dwelling on the matter. Was there something insidious about the girl going off? It would be prudent, she thought, to make discreet efforts to discover what had happened.

Lydia had intended to begin her enquiries at breakfast. She would raise the subject of Rose with her father-in-law to gauge his reaction. But now, seeing his black look, she resolved to bide her time.

Nicholas broke the seal on his first letter and scanned it, while John poured him a cup of chocolate. The missive did not improve his temper. 'Damnation!' he declared, more to himself than Lydia. 'The devil it was!' Then, jerking his head up abruptly, he tossed the letter in Lydia's direction. 'Put this in Theodore's place, would you? It concerns a customer's grievance. There were never half so many complaints when I had charge of the business.'

Lydia glanced at the letter. Finding it described nothing more dreadful than a broken handle, she nodded dismissively and murmured half to herself, 'A trifling matter – one that will be easily remedied.'

Nicholas affected not to hear. He took a sip of his chocolate and instantly spat it back. 'God damn it, this is stone cold! Take it away, call for some hot milk – and let it be *properly* heated this time.'

Helping himself to a couple of rolls from the basket on the table, he was further distressed to find that the butter had not been impressed with the family crest, but lay on a serving dish entirely undecorated. 'Dear God!' he exploded. 'Has Mrs Meadowes taken leave of her senses? Lydia, you are too lax with her. I always said she was inadequate to the task. I never understood what possessed you to take her on as cook rather than engage a decent French chef.'

'The fault doesn't lie with Mrs Meadowes.'

'Then where?'

Lydia gave him a sweet smile. There was no avoiding the

subject now. 'Perhaps you are unaware that Rose Francis the kitchen maid has run off. There was only Doris, the scullery maid to assist Mrs Meadowes at breakfast. No doubt that is why the butter was not moulded as usual, and the milk is a little cooler than it ought to be.'

'The maid has run off? Are you certain?'

'Patsy told me this morning,' said Lydia, watching closely for Nicholas's reaction. He frowned, seeming surprised and puzzled, but no more. If there had been something between him and Rose, he masked it admirably. 'Have you knowledge of this, John?' Nicholas said, turning for affirmation to the footman, who was hovering by the side table.

John exchanged a brief glance with Philip, who was disappearing with the milk jug. He was unaccustomed to being engaged in conversation while the family were at the table, and his expression revealed his unease. ''Tis true enough, sir. The girl is gone.'

'Can you add anything to Mrs Blanchard's account?'

'No, sir.'

'Most likely she will have stolen something of value to take with her. Have you made checks, Lydia?'

'I regret not yet, sir. I am only just risen.'

'Then please do so forthwith.'

'As you wish.' She hesitated. 'I wondered if perhaps *you* might know why she went, sir?' she added.

Nicholas Blanchard raised his bushy brow and subjected his daughter-in-law to an indignant glare. 'What on earth can you mean, madam? Do you imply I have some insight into the mental workings of a kitchen maid that you, as mistress of this household, lack?'

Lydia swallowed. It was on the tip of her tongue to reply that, yes, she did believe Nicholas might have an insight into the reasons for Rose Francis's departure. And, for that matter, an intimate knowledge of Nancy the housemaid. But then she saw that there was no reason to further rouse her father-in-law's temper, when there were others who might make discreet enquiries for her. So she replied demurely, 'No, sir, but I understand the girl was seen going on unauthorized excursions

– I have reason to believe she ventured into the drawing room; and only yesterday Mr Matthews caught her upstairs.'

'Upstairs? What for? I have no knowledge of it. You must get to the bottom of this.'

'I intend to,' said Lydia, still uncertain whether or not her father-in-law was as innocent as he professed to be. How was she to discover what had become of the girl?

Before she had a moment to reflect, Theodore burst into the room in a state of unusual dishevelment. He wore no wig, his hair was uncombed and his coat flapped open. But it was the dreadful look on his face that chiefly distracted Lydia and Nicholas. His complexion was mottled and his eyes puffy, as if he had hardly slept all night. 'Good morning, Father – and Lydia,' he whispered in a strangely hushed yet agitated tone. He lowered himself into the chair John pulled out for him and, ignoring the astonished scrutiny of his wife, regarded Nicholas glumly. 'Father,' he declared, 'I fear I have some news of the utmost gravity.'

Chapter Ten

IT WAS AGNES'S HABIT, ONCE BREAKFAST HAD GONE UPSTAIRS, to drink tea and glance through her book of recipes. This was how she inspired herself before arranging the next day's menu with Mrs Tooley. She had just begun to contemplate ham and capon pie, pigeons the Italian way and palates of beef ragout, when she was disturbed by Mr Matthews soundlessly descending the back stairs and entering her kitchen.

As a rule, the butler was not a man in whom age seemed a weakness. His hair was all his own, a thick white mane that made his head appear magnificently large, and taken with his jutting brow, high-bridged nose and sternly set chin, he resembled one of the statues in St Paul's Cathedral. Yet now, Agnes observed, he seemed not at all his usual commanding self. Quite the contrary. His mouth was unusually puckered, his forehead strangely taut; something had unstrung him. Perhaps, she thought, Rose Francis's departure has vexed him as much as me.

Agnes poured him a cup of tea and stirred in two large spoons of sugar. 'Here you are, sir,' she said, handing him the mug and an oatmeal biscuit to go with it. 'It might not be as hot as you like, but I trust it's brewed to your liking.'

Mr Matthews thanked her, placed them on the table and

felt in his breast pocket for the silver flask he always kept there. He unstoppered the lid, and with trembling fingers added a hefty tot of brandy to his mug before returning the flask to his pocket.

'Awkward, Rose leaving like that, isn't it?' ventured Agnes, shocked to see him needing a nip so early in the day.

Mr Matthews looked up from his tea. He shrugged. 'For you it must be,' he replied tersely.

Ignoring his unsympathetic tone, Agnes tilted her head slightly in a confiding manner. 'I believe your second footman, Philip, was sweet on her.'

'That may have been so,' said the butler, looking pointedly at the clock. 'But since Philip is here and Rose is not, we may assume he hasn't played a part in her leaving.'

'I suppose not. Apparently there was an altercation between Nancy and Rose yesterday. Perhaps that played a part.'

'I have no knowledge of an altercation,' said Mr Matthews. 'And what's more, I fail to see why, when you are one wayward maid short and there are so many graver matters to consider, you are wasting my time and yours on idle gossip.'

The harshness of this remark took Agnes by surprise. The butler might bully his footmen where necessary, but he had no need to be abrupt with her. 'The girl worked for me, Mr Matthews. I am not gossiping, simply wondering what's become of her.' The unusual vehemence with which she said this took them both by surprise. It was only a pinch short of rudeness, and Agnes was never rude.

The butler's pinched lips squeezed tighter still. His manner showed he had no wish to discuss the wretched Rose. 'Your duties, Mrs Meadowes, are not to wonder. They are what Mrs Tooley and I tell you. Your maid may be missing, but that does not give you the right to abandon all decorum. Unless, that is, you wish to follow her pernicious model.'

Agnes sat up straight and closed her book of recipes. 'I don't comprehend your meaning, sir,' she said softly, her eyes holding his.

Mr Matthews half-lowered his lids. 'Come, come, Mrs

Meadowes, you know as well as I that your maid was hardly a model of propriety. *You* have already mentioned Philip.'

She swallowed. 'Were there others?'

'I believe she numbered the journeyman Benjamin Riley among her intimate acquaintances, and I hazard there was another gentleman, with whom Mrs Tooley observed her in conversation last week. Only yesterday I caught her outside the master's room; furthermore she made other unnecessary journeys upstairs. We may only surmise what took her there. On several occasions I scolded her, so too did Mrs Tooley. But in my opinion she would have benefited from a more watchful eye than you gave her. Having allowed her too much freedom, you should not be surprised to find yourself inconvenienced now she has gone.'

Agnes looked down at the book that lay closed on the table before her. Rose's intimacies with Philip were bad enough, and Agnes agreed that in her general manner Rose often lacked in modesty. But this was something else entirely. It bordered on depravity. 'Thank you, Mr Matthews,' she said, as she rose slowly from the table. 'I had no idea of these transgressions. Had I known, I should of course have spoken to her – taken a firmer hand. Nevertheless, I understand the reason for your disgruntlement. We should all be glad she has gone.'

Mr Matthews, mollified by Agnes's submission, grew unexpectedly contrite. 'The reason for my agitation is not simply that wayward girl,' he said. 'Something far more dreadful than her running off happened last night; something that might threaten all our livelihoods. I intend to tell the rest of the staff at dinner. Until then you must keep it in confidence . . .'

Chapter Eleven

NANCY BLAMED HER LATENESS SQUARELY ON ROSE FRANCIS running off. If the bitch had got up when she ought, Nancy would not have overslept and be rushing now. It was her fault – it was always Rose's fault – and it was Nancy who bore the brunt of her failings.

In the drawing room, dropping her housemaid's box on a cloth by the hearth, Nancy kneeled down, feeling her belly press against her stays. She tried to ignore the discomfort, hurriedly raking out the ashes and sieving them so that the cinders could be used in the kitchen. She sneezed as the dust invaded her nostrils, then fluttered a rag to disperse it, before oiling the metal bars of the grate and rubbing them with emery paper to make them shine. Then she laid the fire ready for later in the day. When she had finished, she stood up too quickly and felt faint, but there was no time for dizzy spells when the rest of the room waited. She rubbed her back briskly, then swept the floor and dusted the furniture, using an old silk handkerchief of Nicholas Blanchard's.

She repeated the procedure in the breakfast room, front hall, library and dining room. When Doris came up with the message that Mrs Meadowes wanted her to come down and help in the kitchen, Nancy's feet felt as if they might burst, like sausages fried too fast. She was flushed and about to drop, and there were still the three rooms upstairs to do. 'Can't till I've done the bedrooms,' she said curtly.

Doris put her plump hands on her bulging hips. 'Ain't you finished yet?'

'Do it look like it?' retorted Nancy, irked by Doris's painful drawl. She noticed that Doris's apron was already stained. The girl was not only a numbskull but clumsy with it.

Doris paused and looked at her in confusion – like a pig, thought Nancy unkindly – a dull-witted, fat sow. 'Late, ain't you?'

'"Late, ain't you?"' mocked Nancy, scowling and mimicking Doris's stumbling tone with uncanny accuracy. 'You're a fine one to talk. Wasn't my doing. Rose was meant to wake me.'

'I already said to Mrs Meadowes why . . . I'll tell that to her now, shall I?'

Nancy tossed her head and flicked her hand disparagingly. 'You poke off an' tell her what you want. What do I care?'

Doris's chin wobbled, but she could think of no answer, so she shuffled off down to the basement. A little revived by this exchange, Nancy crinkled her nose and climbed the stairs. Her routine was always the same. Theodore's bedchamber first, because he rose early for the workshop; Nicholas's next, Lydia's last, on account of Patsy, who liked to fiddle about, arranging Lydia's clothes – and trying them on if she got half a chance – after Lydia had gone down to breakfast.

In each room, Nancy took care to notice how everything was arranged, so she could replace things exactly as they were. The Blanchards were most particular on this count. 'If a door is open when you enter a room, leave it so when you leave, unless you are told otherwise,' Mrs Tooley always said. 'Likewise, if a dish is put beside a plate, do not put it back next to the candlestick.'

Being quick-witted, Nancy reckoned she knew every inch of every room of the Blanchard house better than her own face. So when she entered Nicholas Blanchard's bedchamber for the second time that morning, she noticed something that struck her as both curious and troubling.

There was a mahogany box that always stood in the centre of Nicholas's dressing chest. The lid was inset with a silver plaque, on which Nicholas's initials were engraved in script so curlicued it was all but illegible. The inside was lined with crimson silk and cushioned like a jewel box, and it was here that Nicholas stored his formidable collection of tie pins. There was one with a gold head shaped like a dog, one with a deep-purple amethyst, another fashioned as a miniature sword.

The box contained little else save a pair of flintlock pocket pistols, the butts adorned with bone inlay and silver mounts. Nicholas kept them wrapped in a pair of silk handkerchiefs. There was a flask of powder kept in the same box. He said the pistols were there in case any villain should dare burst into his bedchamber in the dead of night. They were always kept loaded, and every week Mr Matthews brought them down to the pantry to clean and reload. Once, when Nicholas was out, Mr Matthews had shown off to the rest of the servants by demonstrating how they worked. He had taken aim at a pigeon in the yard outside. Feathers and blood had sprayed all over the flags, and everyone had cheered, although the bird had flapped about refusing to die. John had eventually caught the bird and wrung its neck, and Mrs Meadowes had turned it into a tasty pigeon pie.

Nancy had no business opening the box, let alone touching pistols; she knew very well that they were dangerous. Dust and dirt were her business, not guns or jewels. Nicholas had Mr Matthews to take care of his personal possessions. Nevertheless, the temptation was too much to resist, and once or twice she had dared to unwrap the pistols and hold them in her hand. She liked to imagine herself pointing one at someone and squeezing the trigger and seeing him flap about like that wounded bird. Sometimes she imagined herself picking up the gun when Nicholas called her over. She pictured his great brow shooting up in fear as she got him in her sights.

But today, when she walked over to dust the dressing chest

and lifted the lid of the box, she saw that one of the pistols was missing. She opened the top drawers and poked about among an assortment of silken handkerchiefs. There was no sign of it. As she got on with her work, Nancy kept wondering what had happened to the missing pistol. Mr Matthews might have taken it away to clean, but usually he did this on a Saturday morning, after breakfast, and today was Tuesday. In any case, why take one pistol and not the other? Nancy had no reason to suppose that Rose had taken the pistol; nevertheless, it was once again her wretched name that came unbidden into her mind.

Chapter Twelve

MRS TOOLEY WAS SO-CALLED OUT OF RESPECT RATHER THAN marital status. A slender, small-bosomed woman, erect of gait, with a dry floury complexion and wispy hair the colour of dusty pewter, she had come to the Blanchards' household as a scullery maid at the age of sixteen, since when, as far as anyone knew, she had never married or had any kind of romantic alliance. She occupied a cluttered suite of rather gloomy rooms, situated halfway along the back corridor in the basement. Her ill-lit, small bedroom was enlivened with cheerfully embroidered samplers, which she had stitched herself, and a shelf upon which stood an intricate shell-work tableau. In her parlour, the chimneypiece was crammed with pottery owls, sheep and dogs, and dishes upon which blue and white Chinoiserie fruits and flowers were painted. Along the picture rail of one wall was suspended an array of brightly coloured plates. Dotted about the other walls were half a dozen engravings of the sea in varying climactic conditions, from violent tempest to glassy calm. To the rear was a store room, containing an enormous closet packed with bottled delicacies such as greengage plums in syrup, quince marmalade, nasturtium pickles and mushroom catsup, and this infused all three rooms with the sharp but tantalizing aromas of vinegar and fruit and spices.

Mrs Tooley's temperament was as fragile as the objects on her chimneypiece. She was likely to grow flustered at the slightest disruption, if she observed a single mote of dust beneath a dressing chest, or the ruffles on a pillowcase were not properly pressed. Her teacup would wobble, and she would be forced to rummage for her salts or a little of something stronger.

Agnes sometimes wondered if Mrs Tooley was quite as frail as she appeared, whether on occasion she exaggerated her weakness to elicit compliance, avoid argument or relieve herself of those tasks she had no wish to carry out. Either way, Rose's disappearance would have given rise to some symptom of alarm. Agnes half thought to find Mrs Tooley already in her bed, lost in slumber with a spoonful of her calming remedy inside her. Having now also learned of the dreadful murder and robbery, Agnes prayed this would not be the case. There was no telling what two calamities in a day would do to Mrs Tooley's nerves, or how long she might be indisposed. She must broach the subject of her day's leave sooner rather than later. She was permitted only one free Sunday a month to visit Peter. That day did not fall due until the week after next.

But Mrs Tooley was not in her bed. She presently stood at a side table beneath a faded print of a brig in a stormy sea. She was counting plates and pickle dishes and jotting the results in a fat, leather-bound notebook. She looked pale and pristine. As usual, her clothes were immaculately clean, a skirt and bodice of charcoal grey, a collar of starched white linen, a pair of metal-rimmed spectacles attached to a black ribbon about her neck.

Agnes was not deceived. Counting china at this hour was an ominous sign, when every day this was when they met to agree the following day's menu, so that on the dot of eleven it could be taken upstairs to the morning room for Lydia Blanchard to approve. There would be a first course, consisting of soup, fish and poultry, with vegetables, pickles, gravies and sauces for accompaniment; a second course of other meat dishes, including a roast, and half a dozen side dishes. And then the dessert, over which (contagions permitting) it was Mrs Tooley's prerogative to preside.

Mrs Tooley turned her head and wagged her finger at the slate waiting on the table, indicating that Agnes was not to speak for fear of making her lose her thread. 'Make a start, Mrs Meadowes. I'll be with you in a jot.'

Agnes nodded dismally and sat down. As a rule, there was little she enjoyed more than cooking. The act of planning and putting food on the table satisfied some craving, although she never questioned what caused that need in the first place. But today she felt no relish at the task in hand. Securing a day off was doomed to failure, how could she have imagined otherwise? The household being Mrs Tooley's entire existence, it was ludicrous to suppose she could ever comprehend Agnes's predicament. Agnes's thoughts drifted away from whether pea soup might be preferable to ox-cheek soup, nor did she speculate upon the disappearance of Rose and the terrible events Mr Matthews had related. How was she to collect Peter? Where would he stay? These dilemmas pressed all other concerns from her mind.

Agnes had no family or friends to call on. Since taking up her position with the Blanchards, she had deliberately shunned society; all her free Sundays were spent visiting her son. Until now she had accepted this state of affairs, viewing the separation from Peter as regrettable but inevitable. She appreciated the necessity for an ordered household. That a resident cook's child be permitted to live with her was unthinkable. It was only now, when the status quo of her daily existence was upset, that the restrictions jarred; she thought it would be consoling to have someone else in whom to confide.

'Well,' said Mrs Tooley some time later, settling herself shakily in a chair, 'I trust whatever it is you have planned can be made without your kitchen maid.'

'Speaking of which,' said Agnes as calmly as she was able, 'I can't manage with only Doris. She is willing but slow. Nancy is much quicker. Could you spare her to help for an hour or two each day until we find a replacement?'

Mrs Tooley's pale cheeks were suddenly suffused with pink. As she regarded Agnes from over the rim of her spectacles, her eyes took on an injured expression. 'Please, Mrs Meadowes, spare me further upset. I am not myself. What of Nancy's other duties? Do you suppose we can leave the beds unmade, the fires unlit, the floors unswept?'

'Of course not, ma'am. But perhaps Philip could help with the fires, so Nancy wouldn't have so much to do upstairs.'

Mrs Tooley's thin upper lip quivered. 'And rearrange the entire household while we're about it?'

Agnes regarded her slate. She willed herself not to succumb, but felt herself yielding to Mrs Tooley's will. 'I am only anxious not to let things slide.'

'I'll speak to Mrs Blanchard and place an advertisement directly,' said Mrs Tooley in a more measured tone.

'Thank you, ma'am,' responded Agnes. 'But what if she returns?'

'She will be shown the door directly,' Mrs Tooley whispered.

This was just what Agnes had expected to hear. She suppressed a flicker of sympathy for Rose, reminding herself that the girl's sins were greater than she had suspected, and that she had caused a great deal of inconvenience. One way or another, Rose was gone from her life. Yet the knowledge did not bring her relief. A niggling uncertainty remained, like a piece of gravel in her shoe.

'Mr Matthews said you observed her last week in the company of a gentleman,' said Agnes.

'That I did,' affirmed Mrs Tooley. 'And he was not from this vicinity, either.'

'Did you upbraid her?'

'Naturally. And naturally, being the brazen girl she was, she denied it. Told me that it was no more than a gentleman asking directions. I gave her the benefit of the doubt then. I see I should not have done so. I should have been firmer. But she could be so very forceful. And you know how arguments distress me.'

'Indeed she could be forceful,' replied Agnes, her sympathies now swinging unreservedly in the housekeeper's favour. 'Perhaps 'tis a good thing she's gone.'

Mrs Tooley nodded, apparently satisfied. Unlike Mr Matthews, she did not chastise Agnes for failing to be stricter with Rose. Adjusting her spectacles, she peered at the slate on the table in front of Agnes, and then looked at Agnes, aghast. 'Why is there nothing on the slate?' she exclaimed.

'Forgive me, ma'am, my mind was elsewhere.' Agnes began to write half-heartedly on the dusty surface.

Chapter Thirteen

IN THE BLANCHARD WORKSHOP NEXT DOOR, NOTWITHSTANDING the terrible events of the night, the journeyman Benjamin Riley was preparing to take newly made items of silver for assay at Goldsmith's Hall. He took out the stamp (a small iron punch with the letters NB raised upon it) and a craftsman's hammer, and laid these objects upon his workbench. From a shelf where various silver vessels were ranged, he selected a tea-caddy spoon with a pierced handle. He placed this upside down on an anvil, fixing it with a vice so that the neck lay across the metal block. Then, positioning the stamp above the neck of the spoon, he raised the hammer and brought it down with a whack, causing sparks to fly and the letters to appear in a small dent of dark metal.

Thomas Williams, the second journeyman, looked up from his bench to regard Riley with baleful eyes. 'Those spoons are delicate at the neck, mind you don't shatter them,' he said quietly.

Riley bristled. 'Oh, pardon me, sir,' he muttered, bowing with mock humility. 'I clean forgot my master was there.'

'I don't have to be your master to see when you're taking care and when you're not.' Williams was put out by what had happened last night and this had made him unusually short-tempered. He had been fond of Noah Prout, and had spent much time teaching the boy the rudiments of his profession. It was also he who had spent most time fabricating the wine-cooler; thus the loss seemed to him a graver blow.

Benjamin Riley scowled, unclamped the spoon and put it to one side, then picked a caddy off the shelf. 'What gives you the right to tell me what I ought and oughtn't to do? You ain't any better than me – despite your airs.'

'God help me. Did I say I was any different?' said Williams. 'Don't you see we both want the same – work, business? And the way you're carrying on, you'll ruin it for both of us.'

'I think the loss of the wine-cooler will have more to do with that than a bloody spoon,' said Riley with vigour. 'Any case, I'm too busy for your nagging. Get off and mind your own affairs. Leave me be.'

'If only I could,' said Williams, returning to his work.

One by one, Benjamin Riley stamped the Blanchard initials upon four small silver boxes, three tea caddies and half a dozen caddy spoons. Then he wrapped each object in a linen cloth to protect it from scratches, and loaded them into his basket. This done, he put on his coat and hat, smoothed his hair in its queue, and telling himself he looked handsome enough to pass for a patron rather than a purveyor of silver, he stepped out into the street.

The Goldsmith's Hall, towards which he threaded his way, was halfway down Foster Lane. It was an imposing structure, built in the classical style, with large windows punctuating the front façade and an inner courtyard reached through a columned portico. Near the entrance Riley caught sight of half a dozen journeymen and apprentices standing in a cluster, all on their way to take their wares to be assayed. He was so bound up with looking to see which of his rivals were there that he failed to observe the comely figure of Agnes Meadowes drawing alongside him on her way to market. Thinking he had spotted a friend, he swivelled abruptly. Agnes caught no more than a glimpse of a dark-brown hat, and beneath it a pock-marked, ferrety face and strands of lank brown hair, before his full basket collided forcefully with her empty one and she was sent sprawling into the gutter. Half a dozen pieces of silver from his basket tumbled alongside her.

'Oh my Lord!' exclaimed Benjamin Riley, as he scrabbled in the mud to retrieve a lid from here and a spoon from there, while keeping an eye on a couple of urchins. 'Get away with you, thieving wretch!' he bellowed at a bedraggled girl. 'Any closer and I'll call the watch and have you branded!'

'All right, mister, only tryin' to help,' said the girl, shrinking away.

'My arse you was,' he glowered.

Excited by the rumpus, a cluster of onlookers gathered, laughing and pointing. Meanwhile, various street children added to the fray by calling out 'Sir – 'e's taking it!' and 'There, sir!', causing Riley to spin round and add to the amusement. When all the mud-stained articles were safely recovered and stowed away, and the children had dispersed, Riley turned towards Agnes, who until this moment he had entirely ignored. By now she was back on her feet, brushing down her mud-spattered petticoats. Since he was still squatting, he took the time to observe her slender ankles before he rose. 'All right, Miss?' he said as he slowly drew himself up, taking in every curve of her.

'No thanks to you,' said Agnes, stepping back.

'Miss Meadowes, the Blanchards' cook, ain't it?' He stepped forward, squeezing her arm with what Agnes deemed to be over-familiarity.

'M*rs* Meadowes,' she declared, jerking away from his grasp.

'M*rs* Meadowes, forgive me. I see your dress is dirty – come back to the workshop with me, and I'll help you put yourself to rights.' He winked.

Agnes bit her lip. She was tempted to tell him to go to the devil – that would take the smile off his greasy face – but she recalled Mr Matthews telling her that Riley was friendly with Rose. Perhaps he knew where she had gone. Agnes did not pause to question why she remained perturbed by Rose's disappearance, when all she had learned of the girl's abundant flaws should have made her glad to forget her. She flashed Riley a half-smile. 'That won't be necessary, thank you, Mr Riley. I haven't time to spare. I'm in a rush on account of my kitchen maid going off. I think you knew her. Rose Francis was her name.'

Riley looked puzzled. 'Gone? Run off?' he said.

'Do you know where she is?'

'Why should I?' he asked warily.

She flashed another appeasing smile. 'I thought you and she were friendly.'

Riley shrugged, but said nothing to confirm or deny this.

'When did you last see her?' pressed Agnes.

'I can't say for certain. Perhaps three or four weeks ago.'

'She gave you no hint of her intentions?'

'None.'

'What was the reason for her visit to you?'

'None, save that she was sweet on me,' said Riley, grinning and exposing his uneven teeth.

Agnes could not prevent an inward shudder. Whatever was it about Rose that made so many men believe she was fond of them? Whatever Riley said, whatever Mr Matthews claimed, she could not conceive that this odious man had ever meant a fig to Rose. Philip was one thing – she could not deny he was well made, or that women generally found him charming. But Riley was quite the reverse: ingratiating, with something palpably unpleasant in his manner. The very idea of Rose and he filled Agnes with revulsion. She thought of Rose and Philip in the larder. Surely Rose would not have stooped . . . would not have allowed him to take liberties . . . would she?

But then, she reminded herself, even if Riley knew more than he revealed, what did it matter? Rose had gone, relinquished her position. Mrs Tooley would not take her back. Agnes, therefore, had no obligation to her. Perhaps she should have taken more of an interest in Rose's whereabouts and paramours before, but they were nothing to her now.

Chapter Fourteen

AGNES STILL HAD NO NOTION HOW TO RECONCILE MRS Catchpole's demand with the limitations of her duties. How was she to find the time to make arrangements for Peter's care if she was not allowed a free minute? As she walked to market with her empty basket and back with her full one, pulverized crayfish shells for her soup and dressed pheasants for roasting, and mixed stock, butter, flour and lemon juice for her fricassée sauce, she mused on this dilemma. The effort was apparent in the rigid set of her jaw and a distant glaze in her eyes, which took on the lustre of polished agate. She was entirely oblivious to the fussings of Mrs Tooley, the clumsiness of Doris, and the quips and banter, and comings and goings of John and Philip. When Patsy asked her for a clove for a toothache, Agnes did not hear her until Patsy bellowed the demand, which made her tooth throb worse than ever. But by the time the sauce had transformed to the smooth, thick consistency she desired, a solution of sorts had presented itself to Agnes.

Lydia Blanchard was a mother herself – her two children were both away at school at present – and Lydia knew that Agnes had a son. When Agnes had replied to the advertisement in the *Morning Post* for an undercook and been called for interview, she had not concealed Peter's existence. Since then, Agnes had seldom conversed with Lydia; that was Mrs Tooley's duty. Occasionally, after large parties, Lydia would descend to the kitchen to thank the staff; or when she wanted something particular for dinner and did not trust Mrs Tooley to convey it properly, she would attend the morning meeting. Such events were rare, however, and in recent months had grown rarer. Thus Agnes did not pretend any close rapport with the mistress of the house; nevertheless, she reasoned, being a mother, Mrs Blanchard might understand the present situation. And if Lydia ruled that she should be granted a day off, there would be nothing Mrs Tooley could do to stop her.

With a renewed sense of urgency, Agnes turned her attention to her immediate surroundings. She made her pastry and set it to rest. Then, having instructed Doris to pick the flesh off a boiled chicken (washing her hands first), and set the brown meat in one bowl and the white in another, she ventured upstairs.

Agnes rarely visited the upper part of the house. The change in temperature between the steamy kitchen and the cool, oak-boarded corridor struck her. She shivered, though whether this was caused by apprehension at the task she had set herself or the sudden chill she could not be certain.

The hall was modestly proportioned, but decorated to impress. The floor and doors were dark; grandiose Italian paintings in thick gilded frames were displayed against grey-blue walls. The only furniture was a pair of mahogany commodes, two hall chairs and a long-case clock. Suspended from the centre of the ceiling was a large silver chandelier. On the left were the dining room, drawing room and Nicholas Blanchard's library. The breakfast room and front parlour, where it was Lydia Blanchard's habit to pass this hour of the day, lay on the right.

Agnes knocked gently, glancing nervously around. She had seen John going out with Nicholas. At this time, Theodore should be at the workshop or busy on his morning's excursions. Philip was downstairs in Mr Matthews's pantry polishing the silver; Nancy was still finishing the upstairs rooms. What would she say if Mr Matthews or, worse, Mrs

Tooley apprehended her? But her fears were unfounded. No one came or caught sight of her before she heard Lydia's muffled voice calling, 'Enter,' from behind the door.

Lydia was embroidering a crimson rosebud on a shawl of pale-blue silk, upon which an intricate pattern of flowers and trailing vines was worked with great delicacy. On a chair beside her, a volume of poetry lay open.

No sooner had Agnes stepped over the threshold than she sensed that her arrival was unwelcome. I should not have come, she thought. Lydia has never encouraged intimacy among her servants. Patsy is her chief ally and confidante; Mrs Tooley's management of the household obliges Lydia to consult with her daily. But what need has she to confer with me?

When Agnes's glance lingered on the open book, Lydia furrowed her brow. 'I thought you were Patsy come to read to me. What on earth do you want, Mrs Meadowes?' She stabbed her needle in the design in front of her. 'I have already approved tomorrow's menus with Mrs Tooley.'

'Thank you, ma'am. My business doesn't concern the menus.'

Lydia shook her head. 'I cannot conceive what it can be, in that case.'

Agnes raised her chin and thought of her son. 'It is a private matter – of some delicacy.'

'Then should not you discuss it with Mrs Tooley?'

'If I broach the subject with her, I have no doubt she will refuse me out of hand. Being a spinster, she has no comprehension of maternal concerns.'

'I'm not sure I follow your meaning,' said Lydia slowly.

'It is my child, Mrs Blanchard,' said Agnes, speaking without pause, so that Lydia had not a moment to halt her. 'I have had a letter from the woman who tends him. She is in poor health and says I must find somewhere else for him to stay directly. I have no choice but to ask for an extra day's leave to make the necessary arrangements.'

Lydia frowned. 'But if it is a day off you want, Mrs Tooley

will have to agree. I cannot upset her; you know that, Mrs Meadowes. She is essential to the running of this house, and with the maid run off there is upset enough without courting more. Besides, even if I grant you an extra day off, where will you take your child? You cannot expect to bring him here.'

'Of course not, ma'am, I wouldn't dream of proposing that. But I would find somewhere to take him. All I ask is for you to put a word in for me, so that Mrs Tooley would be amenable.'

Lydia's face took on an air of regret. 'How would Mrs Tooley cook for all three of us with Rose gone and only Doris to assist?' she said helplessly.

'I can prepare everything so it's ready the night before. And with a little help from Nancy, Mrs Tooley and Doris would manage.'

Lydia appeared to give the matter her consideration, but in the end her decision was not what Agnes had hoped for. 'I see your dilemma; naturally, I am not unsympathetic. But under the present circumstances, it is impossible. You will have to find another means to resolve the problem.'

Agnes was at an impasse. Part of her wanted to plead, to implore, but she knew there was no purpose in losing her dignity and pursuing the matter. Lydia would not yield. 'Very well, ma'am. Forgive me for interrupting you,' she said, curtseying and making her way to the door.

But as she placed her hand upon the knob, Lydia summoned her back. 'One moment, Mrs Meadowes. There is another matter I would discuss with you.'

'Yes, ma'am,' said Agnes, wheeling round.

'Regarding your maid, Rose – have you any idea where she went off to?'

'No, ma'am, none at all.'

Lydia frowned disappointedly. 'Mrs Tooley told me the same. And the other staff – I presume it has been the talk of the kitchen – has no one any notion?'

'Not so far as I've heard, ma'am.'

'Do you think,' here Lydia lowered her voice confidentially, 'she might have been – in trouble – you know what I mean?'

Agnes's blush showed she understood perfectly. 'If so, I was not aware of it.'

'You noticed nothing different about her – in recent days or weeks? No sickness, no swelling . . .'

'Nothing, ma'am.'

Lydia seemed disappointed. Her mouth made a small moue. 'Is there any talk about her and my father-in-law? You may speak frankly to me, Mrs Meadowes. I am sure we are both cognizant of his tastes.'

Agnes felt her cheeks flame. Intimacies of this kind were not something she discussed with anyone, let alone her mistress. 'I don't know, ma'am,' she said nervously. 'I don't think so.'

Lydia tilted her head, her grey eyes seemingly riveted by Agnes's discomfort. 'Have you heard of the catastrophe that took place last night?'

'Yes, ma'am, although the other servants have not yet been informed.'

'Do you think Rose might have had a hand in last night's robbery?'

Agnes was jolted from her embarrassment by surprise. She answered after only the briefest consideration. 'Whatever else she was, I do not believe Rose Francis was a thief or a murderess,' she declared, startling herself as well as Lydia by the emphatic tone of her voice.

'That remains to be seen. Has anyone made a search of her possessions?' said Lydia, sharper now as she grew frustrated by Agnes's determined discretion.

'I don't believe so, ma'am.'

'Then be so kind as to look. Perhaps something there might tell us what has happened to her. I ask you as the person for whom she worked, who must have known her best. Her departure on the same night as the robbery next door strikes me as a strange coincidence. Should you find anything, I would make it worth your while.'

Lydia made no specific reference to the day off that Agnes had requested, but that was what immediately sprang into

Agnes's thoughts. Was that what Lydia intended? Agnes knew too little of her mistress to be certain; she could only pray.

Agnes began reluctantly to mount the stairs, clenching her fists as she did so. She was not generally prone to self-pity, yet she felt in danger of succumbing now. Lydia would not spare her time to find a new home for Peter, yet on some inexplicable whim was adding to her duties. And what an unwelcome task it seemed. Agnes had no inclination to involve herself in the private affairs of others. It went against her natural grain. With so much pressing upon her, how could she fail to feel sorry for herself? Nevertheless, Agnes could not forget Lydia's inference: please me in this and I might reconsider your request.

Why should Peter suffer because of Rose's misdemeanours? Surely the household could manage for a few hours without a cook and a maid. She wanted only to settle her son elsewhere, so that she might continue carrying out her duties as diligently as she had for the last five years. For a fleeting second, Agnes contemplated behaving like Rose – ignoring her duties, leaving the house and travelling directly to Twickenham to whisk Peter away. Then common sense reasserted itself.

She was still mounting the stairs, weighed down by indecision, when Nancy came clattering down, a broom clutched in one hand and her housemaid's box in the other, and nearly collided with her. The various bottles and brushes in Nancy's box rattled. Her small, sharp features registered surprise at coming upon Agnes on the back stairs when she should have been busy making dinner. 'I've only just finished tidying up there, Mrs Meadowes. Sorry I couldn't come down and help before. Was there anything in particular you're wanting of me now?' she said, unable to keep the curiosity from her voice.

'Yes,' Agnes replied crisply. 'If you've a minute to spare, I should like you to point out Rose's bed and belongings to me.'

Nancy's eyes grew round. 'Whatever for?'

There was no reason, thought Agnes, to mention Lydia Blanchard's interest in Rose's whereabouts. If she breathed a word of it to Nancy, it would soon be common knowledge and everyone would grow wary of revealing what they knew. 'I think it only right that I should try to discover where she's gone,' she replied cagily.

'You ain't wanting to get her back – not after all the trouble she's caused?'

'No, but suppose the poor girl's met with some misadventure.'

'Didn't seem much of a poor girl to me,' muttered Nancy.

'What was that?' Agnes quickly asked.

'Nothing,' replied Nancy airily.

'I gather you and she had an argument yesterday.'

'That were over nothing much – only my ticking her off for not tidying her bed. And I'd every right to do so. She was in a state over something – don't know what – and suddenly went for me. Good job John were there to pull her off.' Unconsciously, the girl raised her hand to her neck, where Agnes caught sight of a livid red line.

'That's a nasty wound. Did Rose do that?'

'Yes,' snapped Nancy.

'Quite a temper over an unmade bed.'

Nancy shook her head. 'Like I said, she were in a state. Probably thinking of going off.' Turning on her heels, she led the way up four flights of stairs to the garret.

There were two attic rooms. 'That there's where Patsy sleeps,' said Nancy sourly, pointing to a door on the right. 'This is ours.' She led the way into a narrow, draughty garret with sloping ceilings and exposed rafters. Agnes shivered, thinking of her own snug quarters in the basement, which were warmed by the kitchen range. 'Her bed is there by the window, and mine here, next to the door. Doris's is over there.' She signalled to a third bed a short distance away by the washstand. 'I made Rose's this morning – Doris and I took turns. Rose was never one for order, and if Mrs Tooley comes up and sees the room in a state all of us get a scolding.'

Agnes looked down at the bed and its thin coverlet, imagining Rose half-asleep first thing in the morning, her hair, the colour and thickness of treacle, sprawled across the bolster. She walked to the casement window set into the eaves. The sky was fine and clear, with only the occasional strand of cloud alleviating the blue uniformity. She gazed out over the street at the dome of St Paul's, squatting like a gigantic toad above the patchwork rooftops of Foster Lane and Cheapside, at the spires rearing above the mottled roofs, at the warren of alleys leading down to the river. The water seemed glassy and still – a band of quicksilver amid a dark sea. Somewhere in this panorama of shadow and light was Rose. But where? What had lured her away? Lydia had hinted she might somehow had been involved in the murder and the robbery. Agnes did not believe Rose capable of such a thing, yet she had to find what had caused her to leave, for Peter's sake. Reminding herself that the answers to these questions might well lie in this room, Agnes turned back to Nancy. 'Where did Rose keep her belongings?'

'In here, like the rest of us,' said Nancy, throwing open the creaking doors of a small deal press cupboard painted a soft shade of green, and pointing to the uppermost shelf. 'Those things are hers.'

Folded neatly was a meagre assortment of clothes: a back-laced corset, a calico petticoat, a cotton slip, a patched under-petticoat, two pairs of yarn stockings and two threadbare skirts and bodices, one of a dark-blue woollen cloth, the other of yellow and green striped cotton. Agnes recognized these as being Rose's usual workday clothes. There was nothing more.

Agnes pointed to the skirts and bodices. 'As I recall, she had a Sunday gown of blue wool, did she not?'

Nancy looked at the shelf and nodded. 'I hadn't looked afore now. And her cloak and bonnet and her best boots are gone. She must have been wearing them when she went out.'

'Shouldn't there be more besides what is here? Underclothes and a nightgown? They aren't here.'

'Perhaps,' said Nancy, looking uncertain. 'I hadn't thought.'

'And had she no personal possessions – no letters, papers, keepsakes from her family?'

Nancy stared at the shelf and shook her head. 'If she had I never saw 'em.'

'She must have had some things,' said Agnes carefully. 'If nothing's here she must have taken them with her, which suggests she did not intend to return.' She paused, looking at the scant belongings on Rose's shelf, and then at the other fuller shelves lower down – presumably Nancy's and Doris's possessions. All were neatly stowed in deference to Mrs Tooley's inspections. She raised her eyes and caught a strange look on Nancy's face. 'What is it? Has something else gone?'

'No, Mrs Meadowes. Nothing from what I can see. It's only you asking me made me recall there was something in particular that was somewhere else. I haven't looked to see if that's gone. I pray you won't scold me for not mentioning it sooner.'

'What do you mean?'

'A week ago, while I was changing the linen on her bed, I found it under her mattress – a purse stuffed with gold sovereigns. There were twenty of 'em.'

Agnes's brow knotted. 'Show me where you found it.'

Nancy stepped towards Rose's bed and rolled the thin horsehair mattress forward to expose the wooden slats beneath. She pointed to the top right-hand corner. 'It was here, Mrs Meadowes.'

'Did you speak to her about it?'

Nancy laughed and shook her head vehemently. 'I wouldn't dare. No point in asking for trouble. She could be ferocious when she wanted.'

How would a kitchen maid like Rose have come by such wealth? The accusations of Lydia and Mr Matthews still rang in her ears. 'Have you any notion how she got the money?'

'Must've been something underhand, mustn't it?'

'Did you mention the matter to anyone else?'

'No,' said Nancy, her head down.

She was holding back something. 'Why did you dislike her?' asked Agnes impulsively.

A sudden flush spread across Nancy's pale face. 'I weren't like her, ma'am – she'd do anything for a man. Philip got taken in by her – more fool him. She were scarce better than a whore at times.'

Agnes remembered now Philip's quip that he was the cause of Rose and Nancy's argument. 'Was Philip the reason you fought yesterday?'

Nancy's gaze flashed towards the window, then she looked quickly back at Agnes. 'I told you that was over nothing more than the mess she made,' she declared. 'But there's something else, Mrs Meadowes . . . although I don't know if it's aught to do with her running off.'

'Yes?'

'There's a pair of pocket pistols that are always kept in a box in Mr Nicholas Blanchard's room, with a small flask of powder. This morning when I looked, one was gone. I didn't say nothing before, on account of I shouldn't have been looking. Do you think she might 'ave took it?'

Agnes hesitated. 'I don't know, Nancy,' she replied.

What she meant, however, was that she did not want to know, but she feared she would be obliged to find out.

Chapter Fifteen

AT ONE O'CLOCK, THE SERVANTS GATHERED FOR LUNCH. DORIS had laid the table, knives and spoons drunkenly askew, and set out yesterday's leftovers on the table – dropping a meat pudding in the process so that it burst all over the flags and turned them slippery as grease. Once everyone was seated, Mr Matthews declared he had an important announcement, and a ripple of unease and excitement spread through the assembly.

The butler stood at one end of the table to say his speediest grace – 'Lord, we give humble thanks for the fruits we are about to receive, Amen' – then without further pause, he cleared his throat. 'Ladies and gentlemen,' he said, with as much gravitas as a judge announcing a death sentence, 'I have news to break of a tragedy.'

After he had finished, Mr Matthews picked up his carving knife and fork and turned his attentions to the bacon while the news soaked in. Mrs Tooley was greatly shaken, and had to forage in her pocket for her smelling salts and take several noisy sniffs before she was able to swallow a morsel. But by and large, Mr Matthews's momentous announcement did not cause the stir he might have expected. By now three hours had passed since the upstairs breakfast, at which Theodore had broken the news to his father. Both John and Philip had been present. Their talkative dispositions had ensured that most of the other servants had already got an inkling of what had happened.

There were, however, certain details which Theodore had neglected to mention and in which everyone took an avid interest. According to Mr Matthews, who had heard it from the apprentice who found Noah's body, the constable had visited the Blanchards' workshop soon after the crime was discovered. The justice had been left undisturbed until nine, by which time the undertakers had arrived and transported the corpse away on their wagon. The only obvious reminder of the tragedy was a large wine-coloured stain on the ceiling of the downstairs showroom, caused by blood dripping through from overhead. Despite the efforts of the other two apprentices, this had so far proved impossible to obliterate.

Agnes rubbed her forehead with the back of her hand, staring unseeingly at the piece of bacon on her plate. Lydia Blanchard's suspicion that Rose was somehow involved in what had happened next door obliged her to take an interest in the conversation. Yet she did so unwillingly. The fact that a young boy had been killed while on watch struck her as tragic, but what seemed more poignant was that his death had been eclipsed by the theft of a valuable wine-cooler, and that everyone appeared to take such vicarious delight in the drama. It seemed somehow indecent.

'John,' Agnes said, in a tone inaudible to the rest, 'do you think it possible that a woman could have had a hand in the murder and robbery?'

John put his knife down softly on his plate and turned to look at her. His face was narrower than Philip's, his features less regular – his nose was long and aquiline, his eyes set at a slanting angle, his lips thin. Yet for all that, thought Agnes, it was a more appealing countenance. John was never presumptuous or unseemly. She could speak to him with an ease she never felt with Philip.

'I doubt any woman would have had the strength,' John answered unhesitatingly. 'Butchering a man requires considerable force, don't it? And from what I hear the wine-cooler was a sizeable one – as big as a bathtub; too heavy for a woman to carry.'

Agnes nodded at this confirmation of her own suspicions. Whatever Lydia thought, Rose alone was unlikely to have been responsible for what happened last night. But had she had an accomplice?

'What do you know of Rose Francis's male acquaintances?' she asked.

John took a bite of bread and chewed it slowly before swallowing. 'You think *she* had a hand in it, do you? Reckon it was more than a coincidence, her going off?'

Agnes shrugged noncommittally. 'Who might have helped her?' she persisted.

John smiled, revealing his teeth. 'There was quite a collection of men friends, by all accounts. But the only ones I know came from this house, or the premises next door, and none of them have disappeared – so I somehow doubt it were any of them.'

Agnes sensed that behind his shrewd grey eyes lay more. But John was never as keen to gossip as Philip. She wondered whether he held back from loyalty to Rose – had he been fond of her too?

'I gather there was an argument yesterday between Rose and Nancy.'

John's thin mouth tensed. He nodded. 'I witnessed it and cooled them down.'

'What was it over – Philip?'

'I don't believe so. Rose and he was no longer sweet on each other. Nancy could have him if she chose.'

'What, then?'

'Something about a letter Nancy had taken that belonged to Rose.'

'From whom? What did it say?'

John regarded her, then smiled again. 'They never said, and I never asked. Just pulling 'em apart was enough to test me to the limit.'

'Did you happen to hear anything about her and Benjamin

Riley, the journeyman next door, or Mr Blanchard, senior?'

John tapped his nose as he had the previous day when informing her of the letter. 'I don't suppose the rumours I've heard are any different from those that've reached you, Mrs Meadowes. Seeing as how we all live in the same place and eat the same food and breathe the same air.' He paused, wiping the rim of his plate with the last piece of bread while Agnes looked on frustratedly. 'And where's the use in picking over the same bone? 'Twould leave us all hungry.' Then, before she could press him further, he swivelled himself pointedly towards Philip and broke into his conversation with the now giggling maids. 'Now, what happened to all them candle stubs in the dining room? Was it you or Nancy that took 'em?'

At the upper servants' tea in Mrs Tooley's parlour an hour later, Agnes did not let the subject of Rose Francis rest. 'Most of Rose's belongings are still in her closet. What do you intend to do with them?' she enquired, while Mrs Tooley unlocked the tea caddy and spooned a mixture of green and black leaves carefully into the pot.

'Nothing, for the time being,' returned Mrs Tooley tartly, for in truth she was tired of the subject of Rose Francis, and now that she had overcome her initial shock, she was eager to press Mr Matthews further on the terrible drama of the previous night. 'But if Doris and Nancy are helpful till we find a replacement, I might offer them the pick of her things.'

'Most of them are too worn to be much use to anybody,' said Agnes. 'She took the best with her.'

'Didn't she ever,' put in Mr Matthews glumly.

'Dusters, then,' said Mrs Tooley decisively, locking the caddy and turning to the butler. 'So, Mr Matthews, you say the apprentice who found the body had no notion of what had taken place until he went in. He heard no sound at all, you say? And then the first thing he saw was Noah's head hanging on by a thread and blood flooding all over the floor?'

'That's according to him,' said Mr Matthews, nodding sagely.

'And the blood was quite prodigious – enough to soak

through the ceiling, you said?' Mrs Tooley shuddered, but did not seem as distraught as Agnes expected.

'There were footsteps all across the floor, leading to the exact place where the wine-cooler was displayed. I saw them quite clearly when I accompanied Mr Theodore last night.'

This gruesome exchange, reiterating much of what she had already heard, was insupportable to Agnes. She got up to leave, but then, remembering her need to ascertain what had happened to Rose, settled down determinedly once more. She attempted to steer the conversation her way. 'Rose leaving those things in her closet shows she no longer needed them. That might mean she had money enough to buy new things.'

As she spoke, she observed that Mr Matthews's expression turned disdainful, as if this were a trivial matter of no interest to him. He picked up his tea and sipped it, gazing into the middle distance. Patsy, tall and elegant, paused with a teaspoon in her hand. She was a dark-haired, somewhat masculine woman with a longish nose. She patted the back of her neat coiffure with her large hands, regarding Mrs Tooley and Mr Matthews thoughtfully. 'Rose Francis must have had a very rich friend indeed, to leave everything behind. Or perhaps she had more than one sponsor.'

'She did not leave everything behind. Only her working clothes,' insisted Agnes.

'Either way, we're all better off without her,' said Mrs Tooley, glancing towards Mr Matthews for approval. But he was maintaining his air of disinterest and gazing at his tea, and thus did not notice her.

'Nancy happened to mention there was a pistol missing from the dressing chest in Mr Blanchard's room. Do you know anything of it?' said Agnes, addressing the butler directly now.

Matthews nodded self-importantly. 'I have been apprised of the loss. Mr Blanchard was as astonished and distressed to discover it as I. Naturally, we can only assume that Rose took it. I must make an inventory of the household silver at the earliest opportunity. We must hope nothing else is gone.'

Agnes remembered that the day before, Mr Matthews had found Rose upstairs, and wondered if stealing the pistol rather than intimacy with Nicholas was the cause. 'Nothing,' she said, 'save a valuable wine-cooler and a life.'

'Upon my soul, Mrs Meadowes!' exclaimed Mrs Tooley. 'You are surely not suggesting Rose—'

But before she could finish, there was a heavy thumping at the door. ' 'Scuse me for interrupting,' said Philip, now dressed in his full afternoon regalia, popping his powdered head around the door of the parlour. 'I've an important message for Mrs Meadowes. Mr Theodore Blanchard asks that she attend him immediately. And by the by, he doesn't want to see you upstairs, ma'am, but in the showroom next door. Ain't you the lucky one. You'll witness the stain on the ceiling. Don't forget to look up so you can tell us all what it's like.'

Chapter Sixteen

AGNES COULD COUNT ON THE FINGERS OF ONE HAND THE TIMES she had entered the Blanchards' business premises. Usually it had been prior to important dinners, when she had been sent to borrow extra items of silverware for the table. Perhaps bowls for sweetmeats or leaf-shaped pickle dishes, or her particular favourite, a series of salt cellars, fashioned like muscular sea gods supporting open oyster shells – so realistically modelled that every stria of the shell was visible.

But she was familiar enough with the premises to know that downstairs was the main shop, where smaller objects were displayed for customers, while leading off from the rear were the workshop and an office where accounts were prepared. Upstairs was a grander showroom, where the magnificent silverware was displayed upon which Blanchards' reputation was founded. She had never entered this hallowed place, but according to Mr Matthews, the pieces exhibited here were of fabulous scale and intricacy, fashioned not simply for sale but to elicit commissions. Almost anything could be tailored to suit. It was perfectly possible to order a set of serving dishes with a border design taken from a tea caddy, legs from a soup tureen, and handles like those on a teapot. In short, there was almost nothing the ingenious Blanchard craftsmen could not fashion, provided the patron could be enticed to commission it.

With a heavy heart, Agnes presented herself in the downstairs shop. She had never spoken to Noah Prout, the poor apprentice who had been murdered, yet the very thought of entering the place where such an atrocity had taken place only a few hours earlier, and seeing the stain on the ceiling, distressed her. Fortunately, however, she was not left to linger. As soon as she mentioned that Mr Theodore Blanchard awaited her (her eyes fixed firmly on her feet), one of the surviving apprentices scurried off to fetch a journeyman. Minutes later, heavy steps clattered down the stairs at surprising speed. She raised her head, and discovered to her relief that it was not Benjamin Riley but Thomas Williams who had come to fetch her.

'Mr Blanchard is almost ready, Mrs Meadowes. He asked me to show you upstairs, and asks that you wait a moment there for him,' said Williams in a sombre tone, after bowing and bidding her good day. He was a stocky man, not much taller or older than she, with rusty coloured hair sprouting from his head in wild curls. His flat, wide face and rather solid jaw gave him a stubborn expression, which contrasted oddly with the somewhat melancholic glow in his green eyes.

Agnes greeted him with a brief curtsey. 'Thank you, Mr Williams,' she returned as he held the door open for her. She was halfway up the stairs before she realized with relief that she had not once caught sight of the ceiling.

Williams ushered her into the showroom leading off the landing. 'Please won't you sit down, Mrs Meadowes,' he said, walking to the far end of the room and arranging a chair near the fire. 'Mr Blanchard is finishing some business in the office. He bade me tell you he will join you shortly.'

The room was long and thin, panelled in oak, with a carved chimneypiece in the centre and a pair of large sash windows draped with elaborate swagged curtains at either end. It was furnished not as a conventional shop but rather as a dining room, with a dark-red Turkey rug, a pair of consoles, a well-polished mahogany sideboard, and a matching circular dining table. Every surface was covered with silver. Small candelabra and silver boxes fashioned in various forms adorned the console tables and chimneypiece. The dining table was set as if for the grandest of banquets, complete with candlesticks, covered dishes, silver wine-coolers, goblets, salt cellars, condiments, plates and cutlery, all made from silver and of the finest design and quality. At each end of the sideboard stood a pair of massive twelve-branched candelabra. The only incongruous note was struck by a space in the middle. This, Agnes supposed, was where the wine-cooler had stood.

Even as she took in the details of the room, Agnes was aware that Thomas Williams observed her. She felt anxious at being thus scrutinized by a man she barely knew. But her preoccupation with Rose remained at the forefront of her thoughts. There were several matters with which Thomas Williams might usefully assist her. Thus she forced herself to make conversation with him. 'I came upon your Mr Riley yesterday. He was carrying a basket of silver and dropped it in the road,' she began.

Williams looked doleful. 'Indeed? He never mentioned it. How unfortunate.'

'It was,' she said emphatically, then after a short hesitation pressed on. 'I expect you knew that he was friendly with our kitchen maid, Rose Francis?'

Thomas Williams turned down his mouth glumly. 'I caught a glimpse of her from time to time.'

'Where did you glimpse her, Mr Williams?'

He frowned and scratched his hair. 'I don't exactly recall. In the street – or was it here perhaps? She visited occasionally.' He hesitated again. 'I hope I am not speaking out of turn – I would not wish to embroil her in any trouble.'

Agnes shot him a piercing look. 'Of course not. I only ask because Rose Francis has gone missing. Compared with recent events here this might seem a trivial matter, but I need most urgently to find her.'

He looked up sharply. 'Did you ask Riley?' he said in a more business-like tone.

'Yes, but he refused to say much. Indeed, he offered no help at all.'

Williams took a deep breath. The soft, mournful expression returned. 'That doesn't surprise me.' He fingered a candlestick. 'I'm sorry to hear that she's gone,' he said. 'Riley has not mentioned the matter to me, and I have no knowledge of their dealings, or what they were to one another. I didn't pay much attention. Why are you after her? Is she in trouble?'

'No, though she caused me a deal of inconvenience. But Mrs Blanchard would like to know what made her go off like that.'

As she had hoped, this mention of Lydia's name seemed to sway Williams in her favour. 'Then if it would assist you, I'll question Riley about it and see if he says any more,' he suggested.

Agnes congratulated herself inwardly. Perhaps she was better than she knew at the art of conversation. She smiled, feeling easier now. 'Anything you discover would be welcome. Rose could be unpredictable, she was inclined to be overfriendly with her men friends. But to go off without a word – none of us expected that. Do you think Mr Riley might have set her up in rooms somewhere close by?'

Williams gave a bitter laugh and shook his head. 'On a journeyman's salary, I doubt it – besides, he has a landlady who's fiercer than a mad dog. He's forever arguing with her. But still, he might know where she is.'

No sooner had Thomas Williams spoken than there was the sound of a door closing and the soft thud of footsteps on the boards outside. He moved speedily to open the door, and the earlier formality returned to his demeanour. 'This will be Mr Blanchard for you. With your permission, Mrs Meadowes, I will take my leave.' His voice dropped to a half-whisper. 'Rest assured, I shan't forget my undertaking.'

As Theodore Blanchard strode in, followed by another man – an elderly gentleman, tall and well built, in an old-fashioned, full-bottomed wig and a dark-brown coat – it was his expression that first caught Agnes's attention. Usually the most easygoing and placid of men, Agnes had never seen him so distracted as he looked today. His face was flushed to the colour of port wine, his jacket half-buttoned, his cravat undone. He appeared to be sweating profusely, for his forehead glistened as brightly as the silver in front of him.

Theodore strode across to the dining table and drew up a pair of chairs for himself and his companion, whom he introduced to Agnes as Justice Cordingly. 'You have heard, I take it, of the robbery last night, Mrs Meadowes?' Theodore said without preamble.

'Yes, sir. Mr Matthews apprised us of what happened.'

'Bad enough to lose the apprentice – he was a good one and becoming better by the day, and boys of such diligence aren't easily come by – but to lose the wine-cooler, that is a veritable calamity,' said Theodore.

'I am very sorry for the loss,' returned Agnes. Inwardly, she was appalled at Theodore's callousness in equating a life with a wine-cooler, but she reminded herself that he was in a state of agitation and not at all himself.

'At any rate, I dare say you want to know why I have summoned you like this,' said Theodore, as if he had read her thoughts.

Agnes glanced nervously at him, then towards the table, where six salt cellars in the form of miniature turreted castles caught her attention. 'I did wonder, sir.'

'It was my wife who first suggested it. She thought you might be amenable . . .' began Theodore.

'Perhaps *I* should explain,' said Justice Cordingly, holding up an intervening hand in a lordly manner. 'It is a measure of the high esteem in which you are held, Mrs Meadowes, that you have been summoned here this afternoon. There is little chance of the forces of justice solving a complex tragedy such as this without additional cooperation. But we must pick our deputies with care. After my preliminary examination of the facts, it appears likely that someone inside this household has assisted in this crime. We therefore require someone inside the household to aid us, someone whose integrity is beyond reproach. Mr Blanchard has consulted his wife and concluded that you should be the one to assist.'

From somewhere nearby, the strident sound of hammering metal could be heard. It was piercing enough to make Agnes blink at every stroke, and she was not at all sure she had heard correctly. She was a cook, her place was in her kitchen – what assistance could she conceivably offer? She felt Justice Cordingly's and Theodore's eyes scrutinize her expectantly. She felt exposed, uneasy. 'I'm sorry, sir, I do not properly understand what you require of me.'

Justice Cordingly scratched his long nose in a contemplative manner. 'As I said before, we believe this was no casual crime. Only the wine-cooler, the most valuable object in the building, was taken. That points to the fact that someone knew of the object and its value, and that the crime was carefully planned, and undertaken with inside knowledge. *You*, Mrs Meadowes, have been elected by us to be the servant of justice; to poke about, ask questions, encourage confidences, and report to one or the other of us anything – anything at all – you think significant.'

Agnes blinked as the metal was struck again and again. She felt her temples flinch and her brain pound, as if the hammer were striking inside her head.

'And, most pressingly, you are to assist in the *recovery* of the wine-cooler,' chimed Theodore hastily.

Having slowly grasped their meaning, Agnes was overwhelmed with misgivings similar to those she had felt after her conversation with Lydia. Once again, she was being forced to act against her natural inclinations, to abandon her private disposition and go against her conviction that there was nothing to be gained by being too friendly. The truth was, she was not interested in others' private lives or dilemmas, any more than she wanted to share her own misfortunes. It was tragic that an apprentice had been murdered, she regretted the wine-cooler's loss – but ultimately, neither of these calamities was anything to do with her. Nor, with all she had to worry over, did she wish them to be.

Dare she make this point to Theodore? Despite her usual

docility, Agnes decided she would. She coughed tentatively and did her best to raise her voice above the noise. 'I am honoured by your offer, sirs. And I am gratified to learn that Mrs Blanchard holds me in high esteem. But I am not at all certain I am suited to the responsibilities of the task,' she ventured.

'What?' said Justice Cordingly, his brow rumpling incredulously. 'What did you say?'

Theodore snorted. The filigree of veins on his nose and cheeks darkened. 'As we see it, you are the only choice,' he declared. 'You are not so young as to be foolish, but more alert and able than either Mrs Tooley or Mr Matthews. Patsy is not below stairs enough to be useful. The others are too lowly to trust.'

Just then the hammering stopped, leaving the room silent. Agnes felt her stomach grow watery. She wished she were anywhere but here. 'Even so, sir, I am not certain I have the confidence of the other servants.'

'In my experience,' said Justice Cordingly in a coaxing tone, 'those who wish to hear confidences have only to make themselves amenable. Most servants in your position would relish the opportunity you are being offered.'

Then perhaps in that respect I differ from most, thought Agnes as she gazed at him in unhappy silence.

Theodore mopped his brow with a crimson handkerchief. 'Before you voice any further reservations, Mrs Meadowes, I will mention one other point. As Justice Cordingly has said, the wine-cooler was the most valuable object ever made by Blanchards. Losing it could well pitch us into bankruptcy, in which case I and my family will land in the Fleet, and every member of staff in the household, you included, will lose their jobs. You have it in your power to prevent that happening.'

There was a pause. Agnes felt as though someone was dragging her hand towards a hot oven and she was powerless to pull back. 'But is it probable that something I hear below stairs will lead to the wine-cooler's recovery?' she asked desperately.

'It isn't *only* listening I require of you. There is someone outside the house who might find it,' said Theodore, again wiping his gleaming brow with his handkerchief. 'I want you to act as my intermediary and pay him a visit.'

Once again Agnes was jolted by surprise. 'Who is this person?'

'A man whose premises are close by here, in Southwark – a place called Melancholy Walk. He goes by the name of Marcus Pitt.'

'Are you acquainted with the name?' said Justice Cordingly.

'No, sir,' replied Agnes, looking in bemusement from Theodore to Justice Cordingly and back. 'Should I be? Is he a servant, or a tradesman or another silversmith, perhaps?'

'His profession is none of those,' said Justice Cordingly, shaking his head bitterly. 'It is far more lucrative. He is what some consider a necessary evil, and others (myself included) a scourge of society – a thief-taker.'

Agnes had naturally heard of thief-takers – men who used intelligence from tapsters, ostlers and every variety of rogue to recover stolen property. Some appeared honourable, holding respectable positions. But while they purported to offer a useful service to the unfortunate victims of robbery, they were rumoured to be less innocent than they seemed, acting as fences, on occasion even engineering the theft of the property they were later paid to recover.

She shifted uncomfortably in her chair. 'I am very sensible of the kind of man to whom you refer, sirs. But I have no expertise in such matters. Why should you wish me to visit such a person for you?'

'Because, Mrs Meadowes, as Justice Cordingly has said, there is no doubt that this murderous robbery has been most carefully orchestrated. Marcus Pitt is the most influential thief-taker in this locality. Few crimes that take place hereabouts are unknown to him. It may well be that whoever inside our business or household betrayed us, conspired to do so with his aid, using a thief under his control. Even if they did not, if anyone can find the wine-cooler it is he.'

'If Mr Pitt is so powerful and influential, is it wise to entrust me to speak to him? Would it not be more prudent for you to approach him directly?'

A shifty gleam appeared in Theodore's eye. 'We would, but Pitt forbids it. He prefers to deal with an intermediary – says it only causes trouble if those that are robbed come too close to those that perpetrated the crime.'

Agnes sensed that there was more to why she had been chosen than Theodore had revealed. 'But as a woman cook, am I a prudent choice?'

Theodore shook his head emphatically and flashed a knowing look at the justice. 'Rest assured, Mrs Meadowes. You are adequate for the task. Mr Pitt is a consummate businessman. He conducts similar transactions every day. Besides, I hear he has a taste for handsome women.'

Agnes recoiled inwardly, trying not to dwell on this last remark, unable to see a way of averting the inevitable. Was she to be offered to this loathsome thief-taker – a man who profited from others' misfortune – as bait to entice him to help? No, she told herself, Theodore would never misuse her in such a way. His earlier arguments – the age and fragility of the remaining upper servants, Mr Pitt's preference for an intermediary – these were the reasons for her unwelcome appointment.

Theodore expected nothing but compliance, and interpreted her troubled silence as acquiescence. 'You should not, of course, reveal that you are my cook – I do not wish him to take insult by my sending a domestic servant,' he continued. 'Rather say you are an engraver from my workshop, come on my behalf. I will notify him in advance. Do what you can to play on his sympathy – it can only help. Let him know you are recently arrived and fear you will lose your position if the business flounders, as it certainly will in the face of such a prodigious loss.'

As she sat before them impotently listening, the hammering started up again. This time it was gentler than before, but Agnes shrank inwardly at the anticipation of every stroke. 'And how much do I offer to pay?' she murmured.

'To begin with he will merely require a fee to register the loss. Assuming he finds the wine-cooler, the negotiations for its return will come later. At very least he will expect the melted value of the metal. I am prepared to offer that sum plus a modest additional payment. But I don't wish you to disclose that in the first instance. Nor do I want Sir Bartholomew Grey's name mentioned. Heaven forbid we attract Pitt's unsavoury attention towards his household or I'll never see another commission from him.' Theodore paused. 'I should also say, if you acquit yourself well in this I shall reward you handsomely. Find the wine-cooler and I undertake to pay you twenty guineas.'

Agnes's stomach tightened, the hammering forgotten; the horror and danger flew from her thoughts. Twenty guineas was six months' wages – it would augment her dwindling savings and assist with the costs of Peter's board and education. She still felt a powerful presentiment of doom, but what was instinct compared to practicality? If she took on this role, she might not only save the Blanchard enterprise but benefit Peter. She nodded hesitantly. 'Very well, sir,' she said. 'When shall I call on Mr Pitt?'

Theodore smiled and mopped his brow again. His mood seemed less fraught. 'Tomorrow at midday. I will tell my wife to inform Mrs Tooley you are to be permitted extra freedom to assist me. Marcus Pitt will be expecting you. Philip will escort you to his premises.'

'I could go on my own if it is more convenient, sir,' said Agnes, who did not in the least relish the prospect of a journey disturbed by the garrulous Philip.

Theodore shook his head. 'Do not underestimate the dangers of this undertaking, Mrs Meadowes. Pitt might pose as an arbiter of the law, but from all I hear he is as much a rogue as those with whom he deals. Heaven forbid the same fate should befall you as that poor fellow last night—'

Chapter Seventeen

SOME HOURS LATER, AGNES STOOD AT THE KITCHEN TABLE WITH a newly boiled calf's head on a platter before her. She inserted the point of a sharp knife midway between the eyes and slowly raised the skin. Faced with the practicalities of preparing supper, she attempted to push all thoughts of Marcus Pitt from her mind. The only matter superseding the steaming head and the forcemeat with which she would stuff it was Peter, and her pressing need to retrieve him from Mrs Catchpole. From this vantage point, Agnes now saw Theodore's proposal in a more favourable light. It offered money and, more immediately, a chance to escape the house and her usual duties. She would thus be able to find somewhere for Peter to stay.

Slowly, her spirits rallied and she began to view the proposed mission with a measure of willingness – gratitude, even. And yet Theodore Blanchard's final thoughtless words of warning were not forgotten. The prospect of venturing out into society and involving herself in matters outside her world frightened her. But she would brazen out the perils for Peter's sake; and afterwards she could return to her former existence.

Agnes's thoughts were then diverted along another path.

Lydia had encouraged Theodore to choose her as his aid. Did Lydia's interest in Rose lie behind her recommendation? Or was she trying to help Agnes gain the freedom she had asked for without offending Mrs Tooley? She had, after all, shown some sympathy to her plight. If Lydia had tried to assist her, it was only right that she should continue her efforts to discover what had happened to Rose. Besides, she could not deny that she too was curious to find out where the girl had gone.

Both Lydia and Mr Matthews had suggested there might be an alliance between Rose and Nicholas Blanchard, and Mr Matthews had seen Rose upstairs the day before she disappeared. But assuming Rose had stolen the pistol, thought Agnes, this was most likely when she had done so. It did not prove there was an improper alliance. Lydia had implied that Rose might have left because she was carrying Nicholas's child. What had caused her to form this opinion? There was only one person who had Lydia's wholehearted confidence, and she was presently standing fifteen feet away in the laundry room, cleaning one of Lydia's hats with a velvet cloth.

Leaving the calf's head to cool, Agnes accosted Patsy. 'Has Mrs Blanchard said anything to you about her interest in Rose Francis?' she enquired with an ingenuous smile.

Patsy looked askance, but a moment later weakly returned the smile. As lady's maid, she liked to pretend she had nothing in common with the other maidservants. She was older and more finely dressed, and to underline her importance she aped Lydia's manners – crooking her little finger when she drank tea, picking daintily at her food as if she had no appetite. Her placid expression and cool manner were also strangely reminiscent of Lydia. Agnes often wondered if this was a further affectation on Patsy's part or whether she had unconsciously grown to resemble her mistress.

When it came to Agnes, however, Patsy was, as a rule, more convivial. Agnes suspected that this was because Patsy longed occasionally to exchange ideas with someone to whom she was not always expected to defer. Doubtless that was why, offered an opportunity to discuss the matter of Rose freely, Patsy seized the offer. 'Yes, but I don't for the life of me see why. I should have thought she would be grateful the girl had gone,' she said candidly, scratching a tiny blemish on the hat brim with the nail of her forefinger with feigned concentration.

'Why do you say that – had Rose annoyed her?'

Patsy gave a small, tight smile. 'Not exactly.'

'What then?' Agnes persisted. 'Had it to do with Nicholas?'

'Mrs Blanchard wondered why the wretched girl had been upstairs,' said Patsy importantly.

'When was this – yesterday?'

Patsy raised her head, but did not look straight at Agnes; she gazed into the middle distance in the same unfocussed way that Lydia had done in response to Agnes's request for time off. 'No, not then. I don't recall exactly. A week or so back, perhaps. I think she mentioned it to Mrs Tooley.'

'Why did she not question Rose herself?'

Patsy paused, as though considering her reply. 'She never caught her. It was something she discovered – a letter, I believe – that showed the girl had been there.'

'A letter?' Agnes recalled John mentioning that a letter had been the cause of the fight between Rose and Nancy. 'Was it Mrs Blanchard who found the letter?' she pressed.

A further pause. 'No, I believe Nancy handed it to her.'

'What did it say?'

Patsy shook her head ruefully. 'It was written by Rose, and concerned a man. Mrs Blanchard read it to me so quickly and I was tidying her things at the time, so I didn't hear exactly.'

Agnes nodded, pondering. A man, she thought; what else would a letter penned by Rose concern? 'And what did Mrs Blanchard say after Rose's disappearance?'

'She was troubled, though Lord knows why. If you want my opinion, Mrs Blanchard hasn't enough to occupy her.'

Remembering the calf's head, Agnes returned to the

kitchen table. She would have liked to keep the conversation going, to discover what else Patsy might reveal, but duty, as always, was uppermost. As she assembled the stuffing with ingredients Doris had prepared for her – a pound of bacon fat scraped to beads, the crumbs of two penny loaves, a small nutmeg grated, a pinch of cayenne pepper and a little grated lemon peel – she thought about the letter Nancy had found. Why had she lied earlier today when Agnes had asked her what the argument was about?

A few minutes later, Patsy emerged from the laundry room with the hat in her hand and the cord of an evening bag draped about her wrist, as if she were off to some grand assembly. She hovered by the table, watching Agnes deftly mixing the stuffing.

'Lord knows why she went off,' she proffered suddenly in a bitter tone, 'or why there's such a fuss over her going. It seemed to me she gave us both the run around on occasion . . . Mrs Blanchard wanted me to ask you whether you found anything among the wretched girl's things to show where she has gone?'

'You may tell her I have looked, but discerned nothing,' said Agnes.

She was now adding the yolks of half a dozen eggs to her stuffing, cracking each one over a small bowl so the white ran into it, then dropping each golden orb into the crumbled mixture, where it gleamed like a small sun. Taking up a long metal spoon, she began to stir the ingredients together, cutting again and again through the mix until it had transformed to a rich yellow-tinged forcemeat. 'Did Rose plague *you*, Patsy? If so, I never knew it.'

'I wouldn't allow her to bother me, Mrs Meadowes. But that didn't mean I was blind to what she was.'

Agnes pressed a small quantity of forcemeat into each ear of the calf's head and the rest into the head cavity, moulding the skin over so that it once again resembled a head. The sharp tone of Patsy's reply made her look up. 'How d'you mean?'

'Rose lacked modesty. She was forever sticking her nose in

matters that didn't concern her. You let her get away with it, but that didn't mean it was right.'

Agnes knew she ought to have been more forthright, but Patsy's criticism galled her. Her feelings towards Rose were ambivalent – the girl had lacked modesty, but had she really been as black as everyone painted her? 'She wasn't all bad, Patsy. She was quick enough around the kitchen, and no worse than you would find in any household.'

Still riled, Agnes picked up the calf's head and plunged it into a pot with white wine, lemon pickle, walnut and mushroom catsup, an anchovy, a blade of mace and a bundle of sweet herbs, then set the pot on the stove. Patsy, meanwhile, seated herself at the table, still clutching Lydia's belongings as if they were a badge of office. She leaned forward towards Agnes. 'Speaking confidentially, it wasn't what Rose did or said so much as what lay in her thoughts that made me take exception to her. She was forever trying to wheedle round me, wanting to know where I went with Mrs Blanchard and who we met.'

Agnes arched a brow. 'You mean her attempts at conversation offended you? That was why you disliked her?'

Patsy frowned. 'It was what inspired the conversation, more like.'

'What, then?'

Patsy fiddled with the brim of Lydia's hat. 'She wanted my position. She thought her duties as kitchen maid beneath her, and wanted to better herself. That's why she sneaked upstairs. She was scheming for my post and trying to engineer meetings with Lydia to get it. I can't pretend I'm sorry she's run off, and that's the reason why.'

After Patsy had gone, Agnes wiped her finger around the inside of the bowl in which her forcemeat had been made and licked it, savouring the mingling of spices. It seemed there was not a soul in the house with whom Rose had enjoyed an uncomplicated relationship. She *should* have reprimanded Rose more. Why then had she shied away from confrontation? Was it only her embarrassment at Rose's familiar manner with men? Agnes did not remember a time when she could speak to a man without self-consciousness and constraint. Her father had kept her apart from them; her unhappy marriage had shown her the dangers of them. And as for acting as Rose had done in the larder – such wantonness was unimaginable. But then a further thought struck her: was a small part of her jealous of Rose?

Unsettled, Agnes posed herself a more straightforward question. What means could she employ to trace Rose? Was there a family to whom the girl might have written of her intentions? She mulled this over for a while before it occurred to her, with a further stab of self-recrimination, that while she and Rose had worked together almost every day for the last year, their conversation had invariably been about food and its preparation. Agnes's dislike of discussing her own history meant she rarely raised personal matters with those around her, and Rose had never volunteered any information. Not once had she mentioned her family, or where she had come from. And Agnes had never asked.

'Forgive me for disturbing you, Mrs Tooley. Might I trouble you for a bottle of preserved plums? I need them for my sauce.'

'I suppose so, Mrs Meadowes,' responded Mrs Tooley, twirling her quill and peering over the rim of her spectacles as suspiciously as if Agnes were asking her for gold rather than a jar of fruit. There were accounts from the grocer, fishmonger, butcher and chandler arranged in exact piles all over the table. She was checking them off against orders recorded in her household ledger; those she had verified had been impaled precisely in the centre on a large iron spike.

Mrs Tooley put down her quill on the pewter inkstand that had been a gift from Lydia Blanchard a year ago. She patted her linen cap and smoothed the lappets, as if reassuring herself of their pristine condition. Removing her spectacles, she bustled to her store cupboard and threw open the doors wide so that they both might properly admire the treasure within: shelves filled with a spectacular array of preserves and pickles as richly coloured as jewels. She brushed a finger over the middle row, where bottled fruits were stored, flitting a proprietorial glance at jars labelled quince, morello cherry, damson, peach, greengage, grape, and finally plum. She selected a jar of ruby-coloured fruit and proudly handed it to Agnes. 'I believe you'll find these as tasty and firm as any you've tried. Anything more you require, Mrs Meadowes?'

Agnes hesitated. Realizing how little she knew of Rose's past had made her conscious that she was equally ignorant of Mrs Tooley. She had known the elderly housekeeper for five years and never once recalled speaking to her about personal matters. Where did the housekeeper go on her days off? On a sudden whim she said, 'I wonder, Mrs Tooley, do you have any family to visit in your free time?'

Mrs Tooley looked puzzled. 'Family? I scarcely have time to visit what little family I have. I have a brother, but the last time I stayed with him I found the disorder in his house most disconcerting. It made me appreciate the tranquillity here. That was two years ago. I have not found the opportunity to go there since.'

'I see,' said Agnes, thinking that a little disorder was not necessarily a bad thing. She moved on to more pressing matters. 'Has Mrs Blanchard spoken to you on my account?'

'She has,' replied Mrs Tooley. 'I understand you are to make an excursion to a thief-taker and might not be back in time to make dinner. I suppose I should be grateful that it is you being sent, not I. But do take care, won't you, Mrs Meadowes? I cannot possibly manage without you.' As she spoke, Mrs Tooley raised a slender hand to her papery cheek and her head began to tremble slightly.

Agnes felt touched, and guilty that she had so quickly given up her attempt at friendly conversation. When she was less pressed she would try again. 'Do not trouble yourself over my welfare,' she said. 'I shall return as swiftly as I can. But there is one other matter I should raise with you. I need to see Rose Francis's reference. Do you happen to know where it is?'

'What possible use can that be now?'

'Mrs Blanchard believes there may be some connection

between the murder and theft and Rose running off, and that she should be questioned on the matter – wherever she is. It occurred to me that her background might help ascertain her whereabouts.'

'There was a written character,' said Mrs Tooley carefully. 'I always insist upon it. As I recall, she stated at her interview that she had no family to speak of. Both her parents had died. She had gone into service for that reason, and came here from a large household in Bruton Street.'

'The family name?'

'Lord and Lady Carew, as I recall.'

'Carew?' echoed Agnes. The name meant nothing to her. 'What reason did she give for her departure from their household?'

'She wanted to better herself and thought a position as kitchen maid might lead to her learning to cook.'

'Who wrote the character? Was it Lady Carew or a member of her staff?'

Mrs Tooley coloured. 'I don't recall. I believe it may have been the housekeeper or steward who wrote it. It was clearly a hand of some education, finely formed and written on paper of quality. There was nothing out of the ordinary about it, if that is what you are implying.'

'I certainly did not mean to imply anything of the kind,' assured Agnes quickly. 'Do you have the letter still?'

Mrs Tooley nodded and moved to the dresser; she opened a drawer and took out a large card folder, untying the tape that bound it. The folder was filled with a sheaf of some twenty or so papers. These she turned over slowly, until at last she came to the one she was searching for. 'Ah yes, as I thought, written by the housekeeper. Here it is.'

'Thank you, ma'am,' said Agnes, taking the paper.

To whom it may concern,

I herby confirm that Miss Rose Francis has been employed as housemaid in this establishment for the past twelve months and is leaving of her own free will. Throughout this time she has shown herself to have an obliging, sober and handy disposition. Her temper is by and large good, her character sociable, she appears sound of health.

Mrs Moore, housekeeper to
Sir Henry Carew.

'There is another letter that interests me,' said Agnes carefully as she handed back the paper. 'I understand Mrs Blanchard recently spoke to you about a communication she found upstairs belonging to Rose.'

Mrs Tooley grew suddenly tremulous again. 'That is an incident I should prefer to forget,' she confessed unsteadily. 'My nerves were dreadfully frayed by it.'

'I do not mean to upset you, ma'am. I simply wondered what was in the letter and whether you kept it?'

Mrs Tooley shook her head. 'I returned it to her after I had given her a talking to. It was a note half a page long, unsigned but written in her hand to someone addressed as 'Dearest'. The contents said little save that she was glad to learn he was well and would think over his proposal. She thanked him for his generous assistance, and hoped to see him on her next free afternoon to discuss the proposal further and give him her decision.'

'Do you recall the address?'

Mrs Tooley swallowed and fidgeted with her spectacles. 'There was none – as I said, the letter was unfinished.'

'And what excuse did she make for the letter being in the drawing room when you spoke to her about it?'

'She was aghast to learn where the letter had been found, and claimed that she had never been in there. She had left the note in her closet. She said that someone must have taken it and put it in the drawing room to cast her in a bad light.'

'Did she say whom she believed had done such a thing?'

'Either Nancy or Patsy, both of whom she declared were jealous of her. But since she had no proof of the assertion I dismissed it.'

'Did you ask for whom the letter was intended?'

Mrs Tooley winced as if the question were painful to her. 'When I asked whether she was writing to the man I had seen her with in the street, whom she had claimed asked her for directions, and whether the proposal was one of marriage, she grew stubborn and refused to disclose anything. I reminded her that maids were not permitted followers, and that if she did not behave properly she would be denied her usual Sunday afternoon off. I had already heard rumours that she had been out without permission on several evenings with Philip.' As she said this, Mrs Tooley began to tremble again.

Agnes recalled her own difficulties with Rose and the confrontations she had avoided, and sympathized. 'What did she say to your admonition?' she said gently.

'She grew heated and said that Philip was neither here nor there. They were nothing to each other. And just because the note was written in an affectionate manner did not mean it was intended for a lover. I was viewing the matter unjustly. Even servants were surely permitted a life outside their place of work. And then she did something most untoward.'

'What?'

'She stamped her foot like a petulant child, and said she had had enough of being put upon and tarnished just because the other maids were jealous of her. And she had had enough of drudgery too. I had made up her mind for her. She deserved a better life. And in front of my eyes, she tore the letter up. I said, "I'll show you drudgery," and set her washing pickling jars for her impudence. And before ten minutes were passed she had dropped a jar of apricots on the floor. It was spitefully done – I've no doubt of that whatsoever. I should have dismissed her then. I would have done if finding new girls was not such a trial . . .'

The effort of remembering and relating all this was now manifest: Mrs Tooley's colour was heightened, and her chin quivered with emotion.

'Of course,' said Agnes, patting the housekeeper's hand. There was nothing feigned in her agitation – it would be unkind to press further. Such a dramatic and defiant gesture was typical of Rose. But if the letter did not refer to a marriage proposal, what proposal did it concern, and why be so secretive over it? It could only mean there was something else to hide. An impending robbery, perhaps?

Chapter Eighteen

ONCE UPSTAIRS SUPPER HAD BEEN SERVED AND ALL THE OTHER evening duties were completed, most of the servants retired to their quarters. Agnes, however, preferred to stay on in her kitchen. The hour or two alone allowed her time to tidy the kitchen, survey the pantry and larder, ascertain what was left and determine what was needed for the next day. Often, too, she used these quiet hours to sit at the kitchen table and write letters to Peter, or to add to her book of recipes, or amend those that were already written with refinements learned by experience. Moreover, to be surrounded by the tools of her trade and the residual smells of cooking, and be warmed by the dying embers of the fire, brought Agnes comfort and a sense of belonging. The kitchen was where she felt most at peace.

But that evening, solitude did not bring Agnes the tranquillity she craved. She rearranged the boxes of spices on her dresser, and stacked the stoneware dishes in a more orderly fashion than Doris had left them, unsettled by thoughts of the visit she had to make the next morning. Noticing to her annoyance that a silver salver had been carelessly left out behind the pestle and mortar instead of being locked in the silver cupboard or taken upstairs, she moved it to a more conspicuous spot where John or Philip would be sure to notice it. When there was nothing more to tidy, she sat at the table with her recipes and papers, still feeling weighed down with dread. To distract herself, she first wrote a brief line to Mrs Catchpole, telling her that she regretted to learn of her ill health, but that she could not come immediately to take Peter away. She was, however, making every attempt to rectify this situation and hoped for Mrs Catchpole's forbearance meanwhile. Putting this letter to one side, she next penned an affectionate note to Peter, writing in large clear script so that he would be able to read it himself.

When this was done, she placed Peter's letter next to Mrs Catchpole's and, to keep her thoughts from returning to Pitt, began copying out a new recipe for orange tarts given to her by the local confectioner.

Agnes had scarcely put down her pen when she heard a gentle tapping at the kitchen door. She picked up the candlestick. 'Who is there and what is your business?' she called out, checking hurriedly that the bolts were pushed to, for after last night's murder she had no intention of opening to just anyone.

'It is I, Thomas Williams, the journeyman.'

Agnes opened the door an inch, then, seeing it was him, opened it further until the gap was just wide enough to fit her head through. 'Yes, Mr Williams?' she said warily.

Williams removed his hat and gave a small bow. 'Good evening, Mrs Meadowes. I have come about the subject we spoke of this afternoon – Benjamin Riley.'

'Oh yes, indeed. Please enter.' She stepped back, cradling the flame of her candle against the sudden burst of air, feeling foolish for her caution yet grateful for the interruption. It was something to keep her mind off tomorrow.

Thomas Williams put his hat upon the table, then prowled around, gazing in turn at the vast range, the ranks of pots and coppers, and all the other equipment as if he had never before seen the like. 'May I take a seat?' he said at length when his survey was complete.

Agnes hesitated, and to her consternation felt a blush begin to spread across her cheeks. She was alone in her kitchen with a man who was not a servant in the household, a man she barely knew, and he wanted to sit down. She found herself wondering where Williams lived and if he was married, then a moment later reprimanded herself for being foolish enough to wonder such things. The admonition did not prevent her heart beating faster. But then she wondered what she would do should he grow over-familiar. If she called, how long would it take Mrs Tooley or Mr Matthews to come? She reprimanded herself again. Williams had come at her invitation. There was no reason to suppose he was anything but a respectable craftsman who had performed a service to help a fellow employee.

'Please, Mr Williams, do sit down,' she said with an air of formality. She briskly closed her book of recipes and, to cover her awkwardness, offered him a mug of ale and a slice of cake. Thomas Williams pulled up the chair closest to her own, while Agnes prepared the refreshment. When she returned to her seat, she shifted it six inches in the opposite direction.

'Well,' she said, sitting straight-backed, watching him drink, 'what have you learned, Mr Williams?'

He put down his mug and examined the backs of his surprisingly clean and long-fingered hands. 'Nothing very much,' he said bleakly.

'Nothing at all?'

'He said she was sweet on him, but that apart from a brief flirtation some months ago there was nothing between them. But his opinion means nothing. He thinks every woman is a captive to his charms.'

Agnes sat in silence for a moment. 'Am I to take it you do not care for him much?'

Williams nodded, meeting her gaze in a piercing manner which disturbed her slightly. 'Or trust him, either.' He paused and looked away, his green eyes seeming to grow more wistful as he did so. 'He and I work side by side, spend hours in each other's company, but neither of us has much time for the other.'

Agnes nodded sympathetically. Feelings of estrangement from those with whom she worked were familiar to her too. She leaned a few inches towards him. 'What gave you the impression he was not truthful?'

'I told you before – I saw Rose come to call on him recently, not months ago as he claimed.'

'Did you tell him?'

'Yes. He said it was nothing – that she had been sent upon an errand by Theodore Blanchard.'

Agnes frowned, instinctively rejecting this as most improbable. 'What manner of errand?'

'Something concerning the pieces to be taken to the Goldsmith's Hall for marking.'

'Marking?'

'Every piece that is fabricated in our workshop, or any other in London, is taken to the Goldsmith's Hall and tested for the purity of its metal. If the piece passes the test it is marked with a lion.'

Agnes furrowed her brow. Despite working for one of the most renowned silversmiths of London, she had no notion of such matters. She vaguely recollected seeing marks on pieces of silver, but had never paid them much attention or wondered what they signified. But perhaps it was only right to take more interest in matters outside her own sphere. Recalling the salver carelessly left on her dresser, she got up and fetched it. Four small symbols were impressed in the surface. Only one resembled a lion. She handed the salver to Thomas Williams. 'But there is more than one mark on this.'

He nodded. 'And so there should be. See, here is the lion, walking to the left. A lion *passant*, it is termed. That is the mark that shows the piece contains at least 925 parts pure silver in a thousand and has been passed as sterling.'

'And the other marks – what purpose do they serve?'

Williams laughed, but not unkindly, and leaned towards her, pointing one by one to the symbols impressed in the salver's surface. She was conscious of his head only inches away from her, and barely heard what he said. 'There is the maker's mark – usually the initials of the silversmith. The NB you see shows the piece was made at Blanchards; there is a date letter which changes with each year – P shows the piece was marked this year – and the last mark shows where the piece was tested: a leopard's head in the case of the Goldsmith's Hall.' As he spoke, he suddenly looked puzzled. He sat back with the salver and held it towards the light.

Agnes grew less constrained, but a dash disappointed. 'And is every piece marked?'

Williams nodded. He was scrutinizing the salver with a strange intensity. 'By statute it should be,' he said abstractedly. 'And the purchaser is well advised to ensure it. The system is designed to prevent unscrupulous craftsmen using less pure metal than they should.'

'But why would Theodore Blanchard send a kitchen maid with a message concerning marking? If he had something of that nature to communicate, why did he not tell Riley himself – he is there every day, after all – or send one of the footmen?' mused Agnes.

'I don't believe what he said any more than you do.'

'What time of day did you see Rose come to the workshop?' she said abruptly.

Williams grimaced, as if racking his brains. 'I can't be certain, but from memory it was early afternoon. Around two or three.'

Agnes half-closed her eyes. Two or three o'clock – the time at which she was busiest, serving lunch and up to her eyes with cooking dinner. At that time Rose might melt away and return again without being noticed. Suppose there *was* a grain of truth in what Riley had said? Suppose Rose had called at the workshop on Theodore's business – it might give credence to Rose's involvement in the robbery. But why would Theodore use a kitchen maid rather than a manservant to convey a message? On balance, she remained sceptical of Riley's account.

'It would be helpful to know exactly what the errand entailed. Would Riley say nothing more on the subject?'

Thomas Williams looked up from the salver and swallowed. 'No. Which is why I don't believe him.'

'No more do I, but whatever he says may shed light on what happened.'

'Then if you wish I will press him again.' His attention strayed back to the salver. He picked it up again, examining the underside intently. Agnes observed him breathe on it, look again, then buff it with his sleeve. Only then did he seem to notice her gaze on him. He put the salver down as if embarrassed.

'The marks on that salver seem to have captured your attention, Mr Williams. Is there something out of the ordinary about them?'

Thomas Williams scratched his head, his brow ruffled in consternation. He opened his mouth as if to speak, then closed it again without saying a word.

'What is it, Mr Williams? I pray that you tell me, for I see plainly there is something,' said Agnes with unusual insistence.

Williams sighed, looking sombre. 'Very well. By statute, before any silver object may be sold it is liable for duty – the sum of sixpence per ounce. The sum is usually paid immediately after the piece has been taken for assay.'

'Go on,' said Agnes, listening intently.

'Unscrupulous silversmiths who wish to avoid duty have been known to cut out the marks from a small marked piece and set them into the metal of an untested piece. That way the heavier piece appears to be legally marked and duty is avoided. The practice is known as duty-dodging.'

'And you believe the salver has been tampered with – that this is an example of duty-dodging?'

'There have been no salvers made to this pattern in the last two years. It was that which struck me as we spoke. Two years ago, the date letter was N, yet the salver has a P impressed upon it – the letter for this year. The only possible reason for this discrepancy is if the original marks have been removed, a new piece of metal inserted and the salver assayed recently for a second time.'

'Why did you breathe on the marks?'

'To verify my suspicion. You will see a slight ridge around the marks.'

Agnes took the salver and squinted closely at the marks.

She breathed on them as he had done, and now faintly detected a dark circle around them.

'I see it. But how does that prove the marks have been inserted?'

'If a new piece of metal is inserted into another, it can never be made as smooth as if it had been fashioned from a single metal sheet. That ridge indicates that the metal on which the marks are impressed has been set into the salver.'

Agnes nodded slowly and looked up. 'Did you know such deception took place at Blanchard's?'

Thomas Williams met her gaze. 'No,' he said. 'I had no notion whatsoever.'

With this he looked towards the fire with a distant, unfathomable gleam in his eye. Agnes too was lost in her own contemplation, wondering at the significance of what he had told her. Did duty-dodging have any bearing on Noah's murder, the theft of the wine-cooler or Rose's disappearance? Was Rose somehow embroiled in the fraud?

But before she could draw any conclusions, Thomas Williams interrupted her thoughts. He coughed loudly, causing Agnes to look up with a start. 'Forgive me, Mrs Meadowes,' he said. 'I was thinking of you going off to visit Pitt, and wondering what made you accept such a dangerous undertaking. Your husband cannot be happy with the situation – or perhaps you haven't told him?'

Agnes was caught unawares. She could not see how this strange remark connected to their recent conversation. Did he now perceive some extra peril? Confused, and hoping she was not blushing, she said, 'Danger? My husband? But I have none. He is dead.'

As soon as these words were out, Agnes caught Williams darting a glance at the letters on the table. The one addressed in a large clear hand to 'my darling child' and signed 'your loving mother' lay in front of him. Immediately she felt exposed, and this made her resentful. Peter's existence was a private matter, one she had no intention of discussing with anyone, let alone a stranger. She should have put her book of recipes on top of it, but had not thought to do so.

'Then if you alone are responsible for your son, is that not even more reason to be prudent?' said Thomas Williams quietly.

Agnes gave him a short hard smile. She had no intention of encouraging him further by asking what danger he might perceive. 'My reasons for going are my own, Mr Williams. But I assure you my son's welfare is at the forefront of my mind. Now, since the hour is late, I believe it is time you left.'

Chapter Nineteen

AT ELEVEN THE NEXT MORNING, AGNES DRESSED HERSELF IN A warm woollen coat and a fine velvet hat (which Patsy had lent her after much prevarication), and strode purposefully down Cheapside with Philip by her side. Unconscious of the tempting window displays of the haberdashers, goldsmiths and linen drapers, she gazed briefly at a windowful of confectionary before turning right towards Thames Street and thence on to London Bridge and Marcus Pitt's office.

It was a fine crisp morning. A heavy hoar frost still glazed parts of the pavement untouched by the sunlight, and the open gutter that ran down the centre of the street was semi-frozen. A flock of sheep and one or two ox carts had recently travelled the route, perhaps on their way to Smithfield, and here and there mounds of fresh dung sent up small steamy wisps like miniature bonfires. The earthy odour mingled with other familiar smells – smoke from countless chimneys, the ovens of Bread Street, malt and hops from the Barclay Perkins Brewery, burning chestnut skins, and above all the dank pervasive smell of the river, which wound its way behind the crowded wharves and warehouses.

'Did you and Rose like to promenade together?' Agnes casually enquired, as Philip loitered at the window of a milliner's shop, pulling faces at a prettily dressed assistant.

Philip was too absorbed to hear her. He was posing affectedly, with his hand on the hilt of his sword. The girl who was the object of his attention blushed, but kept stealing glances at the tall, well-built young man with the ready smile paying court to her. Agnes, annoyed, repeated her question more loudly, nudging his side discreetly in the process, causing his sword to clash on the glass. The physical contact rather than her words seemed to penetrate his consciousness. Tearing his gaze from the window, he gave Agnes an amiable smile. 'Beg your pardon, Mrs Meadowes? Did you say something?'

'Yes,' said Agnes, beckoning with her hand and walking on, slowly at first then faster once she was sure he wouldn't straggle behind. 'How often did you and Rose walk out together?'

Philip shot a rueful glance back at the window and then hurried to keep pace. 'To begin with it were once or twice a month. Whenever we was both off together on a Sunday. She liked somewhere lively: the pit at the Newgate Theatre, an excursion to Vauxhall.'

Agnes watched as a sedan chair drew to a halt on the pavement beside them and a gentleman in a heavily powdered wig, dressed with foppish elegance, descended directly in front of them, forcing them into the doorway of an undertaker's. Without so much as a word of excuse the gentleman darted into a coffee house. Philip yelled an insult and stepped after him. Agnes grabbed Philip's arm, yanked him back and told him to mind his manners in her company.

'Did she ever mention family or friends?' she continued once her thoughts had reverted to Rose.

'Never,' said Philip, after thinking for a moment. 'It wasn't a subject either of us raised. I wouldn't want her thinking I had intentions when I hadn't. I enjoyed her company right enough, but I enjoy the company of others too. And I can't marry or I'll lose my position, won't I? I reckon that was why she cooled towards me.'

A sudden disturbing vision sprang to Agnes's mind of the pair of them in the larder, Philip with his breeches open and muscular buttocks on display, Rose's pale thighs spread wide. She could not conceive of Rose disporting herself in such a manner if she did not at least hope it would lead somewhere permanent. But the subject of physical love was one in which she was ill-equipped to judge others. Nevertheless, she unwillingly recognized she needed to know more. 'Then when you went out on your excursions, was it just as companions – no more?'

Philip winked. 'Depends what you mean by companions, I s'pose. I kissed her, and did more than that if she was agreeable and we could get somewhere out of the way. Mind you, it wasn't only me – she relished a good tumbling as much as I. At the beginning, that was.'

'Did she change, then?' said Agnes, remembering that John had said their affair was over and trying to ignore the memory of ecstatic moans and grunts.

'In the past few weeks she did. She went out the afternoons she was allowed, but it was never with me. And she wouldn't let me near her.'

Agnes recalled Lydia's suspicions. 'You don't think she might have been carrying your child?'

Philip grinned as though the thought amused him. 'No – not that. I reckon she found someone new.'

'Did you not ask who it was?'

'Of course. But she was devilish secretive on occasion – she wouldn't say.'

'Perhaps it was Riley she was set on?'

Philip regarded Agnes from the corner of his eye. 'Like I said, she never let on anything to me. But as far as Riley goes, I should doubt it. She said she'd tired of him or he of her – I forget which – before we became friends. I saw them talking once or twice, a while since, but that was all. And from the look of things there was nothing between them.'

'And what about Nicholas Blanchard? Did she ever mention him?'

'The old goat? It wasn't Rose that interested him, it was Nancy – though he won't be happy with her for much longer, I'd say.'

Agnes remembered Nancy's jealousy at being spurned when Rose arrived. 'Why? Are you and she friendly again?'

'A bit, maybe, but that don't mean she'll pull the wool over my eyes. You asked me if Rose was with child. Ain't you remarked how Nancy's filled out? And you a mother too?'

Doubtless Philip did not intend this remark to be as hurtful as it was. But whatever his intention, Agnes was disconcerted. How was it that Philip had a better understanding of what drove both Rose and Nancy than she did?

But then as they continued on at a brisker pace, Agnes's consternation yielded to other thoughts. If Nancy were with child, she must be in a state of turmoil wondering what would become of her. Knowing the difficulties of raising a child alone and holding a position in service, Agnes commiserated. And *she* was a respectable widow, and an upper servant at that. Nancy was neither. She remembered Nancy's resentment towards Rose. But even if Nancy did feel bitter about Rose coming between Philip and herself, she surely could not blame the girl for forcing her into Nicholas's bed or her present predicament.

Soon the Monument and the church of St Magnus the Martyr came into view in front of them. They veered sharply to the right towards London Bridge, Agnes still lost in thoughts of her own. She gazed between the gaps in the decaying wooden houses that lined the bridge, out across the sparkling sweep of the river, and tried to think freely. She thought again of the money Nancy had reported seeing under Rose's mattress, and wondered how Rose had come by the hoard. The disturbing notion occurred to her that if Rose was as fond of intimacy as Philip implied, perhaps she had come by her fortune by selling *herself*. Perhaps, thought Agnes with a shudder, she had interspersed her life as a maid with the existence of a whore. Perhaps it was this other life that had taken her away.

She turned back to Philip. 'By Nancy's account, Rose had a large sum of money in her possession – about twenty gold sovereigns. Did you ever see it? Did she mention how it came into her possession?'

'A large sum of money?' Philip's eyebrows shot skywards. 'Twenty sovereigns? God's teeth – the bloody jade! And her grumbling on about how little she had and how she was born to better things.'

Agnes was as astonished by the fact that he knew something of Rose's past as by his outburst. 'To what better things was she born?' she said quickly.

Philip shrugged. 'I don't rightly recall. She'd had a maid of her own. Her father had died, and she had been forced to seek employ.' He shook his head and laughed. 'I shouldn't give it much credence if I were you. She was always one to give herself airs if she thought it would get her out of a chore.' His eyes glistened with tears as he spoke. Beneath the anger, thought Agnes, he is hurt too.

'Then could not the money have been an inheritance?'

'No,' said Philip unhesitatingly. 'That was one thing I never doubted about her story. There was no inheritance. She had to work and she detested it.'

Once across London Bridge, they headed towards the Borough. In the distance were St George's Fields, a black latticework of leafless trees in front of the wintery slopes upon which a scattering of cows and sheep grazed. Philip's eye, meanwhile, settled on a cluster of pretty girls outside the George Tavern, one of whom winked at him and raised her skirt a couple of inches to expose a well-turned ankle. Agnes caught Philip blowing her a kiss. She strode briskly to the tavern courtyard to ask for directions to Melancholy Walk.

Agnes narrowly avoided collision with all manner of men and conveyances, all jostling and barging in their efforts to load or unload, water, feed, harness or unharness their horses. She found a groom who was able to direct her, but when he tried to engage her in further conversation she cut him short. 'Philip,' she cried out brusquely, waving her arm to summon him hastily to her side, 'this gentleman informs me the place we are looking for is this way. Let us leave now. There is no time to waste.'

Melancholy Walk was a narrow alley nestling in the shadow

of the Southwark Glass House and the Clink prison. The houses here were newly built – tall, narrow structures, four storeys high, with a single window on each floor. According to the directions that Theodore had provided, Marcus Pitt's office was the fourth house along.

In answer to Agnes's knock, the door edged open and a puffy, pock-marked, unshaven face peered out. Taking a deep breath, Agnes announced stoutly, 'I have an appointment on behalf of Mr Theodore Blanchard. My name is Agnes Meadowes.'

'That so?' replied the man, stepping back and opening the door with a smile that revealed a gash of blackened teeth. 'And mine's Grant. If you're expected, I s'pose you'd better come in.'

Grant's physique, Agnes now saw, was as unwholesome as his face. His body was vast and round; the coat and shirt he wore were incapable of covering his girth; and slivers of hairy flesh protruded where buttons were missing and fastenings undone. Agnes averted her eyes and stepped into the hallway. Philip made to follow her, but Grant stepped forward, blocking his path. 'Not you. He wants her alone. You wait here,' he said abruptly, shoving him in the chest.

Throughout the journey, Agnes had deliberately preoccupied herself with thoughts of Rose to prevent herself from dwelling on the meeting that lay in store. Now poised on Marcus Pitt's threshold, and separated from Philip, her pulse quickened and darts of apprehension pricked her spine. However, she had no choice but to face the ordeal. She turned back and peered round Grant's bulky mass. 'It's all right, Philip,' she said. 'Do as he says. I'll call if I need you.'

She found herself in a long narrow corridor, sparsely furnished with two seats set against the wall close to the front door and nothing else save at the far end, where stood a pair of benches presently occupied by three boisterous boys playing a game of dice. They were all dirty and raggedly dressed, aged about twelve or thirteen, she guessed. Had she seen them in the street she would have kept clear, assuming they were pickpockets. Presumably, thought Agnes with an apprehensive shudder, it was by keeping lads such as this in his pay that Pitt derived his insight into London's murky goings on.

'If you would care to wait a moment,' said Grant, signalling to the chairs by the door, 'I will inform Mr Pitt you are here.' Then, turning towards the lads, he bellowed, 'You lot, mind your manners – there's company here.'

Agnes sat down gingerly as Grant sidled through an entrance leading off the corridor, yanking the door shut so swiftly behind him that Agnes had no opportunity to glimpse the man or room that awaited her. Despite his warning, the boys paid no attention to her presence, but continued their unruly brawling.

From behind the closed door, Agnes could hear the low sonorous sound of conversation, although the subject was impossible to discern above the racket. Then there was the crash of a door and the sound of heavy footsteps on wooden boards.

'He's ready for you now,' said Grant, poking his head out of the doorway. 'This way, if you please.'

It was not at all what she had expected. The shutters in Marcus Pitt's office were half drawn across the window. Nevertheless, there was enough light for her to see that the room was orderly and the furnishings were of quality. There was a mahogany desk; two or three carved chairs; a cabinet, upon which stood a row of cut-glass decanters and half a dozen wine glasses, two of which were half full; and a coat stand, upon which was suspended a long black cloak, a tricorn hat and a silver-topped walking cane.

The air was stuffy and sweetly scented, thanks to a blazing fire and a pastille burner that gave off a strong, sweet perfume – sandalwood or musk, Agnes guessed. The walls were lined with bookshelves, upon which stood row upon row of identical dark-blue volumes. Agnes noticed that the spine of each was marked with two dates and that the books were ranged chronologically. The significance of the dates was not clear, but the care with which they were ordered brought a certain sense of formality to the room that she found reassuring.

Marcus Pitt was seated at his desk. A volume identical to the ones around the walls was open in front of him, and he was engaged in writing in it. Agnes recalled the voices she had just heard. Judging from the wine glasses, Pitt had been entertaining company before her arrival. There was, she now observed, a small door set into the panelling. Presumably his previous visitor had left through it.

Pitt put down his pen, rose to his feet, bowed and held out his hand to greet her. He was tall, long faced and clean shaven, with a thin nose, well-defined mouth, deep-set dark-grey eyes, his hair impeccably dressed in tidy rolls over his ears and caught back in a shiny black ribbon. 'Mrs Meadowes, good morning to you. I received word of your visit from Mr Blanchard. Allow Mr Grant to take your cloak and hat.' The voice was surprisingly genteel, and the hand that shook hers well manicured, its grip authoritative and cool. His dress befitted a well-to-do gentleman: a fine blue velvet coat, silk waistcoat, buckskin breeches.

'That is quite all right, thank you, sir,' she said, shivering inwardly despite the fug in the room. 'I prefer to keep them.'

Pitt smiled indulgently. 'You have travelled some distance,' he continued with a look of solicitude. 'Perhaps I can offer you some refreshment. A glass of wine?'

'Thank you, no,' said Agnes, reddening at his politeness. 'I am pressed for time. Mr Blanchard is most anxious I return as speedily as I am able.'

'Naturally.' Marcus Pitt bowed slightly. 'How could he fail to be eager for so charming a lady's swift return?'

Notwithstanding her deference, Agnes was adept at maintaining an air of aloofness. She was quite capable of curtailing unwanted compliments with a chilling look or cutting remark. But remembering the delicacy of her commission, and that Theodore had expressly ordered her to capitalize on her charms, she suppressed her instinct and responded with quiet circumspection. 'You are mistaken, sir. I come on business. I speak in a professional capacity.'

A slight twitch now played at the corners of Marcus Pitt's mouth, as though her formality amused him. 'Your propriety is commendable; it must come as a great relief to your husband. I take it you are both in the same profession?'

'My husband is dead,' replied Agnes diffidently, recalling that this was the second time she had been obliged to mention him and finding the subject no more welcome now than it had been the previous night. She hurried on, feeling herself blush as she spoke. 'I have recently joined the Blanchard workshop as an engraver. This robbery threatens their business and thus I am fearful it might also jeopardize my position. As a widow, with a child to support . . . you will appreciate my concern.'

'Indeed, and I admire your fortitude, Mrs Meadowes. You are most courageous. Now tell me properly about the business that brings you.'

'I have come, sir, to enlist your assistance in retrieving a valuable silver wine-cooler that has been stolen from the Blanchards' business premises in Foster Lane.'

Pitt nodded. 'Blanchard referred to the matter in his letter. He knows, I presume, there is a fee for my services? One guinea, payable in advance.'

'I have it in my purse,' said Agnes. Her pulse was beginning to race under Pitt's scrutiny. She felt in her pocket, deriving a moment's comfort from the cool disc of gold that Theodore had given her for this purpose. She placed the coin on the desk in front of her.

Marcus Pitt took a brass key from a bunch attached to his belt, unlocked a drawer and took out a metal-bound strong box. Selecting another key from his collection, he unlocked the strong box, placed the coin inside then secured the box again. 'Now tell me more precisely what happened; describe the stolen property in as much detail as you recall. Not too fast, mind, I must write it all down.'

So Agnes explained the events as they had been told to her, recounting how the shop had been broken into, how the apprentice who had been guarding the shop at that hour had had his throat cruelly cut from ear to ear, and how nothing but the wine-cooler had been taken. Mr Pitt recorded the details in his book, writing with swift fluency in a small spidery script without passing comment. When his pen drew to a halt, he looked up. 'And describe the appearance of the wine-cooler, if you please.'

By good fortune, Theodore had shown her a detailed drawing. Concealing the fact that she had never set eyes on the object, Agnes described it as best she could. 'It was most expertly wrought, measuring three and a half feet long and nearly two feet wide, adorned with mermaids, dolphins, tritons, horses and a figure of Neptune bearing a shield with the patron's armorials.'

There was a short pause while Pitt wrote rapidly in his ledger. Then, sitting back in his chair, he linked his hands, steepled his forefingers under his chin and regarded her with a directness she found most unsettling. 'You haven't told me yet the most crucial detail of all.'

'And what, pray, is that, Mr Pitt?'

'The weight.'

Agnes flushed awkwardly but did not avert her gaze. 'Twelve hundred ounces.'

Pitt blinked, his eyes wide in mock astonishment. '*Twelve hundred ounces*,' he repeated slowly. 'No wonder then that Theodore Blanchard is in a lather. What will Sir Bartholomew Grey say when he knows it has gone missing, I wonder? I take it the wine-cooler was assayed and the duty properly paid?'

'I beg your pardon, sir?' Agnes said, remembering in a flash her conversation with Thomas Williams the previous night. Was Pitt suggesting that the duty might have been avoided? Why should *he* care? Then, not wishing to alert Pitt to her thoughts, she swiftly replied, 'I assume so, Mr Pitt, though I don't see why that should be significant. The wine-cooler is unique. You have certainly enough to identify it, with or without marks.'

'I expect you are right,' conceded Marcus Pitt, scratching his brow as though deep in thought, the suspicion of a smile still playing about his mouth. 'Now, Mrs Meadowes, if you would allow me to explain how my system works.'

'Very well, sir.'

'I will ask around among my numerous contacts and perhaps place an advertisement in a publication or two. When I've found something I shall send one of my young assistants to fetch you.'

He said all this with an air of solemnity better suited to a man of law or a physician than a man who held sway over the city's underworld and employed a retinue of rogues to assist him.

'How long is this process likely to take?' Agnes enquired deferentially.

'No more than three or four days. I wager we'll be enjoying each other's company again before the end of the week.'

'Mr Blanchard will be delighted to hear it.'

'Of course he will,' responded Marcus Pitt with alacrity. 'He's twelve hundred ounces at stake. By anyone's standards that is a considerable sum, not to be taken lightly.'

'Will the villain responsible be apprehended at the same time?' asked Agnes.

Pitt's expression turned suddenly grave. 'That question, Mrs Meadowes, is much trickier. Sometimes it is best to be content with the property and not look further. My business, you see, depends upon the trust of rogues. Mr Blanchard will understand.'

Agnes nodded in silence. So the murderer of Noah Prout would go free in order for Pitt's business to prosper. And Theodore would raise no objection, provided he recovered his wine-cooler.

Pitt seemed to sense her misgivings, for he did not allow her time to dwell on the injustice of this procedure. He rose and bowed to her. 'I will be counting the days – unless, that is, you would consent to put me out of my anguish before.'

Agnes regarded him uncertainly. 'I don't think I follow you, Mr Pitt.'

'Then the fault is mine for not making myself clear. What I want to do is offer you an invitation. Would you care to accompany me to the New Theatre on Friday? I will send a couple of assistants on ahead to keep our places in the pit, and we can dine first. I guarantee I'll entertain you royally and give you a night you won't forget.'

Agnes was dazed; she could not remember the last time a gentleman had invited her on an excursion. Her manner warned most suitors off long before they dared make such a proposal. A flush of flattered astonishment spread across her cheeks. But she reminded herself sternly that for all his posturing, Pitt was not a gentleman but a villain, and she too was masquerading as something she was not. No doubt Pitt was as much drawn by her supposed profession as by her charms. 'That is a most generous offer, Mr Pitt, and please don't think I am ignorant of the honour you pay me. Nevertheless, I regret I am not at liberty to accompany you. I have commitments that proscribe evening excursions.'

Even as she spoke, Agnes knew there was too much regret and not enough distance in her tone. She sensed that Marcus Pitt was well versed in feminine wiles and would notice this. He nodded, shrugged his shoulders and sighed with mock chagrin. 'The ripest fruits are always the first to be picked. 'Twas ever thus,' he declared. Striding round his desk, he helped her from her chair. Then, before she knew it, he had taken her bare hand in his and kissed it. 'Until Saturday then, God willing. Good day to you, Mrs Meadowes.'

'Good day, Mr Pitt,' said Agnes, drawing back her hand as if she had burned it. The sensation of his soft lips and scratchy chin touching her hand had not been unpleasant. Agnes had not felt the repulsion she'd expected at the physical contact; instead an unmistakable thrill had rushed through her veins, as though she had gulped a mouthful of brandy. She swiftly chastised herself for being a fool. This was the allure of dissipation, she told herself sternly. Why had she not put her gloves on sooner? She had a sudden vision of herself with a blackened eye and split lip. Being beaten was no less painful if the man who struck the blows was handsome and on occasion charming. She had fallen prey before, but would not do so again.

Chapter Twenty

TAKING HER LEAVE OF MARCUS PITT, AGNES FELT NEW FEAR, AND new puzzlement too. Quite apart from Pitt's question concerning duty, another comment of his resonated in her mind, for she could not explain it: '*What will Sir Bartholomew Grey say when he knows it has gone missing, I wonder?*' On Theodore's emphatic instruction, she had never mentioned that the wine-cooler had been made for Sir Bartholomew Grey.

Pitt's knowledge was most obviously explained by an illicit involvement with a member of the Blanchard staff; someone who knew the wine-cooler had been made for Grey. It seemed that Pitt had unwittingly confirmed Justice Cordingly's and Theodore's suspicions that the robbery was no casual crime. Duty-dodging was neither here nor there. Pitt must have been commissioned to orchestrate the robbery of the wine-cooler, which he had now been employed to recover. The question was, by whom?

In the hallway, the towering bulk of the manservant Grant stood sentinel outside the door. Agnes opened her mouth to tell him she was leaving. Just at that moment, her eyes flickered past him to the three boys who were still rough-and-tumbling at the end of the corridor. But now, she observed, they had been joined by a fourth person. Sitting quietly watching their capers was a young, dark-haired girl. She had a long thin face, straggly unkempt hair and cat-like eyes. Her mouth was small and round, her feet bare, her clothes ragged and nondescript, apart from a crimson shawl wrapped about her shoulders. It was this shawl – a splash of glowing colour amid the monochrome gloom – that caught Agnes's attention.

She was the girl Agnes had seen waiting outside the day before the robbery. The girl to whom she had offered three farthings, and who had stolen her purse and an orange. In an instant, the humiliation and outrage she had felt at being robbed came flooding back; she half-wanted to go up and take hold of the girl and shake her. But prudence got the better of her. Remembering where she was, and anxious not to draw attention by staring, Agnes briskly turned away from the girl. She pulled on her gloves with trembling fingers, adjusted her hat in the looking glass, noting how darkly her eyes gleamed against her pale complexion and how fast she was breathing. 'I am ready,' she said quietly to Grant, who opened the front door for her.

Philip was slouched against the railings outside. Catching sight of Agnes, he leaped up. 'All go well, Mrs Meadowes?'

She nodded curtly. 'I believe so, thank you, Philip. But I don't wish to waste a moment more. Let us go.'

As they headed back towards the Borough, Agnes's mind was racing. Coming so soon after Marcus Pitt's slip, the significance of the girl's presence was clear. It was further evidence of a link between the robbery and Pitt. Thank God, Agnes thought, I had the presence of mind to say nothing! Had I revealed that I knew her while I was still on Pitt's premises, heaven knows what might have happened. Pitt would surely not have let me return in safety. The girl must have been set to observe the comings and goings at the Blanchards' premises so that the most opportune moment for the robbery could be chosen. Agnes recalled the girl mentioning she was waiting for her pa, and the shadowy, long-coated figure glimpsed just before she had run off. Had he been the perpetrator of the dreadful crime? She resolved to mention the matter to Justice Cordingly at the earliest opportunity. There might not be proof, but at the very least, she thought, the girl's father should be identified and questioned over the matter.

Within ten minutes they had arrived at London Bridge. They were a quarter of the way across when a man wheeling a barrow piled high with old rags trundled past with a couple of dogs growling at his heels. From the opposite direction, a sedan chair careered up at considerable speed, just as a large wagon, drawn by a couple of oxen, creaked to a standstill behind the man with the barrow. To avoid the obstruction, Philip and Agnes crossed to the other side of the road, skirting several stalls selling quack remedies, gloves and ribbons. The air reverberated to a mêlée of shouts – *Make way! . . . Move over! . . . Make haste! . . . Watch behind you!* As the barrow drew alongside her, Agnes became conscious that a thin high voice was yelling out to her above the cacophony of sound, 'Wait, Missus! For Gawd's sake, stop! A word, if you please.'

Agnes peered round the swaying wagon and the oxen's bony haunches and caught a flash of crimson cloth – it was the girl again. She had no desire for Philip to see her in discussion with the child. Doubtless Philip already knew that an urchin had robbed her; John and he had few secrets. Given half a chance, they might well ridicule her about a second encounter. 'Continue on, Philip,' she said as the traffic passed and the way ahead cleared. 'There is an order I want to place at the chandler for Mrs Tooley. I'll catch you in a minute.' Without further explanation, she darted into a nearby shop.

The girl came charging up, but when she saw Agnes inside the shop she did not enter. Agnes waited until Philip was out of view before she emerged. 'So, Miss,' she said warily, 'What is it you wish to say?'

The girl had evidently run all the way from Melancholy Walk, for she was panting and her cheeks were flushed. 'You know who I am,' she said between gasps, meeting Agnes's scrutiny boldly.

'I saw you outside the Blanchards' shop two days ago,' Agnes crossly acknowledged. 'You stole an orange and my purse, even though I gave you three farthings.'

The girl did not bother to deny the charge. 'I want to know what you're intending to do about it. Did you tell the man you're with?' She jerked her head in the direction Philip had taken.

'No.'

'Then who will you tell?'

Agnes pondered. The girl's presence at Pitt's could not be overlooked. She could not be allowed to escape as she had before. Agnes had already resolved to tell Justice Cordingly; Theodore Blanchard should also be informed. What steps were then taken to discover who had helped Pitt and this girl's father was for them to decide.

Then it occurred to Agnes that if she played along with her, the girl might inadvertently confirm her father to be the murderer and reveal the name of the insider who had assisted. But she was uncertain how to go about extracting information from a wretch who would no doubt rob her again given half a chance. 'Tell me first, what's your name?' she said cautiously.

'Elsie,' said the girl.

'Elsie what?'

'Elsie Drake.'

'So, Elsie Drake, whom do you advise me to tell?'

'I suppose you think you should tell your master, so's he might try and nab my pa, but I've come to warn you not to. Not yet, at any rate. It won't help your chances.'

This was the last thing Agnes expected to hear. 'Why not?'

'If Mr Pitt gets wind of it, he'll have the wine-cooler melted down and sold for bullion and then Mr Blanchard'll never get it back,' replied Elsie without hesitation.

The girl's logic surprised Agnes, not to mention her nerve, which was quite beyond expectation. 'What does the wine-cooler matter to you?'

'It don't, but my pa do, and he's all I got. If Mr Pitt finds out the justice is after my pa, he'd most likely give him up to be hanged just to get the forty guineas reward, rather than let the justice take him and get nothing. And if that happens he'll melt the wine-cooler down, just to keep himself on the safe side, so we'll all be the loser.'

Agnes grasped what the girl was saying. As a thief-taker, Pitt received payment from the authorities for any criminal he apprehended. This was how he disposed of villains who rebelled against his control, or any he suspected might be apprehended and incriminate him.

'Your father – what's he called?'

'Harry.'

'Harry Drake?'

Elsie nodded, looking at her feet.

'And what does he do for Mr Pitt?'

She shrugged sulkily. 'I don't know much. He don't talk about it.'

Agnes had no doubt this was a lie, but then, she thought, what else could the girl say? Her father, despite being a murderous thief, was all she had. 'Did someone else help your father? Someone inside Mr Blanchard's shop?'

'How should I know? I just watched outside an' told 'im what I saw.'

'Told who?'

'My pa.'

Elsie looked at her, unblinking, hostile. Sensing she would get no further, Agnes changed tack. 'What time did you start watching?'

'He wanted me sitting there most of the night – said the night was what interested him most.'

'And the night of the robbery, were you there outside?'

'No.'

Agnes's disappointment must have shown. 'Why d'you ask?' said Elsie craftily. 'Feeling guilty? Worried I saw you do summat you shouldn't?'

'Did your father mention seeing a woman leave the house? She was young and handsome, dressed in a cloak and a dark-blue dress,' persisted Agnes firmly, without responding to this taunt.

Elsie's eye flickered for a second, but she held Agnes's gaze. 'No, he never said nothing,' she said. 'I said before, never does.'

Agnes looked at the miserable face, the ragged costume, the bare feet blackened with grime. Her willingness to risk approaching Agnes and answering her questions showed her anxiety for her father's well-being. Agnes had no doubt that Harry Drake must have been the murderous thief who stole the wine-cooler. Bitter experience had shown her that his daughter was inherently untrustworthy and far from innocent. But it struck her that given Elsie's circumstances, the loyalty and affection she felt towards her father was remarkable – touching, even. Regardless of rights and wrongs, Noah Prout was dead; the wine-cooler was gone, and the Blanchards were prepared to pay for its recovery. If Harry Drake swung for the murder Elsie would be fatherless, but Pitt would still have profited. Where was the justice in that?

'So, Missus,' pressed Elsie. 'You won't say nothing, will you?'

'No,' said Agnes wearily, 'I won't.'

Agnes soon caught up with Philip, and as they appoached Foster Lane she sent him on to the house to resume his duties while she went next door. Eager for news, Theodore had instructed her to report to him the minute she returned. But Agnes's mind was only partly on what she would say. Now that her perilous meeting was over, she was preoccupied once more with Peter and Mrs Catchpole, and the problem she had yet to address. Perhaps, she thought, since she had acquitted herself well on Theodore's behalf this morning, he might spare her tomorrow to resolve matters in Twickenham. But on further reflection, she resolved that rather than ask him directly and risk having her request turned down, she would make finding Rose her excuse for leaving the house next day. If Theodore believed that letting Agnes out of the house was in his interests, he would be less likely to refuse her. How devious I am becoming, she thought as this plan took shape, how quick to embrace subterfuge!

When she entered the shop, Thomas Williams was the first person she saw. Judging by the neatness of his dress – hair tied back in a queue, blue coat, black cravat, black breeches – he had been attending to customers rather than working. 'Good day, Mrs Meadowes,' he said, bowing decorously. Then in a whispered undertone he added, 'I am relieved to see you safely returned.'

He seemed to have forgotten the brusque curtailment of their conversation last night. Torn reluctantly from her worries, Agnes frowned at the intimacy his whisper implied. Here was a further complication she would be wise to avoid. 'Good day to you, Mr Williams. I have come to speak to Mr Blanchard,' she responded coolly.

He bowed again, more stiffly this time. 'I shall tell Mr Blanchard you are here.'

As he turned, she thought suddenly how solid he looked, with his broad shoulders, silver-buttoned coat and stocky calves clad in white stockings. How different he was from the languid, elegant, dangerous Pitt. The moment when Pitt had kissed her hand reared into her thoughts. She felt a knot in the pit of her stomach and tried to push it away, but then another memory surfaced: the curious remark that Pitt had made. 'Before you announce my arrival, Mr Williams, there is something else I should like to ask,' she said, addressing him now in an easier manner.

He turned back, his face registering surprise at her change of tone. 'Very well. What is it?'

Agnes scrutinized a row of snuff boxes in the window, conflicting sentiments battling within her. Williams had the appearance of an honest kindly fellow – but so had her husband when she'd first set eyes on him. It was always prudent, she told herself, to confide as little as possible, to keep as much back as you could. She steadied herself and met his gaze. ''Twas nothing of significance,' she said casually. 'Only today, when I called on Mr Pitt, he mentioned something surprising – the subject of marking and duty. Bearing in mind our conversation on that subject last night, can you hazard why?'

William drew his brows together. 'As I told you before, the duty must be paid according to the weight. The rate is sixpence an ounce. On a wine-cooler weighing twelve hundred ounces, that would be a considerable sum – thirty pounds. Perhaps Pitt was curious to know whether Theodore had already paid the duty, so as to calculate what to ask for its return. Duty would add to the total loss if the wine-cooler were not recovered.'

'Was it you or Riley who made the wine-cooler?' asked Agnes suddenly.

'Mostly it was me, though he helped with some of the first castings.'

'And you that took it to assay?'

'No. Riley usually goes. He says he likes the change, and I've no inclination to stand in line for an hour if I don't have to.'

'Then perhaps Rose Francis's business with Riley had something to do with duty-dodging; it might explain her visits to him and why he is reluctant to speak of them. And perhaps it also explains the gold in her possession.'

'What gold?'

'One of the maids recalled seeing twenty sovereigns in a purse hidden under her mattress.'

She noticed that this did not seem to surprise him in the least. 'Come, come,' he said, shaking his head and folding his arms across his chest. 'It is surely far-fetched to believe a kitchen maid would be caught up in a matter such as this. If you do not understand the marking system, why should she?'

'Riley could have taught her; if he somehow enticed her to bring him articles from the Blanchards' house for the marks to be removed and placed on more valuable items, that would explain their discussions. Why else would she have called on him?'

'Hmm,' said Thomas Williams uneasily. 'It is possible, I suppose. But I confess I do not give it much credence. Blanchards sell few items more sizeable than a salver. The wine-cooler is an exception. Besides, even if they did operate such a scheme, how would they profit from it? All the objects made and sold here are listed in the accounts, which Mr Theodore Blanchard keeps.'

'Then perhaps he was involved too.' Agnes walked away from the window and gazed at an arrangement of silver candlesticks on a mantelshelf. Even to her, the theory seemed far-fetched. And there was no proof, apart from the visits to Riley and a single salver. Surely, she thought, Rose could not have been embroiled in such an intrigue.

Footsteps sounded on the landing upstairs, a stiff cough wafted down and Theodore's voice called out, 'Mrs Meadowes? Is that your voice I hear? What are you doing down there? Williams, bring her to the upstairs showroom forthwith.'

Theodore was slumped in a leather armchair by the fire. The same place, reflected Agnes, where Noah Prout had sat two days earlier before Harry Drake had cruelly slit his throat. 'Well,' he said, waving her impatiently in the minute the door closed behind her. 'Come, come, Mrs Meadowes. Sit down. Tell me, what did Pitt have to say for himself?'

Agnes perched on the edge of a seat. 'He gave the impression he was confident of recovering the wine-cooler,' she said cautiously. 'He expects to have news within the next few days. Most significantly, however, he knew without my telling him that the wine-cooler was intended for Sir Bartholomew Grey.'

'Did he, by Jove? So our suspicions were correct, there is a traitor here.'

Agnes nodded. 'A traitor is here or *was* here. Mrs Blanchard suggested Rose Francis's disappearance might have some bearing on the theft, and requested that I should try to find her. I wondered whether tomorrow morning would be an opportune moment to—'

'No, no, no, Mrs Meadowes,' broke in Theodore, thumping his fist on the armrest of his chair and shaking his head so violently that his chins wobbled like blancmange. 'Let us get one thing clear. I do not wish you to waste time or deliberately divert your attention from what is paramount: namely acting as an intermediary with Mr Pitt. Moreover, my wife was most concerned that Mrs Tooley should not be unnecessarily upset. She says I should make only sparing use of your services. Therefore, let us wait to see whether Pitt recovers the wine-cooler first, then if the traitor is in the vicinity and chasing after him is necessary, Justice Cordingly will decide how best to do it.'

It went against the grain to argue with her master, but in this instance Agnes was spurred to make a stand. All she required was a few hours free. After the dangers she had braved for him, was that so much to ask? 'But if Rose Francis was involved in the robbery, she might lead us to the wine-cooler without you having to pay to recover it, and Pitt would not profit from his crime,' she protested.

Theodore snorted. 'Have I not told you clear enough, Mrs Meadowes? Whether or not the girl was involved is irrelevant. She is gone. She cannot help us. Looking for her will waste time and cause disruption in the household. More importantly, if word reached Pitt it might cause him to melt the wine-cooler down and sell the silver for bullion. I cannot afford to take the risk. If you wish to keep your post you would be wise to remember it.'

Agnes turned her head sharply, as if slapped on the cheek. She regarded the prospect from the window; a grey fog had descended that half obscured the façades opposite. Elsie's words of warning rang in her head. She too had mentioned the possibility of the wine-cooler being melted down. Confronted by Theodore's intransigence, there seemed little purpose in openly requesting leave to visit Peter. Common sense told her he would say no, and that she had no alternative but to submit to his will.

Sensing unspoken acquiescence, Theodore cleared his throat. 'Did Pitt pass any other remark of interest? he asked.

'He wondered if the wine-cooler was marked and the duty paid,' said Agnes nervously.

Theodore clenched the armrests of his chair and his eyes bulged. 'Duty? *He* mentioned duty? I can scarce credit it! And what did you say?'

'That I assumed it was.'

Was Theodore aghast at the implication that such a nefarious practice as duty-dodging might have been perpetrated on his premises out of concern for his reputation, Agnes wondered. Or was he worried that his own involvement in such a scheme might be exposed? 'What do you suppose he meant, sir?' Agnes probed warily, curiosity overcoming her trepidation.

'Meant?' said Theodore indignantly. 'How in heaven's name should I comprehend the workings of a mind such as Pitt's? Naturally the wine-cooler had been properly marked. But that is by the by. So long as he recovers it, that's all that need concern any of us. You included, Mrs Meadowes.'

Chapter Twenty-one

MRS TOOLEY HAD STOOD IN FOR AGNES AS, ON SO MANY previous occasions when contagions had struck, Agnes had stood in for Mrs Tooley. A simple dinner had been arranged. The first course comprised soup *à la reine*, chicken stew with celery, fried tripe and boiled cauliflower; the second course, a wholesome ragout of pig ears, macaroni pie, roast mutton, mushrooms and cabbage in butter sauce; for dessert there would be jam tartlets and apple pie. Mrs Tooley had enlisted the help of both Doris and Nancy and they had made a good start. The desserts were prepared, the stew set to simmer, the mutton already darkening on the spit.

With only an hour left to complete the rest, Mrs Tooley and Nancy melted away. Agnes, undaunted, rose to the challenge, which she felt better equipped to handle than consorting with thief-takers and street rogues. Turning first to the soup, she picked up a pot containing lean beef and a knuckle of veal, onions, carrots, celery, parsnips, leeks and a little thyme, which had been simmering for most of the morning. She strained it through a muslin cloth, then thickened it with breadcrumbs soaked in boiled cream, half a pound of ground almonds and the yolks of six hard eggs. This done, she dipped in her little finger, licked it thoughtfully and adjusted the seasoning, while issuing Doris with a barrage of further instructions. 'Water on for the vegetables, then slice up the ears in strips; then baste the joint – careful, mind – so the fat don't catch on the fire.'

Cheeks glowing from steam and heat, Agnes wiped a damp hand across her brow, then began on the gravy for the pigs' ears, adding a pinch of mace and a glassful of claret as the French chef had taught her. She poured the gravy over the sliced ears. 'Into the hot cupboard with this, Doris. And then get me the cabbage and cauliflower, please.' She basted the mutton with a long-handled spoon, and set to frying the tripe in a deep pan of lard until it was brown and crisp. She set a pan of mushrooms alongside, and tossed the cabbage leaves in a pan of boiling water and the cauliflower in another. 'More cream, Doris. Are the plates warmed?' called Agnes, shaking the mushrooms while tasting the macaroni. 'Vegetables need draining. Where are John and Philip?' Without waiting for a reply, she garnished the tripe with parsley and poured the soup into a large tureen. 'It's nearly time, Doris.'

As if he had heard, Philip burst in through the door. He had just finished setting the table under the eagle eye of Mr Matthews, who had chastised him roundly for his carelessness in not keeping the dessert spoons at perfect right angles to the knives and exactly one inch distant from the forks. Philip threw himself into a chair, sighing exaggeratedly as though he was all done in, his large muscled legs apart.

'At last, Philip! Sharpen the carving knife, if you please, in readiness for Mr Matthews to carve the mutton,' said Agnes, avoiding his eye, irked by his lack of decorum. 'Dear God, the stew must be ready by now. Take it off the heat please, Doris.'

By now her dress was sodden with steam, and her forehead and face burned with the raging heat of a kitchen in full spate. And yet in the midst of all this activity, she found an unlikely sort of peace. Although Peter, Marcus Pitt and Rose Francis formed a knot in her mind that she could not entirely ignore, being caught up by the demands of dinner brought solace of a kind. For the time being she could not fret – she had to get on.

*

Compared with the clutter of Mrs Tooley's parlour, the butler's pantry was altogether a more spartan, less homely place. There were no colourful samplers or seascapes hung upon the walls, no saucers or teacups, or ornaments on the mantelpiece. Apart from a single uncoloured engraving showing George II in his coronation robes, all the furnishings were strictly functional. There was a silver cupboard, which was always kept locked unless something was being taken out or put away; a table upon which Theodore's and Nicholas's clothes and the menservants' liveries were pressed; a lead-lined sink, where the footmen washed the glasses; a wooden horse, where sundry articles were dried; and besides these, three wooden chairs.

This is not to say that Mr Matthews's life was devoid of decoration. Unrolled and laid out on the table beside him, weighted down with two dessert knives and a lump of beeswax, was a gaudily coloured print depicting the same monarch as the engraving on the wall. Only here he was displayed half unclad, clutching a string of German sausages and engaged in the clumsy seduction of Lady Yarmouth.

Mr Matthews enjoyed looking at such scurrilous images. He subscribed to a nearby print shop which provided a selection on loan for a modest tuppence a week. Usually he kept his images tightly furled in his cupboard. Mrs Blanchard had instructed him to make a tally of the silver to ensure nothing was missing. He saw no reason not to interrupt his task with occasional glances at something a little more entertaining.

Mr Matthews had counted the knives (sixty-eight of them) and forks (fifty-four) without incident. He had just reached the twenty-second spoon when John barged in, wanting candles to replenish the sconces in the hallway. A sudden gust of wind entered with him, blowing the print onto the floor. Mr Matthews started guiltily, recovered the print and had begun to roll it up before he realized it was only John. 'You!' he exclaimed. 'See what you made me do!' But once the door was firmly closed behind him, he said in a more convivial manner, 'Take a look at this, dear boy, and tell me if you ever set eyes on anything half so droll before.'

John's sudden entry and his subsequent guffaws and exclamations at the parted thighs, the unbuttoned breeches, the dog running off with the king's garter, further distracted Mr Matthews. The butler sneezed and wiped his nose, shaking his venerable head. As a rule his memory was sharp, but the distraction had caused him to forget where he was with the spoons. He replaced them hurriedly in their box, locked it and returned it to the silver cabinet, resolving to allay Mrs Blanchard's fears and tell her the silver was untouched. She would be none the wiser. He turned then to the more enjoyable task of pouring a bottle of port through a silver funnel into a cut-glass decanter.

Just then the door reopened and the curvaceous figure of Agnes Meadowes appeared on his threshold. At this second interruption, the butler's face fell; he smartly whisked the print from John's grasp and slapped it upside down on the table. Agnes was surprised to find the pair of them standing so close and the atmosphere so jovial. As a rule, Mr Matthews preserved his authority by maintaining his distance.

'Excuse me, sir,' she ventured with an apologetic smile, 'may I have a word alone?'

'I am engaged, as you can see.'

'It is a matter Mrs Blanchard has asked me to discuss with you,' said Agnes, not entirely truthfully.

Mr Matthews frowned and heaved a sigh. He turned to John. 'Best be off with those candles then, eh.' John nodded, grabbed a handful from the box and left.

'Well, Mrs Meadowes, what can I do for you?'

'Mrs Blanchard believes Rose might have had some involvement with the murder and robbery. She has asked me to discover what I can of her whereabouts.'

Mr Matthews hesitated, sucking in his haggard cheeks. 'And you suppose *I* know the answer to that, do you?'

'Of course not,' said Agnes. 'Only you may unwittingly know something that will shed light on it.'

Mr Matthews tutted with disapproval and returned to his

decanting. 'Well I grant you it would provide a reason for her running off. But it seems implausible to me. A woman could not have carried off something so heavy.'

'She might have called upon an assistant.'

He was nearly at the end of his decanting – the most delicate part of the operation – thus for a minute or two he said nothing. Agnes noticed how deftly he performed this operation, his long slender fingers cradling the bottle, delicately supporting the funnel. Plainly, she thought, he has yet to sample the contents, or his hand would not be so steady. Eventually, when the last sediment-free drop was safely in the decanter, he turned to her. 'Whom have you in mind?'

'Mr Riley – the journeyman next door.'

Mr Matthews looked unconvinced. 'I doubt Rose had anything to do with the robbery. There is a far simpler reason for her departure, in my opinion.'

'What, then?'

'Guilt,' said the butler flatly. 'Have you forgotten that she stole the pistol from Mr Blanchard's room?'

'I have not forgotten its loss. But can we be certain it was she who took it? And if so, what was her motive for the theft?'

'I told you, I saw her upstairs on Monday morning while you were out at market. She had a furtive manner; she must have taken it then.'

'You implied before that her sorties upstairs were because she engaged in intimacies with Nicholas Blanchard.'

'I was not aware then that the gun was missing,' replied Mr Matthews smoothly. 'Besides, one misdemeanour does not preclude the other.'

No, thought Agnes, but it stretches credibility, and Philip – an undoubted expert in such matters – had said there was nothing between the pair. 'Perhaps not,' she said, nodding understandingly. 'Although I would hazard Rose did not run away because she took the pistol. Rather the reverse – she took the pistol *because* she was running away.'

'Come, come, Mrs Meadowes,' said Mr Matthews. 'Surely you are splitting hairs. Whatever way you turn it, the girl was guilty as sin.'

Agnes bit her lip, an obstinate gleam in her eyes. 'Apart from Monday, did you see Rose upstairs on other occasions?'

'No, but Nancy did – and gave proof of it, too.'

Agnes nodded. Presumably he was referring to the letter. 'Might it not have been something quite innocent that took her upstairs? Perhaps there was some matter on which she wanted to speak to the master or mistress.'

'What concerns might a kitchen maid have had that she could not discuss with me or Mrs Tooley – or you even?'

Heaven knows, thought Agnes. But just suppose Rose had had a personal matter that bothered her. How easy would it have been for her to discuss it with an ailing spinster housekeeper, an elderly butler, or an introverted cook who shut herself off and knew so little of the ways of love? Perhaps Rose *had* tried to seek out Mrs Blanchard, as she herself had done, hoping that her mistress might view her predicament more sympathetically. Perhaps that might explain why she had questioned Patsy about Mrs Blanchard's comings and goings – she did not want Patsy's position, merely a moment or two alone with her mistress.

Mr Matthews was pondering too. 'Now I think on it, I recall that one time Nancy caught her upstairs, Rose was carrying away a small silver salver. It was the one from the hallway upon which visiting cards are presented. She wouldn't have done that if she was so innocent, would she?'

'When was this?'

'A week or so ago,' said the butler vaguely.

'Did you confront her?'

'Naturally. She said she was not taking it away but putting it back. Riley had repaired it and had given it to her to return. She said that Nancy was a liar and was only trying to get her into trouble because Philip preferred her. And I need not think she was sweet on Philip, for she wasn't; they were friends and no more than that. The impudence of her manner, I'm sorry to say, was not unusual. I checked the story with Riley and he backed her up. It was that which made me suspect there was something between them. I contemplated telling her there and then that there was no place for such insolence, but Mrs Tooley begged me not to, saying you and she would never manage without her.'

Was this proof of Rose's involvement in duty-dodging, wondered Agnes. But then, bearing in mind Nancy's resentment of Rose, how trustworthy was her testimony? How likely was it that Nancy had really found the letter in the drawing room, *and* seen Rose with the salver, *and* discovered the cache of money under her mattress? The menservants came and went upstairs, yet had seen nothing. Doris shared a bedroom with Nancy and Rose, yet had not seen the purse. Plainly Rose was capable of untruths – she had lied brazenly over her friendship with Philip. But was Nancy lying too, in the hope of discrediting Rose, whom she hated, in the eyes of Mrs Tooley? 'Was it the same salver that was left out on the dresser last night?' she enquired.

'Yes,' said Mr Matthews. 'Philip is prone to almost as many lapses as your Rose. He brought it down yesterday to polish and carelessly forgot to put it back. I have already reprimanded him most sternly on the matter.' He paused. 'It was a pity you did not take a similarly strong line with Rose.'

'I did not need to,' said Agnes. 'She went anyway.' Then, embarrassed by the boldness of this reply and wishing she could retract it, she curtseyed hurriedly and returned to her kitchen.

Chapter Twenty-two

WHEN THE TIDE WAS LOW, SOMETHING OF VALUE MIGHT OFTEN be found a few yards out from the steps at Three Cranes Wharf. A bucket of coal, a handful of nails (copper ones were best), a piece of rag, a foot of rope or a few bones washed down from the abattoir – such riches awaited anyone willing to scratch about on the stony, rubbish-strewn mud flats of the River Thames.

The most fruitful place was the most precarious: between the moorings, beyond the shoals, where the retreating tide etched small channels that intersected and merged like the frayed fibres of an old piece of rope. Those who ventured here trod with care; for there were quicksands and channels that might pull a person down and drown them before they had time to call out. One day it might be safe to scrabble in a certain spot, the next the river would alter its conflagration, moving and shifting with the wind and tide. Only the boldest dared venture in this direction on an ebbing tide, when the water still concealed what lay beneath. This was where Elsie Drake had come.

She walked alone, towards the receding water whipped by the stiff wind into angry peaks and troughs. Wading barefoot through the noxious slime, she avoided the bricks and sharp stones that might cut her feet, her head hunched forward, thin shoulders bent double, hair streaming in the wind. She carried a willow basket on her back and a stick in her hand. Being accustomed to the dangers, she advanced slowly, poking the stick in the mud ahead, then swishing it from side to side so that she could test the firmness of the mud and feel for anything hidden beneath it.

This time, however, Elsie's search was not for the usual flotsam. She had something particular in mind. Mrs Meadowes's question regarding the woman in a blue dress had triggered her recollection of an event she had witnessed and then forgotten. If the tide was low in the early hours, Elsie occasionally ventured out with a lantern, knowing no one else would follow and anything she discovered would therefore be safe. On Monday night, the night of the robbery, she had observed such a woman. Elsie had come down to the river before dawn in search of coal. The woman had caught her attention by crying out, then stumbling and falling down the steps. Elsie had seen her pick herself up, gather her possessions and run off over the mud. It had been too dark to see the colour of her dress, but not too dark to observe the figure pursuing her – a tall man, Elsie remembered, though owing to the gloom, anything more precise had been impossible to discern. Assuming that they were lovers having a tiff, or that the woman was a whore who had tried to fleece him, Elsie had thought little of the episode at the time. But Agnes had brought it back to mind.

Elsie had worked herself into an almighty stew over Agnes Meadowes. The minute their discussion on London Bridge was over, Elsie had kicked herself for initiating it. Why should Agnes keep quiet about seeing her outside Blanchards' shop and again at Marcus Pitt's? Why had Elsie been so foolish as to run after Agnes and beg (so far as she was capable of begging) for her silence. It was all down to the charity Agnes had displayed towards her. Few servants deigned to give Elsie a kindly look, let alone three farthings. But Agnes's gesture, Elsie now saw, had been her undoing. She had given Agnes the opportunity to betray her.

Nothing prevented Agnes Meadowes from changing her mind and handing Elsie and her father to the justice. One way or another, her pa was dead, and she would most likely be transported. Elsie had passed several hours dwelling on this before a means of altering her fate came to her. What if the woman she had seen running over the mud was the same one Agnes was asking after? It was the same night, after all, and very few people were out at that hour. What exactly the woman was to Agnes, Elsie was uncertain, but cunning told her that she was important. And that being so, if Elsie could find some evidence of her, she might use it to keep Agnes quiet.

When Elsie had last seen the woman, she had been running over the mud near the grounded barges, and had dropped the bag she was carrying. Elsie was not certain whether or not the woman had halted to recover the bag, or had abandoned it. It had been too gloomy to see. But it occurred to her that if the bag *was* still there and she could recover it, the contents might serve her very well.

Ignoring the freezing water and oozing mud, and the salty spume whipped in her face by the north wind, she directed her steps towards the dark hulks where the woman had disappeared from her view. There were three boats moored side by side, with ropes dangling over their hulls like garlands on a door. There was no watchman she could see, but for once Elsie made no attempt to filch the ropes. Instead she began prodding around in the mud with her stick. The water in most places was still six inches deep, although here and there banks protruded from the water like smooth grey islands. She walked slowly forwards, poking, then stooping down when the stick met resistance to grope in the muddy slush for whatever lay concealed there. Then she poked again.

Half an hour later, her basket was a quarter full with an assortment of sodden wood and coal that she could not resist picking up, but she had found no trace of the bag. Knowing that she did not have long before others came, Elsie walked back towards a spit of mud jutting out into the water beyond the barges.

For some time, she poked around. Presently her stick struck something soft lying six inches or so beneath the surface. Elsie took a board from her basket and used it to scoop away the mud. At first she saw nothing, but as she dug deeper she came across a patch of sodden, silt-encrusted black cloth. She began to scoop out a wider circle, using her board to scrape away at the mud. More folds of dark cloth became visible. Perhaps it was the bag she'd been hunting for. She dug on, revealing a still larger expanse of the cloth. But then came something more disturbing – a flash of something mottled and purplish-grey in hue.

Elsie stopped digging and squinted down, uncertain, fearful, yet hopeful, then wiped away a little more of the mud with her numb fingers. More urgently, she excavated around the object, examined it closely, then nodded and knelt back on her frozen heels. She seemed calm, but her pulse was pounding and there was an empty feeling in the pit of her stomach. It was not what she had been looking for – not the bag, but a body.

The small mottled corner she had uncovered first was the tip of a finger. Ten minutes and much careful excavation later, Elsie had revealed most of the corpse. The woman was clad as Agnes had described, in a blue dress and black cloak of middling quality; her hair was chestnut brown. Even if she had wanted to, it would have been difficult for Elsie to discern much more about her, her features were so distorted by mud and water. Her hair was tangled with mud and grit, her lips puffed and purplish-black, her mouth, nostrils and eyes filled with mud.

Not far away from her claw of a left hand lay the bag for which Elsie had searched. It was made from brown canvas; there were letters stencilled in black upon it, but Elsie could not read them. She had seen plenty of bodies before in the dingy parts of the city she inhabited. Thus she felt no immediate revulsion or fear, but wonderment rather at the opportunity she had stumbled upon. Without pausing to consider what had caused the woman to die, Elsie deftly unbuckled the bag and found inside several items of clothing.

Then turning back to the corpse, she unlaced its boots and tugged them off, then briskly unfastened the bindings of the cloak and, grasping one edge, yanked sharply upwards to free it. The body rolled slowly onto its side and then tipped back again – but not before Elsie noticed that the woman had been slashed across the neck. The wound had been so ingrained with silt that she had not seen it at first, but moving the body had made the head loll back, revealing a wide incision so deep the head seemed to be hanging on by the merest thread. There was no sign of blood – presumably it had all been washed away. Instead the flesh had a strangely inhuman, spongy appearance.

Elsie had seen several bodies hauled out of the river before, but never one so brutally damaged. She was surprised how much the sight disturbed her. She felt her heart race and a sickening sensation in her belly. Presumably the man she had seen chasing the woman that night must have done this. She considered telling Agnes what she had seen and found. Perhaps then the murderer would be caught and punished for his wickedness. But if she did tell her, Agnes might force her to give up the clothes and boots. Elsie glanced down at her feet, bluer than the lips of the corpse from walking through the freezing mud. She would keep the boots for herself and reckoned that if she dried the other clothes, the ragman might give her enough for them to keep her from having to return here for most of the winter.

Elsie then turned her attention to the laces of the bodice. Once the skirt was off, she felt in the pockets and found them to be empty save for a small black heart-shaped object. A brisk rubbing revealed this to be a small silver box, decorated with leaves and flowers. Elsie opened the lid, which was engraved inside with some writing – the woman's name, she guessed. Here was all she needed to weave a tale for Agnes. Never had the mud seemed so bountiful.

Good fortune did not turn Elsie's head. Rather it caused her to become more vigilant. She glanced back in the direction from which she had come, and against an angry yellowish sky perceived a straggling line of five or six people standing on the mud flats, surveying the shrinking river and peering in her direction. They had probably been watching her for some time, and as soon as the water was low enough would follow her to see what had drawn her here. From their present position they would not be able to make out the body, sprawled out on the mud and covered in dirt. But once they approached and saw what it was, they would want to know what she had found on it. If they discovered her haul they would force her to share it between them; or, worse, they might try and steal it from her.

Elsie decided the corpse might stay in her chemise and petticoat. There was no time to remove them. She stowed the silver box inside her bodice, stuffing it down deep so that it rested safely on the waistband of her skirt. She tipped the coal and wood chips in her basket out onto the mud and packed in the clothes and boots, pressing them down as far as she could, then covering her treasure with a layer of coal and wood. The task took no more than a minute or two. When she had finished, she glanced up. The group was still waiting back at the steps, but they looked ready to start out at any moment.

Using her board, Elsie hastily began to replace the mud. Covering the corpse's head came as a relief – it prevented her from looking on those mud-filled eyes and the dreadful wound. Once the body and bag were safely interred, she smoothed the mud with the flat of the board until she was satisfied her excavations were no longer visible. For good measure, she scattered a few bricks and stones on top.

Taking up the straps of her basket, she slung it on her back. Then, bowing her head and forcing herself to walk as slowly and miserably as if there were only coal and bones and chips of wood inside it, she turned back towards the bank.

None of the other river-finders said a word, save Marge, the oldest and most garrulous, who was picking over some empty crates close to the steps. There was a mud-stained lantern with a broken glass tied around her waist with a piece of string. 'Get anything?' she enquired as Elsie trudged past, head bent low against the wind.

'Nought special,' returned Elsie, resisting the urge to run. If she did not brazen this out, Marge might say something to the others and they would strip her of all she had in a flash.

'You're back up quickly, then,' said Marge. Her eye darted over Elsie's basket. 'You wouldn't be back 'less you'd got summat.'

'Hush,' said Elsie. 'I ain't got nothing. Hand on heart I ain't.'

'Yes you 'ave. Show old Marge now. Ain't I been good to you, letting you share my fire? What is it you got?'

Elsie shivered as a gust of wind stabbed through her thin bodice. She looked glumly at her feet. 'Went out an hour ago, found a load of wood wedged under one of them boats,' she mumbled. 'Won't all go in the basket. Thought I'd go back once I'd got rid of this.'

'Where?' whispered Marge, taking hold of Elsie's elbow.

'Don't say nothing to the others.'

'Not a word.'

Elsie pointed wordlessly towards the barge furthest away from the spit where the corpse was buried. She guessed several of the others standing nearby must have heard snippets of their conversation. Two or three trudged off in the direction she had indicated.

Elsie left Marge hobbling behind them. She shuffled up the steps as slowly as if there was nothing but coal and sodden logs in her basket, although at that precise moment it felt as light as a bundle of twigs. Suddenly she did not feel the chill wind or her damp clothes or her icy feet. It would be a long time, she thought, before she would have to poke about in the mud again. She had boots to wear, clothes to sell, and she had unearthed the means to keep Agnes Meadowes quiet.

Chapter Twenty-three

IT WAS SOON AFTER ELEVEN O'CLOCK WHEN AGNES SET OUT TO market next morning. Elsie Drake was lingering on the corner of Foster Lane and Cheapside. 'You still after the woman with the blue dress?' she queried, popping out of a dark doorway and giving Agnes such a fright she nearly dropped her basket.

'Yes,' said Agnes breathlessly, surreptitiously checking her purse was still in her pocket. 'Have you remembered something about her? Did you see her, after all?'

'Better'n that,' said Elsie proudly, 'I've got summat to show you.' She turned her back on Agnes and with head slightly bent rummaged among the grimy folds of her skirt, extracting an object wrapped in a square of hessian. She unwrapped the cloth, letting it drop to the ground while she placed its contents on her palm. Then with hand outstretched, she spun round for Agnes to see.

A small blackened heart-shaped box engraved with leaves and flowers lay upon Elsie's hand. Agnes had never seen it before. 'What's this? Where did you find it?' she quizzed.

'I didn't find it. She gave it me to show you.'

'*Who* gave it to you?'

Elsie looked perturbed, as if this was not the reaction she had expected. 'That woman in the blue dress, the one you asked after. Take it an' 'ave a look – it's got some writing on it – her name, I'll be bound.'

Agnes took the box and opened it. She saw then that it was made from silver and contained a perforated grill. It was a vinaigrette, in which a lady might keep her smelling salts. Engraved upon the inside of the lid were the words *Forever Yours*. Nothing that linked the box to Rose. 'Where is she?' said Agnes distractedly. She did not give the girl's tale much credence – if her father was a thief it would be easy enough for her to get her hands on some valuable trinket like this and pretend it was Rose's.

'That I can't say.'

'What d'you mean, you can't say? You must know if she gave this to you. If it *is* hers.'

Elsie regarded her feet. 'She told me not to let on,' she mumbled. 'Made me give my word.'

'So you have spoken to her?' said Agnes sharply. 'What else exactly did she say?'

Elsie kept her head bowed. 'Just that I was to show you this – a sign she's well. She knows you're looking for her, and says she wants you to stop. She says she don't want no one from Blanchards bothering her now, however fond they may be of her. But if you've a message from time to time, you might pass it to me to convey,' she mumbled.

Agnes looked again at the box. The outside was filthy, but she was struck by the beauty and delicacy of the decoration. She could see it was valuable, not the sort of thing a kitchen maid might be expected to own. But even if something so precious did belong to Rose, why would she entrust it to such a disreputable urchin as Elsie?

As she looked down at Elsie, Agnes observed something that made her take sudden note. Where before the girl had always been barefoot, now she was wearing a pair of stout brown leather boots that seemed a little large. Agnes's distrust grew more powerful. 'I don't believe Rose told you any such thing,' she said sternly to the girl. 'She and I were not friends. She would not expect me to send her messages, or send them to me. She worked as a kitchen maid, so how would she have something like this in her possession? And why would she send it to me?'

Elsie looked surprised and disappointed. 'You deaf or summat?' she said rudely. 'That's what I said. I said she's had enough with you. She don't want nothing more to do with you . . . And you ain't keeping that box – she only wanted me to show it to you.'

She made a sudden snatch for the box, but by some miracle Agnes anticipated it. As Elsie's small brown hand grabbed for her palm, Agnes clenched her fist and raised it over her head so that the box was safely out of reach. 'I'll keep hold of this, if you don't mind. You can tell Rose it's safe with me. And tell me, by the by, where did you come by those boots?'

Agnes observed Elsie's darting eyes, her knowing demeanour, the thin curve of her mouth, which suddenly seemed unaccountably cruel. She perceived that the girl was performing a charade, manipulating her for some malign purpose. Agnes looked at the box and the boots, then reached out and clasped Elsie by her bony shoulder, forcing her to meet her gaze. 'You stole this, and those boots too I wager. They *are* Rose's, even if this isn't. You stole from me once before.' Agnes brought her face close to the girl's. 'And just now you tried to do the same. Now unless you want me to call the constable, tell me where Rose is and when you robbed her.'

The girl could not hide a flicker of shock. 'I never robbed her,' she said unconvincingly.

'Then let us call a constable to ask the same question. He might well take you to the Round House. And while he's at it have your father arrested.'

'But you promised you'd keep him out of it,' said Elsie, trying frantically to squirm from her grasp.

But Agnes only tightened her grip. 'What makes you think I am any more trustworthy than you? Tell me where you came by those boots and this box, or I'll send for the constable directly.'

'I never robbed her. What makes you say I robbed her?' squealed Elsie, writhing and kicking out clumsily with her oversized boots.

'Boy!' called Agnes to an errand boy a few yards distant. 'Here's tuppence if you run now and fetch the constable. This creature just tried to rob me of my silver box. I'll see to it she's taken before the justice and branded.'

'I never!' squealed Elsie, enraged. 'She's tricked me up! I give her the box and she's gone mad.'

''Course you did,' said the lad, winking at Agnes. 'An' I'm Dick Turpin back from the dead and just gave her a sovereign to boot.'

With this, the weakness of her situation seemed to dawn on Elsie. She stopped struggling, then glanced at the boy and Agnes, then at her feet. 'I'll give you the lot if it's what you want. But you're a bitch an' a half to take it off me.'

Agnes ignored the insult. 'So you robbed her of more, did you? I want nothing except for you to tell me what you know. Where is Rose?'

'I never robbed her, and you won't never speak to her,' said Elsie, half spitting the words.

'Why not? Explain yourself properly.'

When Elsie spoke, her words cut Agnes to the quick. 'She's dead. I found her. That's all there is to explain.'

There was silence for a minute, after which the lad began tugging at Agnes's basket. 'So, ma'am, am I going for the constable or not?' he said.

'No,' replied Agnes, handing him a penny. 'Now be off with you.' She turned back to Elsie. 'Where is she?' she said, trying to steady her voice.

'Down on the mud flats. Near the barge mooring at Three Cranes Wharf. I found her yesterday at low tide. She was buried. I uncovered her.'

'Dear God! She must have fallen into the river and drowned.'

'No, she never. Her throat was slit from ear to ear.'

Agnes felt faint. Her mind flooded with gruesome images of Rose bleeding, her blood seeping into the mud and being washed away by the grimy river. Her heart began to race and a bitter taste rose into her throat. Still conscious, however, that Elsie was a slippery customer who would run off if she gave her an inch of leeway, she tried to push these disturbing thoughts from her mind and concentrate on less distressing details. 'I suppose you also found her twenty sovereigns. I take it that was the reason for your reluctance to reveal this discovery?'

'No,' said Elsie quickly. 'There was not a penny on her. I swear.'

Agnes sighed, unconvinced. 'I do not want the money, Elsie – so far as I am concerned, even if it was a hundred guineas you might keep it. Just tell me frankly how much there was. Remember the constable, Elsie. Remember your father.'

'I told you, said Elsie stubbornly, 'I still got the clothes, if you want to see. But there was no money.'

Agnes could see she would get no further. 'What else did you find – a pistol and a bag, perchance?'

'The bag was there,' said Elsie, 'but no pistol. Although I think I saw her drop it and pick it up. It's my guess the man chasing after her nabbed it. And the money, too.'

'You saw her? When? What man?' said Agnes, unable to mask her surprise.

'I never saw much,' said Elsie. 'But he were tallish and dressed in a cloak, with long dark hair tied back in a queue, and he ran like the blazes . . .'

Chapter Twenty-four

HAVING LEARNED THE FEARFUL TRUTH ABOUT POOR ROSE'S fate, Agnes was thrown into a state of unusual indecision. She could hardly leave the poor girl's body to rot in the mud without a proper burial. A murder had been committed. Something had to be done. But if she observed convention and told the justice, he would demand to know how she had made the discovery and Elsie's involvement would be impossible to conceal. Elsie's pathetic attempts at deception had infuriated Agnes, but she had no real desire to see the girl apprehended.

Torn by conflicting loyalties to her disreputable kitchen maid and the equally disreputable Elsie, Agnes fretted over how best to proceed. Furthermore, she still had the matter of Peter's living arrangements to resolve.

In the market, Agnes was scarcely aware of whether the pears she purchased were worm eaten or the cardoons stringy; she neglected to squeeze the mutton for tenderness, nor did she ascertain whether the eels were as lively as she required. She drifted blindly on, aware that for once in her life she did not feel separate, but entangled in the muddy world surrounding her. With all this to preoccupy her, how could the Blanchards' menu take first place?

Returning to Foster Lane, Agnes was still so engrossed that the faces she passed were invisible to her. It was only when a firm hand clutched her elbow that she took note of her surroundings and realized that someone was addressing her.

'Mrs Meadowes, might I have a word? Mrs Meadowes, did you hear me? Are you quite well? Has something distressed you?'

'What? Oh, Mr Williams,' said Agnes, blinking vaguely. 'Forgive me, but I didn't hear you. My mind was in another place entirely.'

'So I see,' said Thomas Williams with a forlorn half-smile.

Agnes spoke without her usual caution. 'My apologies, sir,' she said. 'I meant no insult. To tell the truth, I have just had a great shock.'

'What on earth was it?'

Agnes related her encounter with Elsie, and how the girl had spotted Rose running over the mud flats on the night of the robbery, and found her body buried there by the barges. She confessed her uncertainty as to what she should do, having promised to keep Elsie out of trouble. Then she took out the silver heart-shaped box and showed it to him.

'Elsie says she discovered this upon Rose's person. Lord knows how she came by it. Do you think Riley might have given it to her?'

'Good God!' said Thomas Williams, eyes downcast. He gave the box a cursory examination, running the flat of his thumb over the engraving. 'I should doubt it. Riley doesn't strike me as the kind to give her such a thing. Perhaps it was a gift from a past paramour.' Then, as if the freedom with which he was speaking struck him, he coloured and altered tack. 'If Drake was responsible for the death of the apprentice, where is the wrong in having him apprehended?'

'But if I do so I will punish Elsie as well. She has no other family, so she would be an orphan and have to choose between the workhouse and the street. Surely it is better to have a parent, however deficient, than none at all?'

'Perhaps,' said Thomas Williams uncertainly. 'But that

doesn't alter the fact that her father is a murderer and she is his assistant.'

Agnes frowned. She did not doubt Drake was the thief, but something in Elsie's description of what she had seen had shaken her conviction that he was the killer. Rather than voice this uncertainty, she concentrated on an argument that she knew held weight. 'If Marcus Pitt hears we know the culprit is one of his men, there is every chance he will melt down the wine-cooler, in which case Mr Blanchard will be ruined and we will all suffer. But I cannot, in all conscience, leave Rose's body in the mud to rot without a decent burial. Something must be done.'

'And so it shall. Rest assured, Mrs Meadowes,' said Thomas Williams, still standing awkwardly, cradling the box in his hand. 'But I hold that if Drake slit Noah Prout's throat you cannot describe him merely as deficient – he is evil, and should be punished for it. I pity anyone with such a man for a father. Do you think he killed Rose too?'

She would have to tell him her thoughts. 'Drake and Rose met identical deaths – their throats were slit, which suggests the same hand murdered them. But I don't believe Drake murdered Rose. Elsie said she saw a man chasing Rose, although she couldn't see who it was. If it had been her father, she surely would have recognized him and said nothing. It follows then that Drake did not kill the apprentice either. Which means that the murderer must be someone else – most likely the person in the Blanchards' employ who involved Pitt and Drake in the first place.'

'Do you trust the girl?' asked Thomas Williams.

Agnes shook her head. 'Truth is not a commodity Elsie holds in high regard.'

'Then do not allow her to deflect you into forming unsound theories.'

'My instinct tells me she isn't lying in this instance, and I don't believe my theories *are* unsound.'

'I comprehend your uncertainty,' answered Williams, scratching his corkscrew curls, 'but murder is a matter for the justice to resolve.'

'Quite,' said Agnes. 'But as I said before, therein lies my quandary. How do I inform the justice of Rose's murder without letting Elsie's identity be known, thus causing the wine-cooler to be lost for ever?'

After a lengthy silence, during which he regarded his boots with great interest and Agnes surveyed the top of his hat, Thomas Williams's head jerked up suddenly. 'I believe I have the resolution,' he proffered, folding his arms across his chest.

'What, then?'

'*I* will tell the constable that I saw the body. I will say I was walking past the river at low tide and caught sight of something that appeared to be the body of a woman lying on the mud, surrounded by river scavengers. The reason for my particular anxiety is that I have heard a kitchen maid is missing from this household.'

'Hmm,' said Agnes. She was not accustomed to receiving assistance from others. Her unhappy marriage had made her guard her independence; she prided her ability to fend for herself and Peter without recourse to others. Nevertheless, she was not so independent as to be foolish. Williams's offer was one she welcomed. She had not known what to do; he had provided her with a workable solution. But still a smattering of reserve remained. Should she trust him? Was he all he seemed? He was, after all, a man. She regarded him uncertainly. 'You are most charitable, Mr Williams, but I hesitate to accept. Your intervention might result in you enduring unexpected inconveniences. I should manage the matter myself.'

'What is life if we don't occasionally engage ourselves in the lives of others and offer our assistance?' said Williams stoutly. His usual melancholy seemed to have left him and a look of unwavering certitude suddenly brightened his expression. 'Besides, I have an hour to spare, and don't want to be cast out without a job any more than you do. Perhaps you should keep this. I am quite certain Rose would have wanted you to have it.'

So saying, he thrust the box back into Agnes's hand. Before Agnes had time to object, he raised his hat, bowed and stalked off round the corner in search of the constable. Just before he disappeared from view, he called out over his shoulder, 'Listen for the door this evening. I will come to tell you what passes.'

The servants ate their last meal of the day at around eight, two hours or so before the upstairs supper was served. Usually the downstairs meal was a simple affair of ale, cold meats, bread and reheated leftovers. Upper and lower servants ate together, seated at the kitchen table in strict order: Mr Matthews at the head, Mrs Tooley on his right, Patsy on his left, Agnes beside Mrs Tooley, and then the others strung out in descending order like pearls on a necklace, with Doris at the farthest end.

It was Mr Matthews's or Mrs Tooley's habit generally to lead the conversation, to prevent an unholy row ensuing. There were times when one of the lower servants spoke out of turn and got away with it, but provided the butler had not sampled too much wine, it was more likely than not they would be sternly rebuked for it.

That evening, however, was not usual. There were two quarts of ale, cold brawn in jelly, cold mutton, a piece of cheese, a loaf of bread and a dish of warm cauliflower set upon the table. There was also Rose Francis's murder to chew over and digest. No sooner had Mrs Tooley asked Mr Matthews why a constable had called than the table was in uproar which even he could not suppress.

'Oh, my heavens!' said Mrs Tooley, crossing herself. 'Who ever would have thought it?'

'Her throat was slit from ear to ear and hanging by a thread?' echoed Doris, looking pale.

'And was there nothing about her person?' asked Nancy. 'No letters, nor nothing to show where she was headed off to?'

'It seems,' said Mr Matthews portentously, 'she was stripped of all her possessions save her chemise and petticoat.'

''Tis a crying shame, that's what it is,' said Philip in a tone entirely devoid of his usual flirtatious sparkle.

'Hear, hear,' echoed John.

Mr Matthews looked stern, but he passed no disparaging remark. He too seemed uncommonly upset, thought Agnes.

'What a horror!' said Patsy, resting her long thin fingers against her cheek. 'Though one cannot say it is entirely unexpected. To go off in the middle of the night, unprotected, is to invite such calamitous events.'

'She wasn't unprotected,' said Nancy flatly. 'She had the pistol. Ain't that nor her bag been found, Mr M.?'

'I haven't heard. No doubt some guttersnipe has sold it for a few shillings,' replied Mr Matthews, head slowly nodding, mouth morosely downturned, 'when at the very least it should have fetched five guineas.'

'All this talk has quite unravelled me. I feel a headache coming on,' whispered Mrs Tooley. 'Perhaps you would kindly all excuse me.'

No sooner was the servants' supper over than the day's final duties were attacked with military precision. Mrs Tooley, having retired to her room, was thus unable to help Agnes and Doris get the dishes ready for upstairs. Patsy went off to tidy Lydia's dressing table, put out her nightdress and take away items that needed her attention. John and Philip, loaded with buckets of coal, replenished the fires in the drawing room, library and dining room, then dressed themselves in their evening regalia for serving supper. Nancy armed herself with three copper warming pans filled with hot coals and three new candles for the night lights. In each of the Blanchards' bedrooms she drew the velvet curtains, turned down the beds, folding a precise triangle of linen sheet over the eiderdown, stoked the bedroom fires (already lit by Philip earlier in the afternoon) and ensured the chamber pots were all in the night tables.

Mr Matthews, meanwhile, put Nicholas's nightshirt and cap to warm, and took out the things ready for his toilette next morning. He folded the towels neatly and laid out the razor, soap and badger-bristle shaving brush. He ran a finger round the wash bowl to make sure there was no trace of scum, then conveyed several items of clothing to his pantry for John to brush and press.

This done, he turned his attention to the more pleasurable duties of the dining room. Proudly, with all the pomp and majesty of a royal attendant, he placed a claret-filled decanter on a silver salver and bore it upstairs. Having set this gently on the side table, he set about trimming the wicks of the lighted wall sconces, and lighting the candles of the candelabra on the table. Then, having bellowed down the back stairs to John and Philip to get a move on, he took up his position by the door, ready to summon the family.

During these preparations, a steady downpour began to thrash the windows. Agnes looked up from the supper trays at the fat drops streaking the glass and shivered, as Doris emerged from the larder with a pat of butter. Just then there was a hesitant tapping at the kitchen door. 'Shall I see who it is?' she said, moving with alacrity towards the door.

'No,' said Agnes, stepping in front and blushing furiously, for she was certain it must be Thomas Williams and was anxious to avoid arousing gossip and speculation in the household. 'I'll see to the door. Leave the butter and go quickly to the scullery now and make a start on those pots. I shall manage quite well here.'

She was correct in her assumption, but only in part. Thomas Williams was not alone. Accompanying him was someone who threw her into a state of great confusion.

A sudden hush descended. She looked from one to the other. Her jaw dropped, yet no words came. She was speechless.

'Well, Mrs Meadowes, that's a strange welcome on a very nasty night. If you can think of nothing to say, perhaps we could come in and sit down until you do. I found my companion on your doorstep. He's quite drenched through – and in urgent need of warmth and food, I'd hazard.'

Agnes could feel the blood receding from her cheeks as she spoke. 'You had best both come in.'

Chapter Twenty-five

THOMAS WILLIAMS ENTERED. BY HIS SIDE, BLEACHED WITH COLD, was a round-cheeked, raisin-eyed boy of ten years old. His dark curly hair (which closely resembled his mother's) was plastered to his head, and rain dripped from his sodden clothing in puddles on the floor.

'Peter!' exclaimed Agnes, scooping her bedraggled son to her bosom. 'What on earth has happened? How did you arrive here?'

Between spasms of shivering, Peter explained that Mrs Catchpole's condition had worsened since she wrote her letter to Agnes. Her sister had been too occupied with looking after the invalid to deal with a child as well. Thus she had put Peter on a coach and paid the driver to see him safe to Foster Lane. But when they arrived in the city, the driver had said he had another urgent vehicle to drive and no time to accompany Peter. He had been left some distance off, at a place called the Strand, and told it would be a simple matter to find his way on foot.

'The scoundrel! The rogue!' said Agnes, pink with outrage. 'To abandon a defenceless child beggars belief. What wouldn't I like to do to such a man . . .' While thus in mid flow, she removed Peter's wet clothing, wrapped him in a blanket and began warming a little broth for him to drink.

She was in the midst of buttering a thick slice of toast when Mrs Tooley entered the kitchen in search of a spoon for her elixir. The housekeeper was dressed in her nightgown and her hair dangled down over one shoulder in a stringy plait of pewter grey. She rammed her pince-nez in position and shot an incredulous look at Thomas Williams and the child wrapped in a horsehair blanket seated close to the fire. Her bewildered eyes slid then to Agnes, whose face seemed to radiate greater warmth than she had ever seen before. In contrast, Mrs Tooley's pale complexion turned as grey as her plait. 'Mrs Meadowes,' she said in a faltering voice, 'I should not need to remind you of all people that servants in this house are strictly prohibited visitors of any kind! This man does not belong here. Neither does this child. I trust you can provide some proper explanation for their presence and that they will be on their way forthwith. You know I am unwell. How could you commit such a grave transgression? I really had thought—'

'May I introduce Mr Thomas Williams,' said Agnes, breaking in. 'He is one of Mr Blanchard's journeymen. He has come to inform me of something pertaining to Rose and the missing wine-cooler. You know I am helping to recover it.'

Mrs Tooley seemed only slightly appeased. Her head oscillated on her neck like a wind-shivered leaf. 'And the child?'

Agnes ladled a little warm soup into a cup. 'Mr Williams rescued him from the doorstep and brought him here because he had nowhere else to go,' she said. She handed the bowl to Peter, who was so upset by Mrs Tooley's unwelcoming manner that he shook his head and hung his hands by his sides, refusing to take it.

'He rescued him from the doorstep? Then may I ask, Mr Williams, what gave you the impression this kitchen doubles as an orphanage or hospital for foundlings?' stuttered Mrs Tooley.

Agnes, crimson now from consternation, took up the spoon and tried to coax a little of the hot liquor into her son's mouth.

'Of course I never thought that for a moment, madam,' replied Thomas Williams, avoiding Agnes's eye. 'I was only trying to help. The child is well cared for, but has somehow contrived to lose himself. I thought we might provide him with a little shelter and then ascertain where he belongs.'

'Your philanthropic aims are most commendable, sir,' said Mrs Tooley, now drawing herself up and contracting her lips as though she were sipping vinegar. 'But what gives you the right to pursue them in my kitchen? No doubt he's brought lice and all manner of vermin in with him. Doris will have to scrub the whole place with caustic tomorrow.

'If you know what's good for you, boy, you'll take your clothes and leave,' said Mrs Tooley, turning suddenly to address Peter in a chilling undertone. 'Otherwise I shall be forced to send one of the footmen out for the watch.'

'No! I won't allow it,' said Agnes, turning abruptly to face Mrs Tooley. 'If he goes, so will I.'

'I beg your pardon?' Mrs Tooley exclaimed. 'What on earth can you mean, Mrs Meadowes? Have you taken leave of your senses? What concern of yours is this urchin?'

Agnes did not allow a shred of sympathy for the housekeeper to obscure her purpose. 'If you must know, he is my son,' she announced firmly. 'The woman who has charge of him is ill and, being unable to care for him, has returned him to me. Therefore I will not have him sent out into the rain. If he goes, so too will I.'

Mrs Tooley gave a gasp and seemed to sway on her feet. She put out one hand to steady herself, and raised the other to her brow. When she spoke again, her voice had dropped an octave. 'Of course, the hair, those eyes – I should have known. How could I not have guessed!'

Having comprehended the predicament, Mrs Tooley's distress did not diminish, but grew. She was too entrenched in her habits to see how she might allow an inch of leeway; yet unaccountably, she felt uncomfortable imposing what she knew to be right. 'The fact that he is yours does not mean he can stay here,' she said, fumbling for her salts.

'But what would you have me do, Mrs Tooley?' demanded

Agnes sharply. 'Send him to the workhouse or out into the street?'

Mrs Tooley unstoppered her salts and sniffed them loudly. 'That is for you to decide, Mrs Meadowes,' she murmured in a feeble voice, designed, Agnes was certain, to evoke pity and thus compliance. 'But whatever you choose, you will have to do something this night or I shall be taken ill, and then the matter will reach upstairs and we shall all have the devil to pay. And now, if you'll excuse me I think I must lie down. I feel an attack coming on.' And with this unhelpful remark, she made her way towards the door.

Agnes lowered herself stiffly into a chair just as Peter, sensing the maelstrom and uncertainty surrounding his fate, began to cry. Thin whimpering sobs racked his little body and turned his smooth complexion an angry shade of red.

'There there,' said Thomas Williams, patting the child briefly on the back with gauche kindness. 'It ain't so bad. Your ma won't leave you at the workhouse or out in the cold. 'Course she won't. Anyway, I believe I have the answer to the problem.'

'What's that?' said Agnes, rubbing Peter's wet curls with a dishcloth.

'My landlady, Mrs Sharp, lives two streets away from here, on Bread Street. She is a sea captain's wife whose husband is away for months at a stretch. She has a child of her own, who is seven years of age, and I warrant she would be quite willing for a short while to look after Peter. I will make the introductions if you wish.'

Agnes could have wept for joy. But a moment later she grew conscious that this was the second dilemma Thomas Williams had solved for her that day. And when all was said and done, what did she know of him? He was a journeyman – shy, somewhat morose, apparently respectable, helpful, and politer than Riley, but that was not saying much. Why would he take such trouble over someone he barely knew? Agnes could only divine that he was trying to ingratiate himself into her favour for some improper purpose of his own. And thus her wariness remained. For all this, she could not refuse his proposal.

'Thank you, Mr Williams. If your landlady is truly willing to take Peter, I would be most grateful,' she said stiffly. Then, to cover her embarrassment, she rubbed Peter's head so vigorously with the cloth that he protested. Here was a chance to see her son more regularly; this realization brought her a surge of pleasure. She flashed a smile over Peter's head at Thomas Williams. 'I can pay ten shillings a week, will that suffice?'

He smiled back hesitatingly. 'Come and discuss it with her now.'

Chapter Twenty-six

AGNES WALKED OUT INTO THE NIGHT WITH PETER TO ONE SIDE of her and Thomas Williams to the other. The rain had eased, but the streets remained wet enough for the lights from houses and shops to streak the ground with reflected light. A keen north-east wind had begun to blow.

'I gather the constable found Rose's corpse,' said Agnes quietly to Thomas as they battled the elements and strode the short distance to his lodgings. 'He paid the Blanchards a visit this afternoon.'

'Yes,' returned Thomas in a subdued tone. 'I accompanied him and showed him the place you described. He ordered the ground to be dug up and we found her without difficulty. I was able to identify the body as Rose's.'

'What condition was she in?' After Elsie's description and the conversation at supper, Agnes did not really wish to know more, but somehow she felt it her duty to ask.

Williams shook his head as if the memory were one he would sooner forget. 'You would not have liked to see her,' he said quietly. 'She was badly disfigured by mud and water, stripped by scavengers of all her clothing save her undergarments.'

Agnes gazed down the rain-lashed street, clutching Peter's

frail hand tighter in hers. There was no sound reason for her to dwell on Rose, yet she could not help herself returning to the subject. 'Unless we understand why she left Foster Lane that night, I cannot see how we will unravel her death. I did think before that a man must lie behind it, and that her going off was quite separate from the robbery. But the fact that the apprentice and Rose were both killed in the same way shows there must be a link of some kind.'

'It is possible, I suppose, that she somehow assisted in the robbery and was killed after serving her purpose,' said Williams.

'Duty-dodging may have played a part,' returned Agnes. 'Mr Matthews told me Rose was caught handling a salver without any convincing excuse – the same one that you examined. '

'Hmm. I should say an affair of the heart was more likely behind it.'

Agnes glanced at him. She said nothing for a moment, gazing instead at the great dome of St Paul's which loomed incongruously large above the diminutive rooftops. Viewed from such close proximity it seemed to belong to another city, a place built on another scale entirely. Was this Sir Christopher Wren's intention, she wondered – to humble and overawe spectators with architectural puissance and majesty, and thereby ensure their submission?

'I did presume, like you, that a man lay behind it,' she said. 'But now I have changed my view. Perhaps love is not involved here. Rose lacked modesty and had an appetite for the opposite sex, but little need for romantic affection. Put together with the salver and the money in her possession, she may have run off as a result of her involvement with duty-dodging and Riley.'

'You believe that having dabbled in a minor duty fraud, Riley suddenly grew more ambitious and organized the theft of the wine-cooler, killing both Rose and the apprentice?'

Agnes ignored his sceptical tone. 'Don't you think him capable?'

'Perhaps,' conceded Thomas. 'But in my experience a

craving for physical affection does not preclude a desire for romance. Rather the reverse.'

Agnes paused awkwardly, uncertain how to respond. She had steered herself onto unsteady ground, where her naivety must be plainly apparent. Was this a preamble to his own improper intentions, she wondered. Thanking God for the dark night, which obscured her flaming cheeks, she avoided this argument.

'Let us ignore Rose's physical desires for one moment, Mr Williams. I told you of Nancy's account that Rose had twenty sovereigns hidden under her mattress. Elsie says she never found this, but I do not give her denial much credence. I still believe it possible she had accumulated that sum from her duty-dodging scheme with Riley. That would give her enough money to live independently of men, for a few months at least. I hazard, therefore, that she was fleeing a threat of some kind. Perhaps she found out Riley's plan regarding the burglary and decided it was too much for her. Perhaps she feared if she refused to help Riley he might turn against her, so she ran off, but he caught up with her.'

'It is a possibility, I grant you,' said Thomas Williams as they stopped outside a dark scuffed door halfway along Bread Street. 'But to tell the truth, I do not believe she and Riley could have accumulated such a sum from duty-dodging.'

'But you told me yourself the duty on the wine-cooler would have been thirty pounds,' protested Agnes.

'Yes, but as I said before, that was an unusually large commission. Nothing close to its size has been made for months, and the wine-cooler itself was far too conspicuous for Riley to risk avoiding duty. And Mr Theodore Blanchard has charge of the accounts.'

Agnes was as ill equipped to counter his superior knowledge on the subject of silver as on love. Frustrated by his disbelief and her own lack of expertise, she nodded, averting her eyes from his. 'God willing, we shall discover the truth when the wine-cooler is recovered, Mr Williams.' Then she whisked away a strand of hair that the wind had blown across her lips, turned to her son and, giving his small hand a squeeze, said, 'Here we are, Peter.'

Ten minutes later, Agnes was sitting in a comfortable parlour before a blazing fire with Peter on her knee. The room was simply furnished with two armchairs, a settle and a circular wooden table. On the mantelshelf stood a jug in the form of a cow, a figurine of a shepherd and shepherdess and a pair of plain brass candlesticks. Mrs Tooley would approve, thought Agnes. The homely surroundings were all she could hope for. Moreover, Mrs Sharp, a placable, buxom, middle-aged woman with sandy hair and shrewd grey eyes, had greeted Peter kindly when Thomas had introduced them.

Thomas was in the kitchen, helping Mrs Sharp prepare refreshments and explaining the situation to her. Above the rattling of the windows, Agnes could hear the gentle murmur of their voices drifting through the door. A few minutes later Thomas returned, carrying a tray with wine and glasses set out upon it. Mrs Sharp followed with a cup of hot posset.

'Here, Peter, this is to warm up those chilly bones of yours. There's milk and honey and nutmeg and a little ale in it,' she said, handing him the posset.

'So, Mrs Meadowes, didn't I tell you we'd find an answer?' said Thomas with a smile. 'Mrs Sharp says Peter is welcome to stay here, provided he is biddable. She'll be glad of his company for her own child, and ten shillings a week for his keep is most satisfactory.'

'I hardly know how to thank you, madam,' said Agnes rising and beaming with relief.

'Never mind that, Mrs Meadowes. Sit down, please do. I'm only glad to be of assistance. Mr Williams has told me the circumstances. 'Tis a crying shame to hear of any respectable mother separated from her child as you are forced to be.'

'My position as cook in the Blanchard household necessitates us living apart, Mrs Sharp. And the lady who had care of Peter was kind enough. There was never a day's problem till now,' said Agnes.

'Even so,' said Mrs Sharp, folding her arms over her

capacious bosom, 'I cannot conceive how I should endure any position that necessitated my being separated from my Edward. Mr Williams says Peter was lodged in Twickenham before. That's some distance. At least here he will be closer. Tell me, why do you not leave service and start an ordinary chop house or something of the kind?'

Agnes had never contemplated what else she might do if she did not cook for the Blanchards. The anchor of household duties had always seemed immovable. 'Are we not all servants in one way or another, Mrs Sharp?' said Agnes. 'Do not all of us endure restrictions? I dare say on occasion Captain Sharp makes requirements of you that, given a choice, you might prefer to avoid.'

'I heartily wish Captain Sharp would make *more* requirements of me,' responded the landlady mischievously. 'But he is away at sea for months at a time and I am mostly left to my own devices. That is why poor Edward has yet to get himself a brother or a sister.'

At this, Thomas's mouth began to twitch in the suspicion of a smile, and Agnes turned scarlet and looked at her wine, wondering if this were quite the place for Peter, after all. She sensed that beneath Mrs Sharp's warmth lay a measure of disapproval, that she deemed Agnes somehow wanting as a mother for enduring such limitations. This was not a view Agnes had ever held of herself, and she found herself unsettled by it.

'Let's drink a toast to the resolution of your worries and your son's happy stay here,' said Thomas, breaking the silence and handing round the glasses. 'Here's to your very good health, Mrs Meadowes – and to Peter's.'

Agnes rarely touched wine or spirits; the taste reminded her of her red-faced husband's freedom with his fists. Today, however, such thoughts scarcely troubled her. With the shock of Rose's murder, Peter's arrival, yesterday's visit to Marcus Pitt and Mrs Sharp's implied criticism, there were too many recent events crowding in for the distant past to occupy her. Her nerves were strung tight. She took the wine, swirled it in her mouth and swallowed, looking at Thomas and Peter over the rim, enjoying the soothing sensation it brought.

Later, when the wine bottle was empty and Agnes's cheeks had coloured, Peter began to yawn and rub his eyes. He was to pass that night in a truckle bed in Thomas's room. The next day he would move in with Edward Sharp.

Thomas went ahead to light the fire and make up the bed. When Agnes arrived, a little unsteadily, with Peter a few minutes later at the top of the landing, Thomas opened the door to his room and ushered them in. Although the fire was lit, the room remained cold, with a masculine smoky smell that Agnes found not entirely unpleasant. From the street outside came once more the sound of rain. Agnes barely thought about where she was. The wine had made her rather dizzy and eased her embarrassment. But all the same, she averted her eyes from Thomas's bed.

Agnes undressed Peter, tucked him beneath the coverlet and kissed his forehead. She snuffed out the candle, so that the only light in the room was the warm orange glow given off by the flames in the hearth. 'Sleep well, Peter. Be good and do as Mrs Sharp bids you. I'll visit tomorrow evening, if I can.'

But no sooner did she get up to leave than Peter grew fretful. His eyes, which a minute earlier had been heavy with sleep, were now open wide, and he begged her to stay until he slept.

With her back to Thomas Williams, Agnes sat down again on the bed, stroking Peter's hand gently. As she watched him, her emotions loosened by the wine, Mrs Sharp's uncomfortable remarks came back to mind. Her comments are well founded, thought Agnes – my previous willing acceptance of the separation has been a sham. But a moment later, confronted by an insurmountable obstruction, she halted. What am I thinking? It is nonsense to question a state of affairs and unsettle myself when there is no choice in the matter. Then she looked down and saw that Peter's eyes had closed and he had fallen peacefully asleep.

Agnes had been conscious all this while of Thomas Williams standing by the fire, watching her. She felt little sense of trepidation, but rather took comfort from his stocky presence. When she stood up, the floor swayed unevenly. Thomas moved forward and took hold of her by the arm. She presumed this was to help her find her way in the darkness, but instead he opened his arms and drew her close, pressing his lips to hers. Agnes was not entirely taken by surprise. Part of her knew she should resist, but part of her welcomed the embrace, and thus she grew muddled and put up no immediate resistance. His earthy smell and the sensation of his lips was comforting; warmth emanated from his body. The longer she allowed his lips to press hers and his arms to enfold her, the greater grew her craving for physical contact. She had not experienced such sensations for many years. What was the purpose, Agnes thought suddenly, in pretending she had not missed them? It was as futile as her pretence that she did not mind her separation from Peter. And so, after the first moment of shock, Agnes abandoned all thoughts of pulling away and passing some outraged remark. Instead she found herself responding.

Chapter Twenty-seven

AGNES WAS MAKING LIVER PUDDING WHEN NANCY STEPPED OUT of the scullery bearing her housemaid's box. Agnes stopped rubbing the suet into her flour and assailed her with unusual forthrightness. 'Did you think I would not suspect you were lying?'

'Pardon me?' said Nancy, swivelling round.

Agnes glared at her. 'I said I believe you to be a liar,' she repeated.

'What do you mean, Mrs Meadowes?' Nancy looked at her in astonishment. 'It is most unjust of you to accuse me of any such thing.'

Nancy was wearing Rose's better working dress, a yellow and green striped cambric. She must have grown plumper, for despite her slender frame it fitted surprisingly well. Agnes glanced downwards – there was no perceptible swelling about Nancy's waist beneath the folds of her skirt, but she seemed broader in the hips. This evidence of Philip's assertion only strengthened Agnes's resolve, and she continued her attack with vigour. 'Some things you have told me concerning Rose may have been true, but others were wide of the mark – deliberately so – weren't they?' she insisted. 'You said them to cast a slur on Rose because you were jealous of her, and,

I presume, to deflect attention from your own predicament.'

Nancy banged down her box and slapped a defiant hand on her hip. 'What predicament?'

Agnes eyed Nancy's belly. 'I think you know what I mean.'

'You've got no proof. Nor any right to speak to me like that.'

'On the contrary, you have given me all the proof I need. Rose Francis was never in the slightest way tidy. You were forever saying how sluttish she was and complaining of the mayhem she created. But when we looked through her things they were all as neat as a sixpence. The only possible reason for that was that you'd been through them already. Perhaps that, rather than oversleeping, was why you were late down for your duties that morning. And as for my right to accuse you – Mrs Blanchard herself has asked me to look into what happened to Rose.'

'We all know what happened to her – the bitch got her neck slit.'

'But we do not know who slit it or why. Perhaps it was your hatred that drove her away, Nancy. Perhaps she could take no more of you meddling with her possessions, stealing her correspondence, quarrelling with her.'

Nancy looked perplexed. 'No, ma'am, you malign me, I done nothing like that. She irked me now and then, but I liked her well enough, I swear. I wouldn't do nothing to—'

'Don't feign ignorance, Nancy. Or would you prefer that I suggest that Mrs Tooley searches through your possessions? She already has her suspicions regarding you. Rose told her you were jealous, and that you took a letter and left it in the drawing room to cast her in a bad light. And John says a stolen letter was the cause of your fight. But I think you took something else of hers as well. Her purse, perhaps? No wonder she wanted to leave.'

''Course I never took the purse. Would I have mentioned it if I had?'

'Then was it another fabrication?'

Nancy scowled. 'No, it was not. There was money right enough.'

'Why then did you quarrel?'

'I told you before, it were nothing.'

Agnes would not be fobbed off. 'I don't believe Mrs Tooley has yet noticed your secret, although I hazard if she did she would not view it kindly.' She disliked threatening the girl, given her predicament, but Nancy was not the type of girl to succumb to an appeal to her finer feelings.

'No, ma'am, don't do that – you know what she's like,' said Nancy, round-eyed with fear.

'Then I repeat, what else did you take?'

'It were a letter, like you said.' Nancy gave a sullen shrug. 'It were nothing but a bit of fun. Patsy told me Rose had been laughing at me with Philip behind my back. And he and I was friendly, till she came.'

'But that incident took place a week ago. Why did Rose wait till Monday to confront you?' She paused as a flash of inspiration came to her. Rose would not have waited. 'That was the second letter you took, wasn't it? Not the one you left in the drawing room, but another. That was what the fuss was about. What was in the letter, Nancy? Where is it now?'

Nancy raised her chin defiantly. 'It ain't as if it was anything much. I only found it 'cos the room were in such a mess, with all her things falling out of the cupboard, and Mrs Tooley got mad at me on account of it. She set me to tidy it 'cos she were afraid of Rose's tongue. And I found it lying under her bed.'

'Do you have it still?'

'It's nothing what'll tell you who slit her throat.'

'Go and fetch it.'

Still scowling, Nancy shuffled off up the back stairs to the garret. Agnes returned to her pudding; by the time Nancy was back she had made her dough and lined her basin. Nancy rummaged in the folds of her skirt and withdrew a sheet of paper. 'Here you are.'

Agnes wiped her fingers on her apron and took it. The letter was dated the day before the robbery and Rose's disappearance.

Dearest Rose
I am much pleased to learn of your change of heart. I will wait for you at the Red Lion at five-thirty tomorrow morning. Our tickets are bought and our passage from Dover arranged. God willing we will be in Calais that night. I need not say how greatly I look forward to that moment.
Yours in affectionate expectation,

The letter was written in a clear strong hand. There was nothing save an illegible squiggle to indicate the name of its author, and no mention of his address. Agnes read this brief communication several times before folding it and placing it in her drawer. Then she stood immobile, lost in thought.

How deluded she had been in ignoring her first instinct that it was an affair of the heart that had caused Rose to run away! Rose had been going off to begin a new life when misadventure and tragedy had befallen her. But then Agnes began to ponder the letter more carefully. Why would Nancy have taken the trouble to steal a letter belonging to Rose? Once she had read it, she could have just returned it to avoid confrontation. She must have had another purpose.

'Did you wait up that night for Rose to leave and follow her?'

'No, course not. I was glad to see the back of her. Why would I go after her?'

'Did you see her go?'

'Yes, but there ain't no crime in that.'

Insight dawned as Agnes slowly began packing her basin with chopped liver. 'You believed this note was written by Philip, did you not?' she said.

''Course not,' said Nancy, blushing scarlet now. 'That thought never came into it.'

Agnes could see she was lying. Nancy was aggrieved that Rose had come between her and Philip, and was distressed to find herself with child. What effect, then, would a letter have had on her which she believed had been written by him arranging an elopement? Had she hoped to entice Philip into marrying her? This seemed unlikely, given Philip's lowly post, which he would lose if he wed. But perhaps in her distress she had believed she could persuade him to seek other employment where marriage was not prohibited. Agnes pressed down the meat and placed a circle of dough on top, pressing it firmly but lightly with her fingertips to seal it. 'If you believed this letter was from Philip, and that Rose was about to run off with him, you might have felt impelled to follow and stop her.'

'That's not only daft,' said Nancy defiantly, 'it's downright impossible.'

But Agnes pressed on, cutting a hole in the top of her pudding as she spoke to allow the steam to escape. 'Philip had gone out earlier that night to the Blue Cockerel, but you were not to know that. Perhaps he had not yet returned when Rose left. You might have followed her, assuming she was on her way to meet him. You might have killed her in order to prevent her taking Philip away from this household and you.'

Nancy shot her a sly look. 'I told you it couldn't be. I never thought he wrote that letter.'

In her agitation, Agnes's hands grew hot. She squeezed too hard on the dough, making it sticky. 'Oh, and why is that, pray?'

There was a long silence. Then, suddenly, Agnes looked up, startled. Nancy was beginning to giggle.

'Stop that and answer me,' said Agnes crossly. 'How did you know this wasn't Philip's hand?'

''Cos Philip don't have no hand save a cross. He don't know how to write, do he?'

With great concentration, Agnes scraped the dough off her fingers, while Nancy went off, humming in what still seemed a scornful manner. Agnes, infuriated and shamed in equal measure, summoned Doris to help her. But even the need to instruct Doris and keep a watchful eye on what she was doing could not prevent her discomfiture. And when she put the pudding in the steamer and scalded her arm, her temper only worsened. It wasn't only Nancy's cutting tone that disturbed her, or the letter that she had just stowed in her drawer alongside her book of recipes and the box Elsie had given her. She was troubled by misgivings that were far less easy to fathom, and, unlike a letter or a silver box in a drawer, impossible to shut away.

She would never have accused Nancy if it had not been for what had taken place last night in Thomas Williams's bedroom. It was his stirring up of sentiments long forgotten which had spurred her to speak out so impulsively. How ridiculous she had been.

When her marriage had ended so disastrously, Agnes had told herself that she had no desire to suffer in the same way again. Since becoming the Blanchards' cook, she had kept strictly to her resolve. Restraint had become second nature to her, and had kept her safe. Last night, however, she had weakened. Agnes thought of the scent of Thomas Williams's room, the wiry feel of his hair, his warmth, the carvings on his headboard, her hair and laces undone. Doubt overwhelmed her. Nothing now appeared as clear or easy as it had been. She was not certain yet which path she should take.

Agnes regarded the pudding steaming on the fire. She had forgotten to add sage and mace, as she usually did. The pudding would not be as carefully seasoned as it ought, but somehow this did not seem to matter.

'Letter's come from Mr Pitt this morning, Mrs M. You heard what it says yet?' said Philip, marching into the kitchen from the yard, dressed in his leather apron. 'Don't suppose you know where my gloves have got to? Mr Matthews is after me for losing 'em.' He reached forward and helped himself to a sliver of pheasant from Agnes's bowl.

Agnes moved the bowl away from him. She was still feeling tetchy after her shaming encounter with Nancy, and Philip, she told herself, was partly to blame. 'Get away. How do you know the letter was from Mr Pitt?'

'It came while I was clearing the dining-room fireplace. Heard your name and Marcus Pitt's mentioned, but Mr

Matthews took it. Suppose that means you and I'll be going back to see him soon.'

'Perhaps,' said Agnes, feeling a prickle of apprehension as the thought of seeing Pitt again distracted her from her worries about Thomas. 'If so, I dare say we shall discover it soon.'

'Go on, Mrs Meadowes. Can't I 'ave summat to eat? I'm half starved. What about that drumstick – there's only pickings on it.'

Agnes opened her drawer and took out the letter she had extricated from Nancy. 'In a minute. Look at this first. Tell me, did you write it?'

Philip regarded the letter, then glanced at Doris and grew awkward. 'Not that thing again.'

'Did you write it?' said Agnes, ignoring his embarrassment.

'No. But Nancy showed it me.'

'When was this?'

'A few days since, as I recall.'

'Monday – the day before the robbery?'

'Reckon so.'

'What does it say?'

A sudden flush spread across Philip's countenance. He shrugged nonchalantly. 'Never learned my letters, did I?'

Agnes nodded. That much of Nancy's story had at least been true. 'Surely you must have asked her what it said?'

Philip seemed to forget his consternation. He smiled and ruffled his dark hair, as if trying to beguile her with his charms.

Agnes was unmelting. 'Well?'

''Course I did. There's no pulling wool over your eyes, is there? Nancy said Rose was planning to go off.'

During their previous conversations, thought Agnes, Philip had never mentioned that he knew Rose intended to leave. Why not? 'So did you follow Rose when she left for her rendezvous?'

He shook his head vehemently. 'No. 'Course not. I told you where I was that night – at the Blue Cockerel in Lombard Street. There's plenty there to feast the eye and more besides . . . You may ask the landlord, if you wish.'

'Then why did Nancy show you the letter? And why did you say nothing before?'

He seemed to ponder this for a minute, tensing his mouth thoughtfully. 'Perhaps she wants to incriminate me as the father of her child. To do so she reckons she has to turn me against Rose. But why would I fall for it? I told you before, things between Rose and me cooled some weeks ago. I didn't say nothing before, because even if our affair was over I was still fond of her. I wouldn't have wanted her to get into trouble with the Blanchards.'

Agnes pursed her lips. Perhaps he was right. Nancy had taken the letter because she wanted to turn him against Rose and rekindle their intimacy. But if Rose was going anyway, why did Nancy need to show him the letter?

Without waiting for further invitation, Philip fell upon the drumstick with a victorious smile and began to gnaw hungrily on it. 'By the way, how's Mr Williams keeping? Coming to visit again today, is he?'

Agnes felt her hand grow unsteady. She noticed Doris's eyes pop open. 'None of your business, Philip. Any more cheek like that and I'll feed you crusts for a week.'

'Beg pardon. Didn't mean to give no offence.'

'P'raps that's why Mr Matthews kept your letter – he wants to tear a strip off you, ma'am,' piped in Doris.

'Why on earth should he want to do that?' said Agnes.

''Cos of what Mrs Tooley told him. You being with Mr Williams and your boy in the kitchen.'

Agnes coloured, and told Doris to stop being foolish and fetch the oysters from the larder. If Doris knew, and Mrs Tooley had told Mr Matthews, then the entire household must be aware of Thomas Williams's presence in her life. Grim-faced, she scattered bay leaves and juniper berries on the top of the shin of beef she was about to stew. She moistened it with pig's trotter jelly, then covered it with a lid and carried it to the fire. She could not contradict the veracity of what Philip and Doris had said. It was the thought of them gossiping about her that irked her. What did they know of her predicament? Or her desire? Was this what

Rose had felt, she wondered – misunderstood in her desire? Besides, what more could she expect? All households thrived upon gossip; it was human nature. She wiped her hands briskly on her apron and went in search of Mr Matthews and Marcus Pitt's letter.

Chapter Twenty-eight

THERE WAS NO SIGN OF MR MATTHEWS IN THE BUTLER'S PANTRY, nor was he to be found in his office. As Agnes returned to the servants' corridor, her eye came to rest on the small panelled door which concealed a narrow staircase descending to the cellar. The door was usually kept locked, to keep the cellar safe from pilfering servants, but now Agnes noticed that it stood an inch or two ajar. She pushed the door open further, so that the first coil of the dingy stairwell was revealed. For a moment she stood on the threshold, peering down and listening. It was dark as soot; a sudden draught of cold damp air struck her. Was that a muffled voice drifting up from below? She called out, 'Mr Matthews, is that you?' and when she heard nothing, called again, this time more loudly, 'Mr Matthews, are you there?' Still there was no reply. Certain nonetheless that she had heard something, Agnes decided to go in search of the butler.

There were no windows in the cellar, Agnes knew; whenever she had ventured down here before on Mr Matthews's instruction it had always been with a candle. But eager as she was to find him, the thought of further delay seemed unbearable. She propped open the door, placing her folded handkerchief as a wedge in the angle near the hinge, and began to descend.

The air became cooler and danker the further she descended. An unwholesome smell of mould and dust caught the back of her nose and made her want to sneeze. She was three-quarters of the way down when the handkerchief slipped and the door creaked closed. Enveloped in chilly darkness, she groped her way forwards, using her hand on the wall for guidance, her nails catching on the peeling distemper. When she arrived at the bottom of the stairs she halted for a moment, peering into the musty gloom to survey her surroundings.

A dim light emanated from a wall sconce in front of her, which had been lit to one side of a half-opened door. The door led to a long narrow chamber, much of which was obliterated by shadows, but halfway along, on the upturned end of a large barrel, a tallow candle flickered. By its smoky halo of light Agnes could see a curved ceiling vault, a long wall lined with racks of wine, and, facing it, another crammed with wooden kegs of varying size.

She squinted beyond the glow for a sign of Mr Matthews, but saw none. From overhead she heard the distant sound of the servants' clock striking, Doris clattering her pots in the scullery, the sharp rap of someone knocking at the door, the faint cry of a knife-grinder in the street outside. But in the cellar itself there was no sound at all, except her own breathing and the soft rustle of her skirts.

It was only after several minutes, once her eyes had grown accustomed to the gloom, that she noticed a niche set into the wall at about waist height, a yard from where she stood. On inspecting the recess more closely, she saw that there was something dark and indistinct, about the size of her fist, ranged upon it. Agnes reached forward quietly and picked up the object. It was wrapped in a cloth and was surprisingly heavy for its size. Leaning to one side so that the light from the wall sconce might reach her, she began to unwrap it. Something had caused the cloth to adhere to whatever lay within. She yanked the cloth away, holding it in her fist while she examined the contents.

It was a pistol. Small enough to fit in a pocket, the hilt

inlaid with silver decoration, filthy with mud and grit. It was the mud that had caused the gun to adhere to the cloth. Was this the pistol missing from Nicholas Blanchard's room? The thought had no sooner struck her than she heard the chinking sound of glasses or crockery from somewhere nearby. Then came the voices again – this time there was no mistaking them: Mr Matthews was in conversation with John, although their voices were too low to be audible. Before she had time to call out, their footsteps advanced; another door creaked open and the pair emerged from the darkness.

They were plainly visible, thanks to the lantern the butler held in one hand. In his other he clutched a pair of glasses and a bottle – the source of the chinking Agnes had heard. John carried a wooden crate in his arms. The pair advanced slowly and unsteadily towards her.

Agnes knew that she should announce her presence. But she held back, wondering how they might receive her, standing here, holding a pistol that everyone believed to have been lost. If Rose had taken the gun to protect herself, whoever had left the weapon here was most likely the person Elsie had seen chasing her on the mud. The murderer.

Mr Matthews had arrived at the keg upon which the lighted candle burned. He was no more than a few yards away from where Agnes stood watching. Sooner or later, she would have to confront him. Anxious not to be caught with the gun in her possession, she hastily wrapped it in the cloth and silently returned it to the ledge where she had found it.

But instead of advancing further in her direction, as she expected, Mr Matthews halted abruptly. Putting down the bottle, the glasses and his lantern on the upturned keg, he turned to John and placed an arm around the footman's shoulder.

'Dear boy,' he said, speaking more slowly than usual and slurring his words slightly, 'leave those bottles now. As soon as you've finished your other duties come back and take a couple of 'em off to Berry's chop house. I'll leave the door unlocked for you. Tell him I said it's to be kept aside for us – ready for our celebration next week.'

John deposited his crate next to the keg and stood up slowly. 'As you wish, sir. But are you not fearful the loss might be remarked?'

Matthews shook his head vehemently, 'Never mind that. Who's there to notice? After all my years of service I'm entitled to a little reward. And if I choose to share it with you, that's my affair.' Matthews advanced unsteadily, until his face was no more than an inch from John's. 'You richly deserve it.'

John was several inches taller than the elderly butler. He stood immobile, surveying him, then he smiled uneasily, licking his lips, and shook his head. The gesture made Agnes shudder, though she could not have said why. She could see the moisture glisten on his lower lip, and a nervous twitch play about the corners of his mouth. 'Thank you, sir,' John said softly. 'I am most grateful.'

With his eyes still locked on Mr Matthews's face, John raised the butler's hand in his own and pressed the palm against his cheek before planting a kiss upon it. 'Where'd I be without your kindness?' he whispered. 'Still scrubbing pots in some hell-hole kitchen.'

The gesture so astonished Agnes that for a moment she half wondered whether it was a trick of the shadows. She had not even been conscious of a special rapport between the two, let alone suspected anything like this. Clearly this was more than the respect of a servant for his superior; more than masculine friendship. She had witnessed something intimate, untoward, something both Mr Matthews and John would desire to keep hidden. She had heard of such alliances, but never had she encountered them first-hand: men in love with each other – Mollies, they called them; even thinking the word distressed her and made her tremulous. She was uncannily reminded of the unsettling kiss that Pitt had placed upon her hand, and involuntarily brushed her palm against her skirt.

She backed slowly towards the staircase, remounting the steps as stealthily as she was able. But shock combined with haste made her clumsy. She had climbed no more than four or five steps when the heel of her shoe caught in her petticoat and she stumbled helplessly forward. Instinctively she put out her hand to break her fall; her hand grazed the wall and saved her, but not before her ankle twisted in the dark and crumpled painfully beneath her. She let out an involuntary cry.

'Who's there?' called Mr Matthews, instantly drawing back from John, grabbing his lantern and turning towards the steps. 'Who is it?' He walked briskly towards her. 'Answer me, damn you! What do you want?'

Ignoring the agony in her ankle, Agnes hobbled further up the steps, and then, when she had almost reached the top, turned and made as if she was descending. 'Mr Matthews?' she called out. 'Where are you, sir? Is that you? I hear there's been a message from Mr Pitt.'

Mr Matthews halted at the foot of the stairs and gazed up at her. 'Mrs Meadowes! What on earth are *you* doing here?'

'I beg your pardon, sir. I didn't mean to trespass. It was only that I've just now seen Philip, and he says there's been a message from Mr Pitt,' she said calmly, hoping she did not sound as though she had something to hide.

'What if there has?'

'Nothing, sir. I only mean, that's the reason I came looking for you. I went to your pantry and office and then, seeing as the cellar door was open, I thought I'd see if I might find you down here. I only wondered if you knew anything about the message, and whether Mr Blanchard will need me to visit Mr Pitt again.'

Mr Matthews began slowly to mount the staircase towards Agnes. The breach in his defences was apparently of greater concern to him than the subject of Pitt. 'The door was open? How curious when I distinctly recall that I closed it.'

'Perhaps the wind blew it,' said Agnes hurriedly. 'At any rate, if it's inconvenient just now I won't trouble you any longer. I haven't much time myself – I would not wish my pie to burn.'

'Not so fast,' said Mr Matthews, reaching forward and clutching her wrist. His iron grip hurt her grazed hand, and Agnes winced. 'What's this? You are very tender. Hurt, are you?' He released his hold somewhat and drew her palm close to the lantern. 'You have a nasty scratch. How did you come by it?'

'It's nothing, sir,' said Agnes. She took a step back and slid her hand from Mr Matthews's clammy grasp.

The butler stepped up next to her and placed an arm behind her so she could withdraw no further. He drew his face close – so close Agnes could smell brandy on his breath, and his pale eyes seemed full of menace; where before he had always seemed stern yet cordial, now suddenly he reminded Agnes of a snake. She looked desperately down at John for help, but his face seemed empty, neutral – it was impossible to tell what he might be thinking. 'It might be nothing, Mrs Meadowes, but I wish to know,' Mr Matthews whispered urgently.

Agnes summoned her resources. She spoke firmly but softly, in a voice she had mastered long ago to mask her inner fright, but had not used for many years. 'I stumbled just now, sir, when I began to descend without a light. And then you came out with your lantern.'

'You weren't spying on John and me, I don't suppose?' he pressed, still speaking in his strange, urgent tone.

'Spying on you? Whatever for, Mr Matthews? I assure you I have no desire to cause trouble. I only wanted to speak to you. If you don't believe me, ask Doris or Philip. They will tell you I was in the kitchen with them not two minutes ago.'

Mr Matthews peered at her edgily a little longer, but finally seemed to take her at her word and withdrew a little. 'Very well,' he said, 'in that case I shall give you the benefit of the doubt and let it pass. But you are not to come back down here without my permission. No matter how urgent the matter seems to you, it's more than likely it'll be a trifle to me. Do I make myself clear?'

'As daylight, Mr Matthews,' said Agnes. Then, emboldened by her narrow escape, she coughed. 'And if I may be so bold, the letter from Pitt, sir?'

'Ah yes, it was nothing urgent or I should have said. Mr Theodore has it. He wants you to go to him directly after dinner on account of it. He did not tell me why. Becoming quite the favourite, aren't you?'

'I think not, sir.'

'Now, just so there are no more accidents, let me light your way.' He edged past Agnes and, reaching the top, pushed open the door. 'This way, Mrs Meadowes, careful now. Dear me, this door seems tighter than usual. Is something caught?' Before Agnes could intercept him, he had bent down and pulled out the handkerchief she had folded and wedged there. 'What's this?' he said, shaking it out. He looked at the handkerchief, then glared at her. 'Has it anything to do with you, Mrs Meadowes? Can you hazard how it came to be so strangely positioned?'

Agnes looked at the white square, the inadequate wedge she had made, now wafting between his finger and thumb. Thankfully she had never been much of a needlewoman, and had never troubled herself to embroider her initial on any of her belongings. 'I suppose Mrs Tooley or one of the other servants must have dropped it, sir. But unless there's a name or initial sewn on it, there's no way of telling. It might belong to almost anyone.'

Chapter Twenty-nine

AT SIX THAT SAME EVENING, AGNES WENT UPSTAIRS TO DISCOVER what the message from Pitt might contain. Snow had begun to fall, small flakes that settled over the rutted street and obliterated all trace of the city's dirt and danger. Inside, Theodore had retired to the library to enjoy a private decanter of port. When Agnes entered the room she found it in semi-darkness, the book-lined walls and velvet curtains lost in shadow. A fire burned fiercely in the grate, framed by a pair of squat brass andirons with lion's paw feet. Light from a silver candelabrum illuminated a drum-shaped table in the centre of the room, on which an opened folio of engravings and other papers was scattered untidily. The engravings were designs for antique urns and sarcophagi, which Theodore was scrutinizing through an ornate silver-handled magnifying glass, making notes on a sheet of paper beside him. At the sound of Agnes's tread he looked up, studying her for a minute with eyes that seemed unfocused and dull. He scratched his wig, raised his glass unsteadily and sipped his port as though his attention was on other matters.

'I've come, sir, because Mr Matthews said a letter was delivered, and you wished to see me on account of it,' Agnes ventured.

'A letter,' echoed Theodore. He set down the glass, belched gently and began rummaging through the papers on the table. 'Yes, yes, indeed. Mr Pitt's communication, delivered by one of his assistants earlier on.'

'It was good news, I hope?'

He nodded morosely. 'Promising enough – and all I had hoped for, given the circumstances. Mr Pitt claims he has located the villains that stole the wine-cooler. It is still intact, and will be returned forthwith, provided we pay the sum required.'

'Is the sum reasonable?'

Theodore's lips puckered as though there were a bitter taste in his mouth. He lowered his eyes to the engraving in front of him and, with his forefinger, slowly traced the curvaceous outline of a funerary urn, whose handles were shaped like elephant ears. 'Two hundred guineas,' he declared miserably.

Agnes could not prevent a gasp escaping her lips. 'A sizeable sum, sir. Will you pay it?'

Theodore's eyes shone as though tears welled in them. He turned to another engraving, of a candelabrum in the form of a Corinthian column. 'If I do not pay, the wine-cooler will be melted down, and then the work would all be lost and the metal untraceable,' he said. 'Pitt isn't prone to making idle threats, he knows precisely what he's doing. I think I told you before, our business is not as strong as it once was. A loss like this might land me in the debtors' prison.'

Theodore's tone made it plain that he had descended into a mire of self-pity, induced by the port he had drunk. His situation aroused a measure of commiseration in Agnes. Had she not recently lapsed after the effects of a glass too many? But the sight of the engraving of the candelabra turned her thoughts to the salver that Williams had examined. If Theodore was operating a duty-dodging scheme, the loss would not be as great as he claimed. The sum he would have charged Grey for making the wine-cooler would have included duty – an extra thirty pounds. Assuming the wine-cooler had never been taken to the Goldsmith's Hall, that sum would go straight into Theodore's pocket.

Agnes thought of Rose's unexplained forays upstairs and to the workshop, and her association with Riley. Much pointed to her involvement in the scheme. Perhaps Theodore had used Rose as a go-between, and she had grown greedy and, knowing she was about to leave to join her lover, wanted more than Theodore was willing to pay for her assistance. In which case, had that greed led to her death? But given that the robbery was most likely orchestrated by the same person who had killed Noah and Rose, this theory fell apart. It was ludicrous to suppose that Theodore would engineer the robbery of his own premises, murder his own apprentice and pay for his own property to be recovered.

Having dismissed Theodore as a possible suspect, Agnes was on the verge of mentioning to him her discovery of the gun. But he had told her unequivocally that his only concern was the wine-cooler. She hesitated. There was nothing to be gained by bringing up a subject certain to rile him.

A sense of gloom overcame Agnes. She should say something, but she feared Theodore's response. The room began to feel stifling, the rich smell of port all-pervasive. She had always detested trips upstairs, and now more than ever wished she could return to the sanctuary of her kitchen. But Theodore was not ready to dismiss her yet. And nor, she reminded herself, was her world as safe as it seemed.

Eventually Theodore found the letter among his papers and put on a great show of perusing it. 'Ah yes, here we are, Mrs Meadowes. What Pitt says is this. If I am in agreement with his terms, you are to send word to him this evening. The messenger who delivered this will be waiting outside to take the reply. Tomorrow morning, first thing, you are to deliver the payment to him and he will then set in motion the return of the wine-cooler. Since it is a sizeable sum, and he has no wish for you to be robbed, he will send his own driver and carriage to fetch you. You may bring a single escort of your own to assist you in recovering the wine-cooler.'

Agnes ignored a sudden burning in her chest. 'Has Justice Cordingly been apprised?'

'Not until the transaction is complete. He might insist upon intervening, and if Pitt got word that the law was involved there would be no chance of a satisfactory conclusion to this business.'

'With respect, sir, two murders have taken place that are almost certainly connected with the wine-cooler. Surely that merits his intervention? Should not Pitt at least be apprehended and questioned on the matter?'

'You know very well that Justice Cordingly has both matters in hand. And why ever would I insist upon Pitt's arrest when there is no evidence to connect him to either crime and he is poised to engineer the return of my wine-cooler? I should be a dolt to do so, Mrs Meadowes.'

Agnes remembered Pitt's kiss, the touch of his lips upon her fingers, the insinuating look in his eye. How could she forget? This, coupled with her increasing disturbance over the murderer's identity, redoubled her agitation, and her thoughts grew confused. She did not want to believe the murderer could be someone with whom she lived and worked. She did not want Theodore or John or Philip or Nancy or Mr Matthews to be guilty. Could Pitt be the murderer? Had he accompanied Drake on his nocturnal adventure, killed Noah Prout, and then murdered Rose for no other reason than that she happened to pass him on her way to her rendezvous? Improbable though this hypothesis was, Agnes wanted to believe it in order to dispel the other more disturbing possibilities. But one obstacle she could not reason away: if Pitt were the murderer, how did the gun arrive in the cellar?

She had only to mention Elsie's name and the link between Pitt and the robbery would be established. But she had given her word, and the repercussions would be terrible for Elsie if she broke it. Instead, she attempted further deferential argument. 'With respect, sir, does not Pitt's proposal strike you as suspicious? He has countless henchmen at his disposal. If he knows I have two hundred guineas on me, even if I have a man as protection, what is to stop him organizing another assault?'

Theodore refilled his glass and sipped it slowly. He fixed her with his bloodshot eyes and shook his head. 'I need hardly say that I too have my concerns. Yet I know enough of Pitt's modus operandi to comprehend that that is not the way he does business. After all, he has a reputation to nurture just as we all do. Besides, I didn't say so before, but his letter shows he is quite taken with you.'

Agnes grew hotter than ever; a pulse began to pound in her neck. 'Then you will let Philip go with me, just as a precaution, won't you, sir?'

Theodore frowned. 'Not Philip. This time I think it better you take one of the journeymen – Williams, I think – he is sharp witted and more diligent than Riley, and knows the wine-cooler well. I would not want Pitt trying to fob you off with a replica.'

Agnes desisted from asking why, if this variety of swindle were possible, being held up with two hundred guineas in her possession was not. Besides, the news that Thomas Williams was to be her escort sweetened the pill. Her spirits bolstered, she bowed to the inevitable.

Theodore waved at a chair on the opposite side of the table. 'Sit down there and read his letter. Then take this quill and paper and write to him. Say that you have discussed the matter with me and I have agreed. He may send his carriage at nine tomorrow. You will see he invites you to step out with him. I commend you on the way you've charmed him. It can only work to our advantage if you give him some hope that he might be accepted. But rather than accepting outright you should remain a little vague – it will help sustain his eagerness.'

Agnes perused the letter. The first paragraph concerned the details as Theodore had described them. The last part caused her cheeks to burn.

> *The nature of my profession ensures I encounter a great many people from all walks of life. At our first meeting you impressed me greatly, not only by your radiance and composure but also by your wit. When I asked you before to do me the honour of accompanying me to the theatre, you declared 'present*

commitments precluded it'. May I query your exact meaning. Does that mean no invitation of mine will ever be favourably received, or was my overture inconvenient in that instance only?

Agnes could barely contain her alarm. She ought to make a fuss and demand that someone else went in her stead. She had a sense of foreboding as real and dark as the liquor in Theodore's glass. Nevertheless, duty overcame her better judgement, and instead of speaking out she deferred and did precisely as he ordered. She wrote concisely in her usual elegant hand, accepting the terms Pitt had stated and concluding with the following:

I am honoured you have taken the trouble to offer a further invitation to me. I cannot promise acceptance. Let us conclude the present business before pursuing our private pleasures.

When she had finished, she sanded the page and read it through. The last words seemed to her larger and less flowing than the rest, as though someone else had inserted them. She handed the sheet to Theodore, who smiled grimly as he read what she had written. 'Very good, Mrs Meadowes. Admirable indeed. The final sentence will have him tossing all night, I wager.' He glanced up and caught her blush. 'Don't look coy when I compliment your skill.' He folded the page into three, tucked the ends over and sealed it with scarlet wax. As Theodore dripped the molten red liquid on the paper, his wavering hand caused several splashes to fall onto the paper. Agnes was uncomfortably reminded of blood. Theodore handed back the letter. 'Take it out into the street. There will be someone waiting for it.'

Agnes rose, curtseyed and retreated. John was waiting in the hall directly outside. From the strange look he gave her, Agnes wondered if he had heard their exchange and knew of her perilous mission next day, or if he was still thinking of their encounter in the cellar. There were so many questions she wanted to ask him. How did the gun arrive there? Did you or Mr Matthews put it there? Did you see Rose leave early that morning and follow her? Did either of you have a hand in her death? But Agnes realized that if either were guilty, to press him in such a way would do nothing but place her own life in jeopardy, and then Rose's killer would never be found. So she swallowed and drew a breath and looked coolly at him. 'Mr Blanchard says there is a messenger waiting outside for this letter.'

John nodded with a faint smile. 'Follow me.' He marched stiffly to the front entrance and pulled open the hall door.

A blast of whirling snow and wind rushed in, and with it a small body that had been hunched up against the door. John took a step back; Agnes, standing behind him, mirrored his action to avoid collision. Peering over John's shoulder, she examined a hunched body swathed in rags, half blanketed in snow, the face scarcely visible. The opening door had jolted the body into life and it sat up with a start, shaking its head and depositing white lumps on the doormat. Agnes recognized the pinched triangular face, the red shawl wrapped around it, the over-large boots.

Elsie had apparently been waiting since midday, when she had delivered Pitt's letter. Having passed an hour or two pacing about to keep warm, she had grown tired and taken refuge on the doorstep. From time to time John or Philip or Mr Matthews had caught sight of her through the hall window and shooed her away. Only when they were engaged with other duties had she at last been left in peace. John was infuriated to see her here now.

'Move off! How many times did I tell you already not to park yourself here?' he said, giving her scrawny haunches a prod with the pointed toe of his shoe. 'What d'you think the master would have to say if he saw you here?' He spoke sternly but not unkindly.

Elsie's face was white with cold, the tips of her fingers and her nose were red, her lips were grey. The crimson shawl wrapped about her head was coated with snow, like flour on raw meat. John's poke made her scramble hastily to her feet as if she expected another harder blow to follow. She shot him an indignant look. 'I told you before,

I ain't what you think. I've orders from Mr Pitt to await a reply.'

John clearly gave this remark little credence. He jerked his chin towards the street to indicate she would be wise to clear off now. But Elsie did no such thing; she caught sight of Agnes standing behind John, staring worriedly in her direction. Elsie returned her gaze with an equal measure of anxiety. Agnes comprehended the underlying reason – her father. 'Tell him, Missus,' Elsie said with a show of bravado. 'It's the least you could do after the age you've kept me waiting.'

'I didn't know you were here, Elsie,' said Agnes, manoeuvring her way past John.

'Never mind that. 'Ave you penned the answer yet?'

Agnes held out the paper. 'I have it here for you.'

No sooner had Agnes uttered these words than Elsie reached forward, plucked the letter from her grasp and stuffed it in her pocket. She started off down the steps. Agnes recalled the orange and the purse, stolen with similar swiftness, and the silver box which she had managed to keep hold of. But the sight of the pathetic retreating figure aroused no anger; an image of Peter as he had appeared in her kitchen last night, bedraggled from the rain, came into her mind. Thomas Williams had helped her then. She couldn't scold the girl for snatching the letter; nor, in all conscience, could she watch her trudge off through the streets in such a miserable condition.

'Wait a moment, Elsie. Have you eaten today?'

'How could I, waiting so long for you?' said Elsie, shooting an accusing look in Agnes's direction as if to say, 'You told them, didn't you?'

'Then won't you let me make amends by giving you something warm to eat before you set off back to Mr Pitt's?'

Elsie wavered on the pavement, her hands tucked beneath her armpits, stamping her boots and looking anxiously in the direction of Cheapside and the river. 'It'd be more'n my life's worth. Pa'll be wanting his supper and Mr Grant said I wasn't to do nothing but go straight here and come straight back with an answer.'

'Mr Grant?'

'The man what tells us Mr Pitt's orders and keeps an eye on us.' She wiped a drip from her nose with the back of her hand, then added in a whisper, 'You didn't say nothing about me or no one else, did you?'

Agnes was conscious of John hovering inquisitively in the background. And behind him she now sensed the shadowy presence of Mr Matthews. How much did they know of these matters? She would be wise not to reveal her familiarity with Elsie's background, or keep her longer in their presence than necessary. John was quick witted. Suppose he remembered Elsie from the morning before the robbery and saw that she was a link between Pitt and the theft. Ignoring her question, Agnes said, 'You'll be dead from cold before you reach the bridge if you don't get something warm inside you first. Come down to the kitchen. I'll give you something to eat on the way.'

Elsie shrugged her bony shoulders. 'I don't mind, then,' said she ungraciously, mounting the steps and placing an ill-fitting boot upon the hall mat.

'Don't think of coming this way,' said John, striding forward and blocking her path. Then he turned to Agnes. 'Pardon me, Mrs Meadowes, I cannot but wonder at you inviting creatures such as this in here, and with so many valuables about.' He spoke softly, as if he did not wish to cause offence but was bewildered all the same.

'Quite right, John,' concurred Mr Matthews loudly from the shadowy depths of the hall.

Elsie flinched as though John had hit her. There was a gleam of fear in her eyes as she stumbled back down the steps. 'I didn't ask – you heard her offer,' she protested.

'Wait, just a moment!' cried Agnes, skidding down the steps and grabbing Elsie's arm.

'Let me alone! What are you doing?' said Elsie crossly, wrenching her elbow free. 'Leave me be and save yourself some bother.'

'No,' Agnes said. She leaned down and whispered in Elsie's wind-reddened ear. 'Go down those steps by the railings, they'll bring you to the kitchen door. Wait there a minute and I'll bring you something to eat.'

Elsie regarded Agnes with doubtful eyes. Agnes patted her on the back to affirm the offer and retreated indoors.

'The recklessness of some people never ceases to amaze me,' said John as he closed the door, fastened the bolt, and watched Agnes stamp her snow-clogged shoes on the doormat. 'You're asking to be done over a second time with that one, Mrs M., you mark my words.'

'Quite probably, John,' said Agnes darkly. There was every possibility he was right. Yet somehow, faced with Elsie's misery, his scorn seemed unimportant.

Agnes descended to her kitchen and surveyed her supplies. Reasoning that one less pasty would not be missed from the servants' supper – and that if anyone went short she would ensure it was John or Mr Matthews – Agnes grabbed one from the warming tray and took it to the door that led out to the street. She threw open the door, expecting to see Elsie waiting, but discovered no sign or sound of her.

For a minute she stood there, with the door open and the cold wind howling in, listening for the sound of a clumping boot or a glimpse of Elsie's red shawl. But there was nothing. She gingerly mounted the icy steps leading to the street. After the heat of the kitchen, the cold seemed more piercing than ever. Snow was falling heavily, large white flakes the size of thumbnails, carpeting the stairs and sticking to the top of the railing so she was reluctant to grip it. At the top were some narrow footprints, descending three steps and no further, as though Elsie had started to step down and had then changed her mind. Where the stairs reached the street, the footprints were indiscernible among other trampled imprints. Had John emerged and frightened the girl away as soon as Agnes had gone? She squinted up and down the street. A man hovered in a nearby doorway, sheltering from the blizzard or waiting to be admitted. In the snowy distance she could vaguely make out a couple of muffled figures walking briskly away, but had no way of knowing whether one of them was Elsie.

Agnes took a frustrated bite from the hot pasty, feeling the meat and potatoes warm her as she had wished them to warm Elsie, then turned and descended the stairs. The girl was nothing to her, she reminded herself.

Chapter Thirty

AGNES HAD NO INCLINATION TO STAY IN THAT EVENING. SHE had promised Peter she would call to see how he was settling in at Mrs Sharp's. Nothing on earth would make her disappoint him – but neither had she any desire to beg Mrs Tooley's permission and have her request refused. She claimed a headache and told Doris to see to the servants' supper. She was going to her room to lie down until it was time to put out the upstairs meal.

She was reluctant to confess it even to herself, but there was more than Peter to draw her out on that snowy night. She had seen and heard nothing from Thomas Williams all day. Several times she had found herself looking up at the windows that gave onto the street. She could only make out the lower portion of passers-by, the tail coats and calves of gentlemen, the hems of ladies' cloaks. Whenever she glimpsed a pair of well-muscled legs marching past, she blushed and wondered if they belonged to Thomas, and whether he might be on his way to call on her, or if he might contrive to send a message on some pretext or other. But if any of the stockinged calves or flapping coat-tails were his, Agnes never knew it. Thomas Williams did not call, nor did he make any attempt at communication.

That morning she had not blamed him for taking what she had freely offered him, nor had she regretted her actions. But now that hours had passed and no word had come, her sentiments shifted and shadows of her old self returned. She went over the events of last night repeatedly, trying to view them objectively. His failure to communicate led her to only one conclusion. Thomas Williams must think she was in the habit of comporting herself thus. He deemed her favours of so little worth they did not require acknowledgement.

She wondered how to correct his mistake. After much rumination, one solution presented itself. Henceforth, whenever she met him, she would be a model of decorum. Last night's aberration would never be repeated. He would not inveigle his way into further intimacy. The bolts would be redrawn.

Despite Sarah Sharp's house being only two streets from Foster Lane, Agnes, being prudent in matters of dress, as in every other portion of her life, retired to her room to put pattens on her feet and a woollen shawl over her head. She fastened her cloak tightly and picked up a muff, in which she inserted a small paper parcel that she had wrapped up earlier. As protection against footpads that might trouble her, she concealed a small kitchen knife in the pocket of her cloak. Then she slipped out.

The snow had ceased falling but lay several inches deep; moonlight mottled its surface with silver, filling the rutted streets with ghostly streams of light, broken only by occasional mounds of horse dung and detritus in the gutter. Against an inky sky, familiar landmarks were transformed to something new. The dome of St Paul's had become a luminous orb, pediments resembled white brows, signboards were wiped clean. Agnes turned left at the bottom of Foster Lane into Cheapside, then, passing Gutter Lane and Wood Street on her left, turned right into Bread Street. She walked with her head down, crunching over snow as crystalline as salt, shoulders hunched against the chill, wondering if the river would freeze, and if so whether Sarah Sharp would take Peter and Edward to see the boats and barges all frozen up at their moorings.

'Mrs Meadowes! What a night to come out on,' said Sarah Sharp, throwing open her door when, two minutes later, a pink-cheeked Agnes knocked upon it.

'Mrs Sharp,' returned Agnes, her eyes flitting over her shoulder to see if she might catch a glimpse of Peter, or anyone else. 'My apologies for coming so late. Duties delayed me.'

'Don't trouble yourself over that. You took me by surprise, that's all. Come in out of the cold.'

The smell of chicken broth and bread filled the narrow hallway, soothing Agnes with its homeliness. The thought flashed through her mind that if her feckless husband had not perished, she might be living in such a house as this. Agnes found herself feeling less stoical than usual. She was disturbed by a certain disgruntlement at the hand fate had dealt her and the choices she had made. Is it possible, she wondered, I have taken the wrong path?

Pushing this worrisome thought away, Agnes removed her cloak and enquired how Peter fared.

'Come and see for yourself. My boy Edward has taken to him very well. They have entertained one another all day.'

The kitchen into which Mrs Sharp led Agnes was lit by tallow candles whose light reflected off an array of shiny copper pots. The fire was low but smouldered comfortingly. The furniture was plain and sparse, but well polished and spotlessly clean. Peter was sitting at the table beside a fair-haired little fellow, with the same round face and pale blue-grey eyes as his mother. Both boys were sipping bowls of broth and were dressed in nightshirts and nightcaps. Peter's cheeks were scarlet, his eyes bright, the hair on his forehead ruffled and damp as though his face had been recently washed. 'Ma!' he cried, leaping up as Agnes appeared at the threshold, 'I thought you'd forgot. This is Edward. I taught him how to play chequers.'

Agnes embraced her son and tried to ignore the image of Elsie in the snow that floated across her thoughts. 'Pleased to make your acquaintance, Edward,' she said. Thomas Williams was nowhere to be seen. Was she relieved or disappointed by his absence? Neither, she told herself firmly. She was unmoved, and would remain so.

She took from her muff the small parcel she had brought, and handed it to Peter to unwrap. 'Here's something for you both – when the broth is finished.'

Peter gulped down the last of his soup and tore away the paper. Inside were two gingerbread figures with currant eyes and buttons down their fronts, and almond mouths and hair. The boys grinned and began a mock fight with them. As biscuit limbs were disengaged and currant eyes came loose, they munched swiftly until there was nothing left but the heads, whereupon the game swiftly altered and they began nibbling as slowly as mice to see whose would last longer.

Mrs Sharp drew up a chair by the fire and indicated that Agnes should settle herself in it. Just then there came the sound of heavy stamping by the back door. A moment later the door was flung open and Thomas Williams marched in. He was carrying a bucket of coal. His hair was in its customary disorder, a mass of chestnut spirals; he wore a shirt and mustard-coloured waistcoat, but no coat, and was shivering from the cold. As he caught sight of Agnes, a new light seemed to enter his eyes. 'Mrs Meadowes, good evening,' he said with a courteous bow as he deposited his load by the hearth. He sprinkled a shovelful on the embers, causing them to crackle and spit. 'I wasn't aware you were intending to visit. Had I known, I'd have come to fetch you. It isn't safe to travel alone – you ought to know that.'

' 'Tis a distance of only two streets, and I'm well acquainted with this district,' said Agnes nonchalantly, responding to his bow with a tiny inclination of her head before turning her attention back to Mrs Sharp.

Thomas's expression was sombre as he regarded her. She knew he had registered the hostile tone of her voice and was surprised by it, and felt a small shiver of satisfaction at having unsettled him. 'Even so, a woman alone, unarmed – and after what happened to your kitchen maid. It is folly to tempt fate in such a manner,' he said.

Agnes thought of Rose and the intrigues in which she had embroiled herself, and of the kitchen knife she had taken the precaution of hiding in her cloak pocket, and the gun in the cellar. With a murderer at large, she was probably no safer in her kitchen than in the street, but she saw no reason to argue the matter. Let Thomas Williams fret a little. Hadn't she passed more time than she cared to acknowledge watching for him?

She regarded him levelly. 'In my son's case it was a risk worth taking. I could not rest easy unless I knew he was well. And now I see him very well, for which I thank Mrs Sharp heartily.'

Mrs Sharp must have guessed from this stilted exchange that there was some misunderstanding between them. She turned the conversation to lighter subjects: the latest entertainment at the theatre, a production by Garrick, which she had heard from an acquaintance was most diverting; the price of herrings at the market; and the likelihood of the river freezing and the boys being able to go skating. When they had consumed the last crumb of gingerbread, the boys traipsed upstairs to bed and Mrs Sharp bustled after them, ordering Agnes to sit a while longer with Thomas until she called.

Anxious to steer matters away from the events of the previous night, Agnes told him matter-of-factly about her discovery of the gun in the cellar, and the letter that Pitt had sent – and that Theodore had decided he should accompany her to deliver the money and collect the wine-cooler.

'Has Justice Cordingly been informed of any of this?' enquired Thomas brusquely.

'No,' said Agnes. 'Theodore can think of nothing but the wine-cooler. He is adamant Justice Cordingly should be kept in the dark until it is recovered. I never told him about the gun – I feared if I did he would have seen it as an effort to undermine this determination and it would only have annoyed him.'

The explanation sounded lame as she said it, but Thomas Williams was gracious enough not to criticize her. 'He is willing to stake our safety against Pitt's integrity in order to safeguard the business – a dubious bargain, in my opinion,' he said. 'And even if Pitt is not the murderer, he surely knows the murderer's identity. It cannot be right just to allow the fellow to evade apprehension.'

'I agree wholeheartedly,' said Agnes, thinking of Rose lying dead with her throat cut. 'Moreover, the gun suggests the murderer is someone in the household. But I dare not contradict Theodore's order. And since we cannot doubt that the business depends upon the recovery of the wine-cooler, your position is as much at risk as mine. But on the subject of the murderer, there is one more thing I would like to ascertain, but I cannot easily do so by virtue of my sex.'

'What is it?' said Thomas.

'There is an ale house in Lombard Street called the Blue Cockerel. Philip was out on the night of the robbery, but he claims he spent the evening there in the company of various ladies. He says the landlord will remember him. Would you be so kind as to call on him to verify it?'

Thomas muttered an inaudible response, poured himself a tankard of ale from a jug on the dresser and silently gulped it, gazing at the fire as he did so. Soon after this the clock struck the half-hour and Mrs Sharp summoned Agnes upstairs. Having bidden her son goodnight, Agnes descended and wasted no time in taking her leave. 'I should return directly,' she said to Mrs Sharp, avoiding Thomas's eyes. 'There is still upstairs supper to put out.'

Thomas helped her into her cloak and then strapped on his sword and donned his overcoat and hat. Agnes feigned nonchalance. 'If you are coming out just on my account, I assure you, Mr Williams, there's no need. I shall be as safe on my return as I was coming here.'

Thomas Williams frowned. His green eyes settled on hers intently, as if trying to convey an unspoken message. 'I insist. It is foolhardy to travel alone at this time of night.'

Agnes ignored his look. 'I am quite able to protect myself.'

'Then humour me and allow me the pleasure of your company,' he said, holding open the door for her. As she passed, he lowered his voice so that Mrs Sharp did not hear.

'Besides, there's something more I wish to say to you – in privacy.'

Few people were abroad now, and Thomas walked close to Agnes's side, holding a lantern in one hand and extending his other arm so that she could rest hers upon it to prevent herself from slipping. She felt uncomfortable taking his support; intimacy was not what she had prescribed for herself. They walked for some moments in silence, their feet crunching over the crusty snow, clouds of white breath mingling in the dark night. Agnes was acutely aware of his stocky presence close to her; from time to time she sensed his eyes slide towards her and then away. She wondered, with a glimmer of apprehension, what it was he wished to say, but offered him no assistance, waiting for him to speak. Thus far not a word had passed between them about the previous night.

When they reached the corner of Bread Street and Cheapside, Thomas coughed and cleared his throat. 'I wanted to tell you to be careful, Mrs Meadowes. I spoke to Riley today regarding the box you showed me. There was something dark in his manner. I don't pretend to comprehend what it was, but it worried me all the same. When I told him Rose's body had been found, he seemed little surprised or sorry to hear it. Soon after that he enquired after you. I don't know how he discovered it, but I had the impression he knew there was something between us.'

Agnes's spirits plunged. Finding herself a subject for rumour was what she had feared almost as much as Thomas Williams's poor opinion of her. She shook her head and managed to cover her dismay. 'Never mind Riley's interest in me – I don't suppose he offered any theory on Rose's death?'

Thomas looked at the ground. 'Nothing. His words, as I recall, were that she was a meddlesome, flirtatious girl who doubtless was killed as a result of one of her intrigues.'

'He made no further suggestion that might help?'

'None. His chief concern was to probe my friendship with you.'

Agnes swallowed uncomfortably. 'He must have heard some idle rumour. Philip, our footman, is friendly with him and one of the apprentices. In any case, Riley is the least of our worries. The assignation with Mr Pitt tomorrow is a far more perilous undertaking.'

'But that at least is an easily recognizable danger.'

They were now halfway down Foster Lane, passing the Goldsmith's Hall. In a minute they would reach the steps leading down to her kitchen. A few yards from the railings, Thomas Williams paused and drew a deep breath. 'It wasn't only Riley I wished to discuss, Mrs Meadowes. There was another subject I wanted to raise.' He hesitated, his arm still supporting hers, looking down at his snow-caked boots. 'It is a delicate matter. But it needs to be said, and I beg you won't think me presumptuous for voicing it.'

Agnes raised an arched brow, but remembering to maintain her detachment, she said nothing. After a minute Thomas hesitantly continued. 'Last night I fear I may have imposed upon you. I never meant to do so. Today the thought occurred to me that perhaps you did not reciprocate willingly, but acted rather from some misguided sense of obligation on account of your son.'

Agnes felt the blood drain from her cheeks. Her lips felt brittle and dry in the frosty night. 'What do you mean, "misguided obligation"?' she asked hoarsely.

'When I embraced you I thought your response spontaneous; but afterwards I wondered if all was as it seemed. I have little experience in such matters, but once before I mistook a lady's purpose. It has made me nervous in affairs of the heart. In short, I wanted to assure you that whatever your feelings may be towards me, I should rather you expressed them honestly. I detest subterfuge in such matters. Your son won't be affected. I would rather know where I stand.'

'Do I understand your meaning, Mr Williams?' said Agnes sharply. 'You believe I behaved improperly on my son's account, and that such liberties as I allowed you were not necessary?'

'Impropriety and liberties have nothing to do with it,' said Thomas, reddening under her harsh scrutiny. 'I only meant that I hold you in high esteem, whatever your feelings towards me.

I don't wish our friendship to be distorted by other matters. I beg you to be straight with me.'

'Nevertheless, you suspect I reciprocated your advances for reasons other than straightforward affection.'

'I said nothing of the kind. You are putting words into my mouth. Don't look for insult where none was intended. I can't say any clearer what I meant.'

But the subject he had raised was one to which Agnes was acutely sensitive. She stood in the snowy street, unable to move or find the words to respond. She grew confused. Thomas seemed to be confirming her earlier conviction that he believed her accustomed to behaving improperly, and this caused her face to burn with humiliation. She swiftly reminded herself of her resolution: she would maintain her indifference. Her mind felt clearer. She raised her chin. 'How can I fail to feel insulted by the opinion you have formed of me? You have said you thought I might be bought by showing kindness to my son.'

'Far from it,' said Thomas, his tone growing louder as his patience wore thin, 'I never had an ungentlemanly thought regarding you, either before or after last night. Whatever caused what happened between us, we cannot alter it – nor do I wish to. And since I see you are determined to think the worst of me, I have as much right as you to feel insulted. Good evening, Mrs Meadowes. I think I shall go now to the Blue Cockerel.'

Without a word, Agnes curtseyed and descended at perilous speed down the icy stairs to her kitchen.

Chapter Thirty-one

AGNES SLEPT FITFULLY THAT NIGHT, GOING OVER EVERY WORD of her exchange with Thomas Williams, wishing she had thought to say this, that or the other, to slight him as much as she felt his words had slighted her. When she awoke next morning it was to a dismal overcast sky and snow that was rapidly thawing to unprepossessing slush.

At ten minutes to nine precisely, Agnes presented herself at the shop next door. Thomas Williams let her in. She noticed that once again he wore his sword for protection. Was this on Theodore's order, she wondered. He greeted her as if they were barely acquainted. 'I went to the Blue Cockerel,' he declared coldly. 'The landlord recalled that Philip was there the night of the robbery with one or two other fellows. He did not remember who they were, save that one of them was Riley. Nor did he know what time any of them left.' It seemed to Agnes that his eyes were cold as flint, and the face that had seemed friendly and reassuring before now seemed utterly impassive, as if it were hewn from marble. 'And now, Mrs Meadowes, Mr Blanchard awaits you,' he said, as he bowed and led her into the small back office.

For one fleeting moment she wondered if she had been too hasty with him. Had she misconstrued his fumbling apology for having made love to her? But no sooner had such a possibility arisen than she coldly dismissed it. Their falling out would not have happened were it not for his crass reference to such a delicate matter. And bearing this in mind, her earlier resolve to behave with detachment and the utmost propriety seemed the only dignified course open to her.

Theodore was in the back office. His wig was hanging on a hook by the wall, his bristly head was bowed over a bench. He looked up briefly as Agnes went in. There was an air of glum preoccupation about his tense mouth and unseeing gaze. The surface before him was crowded with dozens of small candlesticks; in the middle a space had been cleared. In this void Theodore had piled up twelve small towers of gold, ten coins in each. He now placed the gold, column by column, in an oak strong box. The chink of metal made a knot in Agnes's stomach. She was conscious of Thomas standing on the other side of the bench, but dared not look in his direction, instead keeping her eyes fixed on the glittering heap in the box.

When all the coins were in, Theodore closed the lid, fastened iron bands over a hasp and inserted a padlock through it the size of Agnes's fist. He locked it with a shiny key and threaded the key onto a length of cord. This he handed to her. 'Put it about your neck, Mrs Meadowes, and conceal it in your bodice.' He spoke in a monotone, as if numb from the enormity of what he was about to do. 'You are not to give the key to anyone but Pitt himself. And only once you have the wine-cooler in your sight. Do I make myself clear?'

'Perfectly, sir,' said Agnes.

Thomas Williams coughed. 'Wouldn't it be more prudent if I were to have the key, sir?'

Theodore turned stiffly. 'Why, Williams?'

'Only on account of her – Mrs Meadowes, I mean – being a woman. It might be safer if a man had it.'

Theodore blinked, astonished that Thomas Williams should question his judgement. 'On the contrary, Mr Williams, it is the fact that Mrs Meadowes is female that makes her so well suited to this task. Pitt is already much stricken with her; I hazard he will be eager to keep to his undertaking partly to ingratiate himself further into her favours.'

Hearing this, Thomas's pale cheeks darkened. 'Forgive me, sir – I was unaware there was something between them,' he said.

'There is nothing between us,' said Agnes hotly, then wished she had kept quiet. She slid the cold metal key beneath her bodice. Thomas avoided her eye and said nothing.

Soon after this, a shadow fell over the shop window and the snorting of horses and clink of harnesses became audible outside. A deep red equipage, drawn by a pair of lively black horses with steaming nostrils, juddered to a halt in the slushy road. The carriage's velvet curtains – of the same hue as the paintwork – were tightly drawn, rendering the interior invisible, but there was a coachman sitting up front, and to the rear a pair of shabbily liveried footmen. Beneath their unbuttoned red greatcoats, both were armed with pistols.

No sooner had the carriage creaked to a halt than the footmen jumped down. One positioned himself close to the carriage door; the other, a portly-figured man with lank hair drawn back in a bow, barged in without troubling to knock or remove his hat. Agnes recognized him as Grant, Pitt's corpulent attendant. 'Mr Pitt's carriage,' he announced.

'She will be with you directly. Kindly wait outside,' said Theodore in a commanding tone. He instructed Thomas Williams to put the strong box inside the carriage, sit beside it and keep his feet on it at all times. Then, turning to Agnes, he said less firmly, 'Well, Mrs Meadowes, are you ready? After the letter you sent, I hazard Pitt will be in a lather of expectation for you.'

Agnes dared not look in Thomas's direction, as she wondered what he must think.

'It won't be necessary for your man to carry that,' said Grant, suddenly barging back into the shop. 'Mr Pitt gave orders we should take it. And he'll only have Mrs Meadowes inside the carriage. Her man is to sit up front.' Without pause, he turned to Agnes. 'This way, madam, when you're ready. Follow me.'

As Agnes was ushered outside, Pitt's second attendant held out his hands for the box. Theodore stood at the doorway of the shop, legs braced, hands on hips, watching as a small fortune in gold was whisked off into the clutches of London's most infamous thief-taker. Confusion was written in the unnatural pallor of his florid cheeks, and despite the winter chill, sweat beaded his brow. He opened his mouth as if to proffer another word of advice to Agnes, but then closed it again without utterance and merely waved her off with his hand.

Agnes's apprehensive gaze swung like a pendulum between the glittering façade of the shop window, resplendent with its silver display, and the ominous carriage, a gash of vermilion set against a bleak winter prospect. She wished she were anywhere but here; a powerful presentiment of misfortune caused a burning sensation in her throat. We are all in turmoil, she consoled herself, all of us groping in the dark, Theodore and Thomas as much as I.

Grant let down the carriage steps and bundled Agnes unceremoniously into the shadowy, curtained interior. Scarcely were her feet both in than Grant cried out. 'Quick now, stand away, ma'am,' and the door crashed closed and was fastened behind her.

Closeted in the dark interior of the carriage, Agnes groped her way round the strong box to her seat. In the fleeting instant before the door was closed, she had gained an impression of a shadowy form seated in the far corner of the carriage. Once she had sat down, she peered towards the corner. But so dense was the enveloping gloom after the daylight, she could see nothing. She reached forward to draw back the curtain on her side. As she did so, a firm hand grasped hers and pulled it unceremoniously away from the curtain. A voice came out of the darkness and whispered directly into her ear. 'I prefer you to leave that for the time being, if you please, Mrs Meadowes.'

The voice was soft but recognizable. Agnes flinched and drew back, her body quaking with the shock of the encounter. 'As you wish, sir.' Then after a pause, she added hesitantly, 'you are Mr Pitt, are you not?'

The voice replied, deeper and stronger now, out of the darkness. 'How astute you are to recognize me, madam. I take that as a compliment.'

'I cannot conceive why. It was nothing but a question, Mr Pitt,' retorted Agnes, forgetting for a moment her fear and that she was supposed to beguile him with her charms.

Pitt laughed but said nothing more. He withdrew and settled back in the far corner of the carriage. His face was still indiscernible, but as her eyes grew more accustomed to the dark she began to distinguish his outline. He was tall and angular, as she remembered; a broad-brimmed hat obscured the upper part of his profile, and he appeared to be wearing a long dark coat. The air in the carriage was scented with the same pungent, sweet, spicy smell as his room had been. In his hand was a cane topped with a silver orb, which Agnes could see gleaming in the gloom like a diminutive moon, with the knobbly shape of his fingers clenched round it. As before, she was conscious of Pitt's allure. What am I thinking? I am in the presence of evil. I ought to be repelled, not drawn, she reminded herself, and turned her head away.

Abruptly, Pitt leaned forward and thumped the orb hard on the window frame. 'Grant – tell the driver to depart directly.'

'Very well, sir,' Grant responded. After that came a muffled shout to Thomas Williams, who was ordered to climb up in front, and to the footmen, who resumed their positions behind. The vehicle sagged and lurched at their weight, then in a louder tone Grant's voice was heard to cry out, 'All in place, let's go!' The coachman cracked his whip and the carriage jolted drunkenly off, metal-bound wheels slewing through the snow.

Agnes was thrown back against the velvet upholstery. The strong box by her feet knocked against the door as the carriage veered into Cheapside. Then it lurched again as it picked up speed. Once they were bowling along, the pace steadied; Pitt pulled the strong box over towards him, stretched out his legs and rested his crossed feet on it as though it were a footstool. 'Forgive me for startling you just now, Mrs Meadowes,' he said.

'Were not the curtains and the dark intended expressly for that purpose, Mr Pitt?' said Agnes, determined not to reveal any sign of the trepidation pulsing in her veins.

'I meant you no harm by them. Only it suited my purpose that Mr Blanchard should remain ignorant of my presence.'

'Oh, and why is that?' said Agnes, recalling that Theodore was equally eager to avoid a meeting with the thief-taker, whom he claimed might derive some profit by their association.

'I find it safer to avoid unnecessary contact with my clients. I prefer to deal with intermediaries. Matters run more evenly and are concluded quicker as a consequence.'

'I confess I still cannot see why such complications were necessary. Would it not have been simpler for Mr Blanchard to hand you the money in person?'

'And deprive myself of the pleasure of your company?'

Agnes tossed her head. 'Whatever your reason for this arrangement, I don't delude myself *I* had anything to do with it.'

Pitt laughed. 'Then if you want the honest truth I shall give it you. Once the money is handed over I make a habit of ensuring all transactions are properly concluded. I won't be with you when you recover the wine-cooler. Should a constable stray into the vicinity, it would not do for me to be found with a large sum of money on my person and stolen property in my presence. Nevertheless, I shall observe proceedings from a distance – and if anything goes amiss you may be assured steps will be taken to rectify it.'

Agnes shuddered, recalling poor Elsie's fears that Pitt would sacrifice her father if he deemed it expedient to do so. What Pitt meant was that he lived and prospered by the terror he engendered in those around him. 'Whatever the reasons for your presence, I assure you I have no intention of duping you, Mr Pitt. My only desire is the same as yours – to recover the wine-cooler and trouble you no longer.'

Pitt laughed mockingly again. 'But therein your desires differ dramatically from mine, madam. Your pretty face and charming ways made an impression upon me at our first meeting. I had hoped from the tone of your letter that our acquaintance would continue. Or was that merely a contrivance to make me more eager to assist you?'

Conscious that she was now on perilous terrain, and that it would be prudent to affect at least some modicum of interest in him, Agnes paused and answered with care. 'It was no contrivance to say our future depends entirely upon how the business is concluded. For as I told you, I am a widow reliant upon my trade. Any person who helps secure my position I will naturally regard with warm sentiments.'

'Then I shall hold you to your promise, Mrs Meadowes.'

Some minutes later, the carriage slowed and Agnes judged they were in the vicinity of the bridge.

'Now we are a safe distance from Foster Lane, you are at liberty to open the curtain if you find the darkness distressing,' said Pitt.

Agnes pulled back the velvet awning on her side and gazed through the window. They were in a place she did not recognize – a narrow alley, lined on either side with tall decrepit windowless buildings, with a maze of small courts leading off. The passers-by were shabbily dressed and gawped with unseemly interest at their elegant carriage. The buildings might be abandoned warehouses, she thought. If only she could get a glimpse of St Paul's, or a church spire or some other landmark with which she was familiar, she might form a more exact impression of her whereabouts, but the low carriage roof and the narrow way obscured her view of the city skyline.

Agnes turned then and regarded Pitt. Half of his face remained in shadow, for he had neglected to open the curtain on his side. His expression was distant, unreadable; he sat erect and alert in his seat, his long slender fingers curled over the knob of his cane, as if he was waiting for something unexpected to happen and was prepared to act at a moment's notice. As Agnes scrutinized him his brooding gaze turned and their eyes locked, before she averted her glance to look again out of the window.

'Where are we?' she said, sitting forward and gripping the edge of her seat. 'Why have you brought me here?'

'Have patience. You'll discover where you are in good time. Each of us knows the other's requirements. Provided you have brought what I asked, you will be safe and your master's wine-cooler will be returned within the hour.'

Agnes might have remonstrated further, but just then the carriage lurched to an abrupt halt. She turned to look out of the window, but the deserted alley into which they had driven was scarcely wide enough for a single carriage. All she could see were decrepit wooden walls, a broken window, a shadowy doorway with a pile of dung mounded to one side. She tried to push down the glass so that she could gain a better view, but when she did so Pitt put a restraining hand on her arm. 'Best not do that, my dear. In time you may descend to admire the surroundings at your leisure. But not just now, eh?'

He tapped his stick sharply on the window. Grant descended, and a minute later his greasy pock-marked face peered in on Pitt's side. Pitt leaned forward to address him. 'Is he still hooded up top?'

'All the way since Cheapside.'

'Any sign of our friend yet?'

'No, sir – but it may be he's there before us.'

Pitt regarded his pocket watch.

'One of you go and look.' He gave the strong box a nudge with the toe of his boot. 'Meanwhile, I'll need help with this.' Pitt turned to Agnes. 'The key, if you please, Mrs Meadowes.'

'I was ordered to hand it to you only when I saw the wine-cooler,' she returned stoutly.

Pitt smiled, lowering his eyelids. 'And so you shall, so you shall, madam,' he said soothingly. 'But as I said, I make a point of never being in the same place as stolen property. You have nothing to fear, provided you do as I ask. Now hand over the key that I may count the contents.'

'But that is not what Mr Blanchard ordered me to do. He said I must see the wine-cooler first,' countered Agnes bravely.

'Don't be rash, Mrs Meadowes. Blanchard doesn't know how my business works. And he didn't want you to vex me, did he? Hand me the key and your worries will cease. The wine-cooler awaits you, even now.' He paused and waited for her to comply. When Agnes still resisted, he drew his face closer to hers and added in a whisper, 'Then perhaps I should look for it myself. There are only a certain number of places a lady may secrete a key upon her person.'

'How dare you!' cried Agnes, alarmed suddenly by what might happen. But for some reason, instead of yielding, her fingers unthinkingly reached into the pocket of her cloak to find the handle of the knife she had secreted there last night.

'Then surrender the key,' insisted Pitt, drawing even closer. 'I repeat, there's not much I don't know about a lady's secrets. I wager I'll find it in an instant.'

Agnes's fingers closed about the handle of the knife in her pocket. As Pitt's face loomed over her, she thought of her husband drunkenly assailing her, and steeled herself and refused to give way. 'Get away from me or I won't—'

'Won't what, my dear?' said Pitt, laughing joylessly as he inserted a hand inside her cloak, splayed his fingers over her breast and squeezed as though testing the ripeness of an orange.

The violation forced a spasm of hatred through Agnes's veins. Theodore's instructions flew from her thoughts. A decade ago she would have surrendered, but now she was different, her reaction impulsive. 'Won't be responsible for my actions,' she said, taking out her knife and holding the blade against his invading hand. 'I dislike being imposed upon, Mr Pitt. Draw back now, or the knife might slip.'

The cold metal blade and Agnes's sudden steel took Pitt entirely by surprise. He let out an incredulous gasp, snatched his hand away and sat back nursing it as if she had cut him. But after a short while he recovered himself and his demeanour altered. His lips drew tight and his eyes gleamed unnaturally bright, the pupils tiny peppercorns of black. 'All right, Mrs Meadowes. A very clever game. But pretty though you are, don't think I have brought you here just for conversation. Perhaps you'd like it if Grant assisted in persuading you to be more obliging.'

Agnes, still trembling from the indignity of Pitt's hand on her breast, did not answer. Tears welled at the back of her eyes. She was enraged with herself for allowing this to happen. Why had she not just given him the key? He could easily take the strong box and break it open if he was so inclined. The battle she had fought with him, she realized, was needless. Nevertheless, she consoled herself, it was a victory of sorts to have caused him consternation. She fumbled for the ribbon at her neck. 'Very well,' she said, slicing the ribbon with the knife and flinging the key to the floor of the carriage, 'if this is what you want, then take the wretched thing.'

Glowering, Marcus Pitt retrieved the key, unlocked the giant padlock, removed the hasp and threw back the lid. Agnes watched as he ran his fingers through the sea of gold, then, still avoiding her eyes, emptied the coins in a mound on the floor of the carriage and counted them back into the box. His muttered counting and the manner in which he deliberately ignored her seemed infinitely more frightening than his threats and advances.

When he had satisfied himself that the box contained the required sum, Pitt snapped the lid shut, locked it again and put the key in his pocket. Then he opened the carriage door and summoned Grant with a tap of his cane. 'Well?' he said.

'A word if you please, sir.'

Pitt descended from the carriage. Agnes heard the sound of a conversation conducted in muffled tones. She could not properly distinguish what was said, but snatches drifted in.

'He was there . . .' said Grant.

'Then you must . . .' replied Pitt.

To which Grant mumbled, 'But I never . . . And how . . .'

'I repeat . . .' said Pitt, and so it went on for several minutes.

From the tone of it, Agnes judged that something unexpected had taken place. The conversation lasted for so long that Agnes's curiosity overcame her fear. She slid across to Pitt's side of the carriage and squinted out from behind the curtain to see if she might discern any more. She could see Grant in full flow, facing Pitt. Grant's face was flushed with agitation and he was gesticulating wildly as he spoke. Pitt's reaction was unfathomable, as his back was turned. All that was visible was the back of his long cloak and his silver-topped cane, which he was twirling thoughtfully in his hand. When eventually Grant halted, Pitt made some staccato remark that sounded like 'You must get it, then.' He jerked his head in the direction of the carriage as he spoke. Grant responded with a nod and stepped round the other side. Guessing that Grant was coming for her, Agnes slid back to her former position. But Grant did not appear, and she judged from the vibrations behind her that he was delving about in the basket at the rear of the carriage. When she summoned the courage to look out of the window again, there was no sign of him. All she could see was Pitt pacing about, still rotating the silver-topped cane in his hand.

A good ten minutes passed, during which Agnes watched from her window, listening intently for any sign of what was to come. But nothing happened and no one outside the carriage spoke a word. Eventually, she heard the heavy crunch of Grant's footsteps returning. Her door was thrown abruptly open and the steps were let down. 'We are ready for you now. Descend, if you please, madam,' said Grant.

Agnes did as he bade, and Thomas Williams was summoned to join her. While she waited for him to clamber down from his platform next to the driver, she noticed something singular in Grant's appearance. When she had observed him earlier, his livery had seemed somewhat the worse for wear, but not unduly grimy. Now, however, his greatcoat sleeves were filthy – the dark-red cloth was almost black and there were damp patches on it. His hands were similarly begrimed, and his face too was smeared with dirt. He looked, Agnes reflected, as though he had been digging in a coal pit.

Williams had travelled with a hood over his head. The driver had only just removed it before letting him descend, and he was still blinking and looking dazed from the sudden daylight when Pitt addressed them. He signalled to a dark narrow passage leading off to the left between two buildings. The opening was barely a yard wide, so narrow that Agnes had not seen it until now.

'A short distance down there is a terrace of three houses by the river's edge. The door of the last building is unlocked; enter it and you will find the wine-cooler waiting for you.'

Pitt spoke formally, avoiding Agnes's gaze. But she wasn't deceived. There was a new coldness in his tone, a steeliness in his expression. In trying to obey Theodore's order she had slighted him, and he had not forgotten it. She was sure that somehow or other Pitt would take actions to demonstrate his displeasure. She wished now that she had not acted with such foolish haste. But the words were spoken, the knife had been brandished; there was no changing any of it.

Chapter Thirty-two

WITHOUT REVEALING ANY SIGN OF THE HESITATION SHE FELT, Agnes plunged down the nameless passage, closely followed by Thomas Williams. As she walked, her confusion intensified. She sensed that even if he had not heard their exchange, Thomas must have noticed the unspoken strain between Pitt and herself. And now that she was alone with him their recent argument came back to her. She knew that in their present precarious predicament, it would be wise to improve matters between them. But she still burned when she remembered his clumsy remarks, and the shock of Pitt's assault had further hardened her against mankind in general. She was not in the mood to soften her manner one jot.

There was not a living soul to be seen. How was it possible, Agnes wondered, to find such a deserted spot in the largest city in the world? With each step they took, Agnes half expected Pitt or Grant to jump out at them. She tried to quell her fears, telling herself that if Pitt wanted to exact revenge he was unlikely to do so while his business might be jeopardized, and while she was protected. Any attack would surely come once her role in this business was played out and she was alone. Nevertheless, she remembered Pitt's words – that he always stayed in the vicinity to make sure the stolen property was returned, although he kept himself concealed. She peered apprehensively into every shadowy gap where a man might conceivably hide. Was he watching even now, she wondered?

For his part, Thomas seemed to harbour no such fears. He remained withdrawn, but appeared untroubled by their present circumstances and impervious to her coolness. He spoke no word until they had passed a large decaying warehouse and the passage widened. 'Have you any idea where we are?' he said eventually, gazing around for a familiar landmark or a street sign.

She started at the sound of his voice, then recovered herself hastily. 'Did you not glean any detail of interest during the journey?' she replied.

'Not a thing. The hood was placed over my head before we left Foster Lane, and the coachman never spoke a word to me, apart from telling me to sit tight. But it doesn't surprise me in the least.'

'What do you mean?'

'It was Pitt's intention to confuse us and make us fearful. It gives him the advantage, helps him conclude his business with a minimum of fuss.'

In that case, Agnes thought, he has certainly achieved his aim.

The passage suddenly opened onto an expanse of marshy wasteland beside the river. The ground was littered with discarded rubbish and traversed by a stinking sewer. Strewn about this vile landscape were skeletons of weeds, broken bricks, old bones, rotten wood, a sliver of orange peel, a mound of rubble, the mangled carcass of a cat. Rats were scurrying boldly about in the murky water. A row of dilapidated houses with boarded-up windows overhung the water's edge. The buildings had been shored up by wooden pilings which thrust up from the muddy water. In between these supports, the structure sagged like a necklace. In the sky flapped and wheeled a dozen or more gulls, their cries carried off like clouds of smoke in the gusting wind.

Agnes walked down towards the water's edge. The tide was

high and the wind brisk. She breathed the air thoughtfully, then, leaning forward, peered up and down the river. Thomas followed her and did likewise. Far off to the left, a fleet of fishing smacks could be seen beating their way upriver into the wind. To the right were moored several coal barges, the men who lowered their brown sails resembling industrious ants. Beyond them, faintly visible despite the curve of the river, were the great pillars of London Bridge and the jagged outline of its shops and buildings.

Agnes turned towards Thomas. 'We have travelled east when I thought we had gone south. I warrant from the smell and the gulls we are not far from Billingsgate market,' she said.

Thomas nodded inscrutably but passed no comment, instead looking back towards the row of decrepit houses.

'The place he means us to go must be there,' he said, striding ahead to the last door in the terrace. 'Let us see if the entrance is unlocked as he promised.' He drew his sword, turned the handle and pushed. The door creaked on its rusty hinges and juddered open.

It led into a dingy narrow passage, with broken stairs rising off to the left and two doors leading off to the right. Thomas pushed open the door of the first room with the point of his sword and glanced in from the threshold, holding his sword aloft. Agnes was forced to wait behind, where she could not see a thing. Then he swiftly closed the door again and progressed several steps along the corridor towards the second doorway.

Doubtless, Agnes thought, he expected her to follow. But she did not. Pitt's assault had left her angry and distrustful of everyone. She wanted to survey the place independently and make certain she was not being duped. Reopening the door to the first room, she peered in. The boards on the windows made the interior seem cavernous and shadowy, but there were enough chinks of light to see that the room was small and unfurnished, and that there was a large damp patch on the floor. The room reeked of soot, which emanated from a mound of black debris in the empty fireplace. There were also, Agnes observed, sooty smears leading from the fireplace across to the damp patch on the floor and thence to the door.

For several minutes Agnes stood in contemplation. She could hear Thomas's footsteps pacing about next door. Apparently he was rummaging about in the corner, for she could hear a scuffling sound. But she had no desire for the moment to follow him. Nor did she call him back to discuss what he had overlooked, although she believed it might be significant.

The pungent smell of soot suggested that it had recently fallen down the chimney. From the marks leading across the floor, it appeared that someone had recently entered this room. Both these details might be explained if that person had concealed something up the chimney – a valuable item, perhaps, something that could not be left on open view in an unlocked house. Agnes remembered the sooty marks on Grant's coat when he had returned to the carriage. And she had felt him rummage about in the basket behind before he left. Had the wine-cooler been in the carriage all along? And had Grant deposited it here for them to recover? But if so, thought Agnes, that meant Pitt had risked being caught with money and stolen property on his person – a situation he claimed he avoided at all costs. And why would he choose such an inaccessible place to hide the wine-cooler? After all, once the money was paid he wanted it to be found. Perhaps, then, something else of value had been concealed here, something Pitt wanted to remain hidden.

Agnes approached the fireplace dubiously and, bending down until she was on a level with the opening, peered up the flue. But she might as well have been wearing a blindfold. She could discern nothing but a yawning sooty blackness. She reached her arm up into the aperture of the chimney. The flue was wide enough, she judged, to hide something sizeable. She groped around, all the time reaching further and further upwards. As she did so, soot and rubble was dislodged and she was forced to turn away her face and press her cheek to the chimney breast to prevent debris falling in her eyes. Still she could feel nothing untoward, nothing to explain the mound of soot or the smudged marks.

At the furthest limits of her reach, the chimney seemed to broaden out sharply, forming a ledge inside. Suddenly her fingers brushed against an unexpected obstruction, a substance that was neither stone nor soot but wood – two planks wedged across the ledge. Further fumbling exploration revealed that they were supporting something. Whatever it was had been wrapped in some variety of coarse hairy fabric – sacking, she concluded. Agnes prodded and felt something hard inside. It seemed her instinct had been right. Grant must have concealed something here only minutes before their arrival.

With renewed determination, Agnes tried to dislodge the planks and then haul the sack and its contents free, but the wood was securely wedged and the tips of her fingers were unable to shove firmly enough to shift them. After some minutes of trying, she was forced to abandon her efforts.

Just as she had withdrawn her arm and stepped away, Thomas's head poked round the door; the expression on his face was less stern than before – relief mingled with bemusement. 'What on earth are you doing, Mrs Meadowes?' he said, viewing the spectacle of Agnes with an arm and face smutted in soot.

'There's something hidden in the chimney,' she said, tasting granules of soot as she spoke. 'Grant had soot on his clothes when he returned to the carriage. Perhaps it is something of value.'

Williams shook his head. 'Whatever it is, it cannot be the wine-cooler; that was what I came to tell you – I have found it hidden in a closet in the room next door.'

'Nevertheless, there is something here. There are planks supporting it. I tried to remove them, but they are beyond my grasp. I think we should discover what it is.'

Thomas heaved a sigh and, unsheathing his sword once more, strode across the floor. 'Very well. Let me try.'

Agnes withdrew and watched him gingerly push his sword up the chimney.

'How far up is it?' he enquired, wrinkling his nose in distaste.

'As far as you can reach.'

To begin with Thomas's face showed his disbelief, and a certain regret at having to dirty his jacket. But then his weapon hit an obstruction and the focus in his eyes altered to a more considered gleam.

'Have you reached it yet?' said Agnes.

'I believe so,' he answered, retracting his sword and feeling with his hand. 'It feels like a sack, and whatever it contains, it is a sizeable object.'

Thomas bent his knees and gave a sharp upward thrust with his arm. A cascade of rubble and soot tumbled to the hearth, along with two wooden boards that had provided the platform for whatever was hidden there. In the dark opening of the chimney a section of brown sacking had also appeared. The nature of its contents remained impossible to guess, since half the sack was still wedged up the chimney and its mouth was twisted and bound by a cord. Nevertheless, it was clear there was something large and lumpen within.

'Allow me,' said Agnes, stepping forward. She felt for the knife in her pocket and with a single swipe cut the string, which fell to the ground. She untwisted the sack and made as if to reach inside. But there was no need. The instant the mouth of the sack was open, part of its contents rolled at their feet, causing Agnes and Thomas to look down and gasp in horrified unison.

A human head. It had been severed from the body. The tongue was half protruding from the mouth and had been nearly bitten through; a stump of spine and a few ragged sinews several inches long emanated from the neck. What was most striking, however, was the surfeit of blood. The hair was matted with it, the features daubed to the extent they were unrecognizable; blood had run into every imaginable cavity: the ears and nostrils and eye sockets, and clogged in the lids and lashes and brows; a trail of thick viscous red seeped from both corners of the lips.

Agnes glanced up at Thomas Williams and saw that his face

was distorted with shock. He was grey as a ghoul and had clamped his hand over his mouth as though to prevent himself from gagging. She too felt an acrid taste rise in her throat, but she swallowed several times and summoned all her resources of detachment. The murderer will escape, she told herself bitterly, if I cede to emotion. Besides, she remained determined to convey a message of invulnerability to Thomas Williams. He might waver and feel ill; she would not.

As it turned out, her aim was easily achieved. Thomas bolted from the room, his hand still gripped over his mouth. Outside she heard the sound of retching. Agnes was quaking and her heart pulsed wildly, but she forced herself to walk calmly over to the fireplace. With trembling hands, she gave the sack and its remaining ghastly contents a firm hard pull.

Chapter Thirty-three

BY THE TIME THOMAS WILLIAMS HAD RECOVERED HIMSELF sufficiently to re-enter the house, Agnes was stooped over the sack, which she had managed to lug from the chimney onto the floor. Biting hard on her lip, she had drawn back the mouth of the sack and was examining the headless corpse. Every now and again she turned to compare her observations with the head. At the sound of Thomas's entry, she turned and looked at him. 'Are you quite recovered, Mr Williams?'

'Of course,' he said, then seeing the headless corpse he took a step back. 'What are you doing?' he mumbled.

Agnes swallowed, breathing deeply to quell the heaving in her own stomach. 'Trying to ascertain what has happened.'

She sensed him wonder how she had the strength to look at such a gruesome sight. It does not mean I am not capable of feeling the same as you, she thought; only that I have learned to exercise control over what I allow myself to feel. I can keep sentiment at bay, and have done so for years.

Thomas coughed uncomfortably. 'Is it not perfectly transparent what has happened? His head has been cut off.'

'Quite so, Mr Williams, but by whose hand? And why?' She paused. Her insides felt molten with the shock of handling the body and there was a burning sensation in her throat. But outwardly she remained composed. 'Does anything in particular strike you about this killing?'

'Not especially,' said Thomas, keeping his eyes glued to the boarded window. 'What do you make of it?'

'It is the same as the others, which suggests it was committed by the same hand,' said Agnes. 'It must therefore be connected in some way. I don't suppose you recognize him, do you?'

'No,' replied Thomas uneasily.

Noticing his returning pallor, Agnes said more kindly, 'You say you recovered the wine-cooler.'

'Yes,' he said, looking at his feet.

'Then while I finish here, may I suggest you go in search of some means of conveying it back to Foster Lane. I shall stay and guard it, meanwhile.'

'Are you not afraid to wait alone?'

'What relevance have my fears? The wine-cooler is too heavy for us to carry any distance.'

It was unlike him to give in to her with so little protest, but either Thomas recognized the truth of what she said or his stomach was heaving once more. In any case, he needed no more persuasion to nod and disappear. Agnes wondered if she had been wise to send him away. What would she do if he didn't return? She felt her own resolve slip, but then she clenched her jaw determinedly. She had no time to indulge her fears; she had to finish the task she had set herself.

The head was sunken-eyed, hook-nosed, and had been unshaven for several days, and – to judge from the smell of tobacco and stale sweat – unwashed for heaven knows how long. But she could conclude little more than that from it. Turning then to the corpse, she attempted to draw an accurate impression of the man's means from his costume. It was saturated with blood, but from the few unstained patches she observed that, while the costume was undeniably shabby, there were curious touches of eccentricity about it. His coat was worn and ingrained with filth, but his lapels were lined with velvet and the cravat was silk. She rummaged through his pockets and extracted a silken handkerchief, a couple of pennies, a small pocket knife, a length of rope, a pair of knitted gloves and a silver wine label engraved *Shrub*. Nothing that shed any light on who he was. She picked up each object in turn and examined it. It was only when she turned over the wine label that she discovered anything of note. The marks were those of Blanchards.

She was still clutching the wine label, but had drawn no conclusions as to its significance, when she heard the sound of a soft footfall close behind her. Swivelling round, her eye caught upon a pair of flawlessly polished black boots standing by the door. She looked up slowly, taking in a pair of black breeches, a black undercoat surmounted by a long black cloak that nearly brushed the ground, a gloved hand holding a cane with a silver knob.

'Mrs Meadowes,' said a suave but chilling voice. 'How very unexpected to find you still here. What on earth are you doing with that corpse?'

Agnes felt as if a hand had gripped her insides. It was the voice she most dreaded – the man she most feared – Marcus Pitt. Not wishing to allow him to glimpse her trepidation, she rose swiftly to her feet and faced him. 'As you see, I am examining it. Do you know him?' she asked unfalteringly.

'May I ask why you think I should?'

'Because you sent us to this house, and the wine-cooler was hidden in the next room. It seems probable to me that he is therefore a member of your confederation of rogues.' As she spoke, she was still clutching the wine label. Suddenly, realization dawned. 'Is he Harry Drake?'

Pitt tensed his mouth and snorted, but did not deny it. 'And you think I killed him, do you?'

'No,' said Agnes, still maintaining her bravado, 'I do not.'

Marcus Pitt nodded. 'Why is that?'

'Why would you have him decapitated, when you might have got a reward for handing him over to the justice?'

'Very good, Mrs Meadowes. Very good. Who would suspect

that beneath that feminine exterior there beats such a steely heart?'

Agnes held her head high on its slender neck. Her eyes narrowed. How could she fail to be hardened after all she had overcome to fend for herself and Peter? 'It has always been my experience that exteriors are deceiving, sir. Most of us, when called upon, can convincingly conceal the person we really are. But that is by the by. May I enquire what has prompted you to return here? I thought you never risked entering a building where there was stolen property still present.'

Pitt flashed a dangerous smile. 'On rare occasions I find it behoves me to take a risk. After all, what would this humdrum existence of mine be without a little danger – a dull thing, a very dull thing indeed. Where one as winsome as you is concerned, is it strange that I abandon my usual precautions?'

'So you expected to find me here,' said Agnes, aware that her control was slipping; her pulse was beating wildly again and fear was encroaching like a stain.

Pitt grinned; the malice in his eye was unmistakable. 'So you know what has brought me here, do you?'

'You wished to see Drake's corpse with your own eyes.'

'Why should I want to do that?'

'Because you are as surprised as I by his death. No doubt you wished to do the same as I – view the corpse to try and ascertain who did kill him. I believe Grant must have discovered the body this morning, lying on the floor, where there is a large dark stain. I hazard it was he that hid it up the chimney, so that Mr Williams and I would not find it and become distracted from the task we were meant to perform. That was the reason you held me so long in the carriage, and why Grant's hands and suit were so noticeably sullied when he returned.'

Pitt gave a non-committal smile. He raised his eyes to the boarded windows and then regarded the severed head and corpse. 'I congratulate you, Mrs Meadowes. Your answer contains an element of the truth. Drake's murder has surprised me, and I dislike surprises. But I also dislike being refused something upon which I have set my heart.'

'Whom do you suppose killed Drake?' said Agnes quickly.

'I have my suspicions,' said Pitt, 'but let us save them for later. You know very well I am taken with you. I think you were teasing me in the carriage.' With this, he pulled back his lips in a leering grin and advanced towards her.

'My apologies, Mr Pitt, if I misled or offended you,' said Agnes, backing away from him. 'I meant no harm; it was only that you took me by surprise when you asked for the key.'

But Pitt seemed not to hear these remonstrations. 'Do you think I don't see the heat in your cheeks, or the desire in your eyes? Come here – let me hold you. But first, let's throw away that knife in your pocket, shall we?'

With this, he grasped Agnes firmly by the wrist and twisted her arm behind her back so that any movement was impossible. He began to rummage in her cloak, and eventually, after much unnecessary probing of her person, withdrew the knife. 'A very nasty weapon,' said Pitt. He examined its blade with his thumb, then flung it away and drew Agnes towards him until his mouth was pressed into her neck. 'Ah, this is what I've waited for!' he said, as he held his other hand against her chin and pressed his moist lips to her cheek.

Once again, Agnes noticed the pungent sweet scent of him. But whereas before in his office he had thrilled her, now she was sickened by his proximity. She shouted and squirmed for all she was worth. 'Release me, Mr Pitt! Let go at once!'

'Such effort is futile, Mrs Meadowes. There's no one to hear and it will only excite me further. Or is a bruising what you want?' he whispered in her ear.

Agnes continued to writhe and squirm, kicking out viciously at his shins, ignoring the fiery pain in her shoulder in her efforts to be free. Pitt clamped his hand across her mouth and pressed her back towards the corner of the room. Seeing what was happening and that she would soon be trapped, she gave his fingers a hefty bite.

'Bitch! What the devil do you mean?' roared Pitt, releasing

his hold at the sudden pain. 'Now I'll give *you* something you don't like.'

'Get away! Leave me be!' screamed Agnes, as Pitt shoved her against the wall and rammed a leg between her thighs. He was searching in his coat pocket, and extracted a pocket pistol.

'Is this what you want?' Pitt cocked the weapon and brandished it in front of her, before pressing the muzzle to her forehead and pushing her head back so that she was wedged in the corner, arms pinioned by her sides, unable to move more than an inch in any direction. 'Now spare me any more theatricals and I'll finish with you more quickly – isn't that what you want?'

He fumbled with his breeches then lunged forward, pressing against her, his mouth on her neck and his free hand probing among her skirts. Mustering all her remaining strength, Agnes lifted her boot and brought her heel down hard on the top of Pitt's foot. The sudden impact gave her a second's advantage. Pitt withdrew an inch or two. Agnes wrenched her arms free and gave his shoulders an almighty shove. He lurched backwards, tripped over Drake's prostrate corpse and fell sprawling on top of it. The pistol was sent flying into the sooty fireplace. Agnes did not bother to recover it – she dodged past Pitt and bolted for the door. She was nearly through, but he clambered after her on his hands and knees and grabbed hold of her skirt. 'Now, my lovely, before you run off, think of this. If you leave, the wine-cooler will be unguarded and any rogue might come and steal it. Then it might be melted down, and what would Blanchard have? No wine-cooler – no money, either.'

'That isn't your way,' said Agnes, hesitating.

'As I told you before, on occasion my ways alter.'

Somewhere in the distance Agnes heard a dog bark and the sound of a barge man shouting. A strange parade of thoughts ran though her mind. If only she were outside, on the river, anywhere but trapped in here with Pitt. Without the wine-cooler, Blanchards would be ruined. And what of Peter – how would she care for him? But then she concentrated her attention on Pitt, sprawled on the floor but still deadly. She would not give in. There was no longer any doubt in her mind what she should do. Her face was as pale as milk as she drew back her leg as he clutched her skirt. Then with all her might she planted a firm kick on the side of his head. There was a thump, then a howl as he released her to clutch at his temple. Agnes, feeling a swell of pride, turned and scrambled for the door.

She careered headlong into a figure coming in the opposite direction.

'Mrs Meadowes, what is it? Where are you going? Didn't we agree you would await my return?'

'Thomas,' cried Agnes wildly, 'do not go in there under any circumstance. Forget the wine-cooler. It is of no consequence. Pitt is there. He is armed with a pistol and in a great temper and will not be afraid to use it.'

'Mrs Meadowes, calm yourself, please,' said Thomas, holding her shoulders. She felt his gaze lingering on her face; she could feel a bruise burning on her neck and an impressed circle pulsing in the centre of her forehead, where Pitt had thrust the pistol at her. 'Wait there,' he said.

'Didn't you hear what I said?' shouted Agnes. 'He has a pistol, he put it to my brow.'

Unmoved, Thomas nodded. 'I have not come unaccompanied, Mrs Meadowes. This morning, prior to our departure, I thought it prudent to notify the authorities. They followed us and were waiting a safe distance away all along. I only went round the corner before I found them. A constable and his two deputies should be more than a match for Mr Pitt, no matter how violent his temper.'

Agnes glanced over his shoulder. Standing in line behind him were two stout fellows holding wooden staves and another leaner man with a pistol in his hand. She recalled Theodore expressly ordering that the authorities should not be apprised of this transaction. Yet Thomas Williams had not been afraid to use his own judgement and defy him. She had never been so glad of insurrection in her life.

'Gentlemen,' called Thomas, 'this way if you please.'

Pitt was on his way out of the back door when the constable and his deputies apprehended him. Realizing there was no escape, he held up his palms in a gesture of mock submission as Agnes and Thomas re-entered the house. 'Very well,' he declared. 'But don't think I am beaten entirely. A certain judge of the King's Bench – a most influential man within the judiciary – happens to be an old acquaintance of mine. I recovered a pocket book of his not long ago; it made most interesting reading. He was so delighted to have it returned, he promised to assist me if I ever fell foul of the law. There's no proof of my involvement in the robbery.'

'There is proof you tried to force yourself upon me,' said Agnes hotly. 'And I shall testify against you.' She paused and shot him a crafty look. 'Unless, that is, you tell me where your carriage has gone.'

'Why do you wish to know that?'

'Because now the thief is dead, you do not need to pay his reward. Your claim to be an innocent intermediary can thus only be credible if you return the gold Mr Blanchard paid.'

At the realization that Agnes had outmanoeuvred him, Marcus Pitt's expression darkened and he scowled. 'You bitch,' he said. 'You're no better than a common whore and a thief.'

'That's no way to address Mrs Meadowes,' said Thomas Williams. Stepping forward, he grabbed hold of the neck of Pitt's shirt and screwed it tight so he had difficulty in breathing. 'Answer her politely. Where is your carriage and Mr Blanchard's gold?'

Pitt coughed and spluttered. His deep-set eyes watered with the discomfort of Thomas's grip. But he spat on the ground and refused to speak.

'So, Mr Pitt, you prefer me to make a statement to the justice, do you?' said Agnes.

Still Pitt said nothing.

Thomas Williams tightened his grip further, until there was a veritable bunch of shirt in his fist and Pitt's face had turned puce.

Eventually, Pitt began flapping his hand up and down, making strange gurgling sounds. Thomas released his hold a little. 'Well?'

'The carriage is in the court at the end of the road,' he stuttered. 'But don't think I'll forget this, Mrs Meadowes.'

Agnes regarded him coolly. 'It strikes me, sir, that unless you tread with care, freedom of memory will be one of the few liberties you have left.'

Chapter Thirty-four

THOMAS AND AGNES TRAVELLED BACK TO FOSTER LANE, TAKING with them the wine-cooler, squatting on the floor like a splendid footbath, the strong box of gold, recovered from Pitt's carriage, and one of the constable's deputies as escort. The constable and the other deputy travelled in a separate vehicle to convey Pitt to the roundhouse and Drake's corpse to a certain barber surgeon, who paid good rates to anatomize the bodies of criminals. According to the constable, Drake's decapitation should not make more than a shilling or two's difference to the sum he would fetch.

For much of the way there was silence between Agnes and Thomas. Agnes was rendered speechless by a jumble of disturbing images. Harry Drake's murder had brought Elsie to mind. The girl was now an orphan. Her father had been brutally murdered. Did she know? Who would mind her now? She thought then of the loathsome Pitt, and wondered how she could ever have thought him anything but repellent. What would have happened had Thomas Williams not arrived with the constable and deputies when he did?

Her resentment over the crass comments Thomas had made the previous night now seemed utterly trivial. She wanted to tell him so, and thank him for what he had done and for the great change he had effected in her. But the deputy constable's presence hampered her; she could not bring herself to raise a subject so personal in front of a stranger. She would wait for a more opportune time.

She regarded the wine-cooler cautiously. She had seen drawings, but this was the first time she had actually set eyes on the piece. She was awestruck by its sheer scale and opulence. Every inch of its surface was rippled with lively ornament – with mermaids reaching out to smooth their hair; dolphins exploding from the waves, shell-wielding tritons astride them; and a great semi-naked figure of Neptune, drawn by a pair of large-eyed, nostril-flaring horses. Agnes pictured the wine-cooler in use at a grand banquet, filled with wine and ice, resplendent on Sir Bartholomew Grey's sideboard. And unlike the magnificent tables of food I create, she thought ruefully, this will not be demolished in a matter of hours. Thieves permitting, it will endure for generations.

She wondered briefly whether or not the marks on it had been transposed from another piece to avoid duty. But amid the riotous decorations, Agnes could discern no sign of any marks. She wanted to ask Thomas where they were, and if he would examine them to determine whether or not they had been tampered with in some way. But here too she was blocked by the presence of a deputy constable in the carriage. Any request of this kind would imply that Blanchards had been involved in illegal practices. Thus for most of the journey Agnes remained silent, pondering the magnificent wine-cooler and dreaming up new plans of which she had never thought herself capable.

When they were nearly back in Cheapside, Agnes cleared her throat and asked Thomas to halt the carriage and set her down. There was a new softness to the timbre of her voice when she explained that she had an urgent commission she wanted to perform before returning to the kitchen.

'What is it? Where are you going?' he replied, astonished.

'I intend to call in at Bruton Street, the home of Lord

Carew. Mrs Tooley told me that Rose Francis used to work there before she came to Blanchards',' said Agnes, aching to be gone now her mind was set.

Thomas looked perplexed. 'But why worry now the wine-cooler is recovered? Whatever Rose's involvement was, it is irrelevant now.'

Agnes was disappointed to hear Thomas echo sentiments that Theodore had expressed. She had expected more of him. 'The wine-cooler is recovered, but three people have been murdered,' she said with a crusading gleam in her eye. 'And we are no closer to knowing by whose hand. I, for one, won't rest until I know who the murderer was.'

Thomas regarded her sternly. 'But that is a matter for Justice Cordingly.'

Agnes turned then to the deputy constable, who was sitting slumped in the corner, plainly agog with interest at the dispute unfolding before him. 'Sir,' she said, 'do you suppose it likely the justice will ever discover who brought about the deaths of an apprentice, a kitchen maid and a thief?'

The deputy, a portly fellow with a broad florid face, shook his head without a trace of hesitation. 'No, ma'am. In my experience, most murderers who are apprehended are caught by someone connected to the victim what makes an effort to trace him. The justice has too many other matters to occupy him. And rich corpses tend to make more racket than poor 'uns, if you take my meaning.'

Agnes turned back to Thomas. 'I recall you once saying we should all occasionally involve ourselves in matters outside our immediate concerns, Mr Williams. I have never done so till now, always believing I was better equipped to manage my own affairs than anyone else. But today, without your assistance, goodness knows what might have happened to me. I thank you heartily for your aid, and for revealing my earlier deficiency. Be in no doubt that from hereon I intend to rectify it. And I shall start by trying to bring the murderer to justice.'

Agnes had expected Thomas to be mollified by this recognition of her indebtedness and the error of her ways. She was mystified, therefore, that he appeared quite unmoved. On the contrary, her gratitude seemed only to cause him further vexation.

'But what makes you believe Lord Carew has anything to do with all of this?' he said, frowning.

'I don't know precisely,' said Agnes. 'Intuition, perhaps. But it strikes me that none of us in the household knows much about Rose's background. I should have asked her more about herself, but I never did.'

'Even so, after all that has happened this morning, now is hardly the time to pay a gentleman such as him a visit,' countered Thomas curtly.

'It is my only chance. Now the wine-cooler is recovered, I will have no excuse to escape the kitchen.'

'Then let me go in your stead.'

'No,' said Agnes, the warm glow of zeal colouring her complexion. 'This is something I should do myself. You were little acquainted with her; it will be easier for me to uncover her past.'

Williams shot her a glance. 'Forgive me for mentioning it, Mrs Meadowes, but what I meant was you are scarcely in a condition to make social calls.'

Agnes realized that this observation was directed at her appearance, of which she was, as usual, entirely oblivious. She peered down at her distorted reflection in the curved bowl of the wine-cooler, and seeing the smuts of soot on her cheek, wet her finger with her tongue and attempted to clean herself. Then she rearranged her hair, pushing a few stray tendrils back into her bonnet. Finally she brushed away the sooty stains from her sleeves as best she could. She was far from pristine, but under the circumstances it was better than nothing.

'Have you money?' said Thomas.

'Enough for a hackney there and back.'

'Then if there's no way I can persuade you otherwise, I suppose I'll have to let you go.' He looked away with an odd expression on his face.

Chapter Thirty-five

HALF AN HOUR LATER, AGNES ARRIVED AT BRUTON STREET, A fashionable thoroughfare of wide houses a world apart from the dismal landscape she had recently visited. Lord Carew resided in the second mansion in the row, a gracious residence five storeys tall, with draped and valanced sash windows on either side of a grand columned entrance. Agnes's hackney drew up at the front of the house, and she spent some moments gazing at it in awe. But then, remembering Thomas's criticism of her appearance, she decided against presenting herself at the front door. Instead she instructed her driver to go round to the mews at the rear, and promised him a shilling if he waited while she made her way to the servants' entrance.

'Looking for summat?' said a plump curly-haired scullery maid who was emptying a bucket of slops into the gutter.

'The house of Lord Carew.'

She jerked her head at an open door set back through a yard. 'Then look no further. You have found the place.'

'Are you employed here?' said Agnes.

'I am,' answered the girl curtly. She looked Agnes over from head to toe. 'But I can tell you straight, we don't give out food to those that come begging.'

'I'm not a beggar,' said Agnes, bristling. 'If I look a little dishevelled, it's only because I've come straight from the Newark coach.' She was surprised at how glibly this lie slipped out.

'Have you, indeed?' replied the girl warily. 'Then what brings you here, may I ask?'

'I seek news of a cousin of mine, who I have reason to believe works here,' Agnes continued untruthfully, her former self forgotten.

'And who might that be?'

'Rose Francis.'

The maid's face relaxed a smidgeon. 'Forgive me, ma'am, if I appeared unfriendly. I meant no harm. 'Twas only my manner. 'Tis true those coaches can turn the best laundered dress into a rag in a few hours.'

'So do you know my cousin?'

'No, but her name is familiar. She quit this house some while ago. I took her place after she'd gone. If it's recent news of her you want, you'll find none here.'

'But perhaps someone who knew her might know where she has gone,' pressed Agnes.

The maidservant shrugged. 'You'd best speak to one of the upper servants. They might know. Come in and I'll see if they've a moment to spare.'

Agnes followed the girl into a kitchen that was four times the size of her own in Foster Lane. An entire wall was given over to the vast fire and ovens, another to dressers, cupboards and shelves. A parade of copper pans and moulds and baskets of every shape and form was suspended from a line of meat hooks strung out upon a wooden beam. Upon a table twelve feet long were set out a bowl of dried fruit, a basket of eggs, a pat of butter, a basin of flour and a half chopped cone of sugar. At one end, a woman stirred a vast basin of ingredients. She was around fifty years of age, stoutly built. Her complexion was pink, and smooth as a sugared almond, her features small and fleshy. She wore her dark hair caught in a plump bun. Two stains the size of apples beneath her armpits bore testimony to the heat of the kitchen and her present exertions.

'Mrs Lugg,' said the scullery maid, raising her voice above the hubbub of half a dozen maids and pot boys, 'I found this lady outside; she wants a word.'

'Does she think I've nowt better to do than prattle to whomsoever comes calling?' replied the woman, sniffing bad temperedly and continuing to jiggle the spoon vigorously in her bowl.

'I'll tell her to go then, shall I?' said the girl uncertainly.

'Should have done so in the first place,' snapped Mrs Lugg. 'Those what have time to waste nattering in the street generally find they're up betimes to catch up on the work they ain't finished.'

'That will be a sizeable cake when you've done,' said Agnes, stepping hastily forward and peering in the basin.

'Reckon you know something about cooking, do you?' said Mrs Lugg, regarding Agnes whilst wiping a drip from her nose with the back of her hand.

'In a manner of speaking, yes,' said Agnes. 'Only I reckon from the proportions of your basin the household I'm used to is not half as sizeable as yours. We've only three upstairs and fewer than ten below.'

'Well, there's more than twice that in this establishment,' said Mrs Lugg. 'So you'll comprehend why I've no time for chit chat. What brings you here? Ain't no good searching for employ without a character, I'll tell you that straight off. And I'd advise you to pay a visit to the bath house before you come presenting yourself to a respectable place like this.'

'It ain't employ she's after,' broke in the scullery maid. 'It's news of one what used to work here – her cousin, she says. She's all messed up from the coach.'

'Oh. A cousin? And who might that be?' said Mrs Lugg, glancing up.

'Her name is Rose Francis,' said Agnes.

Mrs Lugg set down her spoon, made fists and placed them knuckle-down upon her hips. 'Rose Francis!' She nodded as though she should have guessed. 'Sharp so-and-so, wasn't she?'

Agnes nodded. 'On occasion, though she was not all bad, I think.'

‘’Tis a while since I heard her name mentioned. After the way she behaved, ’tis a wonder she’s the nerve to own to having anything to do with us here . . .’

‘Who in heaven’s name is this person?’ said a clear, somewhat shrill voice.

Everyone from the pot boy to the cook fell silent.

‘Mrs Moore!’ said Mrs Lugg, looking as guilty as if she’d been caught with a finger in the treacle. ‘I was just about to send a maid in search of you, ma’am. There’s a visitor come. She wants a word.’

The newcomer was a woman considerably younger than Mrs Lugg, slender as a lily and infinitely more regal in bearing. Her dress was of fine-quality wool, dyed an attractive shade of pale blue and buttoned high about her neck. Her cap and collar were of fine lawn, freshly laundered and pristine. Her features were strong and striking, a straight nose, well-chiselled lips, grey eyes. A large bunch of keys tied about her waist dangled in the folds of her skirts. This, Agnes supposed, must be Lord Carew’s housekeeper.

‘Oh, and why’s that?’ said Mrs Moore, looking Agnes briefly up and down. ‘The kitchen is not a place for visitors – especially not those of disreputable appearance. Go away, please, this instant. There’s no takings to be had here.’

‘’Tis news of Rose Francis she’s after. Says she’s her cousin,’ interposed the scullery maid.

Ridges of surprise erupted suddenly on Mrs Moore’s smooth brow. She scrutinized Agnes more searchingly and then looked around the kitchen at the other servants, who though busily engaged were surreptitiously riveted by this exchange.

‘It’s Rose you’re interested in, is it?’

Agnes nodded.

‘And your name is?’

‘Mrs Agnes Meadowes.’

‘In that case, Mrs Meadowes, you’d best come with me.’

Mrs Moore led Agnes down a labyrinth of back corridors to her parlour. No sooner had she crossed the threshold and closed the door behind her than she rounded on Agnes with a look of ominous determination. 'And now, Mrs Meadowes, may I enquire as to your real reason for coming to Bruton Street?'

'I believe my cousin once worked in this household,' answered Agnes guardedly.

Mrs Moore compressed her lips and shot Agnes a withering glare. 'You are correct in that respect. But why should it concern you? I may say your assertion that she's your cousin cuts no ice with me.'

'What makes you say that?'

'Because Rose has no family – that was how we were persuaded to take her in. But that is by the by. I ask again, what is your interest in her?'

Agnes wavered, glancing about the room. The only adornment on the walls was a series of five silhouettes in oval frames hung on either side of the chimney – two were of men, two of ladies, one of a child. Was this Mrs Moore's family, Agnes wondered? Or was Mrs Moore as alone in the world as Mrs Tooley? Will I become someone hard and intractable like this, or fragile and fussy like Mrs Tooley, with nothing to show for my life save a few ornaments and years of service? But no, for at least I have Peter. Then, seeing suddenly that unless she spoke firmly she would get nowhere, Agnes said, 'To tell the truth, Rose worked under me when she left you. I am the cook at a house in Foster Lane where she took up her position. She disappeared a week ago without explanation. We subsequently found a letter that showed she had an assignation with a lover with whom she intended to run off. I hoped perhaps someone here might have had news of her that mentioned his name and would help trace her.'

Mrs Moore regarded Agnes unblinkingly. 'Rose Francis left this house a year ago. We've heard nothing since. That is all I can tell you.'

Agnes had avoided mentioning the full catalogue of events on purpose, to avoid causing unnecessary distraction and upset. But with Mrs Moore being so unforthcoming, she found it hard to fathom what else she should ask without mentioning them. Had she once been as awkward to converse with as this? No wonder, if she had, that Rose had never confided in her. Even now, her attempts at conversation sounded ungainly.

Suddenly the events of the day took their toll. Agnes felt exhausted; all the determined vigour that had brought her here seemed to have seeped away. She wished for a moment that she had heeded Thomas Williams and not come, or that she had considered more carefully how to approach the household before calling. If only she had sent word beforehand advising of her interest and the reason for it, Mrs Moore might have greeted her more openly.

But just as she was poised to rise and take her leave, Agnes reminded herself of why she had acted so precipitously. The wine-cooler was recovered. On her return, she would be expected to resume her usual duties; it might be days before she had the chance to come again. She had to discover all she could now, even if it meant revealing more than she would have liked.

Mustering all her flagging energy, Agnes drew a deep breath. 'Let me explain more plainly what I meant to convey. The same day Rose left, a valuable wine-cooler was stolen and an apprentice was murdered. A few days later, Rose herself was discovered dead. My employer, Mr Blanchard, will not rest until he knows the exact circumstances of the robbery and the deaths. He believes that someone inside the house may have been involved, and that perhaps Rose was somehow embroiled. Were there any signs of dishonesty when she was with you?'

Agnes had noticed Mrs Moore start slightly at her mention of murder; but no sooner had she finished speaking than the housekeeper's stony manner returned. 'Do you ask these questions with your employer's authority?'

Agnes nodded. 'Both Mr Blanchard and Justice Cordingly have sought my assistance.'

'I see,' Mrs Moore conceded. 'Then I suppose that does alter things.'

There followed a long, long silence while Mrs Moore, paler but no more friendly, indicated that Agnes should sit down.

Agnes waited patiently while Mrs Moore toyed with a narrow silver band on her finger. She did not reply to Agnes's question. Instead she said slowly, 'I suppose I ought not to be surprised at her demise.'

'Why is that, Mrs Moore?'

The housekeeper did not answer directly, seeming instead to wander off on her own train of thought. 'Rose Francis worked here for less than a year,' she declared at length. 'I expended considerable energies on teaching her how to carry out her duties. When she left without so much as a day's notice I felt let down – deceived, even. But then, judging by your account, she made a habit of mysterious departures.'

Agnes let this pass, though the bitterness in Mrs Moore's tone did not escape her. 'Under what circumstances did she come to you?'

'She applied for a post in writing. As I recall, the letter declared she had been raised in the north of England, but sought a position in a London establishment, there being no permanent vacancies in the vicinity and all her family having recently perished in an outbreak of cholera. Her mother had taught her the rudiments of domestic economy. She had been to school until the age of thirteen, could sew neatly and read and write fluently. Her letter was well penned – her hand was one of the neatest of any servant I've ever known; it could have passed for that of a lady. As I later had reason to believe it did. For you asked me if she was dishonest. That was her first transgression.'

'What makes you say so?' said Agnes with interest.

'Her letter enclosed a character. It purported to be written by the housekeeper of a north-country mansion. She claimed she had worked there during the summer months when the house was in use. I made attempts to contact this person but received no response. After some weeks I contacted the local rector. From him I learned that not only had the housekeeper never written the character, but such a mansion never existed. But he did reveal that there was a girl by the name of Rose Francis in the vicinity. She was the daughter of the local schoolmaster. Both parents had died from cholera while her brother was abroad. She had thus been forced to leave her home and seek employ elsewhere. As far as the rector knew, she had cut herself off entirely from all previous acquaintances. Nobody had heard where she had gone. But since work was hard to come by in that part of the country, it was assumed she had gone to London.'

Agnes was struck by a strange thought. She had never dreamed she and Rose had anything in common. Yet now she saw similarities in their sad pasts she had never recognized. Rose had been forced, as she had, to leave the genteel life into which she was born and enter service. But where Agnes had resigned herself to her fate, Rose, evidently, had not.

Agnes studied Mrs Moore thoughtfully. Her eyes appeared fixed on some distant spot. Beneath their coolness, Agnes detected a gleam of wistfulness. Perhaps beneath the housekeeper's implacable exterior lay someone as torn as Agnes herself.

'What impressions did you form of Rose when she first began working here?' said Agnes.

Mrs Moore gave a brief smile. 'She was clever, quick, winsome when she desired to be, but, as I soon discovered, lacking in constancy.'

'In what way?'

Mrs Moore sniffed. 'No sooner had she grown accustomed to the duties expected of her than she began to behave as if she deserved something better. She turned into a troublemaker, resentful of being ordered about, ignoring household rules and inciting others to act as wilfully as she did. And whenever I reprimanded her or punished her, she was without remorse or contrition.'

'What kinds of rules did she transgress?'

'She went out at night time without permission. She was bold, and caused ructions among the male staff. She was often negligent of her duties, and ill tempered with her superiors when reprimanded. Need I continue?'

'No,' said Agnes, thinking all this sounded remarkably familiar. 'But can you fathom why, if she wished to improve herself, Rose took another post as a kitchen maid in a smaller establishment than this? Surely that was a backward step.'

Mrs Moore shrugged her shoulders. 'That is why I am astonished to learn where she went. She left here without giving any notice or a word to any of us as to where she was going. Nor did she ask for a written character. To tell the truth, I would not have written a kind one. I was on the brink of dismissing her anyway. I always assumed she had gone to get married or take up a more lucrative position. The first news I've heard of her since she left is from you.'

Agnes sighed. Rose had plainly forged the character Mrs Tooley had shown her, just as she had done to secure the post with Lord Carew. But something must have caused her to leave Lord Carew's household so precipitously.

'You mentioned you thought she might have run off to get married. Had she a sweetheart that you knew of?'

Mrs Moore sat up stiffly. 'Servants are forbidden alliances in this household, as in most other respectable establishments of my acquaintance.'

'I did not wish to cast aspersions upon the propriety of this household,' said Agnes soothingly. 'But those determined to pursue affairs of the heart invariably find ways to avoid apprehension. Servants *do* marry; and as you have already stated, Rose was flirtatious of disposition.'

Mrs Moore regarded her hands, stony-faced. 'I did not press her on the matter, but there may have been someone.'

'Did she mention a name?'

'No, but when she arrived she wore a silver band on her engagement finger. I asked about it when I first saw her. Naturally, I wouldn't have taken her if I knew she was engaged. But she said the ring had been left to her by her mother.' She paused. 'A day or two before she left, one of the maids found her sobbing on her bed. And when she asked what the matter was, Rose threw something at her and stormed from the room. The other maid retrieved the missile – it was a silver ring – from under the bed. She left it for Rose on the night table by her bed. After Rose had gone, the same ring was found hidden under the mattress.'

'Are you certain it was hidden? Might it have been mislaid inadvertently?'

'I suppose so. But in any case, she never asked for it to be sent to her.'

'Where is the ring now?'

'I have it here.' She slipped the silver band off her finger and passed it to Agnes. 'I looked, but there is no inscription on it.'

'Peculiar that she should leave it,' said Agnes, examining the inside of the ring. There were five marks instead of the four she expected, and only two – the leopard's head and lion *passant* – did she recognize.

'Would you consent to lend me this for a day or two?' said Agnes, wondering what the marks signified.

'By all means, if you think it will help you,' said Mrs Moore. 'I only wore it to keep it safe. I always expected that one day she would send some communication and then I would return it.'

Agnes cradled the ring carefully in her palm, then threaded it onto her ring finger. Her hands were larger than Rose's and Mrs Moore's. As she tried to push it on, the ring bit painfully into her flesh; nevertheless she persisted and eased it over her knuckle.

'Now I think on it, she had another unusual possession – a small silver box – a vinaigrette, I believe it was, heart-shaped, prettily engraved with flowers and leaves,' said Mrs Moore.

Agnes recalled the box Elsie had found in Rose's pocket. 'Did she ever say where it came from?'

'I did ask her where she got it,' conceded Mrs Moore. 'She said it was a parting gift from the mansion where she had worked before coming here, but I suspected she wasn't telling the truth. I had yet to learn that the character she had written was a fabrication, or anything of her probable history. But since the box was not the sort of thing most servants possess, I felt it my duty to take it to Lord Carew and ask if it belonged to him or one of his guests.' Two crimson stains had appeared suddenly in Mrs Moore's pale cheeks. Agnes was reminded of Mrs Tooley's discomfiture when she had interviewed Rose over the letter. Plainly Rose did not take kindly to being questioned over private matters.

Agnes shifted in her seat. 'And what did he say when he saw it?'

'He looked long and hard at it, and declared that though the work was extremely fine, he didn't believe he had seen it before, nor to his knowledge had any of his friends lost it. He surmised that far from being what she said – a gift from her previous employer – the box might be a love token and that I should give the girl a talking to over consorting with the opposite sex.'

'I see,' said Agnes thoughtfully. 'And how long after this did you discover the matter of the forged character?'

'A month or two – it was partly seeing the box and sensing there was something unusual about it that made me pursue the matter.'

'And having found that Rose's character was forged, did you raise the matter again with Lord Carew?'

'I would have done so, naturally, but he was absent at the time – visiting his country seat in the North, as I recall. By the time he had returned, she had gone.'

Chapter Thirty-six

ON RETURNING TO FOSTER LANE, AGNES SCARCELY HAD TIME TO change her dress and wash her face before she was thrown into the thick of it. Mr Matthews was complaining loudly about a wine label missing from the dining room, while instructing John on the art of cleaning two claret jugs by mixing a confetti of brown paper with soap, warm water and a little pearl ash. 'Mr Blanchard will expect you at one in the library,' he called out when he caught sight of Agnes passing his pantry door.

'What wine label has been lost?' said Agnes, recalling the trophy retrieved from Drake's pocket and now lying in her own.

'Shrub wine,' replied John. 'Missing since yesterday. You seen it on your travels?'

'I'll keep a look out,' she replied. Trying not to blush, she hurried to the kitchen.

Agnes supposed that Theodore had summoned her in order to thank her for recovering the wine-cooler and his money. To be called upstairs was a remarkable event, but she took it as a measure of his pleasure. Retrieving both the gold and wine-cooler was a better result than he could possibly have hoped for. Undoubtedly, the future of Blanchards would now be secure. But an appointment in half an hour scarcely allowed her time to peruse the slate upon which Mrs Tooley had written the dinner menu and discover what had still to be done, let alone make a start on it. 'Very well, Mr Matthews,' she said, while glancing over what Mrs Tooley had written:

> <u>First course</u>: *leek potage, broiled eels, small salad, Scotch scallops*
> <u>Second course</u>: *mutton with haricots, calf's liver stew, cardoons, dish of jelly*
> <u>Dessert</u>: *flummery, brandied apricots, Spanish biscuits*

Agnes surveyed the table, the range and the larder. Mrs Tooley appeared to have done nothing save put the haricots to soak and make the jelly. According to Philip, she was presently occupied with checking the linen with the laundry maid who came once a week. Doris was in the scullery, scouring the tray on which the breakfast rolls had been baked with soda and water. The dresser and kitchen table had been scrubbed and the floor mopped, but she had yet to make a start on the vegetables. Agnes felt none of her usual enthusiasm for her work. Her limbs were leaden; her feet heavy in her boots; her neck had been jarred by Pitt and there was a sharp pain if she moved her head a certain way.

Wearily, she instructed Doris to wash the leeks, peel the potatoes and string the cardoons. Turning her attentions to the mutton, she unlocked the meat safe, unwrapped the joint from its bloody muslin and set it in her copper stew pot, adding onion, carrot, celery, bay and thyme, half a dozen peppercorns and the soaked beans. Then she filled the pot with water and put it on a low hook over the hottest part of the fire to come swiftly to the simmer.

Her discovery of Drake's decapitated body, Pitt's assault, her visit to Lord Carew's residence, all this distracted her, so that she was vague and restless in her manner, scarcely conscious of what she said to Doris, and when it came to her own duties, unusually maladroit in performing the simplest of tasks. She cut her thumb while she was slicing the onion for the mutton, and it bled so profusely she was forced to wrap a bandage round, which only added to her clumsiness and made her drop a basin of eggs on the floor. Under more usual circumstances, Agnes might have chastised herself for such a waste. But as she mopped up the slimy pool she told herself that half a dozen eggs was a trifling matter, unworthy of a minute's consideration.

Philip stood in the hall trimming the lamps when a heavy-limbed Agnes presented herself for her appointment with Mr Blanchard. 'I see you are returned from your morning's adventures. And I gather the wine-cooler was recovered,' he said amiably.

'Indeed it was,' said Agnes. 'And the money, too. I presume that is why the master has asked me to see him in the library.'

'Has he? Then you'll have to wait. He ain't come yet.'

Agnes entered the library. Dark-red velvet curtains fringed with gold tassels were pulled back to reveal the misty winter street beyond. The panes were fogged with moisture, but through them she could dimly discern icicles strung along the top of the window-frame, thawing and dripping noisily onto the outer sill. Beyond was the usual traffic of the street: an urchin wheeling a barrow of cabbages; an ox cart laden with barrels of water; a cart full of cackling poultry, trussed up for market; a coach and four, the horses' heads rearing in the bitter wind, the coachman so swaddled by scarf, hat and coat that only the tip of his nose and brows were visible.

Agnes stood for a moment, surveying the brown streaks left by wheels in the muddy snow; then, shivering suddenly, she moved towards the fire. She examined the large desk, its leather surface burnished by the countless layers of polish Philip and Nancy applied. She regarded the mahogany book-cases, and the volumes meticulously ranked upon them. She thought about Peter, and wondered whether Theodore would keep his word and pay the twenty-pound reward he had promised. Theodore's money should be set aside for Peter's schooling; she would ask Mrs Sharp if she would keep

Peter on. There was no reason to send him back to Twickenham if he was settled round the corner, where she might see him three or four times a week. Why had she never thought to look for somewhere closer before now?

She put her hand in her pocket and rubbed her thumb over the label recovered from Harry Drake's pocket – apparently the same one lost from this house yesterday. What was its significance? Drake was a well-known thief. Either he had somehow entered the house before meeting his death, or someone had given it to him. But why? Was this the reason he had died? Should she give it to Mr Matthews, or mention it first to Mr Blanchard?

Glancing up, she caught sight of her reflection in the looking glass. Her eyes were dark as walnuts and circled by shadows, her complexion chalk-pale, visible evidence of her recent ordeal. I am no longer the person I once was, she thought. I am treading on unfamiliar ground, yet no longer feel impelled to retreat. My world has become more uncertain and dangerous and complex, but I am a part of it.

Still shivering, she regarded the ornaments upon the mantelpiece. A pair of silver candlesticks embellished with shells reminded her of the wine-cooler. She wished she had found the means to ask Thomas to examine the marks, and confirm whether or not they had been transposed. If they had been, then Theodore must be behind the fraud; but what would his motive be for perpetrating it? She had heard that there was often friction between Theodore and his father, and that Theodore wanted to move the premises west, while Nicholas desired the business to remain as it always had. Was this sufficient reason for Theodore to operate a scheme to cheat his own father?

Agnes had broached this possibility before and dismissed it. Now, when she turned the theory over, it seemed no more probable. She remembered Thomas expressing doubts that such fraud could be perpetrated on such a sizeable object. Now that she had seen the wine-cooler, and appreciated its magnificence, she agreed. In their present straitened circumstances, the Blanchards would want to advertise the commission, not keep it secret. In which case it would be impossible not to pay the duty owed.

But Agnes could not dismiss the matter entirely. Small details were important to her. Thomas had been in no doubt that the marks on the salver *had* been transposed; therefore someone had been profiting. And since Theodore had control of the books and all marked items were listed, it seemed probable he was the guilty party. But if he was culpable of such petty crime, was he also capable of something graver? Suppose Theodore, tired of the small sums gained from duty-dodging, had engineered the theft deliberately, in order to take a share of the reward behind his father's back and thus gain the wherewithal to move the business without his father's approval. It would mean that the theory she had previously dismissed as implausible might be correct, and that Theodore had committed all three murders.

Agnes did not want to believe Theodore to be guilty. Her livelihood and that of all the other servants in the household depended on him; she owed him her loyalty. But then she recalled Thomas's timely defiance of Theodore's order, his summoning of the constable and deputies, without which heaven knew what might have happened. Loyalty was all very fine, she reminded herself, but not if it defied reason.

Soon after this, the door swung open and Theodore, Lydia and Nicholas Blanchard entered, accompanied by Justice Cordingly. Agnes expected smiles and congratulations. But as her eyes switched from one to the other, it was immediately apparent that they had summoned her for another, less happy purpose. Nicholas's face was ominously set, Lydia glowered, Theodore looked uncomfortably at the carpet. Only Justice Cordingly had arranged his features in an expression of neutrality.

Her stomach drawing itself into a knot of apprehension, Agnes bobbed a curtsey, bade them good afternoon and waited. It was Nicholas Blanchard who first addressed her.

'Justice Cordingly desires a word with you. But it wasn't he that sent for you in the first instance, Meadowes. It is I who has a grievance which I wish to convey in person to you,' he growled.

'A *grievance*, sir?' she echoed, unable to prevent a note of incredulity creeping into her voice. Nicholas Blanchard had no reason she could think of to be annoyed with her; she had just saved his family from ruin.

'I have just received word from Lord Carew. He tells me that this very morning you went uninvited to his house and subjected his housekeeper to a rigorous interrogation. The poor woman was so disturbed by your visit she mentioned the matter to him – and he, being curious and concerned as to your purpose, apprised me of the fact. It seems you deliberately duped her into believing you were authorized to act as you did by Justice Cordingly and my son. Do you disagree with my account in any way so far?'

Agnes looked helplessly at Justice Cordingly and Theodore, but their attention was fixed upon Nicholas. 'I did not dupe her, sir,' she quietly replied. 'Mr Blanchard and the justice did ask me to assist, by reporting what I knew and helping with Mr Pitt.'

'One moment,' said Theodore, interrupting. 'You twist the truth, Mrs Meadowes. I gave you no such authority to pursue the matter as you please. Indeed, I recently ordered you to leave the subject of Rose Francis alone. I certainly never would have sanctioned such a visit had I been forewarned of it.'

Agnes looked at Lydia. 'Mrs Blanchard also requested that I should find out what became of Rose.'

'Did you, Lydia?' said Nicholas sharply. 'What was your reason for that?'

'I asked her to search the girl's room,' said Lydia, nodding her head. 'But I certainly never gave her authority to chase across London calling upon whomsoever she chose.'

Nicholas nodded at this further affirmation of his suspicions. 'I have striven to discover a reason for your duplicitous actions, Mrs Meadowes. Lord Carew is a man of considerable influence; if Blanchards' irk him, he has it within his power to ruin our reputation.'

Agnes stood in bewildered silence, unable to believe her ears. The morning's exertions had worn away at her usual circumspection. After all she had endured on this family's behalf, what right had any of them to speak to her in such a tone? 'I would not have called on Lord Carew's housekeeper unless I thought it useful,' she said carefully. 'After all, unless the murderer is captured, what is to prevent such a thing happening again?'

This reply caused Justice Cordingly to regard Agnes with sudden interest, though it did little to appease Nicholas Blanchard. He paced up and down the room, pondering and pretending to examine papers and objects. Then he came to rest directly facing her, his thumbs hooked into the armholes of his waistcoat, his fingers drumming, louring over her like a malevolent colossus. 'I do not comprehend your meaning, Mrs Meadowes. Cordingly tells me the dead man in the chimney was Drake, a notorious housebreaker. Undoubtedly it was he that committed the theft, killed the apprentice boy, and perhaps also killed Rose Francis, who I gather was on her way to some romantic assignation. And Drake was killed no doubt by Mr Pitt or one of his henchmen. In what way, therefore, could such an unauthorized visit have conceivably proved useful?'

'Harry Drake committed the robbery, but I do not believe he killed Noah Prout or Rose. Nor do I think it creditable that Mr Pitt murdered Harry Drake,' said Agnes.

'Have you evidence for this assertion?' said Justice Cordingly, now intruding in a less intimidating manner than Nicholas.

'Yes, sir,' Agnes replied. 'I went down to the cellar yesterday and saw the pistol that was taken from Mr Blanchard's room. Assuming it was Rose Francis who took it, how has it returned here? The only explanation I can fathom is that whoever killed her has been in this house since the robbery – and most likely lives here. Moreover, the apprentice, Rose and Harry Drake were killed in an identical manner. This surely points to the same hand. Therefore it is my belief that Drake was merely a servant in the scheme, not the murderer; the murderer lives among us.'

At this shocking announcement, Justice Cordingly raised an eyebrow and sucked in his cheeks thoughtfully. But Nicholas remained stormy.

'I always thought something of the kind was the case,' said Theodore with a look of satisfaction.

'Be quiet, Theodore,' said Nicholas, glaring brusquely at his son. He swivelled his gaze back to Agnes, thumping his fist on the table. 'You discovered my gun!' he exclaimed, balls of spittle spraying from his agitated mouth. 'Then why on earth did you not say so sooner? Why was *I* not informed of it?'

Inwardly, Agnes quivered with indignation, but outwardly she remained cool. 'I assumed, sir, that Mr Matthews knew it was there and that he would return it to you. It was encrusted with dirt when I saw it. Perhaps even now he is cleaning it for you.'

Nicholas looked apoplectic. Agnes glanced at Justice Cordingly, as though expecting him to defend her. But the justice was still musing, stroking his mutton-chop whiskers as he did so.

'Your silence was foolish, Mrs Meadowes,' blustered Nicholas. 'Common sense seems to have abandoned you. You saw a valuable gun that you knew was missing and said nothing of it. I find that quite incomprehensible. I want no repetition of such misdemeanours, and no more harrying of important personages. Especially not Lord Carew. If you value your position, you will remember that.'

Agnes did not know what to say, but anger now began to cloud her mind like a fog. And in its midst came an image of Pitt's leering face as he wrestled with her, kissed her neck, rummaged among her skirts and pressed the muzzle of his pistol to her brow. Was she not due at least a word of thanks for what she had endured? Were her opinions so worthless as to be ignored? She opened her mouth to say as much, but just then, as if he had read her thoughts, Theodore rose and interceded on her behalf.

'Enough, Father! We should be grateful to Mrs Meadowes for recovering the money as well as the wine-cooler. Undoubtedly she has saved us from ruin.'

'Ruin of your making,' muttered Nicholas.

Theodore ignored him. Turning to Agnes, he added in a more sympathetic tone, 'I regret our having to speak to you like this, Mrs Meadowes. Your actions were certainly misjudged. But now we must all let this matter rest. I will endeavour to smooth things with Lord Carew – perhaps I might invite him to visit our showroom and he will offer us a further commission and this business will have a happy conclusion.' With this, Theodore gave a brief laugh and began rummaging in his pocket. He extracted a sheaf of folded banknotes and peeled one from the pile. 'Here is the reward I promised, Mrs Meadowes. And as a further sign of our gratitude you may have tomorrow off. I understand you requested it of my wife. All things considered, apart from your last error, you have acquitted yourself satisfactorily.'

Agnes's temper subsided as rapidly as it had arisen. She took the money with murmured thanks, noticing that he had given her five pounds instead of the promised twenty guineas. At least tomorrow would be free to see Peter. She examined Theodore intently as she did so. Did the face of a swindler or a cruel murderer lie behind his placatory smile, she wondered, and was jettisoned into further doubt.

Nicholas glared at his son, as though his mediation were not at all desirable. Wordlessly, he stepped to the other side of the fire and tugged at the bell pull. John entered immediately, which made Agnes suspect he had been listening to the entire exchange outside. In a curt tone, Nicholas ordered him to fetch his cloak and hat and call a carriage, then he shot his son another venomous look. 'Good day, Theodore. I'll leave you in conference with Mrs Meadowes, who appears to have taken over at the helm of our family's business.'

A sudden colouring of Theodore's cheeks showed that he was deeply aggrieved at this public criticism of his actions. He looked fixedly at his father, the veins in his neck pulsating visibly. 'Come, Father, can you deny she has acquitted herself well and deserves our hearty thanks and reward?'

'I cannot say Williams or Riley, alone or even acting together, wouldn't have done as well – and made fewer blunders,' retorted Nicholas.

'I told you before, I suspected that they or one of the servants might have been involved. Someone inside the workshop or this house must have told Pitt the wine-cooler was ready. Mrs Meadowes is only reiterating what I believed all along,' he said in a low, tremulous voice.

'Then why in God's name did you not send a man from the household – Matthews, for instance?'

Theodore looked up and met his father's eye. 'But Father,' he said incredulously, 'Matthews is not what he once was. He is too old to be capable of such an onerous duty. It is all he can do to mount three flights of stairs. Besides, thanks to Mrs Meadowes and Thomas Williams, this situation has been resolved more successfully than any of us could have hoped.'

'That it ended thus owes more to luck than good judgement – or Mrs Meadowes's doubtful skill,' retorted Nicholas. Then he shook his head as though he could not be bothered to argue any more. 'I am going to Whites – I trust I shall find someone there with whom to talk sense.' And with this he stalked out.

'Returning to your earlier conversation,' said Justice Cordingly the moment the door closed behind Nicholas, 'if the gun Rose Francis supposedly stole is in the cellar of this house, where is the proof *she* took it? Might not one of the other servants be guilty?'

Agnes blanched, thinking of her promise to Elsie and wondering how she would parry this question when she was already so confused it was an effort to formulate a coherent response. But then she realized that, with Harry Drake dead, there was no longer any reason to keep Elsie out of it. Rather, with judicious promotion Elsie might gain a position in the household. 'There was a witness to Rose running off,' she replied. 'A most obliging young girl I happened to meet. She saw Rose down by the river close to where her body was found. She saw her being chased by a man and dropping a gun, which she believed the man pursuing her recovered. The pistol I saw in the cellar was ingrained with mud. It seems probable, therefore, that the same man who pursued and killed Rose put it there.'

'And since the same person, we believe, killed the others, it follows that the murderer resides in this house, or has frequent access to it,' said Cordingly, drawing the same inevitable conclusion as Agnes. 'Is the pistol still there?'

'I have not returned to the cellar since.'

'Then let us send someone to retrieve it.' He turned to Theodore and requested that a servant be sent to find the pistol and bring it hither. Theodore nodded, strode to the fireplace and tugged the bell pull. John appeared again almost immediately. 'It seems the weapon that went missing from my father's room is secreted in the basement. Mrs Meadowes saw it there. She will go with you and show you where it is. Be so kind as to bring it here immediately.'

'Very well, sir,' said John, shooting a look in Agnes's direction.

Agnes felt cornered. John would report all this to Mr Matthews and more questions would inevitably follow. She nodded to Theodore and Justice Cordingly and Lydia, and turned to the door. Theodore sank into an armchair, his eyelids drooping with fatigue. Forgetting to make a curtsey, Agnes left the room.

Chapter Thirty-seven

AGNES MADE HER WAY TOWARDS THE BACK STAIRS WITH JOHN trailing close behind. She hurried across the empty hall. Neither Philip nor Mr Matthews were anywhere to be seen, though to judge by the clatter coming from the dining room, one or both were engaged in laying the table.

Glancing through the dimpled panes of the window, Agnes caught a view of the misty street and the profiles of two men standing on the pavement on the opposite side of the street. The glimpse was sufficient for her to recognize Mr Matthews deep in conversation with Thomas Williams. Intrigued, Agnes drew closer to the window. Mr Matthews was turned slightly away; he appeared to be listening intently and was nodding his head, while Thomas, his wiry hair caught in a riband, was speaking. To judge by his gestures and the look of concentration on his face, he was relating a matter of some significance. Most probably, Agnes thought, they were discussing the recovery of the wine-cooler. Mr Matthews always liked to be well informed of events concerning the household. Or perhaps Thomas was asking Mr Matthews to convey a message to her.

'When you're ready,' said John impatiently.

'Isn't that Mr Matthews outside, with Mr Williams?' said Agnes, still staring out at the street.

'What?' said John. 'Where?' He strode over and peered suspiciously through the glass.

Just then a wagon drawn by a pair of oxen and laden with sacks of coal trundled ponderously by, temporarily obscuring her view. The driver whipped them along, but his cracking leather and discordant shout wrought little change in pace. The animals tossed their heads against their wooden yokes, chains rattling, bellowing clouds of breath into the cold winter afternoon. By the time the vehicle had passed, the two figures had gone.

'I see nothing,' said John firmly. 'Now shall we get on?'

They descended to the basement and found no sign of Mr Matthews in the pantry, though a dish of chalk and camphor mixed together to make tooth powder indicated he could not be far away. He came in a minute later. 'There you are, sir,' said John.

'Why, where else might I have been?' replied Mr Matthews sharply.

'Mrs Meadowes fancied she saw you in the road with Mr Williams.'

'Nonsense,' said Mr Matthews crossly, picking up his pestle then dropping it so that the fine white dusty powder sprayed onto the table.

Lowering her eyes, Agnes noticed that the back of his white stockings were splashed with mud. He is lying, she thought, but why?

John nodded. 'I told her the very same. And now, sir, may I trouble you for the key to the cellar.'

Mr Matthews set his lips firm. 'Oh, and what for?'

'Mrs Meadowes believes she saw Mr Blanchard's pistol hidden there. She has said as much to Mr Blanchard and Justice Cordingly and now they both wish to see it,' said John, interchanging a meaningful look with his master.

'Saw the pistol down there, did you? When was that?' said Mr Matthews, turning his watchful gaze on Agnes.

'The other day, sir. When I came to find you – I chanced to see it.'

'Then why did you not say so at the time?'

'I thought you must already know it was there,' said Agnes, arranging her features to suggest chagrin and deference.

''Course you did,' muttered John.

'I hope that was all you saw,' said Mr Matthews darkly, his eyes flashing from her to John.'

'Yes, sir. I would never pry.'

'Good,' said Mr Matthews. 'You're a fine cook, but that don't mean I want ructions below stairs. Now *where* exactly did you see this gun?'

'There is a niche at the foot of the stairs. It was lying there wrapped in a cloth.'

Mr Matthews wiped his forefinger through the gauzy dust on his table. Then he paused and turned to his footman. 'Hmm,' he said, furrowing his brow. 'Very well, John, I shall accompany her myself. If you would be so kind as to put this powder into this silver box. Leave it here and I'll take it up to Mr Blanchard's dressing room later.'

And so Mr Matthews lit a lantern and led the way slowly down the stairs to the cellar. Agnes followed close behind, trying to peer over his shoulder for the ledge where she had last spied the pistol. When they reached the bottom, the butler turned round to face her, his light held aloft. 'Now where did you see this weapon?' he demanded with undisguised disbelief.

'It was here, sir.' Agnes pointed to the deep ledge where she had observed it. 'Wrapped in a cloth. I only caught sight of the handle.'

Mr Matthews stretched his lantern towards the recess so that the cobwebs and the flaking whitewash and render were brightly illuminated against the surrounding dark. A lumpy bundle appeared in the flickering glow.

'There!' said Agnes, unable to keep the excitement from her tone.

Mr Matthews reached forward, took hold of the parcel and unwrapped it, letting the cloth fall to the floor. It was encrusted with mud and the barrel was rusted, but it was indeed the missing pistol belonging to Nicholas Blanchard. 'Terrible,' he muttered, 'the damage that water can do. Even with oil and spirit and pumice I doubt I shall ever get this right again.'

Agnes murmured something non-committal, but only half heard him. She was busy examining the cloth in which the weapon had been wrapped. It was a square of chequered muslin, of the variety Mrs Tooley preferred for dusters.

Back in her kitchen, Agnes was so preoccupied by thoughts of who had wrapped the pistol in one of the household dusters, not to mention Thomas's conversation with Mr Matthews and why the butler should have been so coy on account of it, that she failed to notice the haricots and mutton simmering faster than they should. It was only when the sound of spluttering and hissing roused her that she remarked they had nearly cooked dry. Absent-mindedly she added more stock and prodded the meat with a wooden skewer. Finding it still firm, she returned the pot to the heat. There was little time left and much still to prepare, and Doris was dawdling in the scullery, pretending to wipe an iron pot with oil when she might have been doing any one of a dozen more useful tasks. The reason for her tardiness was easy to discern. Philip, wearing a leather apron and with shirt-sleeves rolled up to reveal his muscular arms, was standing at the adjacent table, mixing scrapings of beeswax with turpentine, resin and Indian red to make furniture polish. The pungent smell of this concoction wafting through the kitchen irritated Agnes as much as the sight of Doris moon-eyed beside him.

'Doris,' she called out impatiently, 'would you leave that and come out here this instant. I asked you to wash the leeks, peel the potatoes and string those cardoons, and they're all still as dirty as they were when they left market. As for you, Philip – why do you choose to do that in my scullery when the proper place is the butler's pantry? I can hardly breathe for the stench of it.'

Doris started guiltily. 'I was just about to do 'em now, Mrs Meadowes. Won't take more'n a couple of minutes.'

'If you do them properly it will.'

'Apologies, ma'am,' said Philip good humouredly. 'No offence intended – I was only keeping this peach company.' He winked at Doris, which made her turn as red as a rump of beef.

Agnes sighed with exasperation. It was beyond her to comprehend Philip's appeal. She went to the barrel of eels she had stored in the larder, caught hold of one writhing body firmly just behind the neck, and transported it to the kitchen, where she gave its head a sharp knock on the edge of the table. Usually she performed this operation without feeling squeamish. Today, however, she breathed in uncomfortably as she swiftly cut round the skin of the neck, turned it down a few inches, pulled away the skin, opened the belly and removed the insides and the long fins and bristles running up the back. Although she knew that the eel was dead from the moment its head struck the table, its spasmodic twitching movements disturbed her. The sight of the dark muscular flesh reminded her of Drake's decapitated body. Had he twitched in such a manner? Had Rose done so too, before her body was encased in its muddy grave? Banish such fancies, she told herself crossly. They help no one and will not let you think clearly. She coiled the eel round in a shallow fish plate, poured enough water just to cover it and set it on a hook over the edge of the fire to come slowly to the boil.

'Put the cardoons in a dish with a little red wine, if you will, Doris,' said Agnes, 'and fetch me the livers.' As Agnes looked up she saw Philip with his arm round Doris, gazing down at the upturned moon of her face and beyond it to the swell of her bosom. He was whispering something, then blowing softly downward, much to Doris's delight. Agnes opened her mouth to scold them, but just then Nancy burst in and caught sight of them. 'Gawd sake, Philip,' she screeched. 'Don't you stop at nothing, not even that dog?'

Philip's head jolted up. 'Don't be jealous just 'cos I ain't with you,' he said evenly. 'We had our fun, and it was you what called it a day.'

'That's a lie,' yelled Nancy as Doris, scarlet and, to judge from her swaying, apparently dizzy with passion, glared angrily in her direction and tottered off to the larder.

'It was you going off with Rose that done for us,' said Nancy in a marginally more measured tone.

'Well, Rose ain't here now, is she? An' I'm sure I could find a moment for you.' He advanced towards Nancy and tried to put his arm around her.

'Not bloody likely,' said Nancy, recoiling. 'Now I see what type o' man you is I wouldn't go with you, not even if you begged me.'

'Is that so?' said Philip, releasing her and rubbing his belly. 'Then I reckon that's 'cos you've more'n me to worry over now.'

'My worries ain't none of your affair,' retorted Nancy, her voice turning shriller.

Philip nodded. 'And ain't I glad to know that.'

Just then a shadow appeared in the doorway. 'What on earth is this racket?' said Mrs Tooley, entering the kitchen with a couple of neatly starched pillowslips folded over her arm. 'Enough, Nancy. Go to your work. And Philip – another word out of you and I shall call Mr Matthews.' Then, turning to Agnes, 'I've no notion what started all this, but one thing I do know – my poor head cannot stand it. I feel quite wretched.' Then after a further pause she added, 'Is all in order for dinner?'

'Yes, Mrs Tooley, perfectly so,' Agnes quietly replied, as Doris plonked the bowl of gleaming livers on the table and the dark reek of blood filled her nostrils.

At a quarter past three, the kitchen was filled with the usual influx. John and Philip entered but immediately disappeared into the butler's pantry to put on Valencia waistcoats, change their gloves for clean white ones and brush their coats until the velvet pile stood up like moleskin. Mr Matthews had already decanted a magnum of claret into a pair of crystal jugs. Since he had filled these vessels only three-quarters full – the rest having been carefully sampled to ascertain its condition – his cheeks had a nicely matching garnet glow. With studied care, he transported the jugs to the dining room, stood them on the sideboard ready for pouring, and then proceeded to light the candles with a taper, paying attention not to spill wax onto the damask cloth. 'First course up in five minutes, Mrs Meadowes, if you will,' he ordered on his return.

'As you wish, sir,' said Agnes, frowning with attempted concentration. She added cream and nutmeg and a little lemon juice to the leek potage, but not minding what she was doing, let the soup boil and the mixture curdle. She added half a pint more cream to disguise it, before ladling the mixture into the tureen and covering it with its lid. 'Scrape me some cheese to finish the cardoons, please, Doris,' she said, while she thrust the salamander into the flames.

Usually she would have warmed the Scotch scallops gently, but today the sauce grew hotter than it should and before she knew it the meat had turned grey and was curling at the edges. 'Ready here,' she declared, nonchalantly scooping the unappetising scallops into a serving dish and covering it over before Mrs Tooley came in and saw.

'Salad, Mrs Meadowes?' demanded the housekeeper, marching up a minute later. 'I don't see it here.'

Agnes pointed with her spoon to a dish on the dresser. 'There, ma'am. I'll leave Mr Matthews to dress it at the table, the cruets have already gone up,' she said as she sprinkled Cheshire cheese over the cardoons, took the salamander out of the fire and pressed it down on the cheese to brown it. 'First course ready, Mr Matthews,' she declared, even though she knew perfectly well nothing was quite as it should have been.

In stately process, John took up the tureen of soup, Philip the eels, Mrs Tooley the Scotch scallops and salad. Agnes heard Mr Matthews knock upon the door of the drawing room and distantly announce, 'Dinner is served.' Then, suddenly remembering that the salamander had been left on the cardoons too long, she lifted it and examined the result: the top was charred and hard.

'Just the jelly we're waiting on now, Mrs Tooley,' said Agnes several minutes later when the housekeeper returned to ensure the second course was as it should be; she had covered her mistake with chopped parsley.

'Scallops looked a little overdone,' Mrs Tooley remarked, adjusting her spectacles on her nose. Then, picking up the lid of the cardoons, her hawk eye remarked their deficiencies. 'That's not like you, Mrs Meadowes.'

Agnes flushed, but made no reply. 'A bowl of hot water, if you please, Doris. Shall I unmould it, Mrs Tooley, or will you?'

'You may as well,' said Mrs Tooley, smoothing down her apron with the air of one with more important concerns on her mind. 'I've deliveries to chase. There's a barrel of candles, two pecks of apples and a firkin of soap on my account that the carrier swears he left and I've never seen.'

Quite right, thought Agnes. There are more important things than jelly. And with this, she dipped the copper mould into a basin of water and inverted it onto a plate. By rights the jelly should have emerged shimmering and tremulous, like a miniature castle. Instead, she had failed to warm the mould evenly and part of one side did not slide away as it should have done.

She surveyed the four dishes set ready for serving upstairs, their domed covers gleaming almost as resplendently as Sir Bartholomew Grey's wine-cooler – although these were a fraction of the size and elaboration. She brushed her sleeve across her forehead, wiping away the perspiration, and walked over to the doorway. 'Second course ready to go up, Mr Matthews,' she yelled up the back stairs.

The first thing Agnes did on finding a moment to herself was not put her feet up, as she had intended to do, but open the drawer in the kitchen table and take out the silver box that Elsie had found in Rose Francis's pocket. She tugged the ring off her finger (using a smear of lard to ease it) and compared its marks with those on the box. They were almost the same: lion, leopard's head, the three tiny crosses in a shield, the initials AW in an oval stamped along the inner edge. Only one was different – the letter mark. The box was stamped with a K, while the ring had the letter M. Agnes tried to recall what Thomas had told her. The pair of initials denoted the maker, the lion represented the silver standard, and the leopard's head showed the piece was made in London. Thus, she deduced, the objects were made by the same maker, but in different years.

What confused her, however, was the fifth mark present on both pieces – a shield impressed with three tiny crosses. She frowned; was there another mark Thomas had explained that she had forgotten? She racked her brains, but remained certain he had mentioned only four. Rummaging in her pocket, she extracted the label she had retrieved from Harry Drake's body. She turned it over, searching for the marks to compare them. There they were as she remembered – four in a row – a lion, a leopard's head, a date letter and the initials NB. What then did the fifth mark on Rose's silver signify? Agnes knew that she would have to ask Thomas to explain, but, having taken out the label, she was now preoccupied with what to do about it. She would be wise to return it at the earliest opportunity; if it were discovered in her possession, it would land her in trouble. She ought to give it to Mr Matthews or Mrs Tooley and tell them truthfully where she had found it, but neither alternative seemed safe. If she gave it to Matthews and he or John were somehow embroiled in the murders, he might see her gesture as a threat. If she gave it to Mrs Tooley and told her where it had come from, she would fly into a state and doubtless tell Mr Matthews. It would be better all round, she decided, to return the label quietly, so that no one knew where it had come from.

But at this hour, with both footmen on duty, it was impossible to venture upstairs and not risk being seen. Instead, she resolved to return the label to Mr Matthews's pantry, where silver was often brought for polishing. With luck, Mr Matthews would still be supervising the men upstairs and she could return the label unnoticed.

Agnes made her way to the pantry, knocked on the door, and when there was no reply, peered cautiously in. But it was not empty, as she had hoped. Mr Matthews was sprawled in a chair with his stockinged feet up on the table. The decanter from dinner stood empty on the table next to him, and beside it an empty glass and a couple of letters. Agnes supposed these must have been recently delivered and had yet to be taken upstairs. Mr Matthews was snoring loudly; his mouth had lolled open and a trickle of wine had dribbled down his chin. 'Mr Matthews,' said Agnes softly, 'may I come in?'

There was no reply. Mindful that Mr Matthews was a light sleeper and had been known on occasion to be napping, then start awake and, finding a footman in the midst of some transgression, box his ears, Agnes tiptoed in. She glanced around for somewhere to put the label where it would not be too conspicuous. The silver cupboard was the most obvious place, but Mr Matthews was fastidious about keeping it locked. On further examination, Agnes observed that the drawers beneath the cupboard had no locks. She moved silently over to them and pulled open the top one very slowly, one hand resting on the underside, one on the knob, so as to make as little sound as possible. Despite these precautions, the drawer's contents rattled as they moved. Mr Matthews stirred, making a throaty groaning noise, and shifted his hand from his armrest to his groin. Agnes turned her head and froze, still holding the drawer, afraid to move in case she should disturb him further. But having stirred again, Mr Matthews seemed to settle down into deeper sleep, and his breath came more evenly. Turning back, Agnes remarked that the drawer was crammed with an assortment of butler's bric-a-brac: several horn buttons, a tangle of twine, a lump of beeswax, dried pieces of soap wrapped in wax paper, morsels of chalk, a phial of camphor, a coiled and cracked razor strop, and a razor with a broken handle. It was a perfect place, she judged, to leave the label.

She dropped it in the drawer, burying it beneath the other contents, then pushed the drawer closed, wincing with every creak and rattle within. But Mr Matthews was snoring soundly and never moved. Agnes swivelled round to return to the kitchen. As she skirted the table, her eyes lingered on the post. The top letter was addressed to Mr Theodore Blanchard. On a sudden whim, she pushed it to one side to regard the one beneath. The hand was vaguely familiar, large and clearly formed and black, but it was the name it was addressed to that made her take note. 'Miss Rose Francis,' it said. It came to her in a flash – the hand was the same as on the letter Nancy had stolen; the person with whom Rose had her assignation on the night of her death.

Without considering the consequences, Agnes snatched the letter and hurried out of the pantry. Returning to her kitchen table, she opened the letter carefully, using her sharpest knife to prise the wax away from the paper.

14 January 1750

My dearest sister,

I was never more surprised than when you did not arrive to meet me. I do not comprehend why you did not at least send me a note to explain your change of heart or circumstance. I can only think that perhaps your engagement is mended, though after all the shilly-shallying I confess I have my doubts it will last. I waited for you all day in Southwark, and next morning, since the passage was booked, was obliged to leave. I write this from Dover, where I await a packet to France. A storm has brewed that makes the crossing impossible. If you change your mind and wish to join me you may write and tell me so at the address written at the bottom of this letter. I must take up my duties as schoolmaster immediately. Do not fear that you will find it hard to adapt to our new life. Any life must be preferable to the one of servitude that you have been forced to adopt since our father died. Your talents will certainly be better employed in teaching than drudgery. I am your faithful brother, as ever.

Having read and reread this communication, Agnes sat for some minutes holding the letter in her hand, staring fixedly at the fire. She thought about Rose and how she had misjudged her. How poignant, thought Agnes; she had been escaping romantic entanglement, when I believed that was what propelled her. But to whom had Rose been engaged? Philip? Riley? Some other person of whom she knew nothing?

Agnes took out a page from her drawer. On it she wrote a note addressed to the name at the bottom of the letter – M. Paul Francis, Vieille Pension, Rue Marte, Calais – in which she outlined the sad fate of his sister. When she had finished her eyes were glassy, but she pressed her fingers on her lids to soothe them, sealed the letter and put it in her pocket. She penned a second brief note to Mrs Sharp, telling her that she would come the next day at ten to take Peter out. Then she put on her outdoor clothes and stepped out in search of the post boy, and to call on Thomas Williams to give him the letter for Mrs Sharp.

Chapter Thirty-eight

THOMAS WILLIAMS WAS NOT TO BE FOUND IN THE WORKSHOP. Benjamin Riley was alone, seated at his workbench hunched over a coffee pot. A flickering lantern was suspended on a hook above his head. He looked up at the sound of the door opening. 'Mrs Meadowes,' he said. 'Returned safely from your adventures this morning, I see.'

Agnes scoured the room. 'Thank you, yes, Mr Riley. Forgive me for troubling you. Is Mr Williams about?'

'As you see, he is not.'

She was uneasy at being caught alone with Riley. His manner towards her had been improper at their last encounter and after her tussle with Pitt she had no wish to entangle herself in further difficulties. Furthermore, with the letter from Rose's brother fresh in her thoughts, her earlier suspicions towards him resurfaced. Whether or not Riley had been engaged to Rose, he was almost certainly involved in a duty-dodging fraud. 'Where is he?' she asked casually, her gaze fluttering over the surface of what she presumed must be his table. It was strewn with an assortment of small articles: pill boxes, vinaigrettes, snuff boxes, patch boxes, bonbonnières.

Riley sat up and folded his arms. 'Why do you ask?'

'No particular reason, only I had something to tell him.'

She knew she should say more, or he would grow suspicious – but what? 'I saw Mr Williams earlier today in conversation with Mr Matthews. I thought perhaps he gave him a message for me, concerning our excursion this morning. Only Mr Matthews fell asleep and has told me nothing. But if he is not here, then I will leave you in peace,' she said.

Riley shot her a curious look. 'I doubt Williams gave Matthews a message for you. It was your butler that had business with *him*.'

'Oh. How can you be sure?' she said. She remembered the furtive look on Mr Matthews's face, and his denials. Any hint of subterfuge made her anxious. Perish the thought that Thomas was somehow embroiled.

'He mentioned it on his return. It seems Matthews has a nephew who is due to come of age in a few days' time. He was enquiring what manner of gift he might give him.'

'A nephew?' said Agnes, temporarily disconcerted. But an instant later she recalled the conversation in the cellar, and Mr Matthews's annoyance at being observed in the street. The gift must be for John – the celebration they planned was to mark John's coming of age. Doubtless the gift was a surprise. That was why he was perturbed that Agnes had seen him talking to Thomas, and why he'd denied it.

Riley was now rising. 'Don't let me delay you, Mrs Meadowes. I'll let Williams know you called for him,' he said abruptly. With this, he stalked to the door and opened it.

The realization that Riley wanted to be rid of her as much as she wanted to get away from him gave Agnes a certain courage. Since Thomas was not there and she had braved Riley thus far, why not broach the subject of duty-dodging? 'One more thing before I leave, Mr Riley,' she said with affected nonchalance.

'Yes?'

'There is a salver in the hall of the Blanchards' house.'

'What of it?'

'Did you give it to Rose not long ago, after some repair?'

Riley's cheeks paled. 'What if I did?' he said rudely.

'What repair did you carry out?'

'That is none of your affair.'

'I only ask because Rose was observed not long ago with the salver in her hand. Mr Williams happened to see the same item and was perplexed at some discrepancy with the marks. He explained a certain fraud to me – duty-dodging, he termed it. He also said it was you who takes pieces to assay. Were you and Rose operating such a scheme?'

'Williams!' muttered Riley, running his hand over his chin. 'Naturally it was he who planted the seed in your thoughts.' He paused, then spoke in a lighter tone. 'Have you mentioned these suspicions to anyone else?'

'Not yet.'

Riley nodded. 'It is well you did not. Has it occurred to you that Williams might have misled you? In our profession, duty-dodging is a widespread and trivial offence – hardly the heinous crime he makes it out to be.'

Agnes compressed her mouth. 'Then it would not matter if I were to mention such a "trivial offence" to Mr Blanchard?'

'Do so and I warrant he would tell you to mind your own affairs. And mention it to Mr Nicholas and you will cause a violent ruction between him and his son which will hardly benefit the business, which is already in a dire predicament. Either way, you would risk losing your position. It may be me that alters the marks, but I do so at Theodore's instigation. He is prepared to go to almost any lengths to salvage his business. Even the few pounds saved from duty are worth it in his eyes. I cannot refuse him any more than you could when he sent you unwillingly to the thief-taker.'

'And what was Rose's role in all this?' she pressed.

Riley gave her a bitter half-smile. 'You are very quick to think the worst of her, but let me assure you she had nothing to do with it, save transporting pieces here and returning them on one or two occasions.'

Agnes raised a sceptical brow. 'Why would a kitchen maid be chosen for such a task? Why not one of the menservants? Or Theodore himself, since he comes here every day?'

'As I said, it was only on occasion – mostly Theodore did bring pieces, or we used those from the workshop. It was

I who asked Rose to return something to the house the first time, when we were still friends. I asked her to put back a box without being seen. She was forever bemoaning the drudgery of her work and saying it wasn't what she was used to, and that she relished a challenge. I never told her why it was important she was not observed, but she must have known there was subterfuge of some kind. Not that it bothered her in the least. After that, Theodore employed her too if it suited him.'

'I see,' said Agnes. 'And when you say you were "friends", is what you really mean that you were engaged?'

Riley shot her a calculating look, then smiled more openly. 'No, it wasn't me that was engaged to her. You ask your Mr Williams who it was.'

'What do you mean?' said Agnes, with as much composure as she could muster. 'What does he know?'

Riley smiled maliciously. 'Rose and he were engaged before either came to London,' he said flatly. He glanced at Thomas's desk, and the array of silver items spread upon it, then turned back to face her. Agnes could feel the blood flood her cheeks, though she tried to maintain an air of calm. 'Williams did not serve his apprenticeship at Blanchards'. He learned the trade in Newcastle under his father, Andrew Williams, a master silversmith. He came here as journeyman two years ago. Sir Bartholomew Grey was somehow involved. I do not know in what manner exactly, but he has an estate in those parts.'

'Go on,' said Agnes. She remembered the strange marks on Rose's ring and box. The maker's initials were AW.

'Before he came to London, Williams was friends with Rose's brother; I think he told me they had met in the classroom. Rose's father was a schoolmaster, I gather. Rose was well educated, and Thomas and she became sweethearts while he was still apprenticed in his father's silversmith shop. They became engaged when he became a journeyman and found a post in London. Soon after, Rose arrived in London. She had found employ as a maid. I do not recall where.' He paused and gazed at Agnes for a moment. The gleam of malice had disappeared. Agnes fancied there was a look of pity in his eye, which irked her even more.

'At Lord Carew's,' she said.

Riley nodded. 'She was not used to domestic drudgery. She hated being a maid. I am not entirely certain what happened between her and Williams, except that there must have been a falling-out. All I know is that one day a year ago she appeared next door, and set to buttering me.' He paused and frowned. 'What is it, Mrs Meadowes? Surprised to learn your Mr Williams isn't all you thought him?'

Agnes shrugged. 'Why didn't you tell me this before?' she said tersely.

'You never asked.'

'I spoke to you on the morning of Rose's disappearance.'

Riley snorted. 'All you asked was if there was something between me and her. I don't know how that notion was planted in your head, but I told you the truth. She and I were friendly at one time, but not for long. That was when Williams took against me. She would flaunt her affection for me in front of him. It was deliberate, what she did, as though she wanted him to see. I enjoyed her for a while, but then I met a pretty milliner in Fleet Street who wasn't half so demanding. After that I think she took up with Philip. She was no more discreet with him, let me tell you – but I dare say you already know that. There may have been others, I cannot say. In any case, if anyone deceived you it was Williams for concealing his engagement. But even if he has, there's no cause to blame me on account of it.'

Agnes was rendered speechless. Rose and Thomas – the very thought of them together was insupportable. Her throat burned and her fingernails bit into the skin of her palm. Rose's ring was still on her finger; it felt as if it was branded into her flesh. She wished she could fling it to the ground and trample on it, but would not give Riley the satisfaction of seeing her distress. But if Thomas were here now, she thought, I should fly at him. She battled to compose herself. Why had she blindly assumed that it was *Riley* Rose was after? The answer was plain. She had been lured along the wrong path by

Thomas himself. By hinting that Riley was dishonest and was involved in some secret affair with Rose, he had deliberately deceived her.

Agnes abruptly took her leave. She strode briskly to Sarah Sharp's house and pushed the letter through her door, unable to bear the thought of conversation. On her return to Foster Lane, she stood for several minutes on the pavement at the top of the steps leading down to her kitchen, mastering her self-control before descending.

Her self-possession remained shaken by what Riley had told her, but she had not entirely lost her powers of reason or forgotten her morning's adventures. Was it possible that what Riley said was true? If so, how did this fit with the theft of the wine-cooler and the murders? Thomas's assistance remained an indubitable fact. And Riley was someone she had never trusted – but nevertheless his account seemed too particular in its detail to be a fabrication. So much deceit, so much lying, so much unfamiliar ground. Agnes felt herself adrift, fumbling for the truth. She told herself she owed Thomas a chance to redeem himself. But then, if he had deliberately lied and deceived her – as it seemed he had – would he tell her the truth now?

She would be wise to arm herself with further evidence before confronting him, she concluded. Who else might shed light on this perplexing matter? In the end, just one name presented itself: Sir Bartholomew Grey, the man whom Riley claimed had been involved in bringing Thomas to London, and for whom the wine-cooler had been made. It was only a few hours since Nicholas Blanchard had warned Agnes against further unauthorized forays. But given the present urgent circumstances, this was a fact she chose to ignore.

Sombre but resolute, Agnes descended to the kitchen. She was unable to taste a morsel of her supper, nor did she feel inclined to get the evening meal ready for upstairs. She was quite prepared to leave most of it to Doris and slip out at the earliest opportunity. But as fate would have it, Mr Matthews roused himself from his slumbers when he was summoned upstairs by a bell. He returned to the kitchen some minutes later with particular instructions from Lydia Blanchard. Nicholas had not returned from his earlier excursion and was presumed to be staying at his club. Theodore had gone after him in the hope of appeasing him. Lydia had accepted an invitation to play cards and would sup elsewhere. There would be no upstairs supper, and Agnes had no further duties that night.

Chapter Thirty-nine

BEFORE LEAVING FOR SIR BARTHOLOMEW GREY'S RESIDENCE, Agnes decided to pay some attention to her appearance for once. She retired to her room to don her finest garb: a bodice and skirt of gold-coloured wool that deepened the amber of her eyes, a clean lawn collar that nicely emphasized the curve of her breast. She regarded herself in the looking glass on her dressing chest and saw that although her cheeks were faultlessly dry, her eyes had a fierce gleam in them. No matter what anger I rouse in the Blanchards, I shall get to the root of this, she thought. Even servants are entitled to justice and to know the truth.

She dressed her hair in a tight knot and dipped a forefinger in egg white and vinegar to coil a single fat tress into a ringlet over one shoulder. She bit her lips and pinched her cheeks to banish the unusual pallor from her complexion – something she had not troubled herself to do for many years. Then, so that no one should remark on her finery and question her destination, she swathed herself in her cloak before slipping out into the night.

It was raining softly as she strode to the corner of Cheapside, her head down to shelter from the fine droplets of rain and avoid the puddles that pitted the thoroughfare.

There were no stars, but by the moonlight filtering through the wafting clouds she could see there was still some traffic about. Agnes sheltered in a doorway and waited. A carriage and four trotted past, whipping up a spray of muddy water to either side, then came a hackney – occupied by a pair of passengers – then several more equipages trundled by. Before long, Agnes's boots and the hem of her cloak were drenched and there was still no sign of an empty carriage. Suppressing her frustration, she waited a short time longer, until at last a hackney with no passenger inside came into view. She darted out and hailed the driver, and having climbed into the vehicle, settled back on the cold seat.

The carriage reeked of tobacco smoke and damp. As it jolted and juddered its way towards Cavendish Street, Agnes clutched the door frame and stared through the rain-speckled window into the passing dark. She caught fleeting glimpses of pedestrians muffled against the weather, hurrying into doorways to avoid the spray cast up by vehicles. She saw barefoot beggars cowering in corners, and drunkards sprawled in the gutter, oblivious to the wet. She listened to the distant curses of watermen, and the occasional cries of the watch, and tried not to think of the risk she was running and why Thomas had deceived her.

Presently the carriage lurched its way past the elegant façades of Cavendish Street. Lanterns burned on each side of the entrance to Sir Bartholomew Grey's house, and through the fanlight blazed a large chandelier, heavily swagged with droplets of crystal. The windows to the main rooms on either side of the hall were dark – was this because the curtains were drawn or because there was no one within? She had no means of knowing.

Telling the driver to wait, Agnes stepped out and knocked at the door. A liveried footman wearing a powdered wig answered, bowing and clicking his heels as he bade her a lofty good evening. As she watched him bow, it struck Agnes that his uniform – deep crimson velvet with gold epaulets and shining silver buttons, and without a single bald spot anywhere to be seen – was ten times more splendid than the

Blanchard livery. Despite her best gown, she felt drab by comparison.

'Good evening. I have come to visit Sir Bartholomew Grey,' she said with as much hauteur as she could muster.

The footman puffed his chest and stared. 'Are you expected, ma'am?'

'A matter of urgency has arisen. There was no time to forewarn him.'

He folded his arms and raised his chin. 'Then I doubt he will see you. He is presently occupied at the card table.'

Agnes had come too far to allow herself to be cowed by a spotless velvet suit. 'My good man,' she said, drawing up to her full height, 'the fact that I have no appointment is neither here nor there. Go to your master, and inform him a Mrs Agnes Meadowes desires a moment of his time. She has been sent by Mr Blanchard and Justice Cordingly, on a matter of grave importance concerning his wine-cooler.'

The footman dropped his arms to his sides. He opened his mouth as if to say something, but then, thinking better of it, closed it wordlessly. Bowing again, briskly and more deeply than before, he ushered her in and departed through a double door, without allowing her a glimpse of what lay within.

Agnes strode about the hall, anxiously waiting. The fire was unlit, the stone floor shiny with polish yet inhospitable. How many housemaids had spent hours scrubbing and buffing here until their arms ached, she wondered? A bracket clock on the mantelpiece ticked with agonizing slowness.

Catching sight of her feverish eyes in the large gilt-framed looking-glass, she turned uncomfortably away to regard a row of marble busts of Roman emperors ranged on columns. She began to pace the corridor, unsettled by the curious sensation that ranks of blank alabaster eyes saw through her ladylike posturing and observed her disapprovingly. It was as she span away from them that she caught sight of the wine-cooler. It stood resplendent on a marble-topped commode, flanked by a pair of blazing candelabra.

So Thomas had been here. Perhaps he was here still. She ran her hands fitfully over the sides of the great wine-cooler, her fingers brushing over dolphins and mermaids' tresses, and the smooth musculature of Neptune's arms and the prickle of his trident. She was uncertain whether she hoped or feared that Thomas had gone. She was not yet ready to confront him. She gazed blindly at the waves crashing over exquisite shells that embellished its surface, her mind equally turbulent. Just then, her eye alighted upon the marks set in a line on a flat piece of rim. There was the leopard, the lion, the letters NB for Nicholas Blanchard and P for the year. Had these letters been transposed? She recalled the way Thomas had ascertained the tampering on the salver. Lowering her mouth, she breathed on the shining surface around the marks. It remained perfectly smooth. There was no ridge to indicate that the marks had been tampered with. No doubt Thomas had introduced the whole business of duty-dodging simply to divert her from the truth.

The footman re-emerged. 'Sir Bartholomew will spare you a moment of his time in the saloon,' he proclaimed in a subdued manner. He rang a bell, and a short while later a second footman arrived and carried off her cloak and gloves. Nervously she adjusted her costume, flattening her collar and smoothing her skirt. When she was ready, she nodded. The first footman threw open the double doors and stood to one side, bowing slightly, arm outstretched. 'This way, ma'am,' he said in an undertone. Heart pumping, Agnes entered.

The room was lit by a chandelier twice as large as the one in the hall, and furnished with carved gilt-wood sofas upholstered in a vivid shade of green, and mahogany commodes with marble tops. One wall was punctuated with two long windows draped in gold damask. Opposite was a grand marble fireplace, and suspended above hung a large dark painting of naked women drinking wine and cavorting with swarthy muscular men, some of whom appeared to have goats' legs, and horns on their heads.

Agnes averted her eyes from the painting, which reminded her uncomfortably of her recent encounter with Marcus Pitt, not to mention her injudicious evening spent with Thomas Williams. She was no more than a foot across the carpet when the footman cleared his throat. 'Mrs Agnes Meadowes, sir,' he announced in a ringing tone, before retreating backwards and closing the doors behind him. Agnes froze, overwhelmed suddenly by a flood of panic. She saw the folly of this visit and longed to retreat. But there was no time to do so. Sir Bartholomew Grey had looked up and seen her.

He was seated at a card table that had been drawn into the centre of the room, in front of the blazing fire beneath the disturbing painting. He was stout and florid of complexion, with a bulbous nose, small blue eyes and a slightly receding chin. He was formally attired in a silk jacket of dark purple damask, black velvet breeches and an old-fashioned full-bottomed wig. There were cards and ivory tokens strewn across the table. The chair facing him was vacant, although there was a black lace fan with silver sequins in front of the empty place. On a sofa nearby a book lay open.

Seeing Agnes standing stock still on the carpet, Sir Bartholomew rose and held out his hand. 'Mrs Meadowes,' he said slowly, with an air of perplexity. 'I have heard something of you from Mr Williams, who left here only an hour since. He never said you would come calling on me in person. You are the family cook, I understand. What brings you out at this time of night?'

'I have come, sir, to ask a favour of you,' replied Agnes uncertainly.

Unease now began to ruffle Sir Bartholomew's ruddy countenance. 'Blanchard said nothing of any favours. Do not expect to take advantage of me, just because you recovered something of mine that should never have been lost in the first place. And if it's a position you are after, I have to tell you I already have a French chef.'

'I do not seek to take advantage,' said Agnes in a firmer tone, as she settled to her surroundings. 'Or a post. Only answers to certain questions.'

Grey blinked. He rested his hand on the table, as though bracing himself against an unfavourable onslaught. 'Questions on what subject?'

'Three murders took place around the time your

wine-cooler went missing. Unlike the wine-cooler, those lives can never be recovered. All I ask is your assistance in finding the killer and bringing him to justice.'

Sir Bartholomew Grey allowed himself a moment to reflect. 'I suppose your aim is worthy. But it strikes me that a woman of your position should not be meddling in such matters. Why has Blanchard never mentioned this? I assumed he would inform the justice, who would pursue the villainous thief. Tell me his name and I'll have him apprehended directly.'

'The thief's name is Harry Drake,' said Agnes, 'a professional housebreaker, who operated with the connivance of the thief-taker Marcus Pitt. But as for apprehending the pair – you need not concern yourself over that.'

'Why?'

'Drake is dead, and Pitt is in the roundhouse awaiting committal.'

'Then I confess myself baffled, Mrs Meadowes,' said Grey, taking out his pocket watch and looking at it. 'What more do you want?'

Agnes would not allow herself to be hurried. She smiled sweetly. 'As I said, the murders are all connected to the theft of your wine-cooler. But I don't believe either Drake or Pitt was responsible for them; I think it was someone inside Blanchards'. The break-in was not fortuitous. Drake was instructed what to steal – he entered knowing that the wine-cooler was the most valuable item Blanchards' had ever made and that Mr Blanchard would pay a sizeable sum for its return. That sum was doubtless to be shared between the three conspirators.'

Grey's attention was caught. 'You mean Drake, Pitt and the anonymous traitor would all have shared in the reward?'

'Precisely.'

'But the money was recovered, I understand. So the plot was foiled.'

'Only in a material sense,' Agnes countered levelly. 'There are still three murders that Justice Cordingly has little inclination to pursue. The murders of a servant girl, an apprentice and a housebreaker do not apparently merit the same justice as the robbery of someone of means.'

Uneasily, Sir Bartholomew nodded. 'But did not Pitt commit the murders?'

'I do not believe so; he tends to keep himself distant from his crimes – though he must know who did.'

Grey paced around the room and, pulling up another chair, offered it to Agnes before sitting heavily in his own. 'Then leave the matter in my hands. Justice Cordingly is an acquaintance of mine. If Pitt has been apprehended, it will be no hard task for one of his constables to wheedle out the identity of the traitor inside Blanchards'.'

'I'm not certain Cordingly will do so when he learns the range of Pitt's influence. I think the chances of Pitt remaining in custody and revealing who employed him are remarkably slim.'

Grey began to pile up the counters, neatening them so they stood in perfect columns. 'Do I take it you have another scheme?'

'Perhaps,' said Agnes, sitting erect in her chair, head held high. 'But first I should like to ask you about another matter, which I believe may somehow have a bearing on these events.'

Sir Bartholomew nodded and waved his hand to indicate that she might proceed. Agnes drew a deep breath. 'What I should like to know, sir, is what you can tell me of the background of the craftsman who made your wine-cooler, Thomas Williams.'

She saw instantly that Sir Bartholomew Grey was taken aback by this sudden change of tack. 'Surely you do not suspect that Williams, one of the most talented silversmiths of my acquaintance, could be a cold-blooded murderer?' he blustered.

She pursed her lips. 'I think there is more to him than we know.'

Grey shook his head. 'I very much doubt it. His father is a craftsman of the highest skill. He supplied me with much of the plate for my house in Newcastle. Thomas is his second son; he served his apprenticeship under his father, but wanted to better himself and thought London was the place to do it.

He asked me for assistance in finding a suitable master who might offer him a place as a journeyman. I was happy to assist and mentioned him to Theodore Blanchard, who was in need of additional help following the retirement of his father. And so he was taken on.'

'Are you familiar with the family mark?'

'Naturally. As I said, I have been a patron of the father's for many years.'

Agnes pulled the heart-shaped box from her pocket and handed it to him. 'Is the mark on this his father's?'

Sir Bartholomew reached out and took up a magnifying glass from a nearby side table. He plucked the box off Agnes's palm and held it between forefinger and thumb close to the candelabra, turning it and raising and lowering the glass to gain the best view of the marks.

After a while he nodded, then put the glass and box down on the table. 'Yes, as far as I can tell the initials are his father's mark. And the extra mark, the one that resembles three small turrets, shows the box was made in Newcastle.'

Hearing Riley's account thus partially confirmed, Agnes's spirits plunged. Thomas had deceived her. Dismay made her reckless, unable to resist pressing further. 'Were you aware of the engagement between Thomas Williams and Rose Francis, who was kitchen maid for Lord Carew and then moved to Blanchards'?'

'A kitchen maid?' Sir Bartholomew scratched his wig and looked at her as if she were mad. 'You cannot suppose I involve myself with maids. I have a housekeeper who takes care of such matters.'

'Do you know Lord Carew?'

'He is a casual acquaintance of mine.'

'But you never set eyes on the girl?'

Sir Bartholomew Grey adjusted his cravat, took out a lace-edged handkerchief from his pocket and blew noisily into it. Then he stood up and began to pace about the room. 'As I've told you, no. I assume you are not suggesting they conspired to aid Pitt to steal my wine-cooler, or that Williams committed the murders. What motive would he have?'

'Money, perhaps,' said Agnes. She sensed his patience was at an end, but there was yet more she wanted to discover. 'And what did you think on learning she was in the employ of the Blanchards?'

'Nothing!' he exclaimed, twirling round with an air of majesty. 'How many times must I say this? You cannot suppose a man of my standing pays attention to the servants of every household he happens to visit. So long as the meat and gravy are on the table, I do not bother myself over who puts them there.'

Agnes recoiled as if he had hit her. At that moment there was an unexpected creak from the far end of the room. She glanced up. A door hidden in the wainscoting was abruptly thrown back and an elegantly dressed young woman stepped through. She was clad in a silk dress of inky blue with a deep ruff of creamy lace around the décolletage; her neck was slender and white, her hair elaborately dressed with black silk flowers. She looked young enough to be Sir Bartholomew's daughter, though evidently she was not. Seeing Agnes, she pursed her lips in a moue of displeasure, walked to the table, picked up her fan and began to fan herself slowly. 'Who is this, my dearest?' she said softly.

''Tis no one but the cook of a tradesman of my acquaintance.'

'Then are we not to finish our game?'

'Certainly we shall finish it,' said Sir Bartholomew, ushering her to her seat then hurrying to ring the servants' bell. Seeing them together made Agnes think of Thomas and Rose; the woman had something of Rose's nonchalant bearing. A knot rose in Agnes's throat. The footman appeared an instant later. 'This visitor has concluded her business, and is leaving,' said Grey. 'Miss Katherine and I will finish our game without disturbance – no matter who calls.' Then, turning to Agnes, 'I do not comprehend your purpose in coming here or what you have learned. But whatever it was, I trust you are satisfied for I have no more to tell you. Good evening to you, madam.'

'Good evening, sir.' She paused and curtseyed, then

remembered Theodore's injunction. 'Before I leave, if I may make one last request.'

Sir Bartholomew looked impatient. 'What then?'

'I would ask that you keep this conversation to yourself.'

Sir Bartholomew regarded her thoughtfully for a moment. 'It is my belief that when servants exceed their duties, only mayhem ensues. Your visit has done little to change my view. Therefore I cannot give you any such assurance. Good night to you.'

Chapter Forty

SINCE THEODORE HAD GRANTED AGNES THE NEXT DAY OFF, SHE sent up a larger breakfast than usual – a cold knuckle of gammon, which Mr Matthews would carve on the side table, coddled eggs kept warm over a dish of hot water, and devilled kidneys. Then, having written down suggestions for the next day's menu on the slate, she headed over to Bread Street to see Peter.

The morning was fine and bright, which made her think of taking Peter for an excursion on the river. But even this pleasant prospect failed to divert her from her preoccupations. Her visit to Sir Bartholomew Grey had borne out Riley's account of Thomas Williams's background, and the fact that the silver in her possession bore his family mark made it likely the rest was true. Rose and Thomas had been engaged. Thomas had lied. He had concealed their engagement. But while this much was clear, she still did not comprehend *why*.

A few minutes later, she presented herself at Mrs Sharp's door. Mrs Sharp seemed puzzled when she saw Agnes standing there, and Agnes wondered if she had inconveniently interrupted her in the middle of her household chores. 'Forgive me for disturbing you, Mrs Sharp. I won't delay you. I trust you got my message. Is Peter ready?'

'What?' said Mrs Sharp, her eyes widening in bafflement. 'But he is already with you – I thought you had returned for something he had forgotten.'

'What do you mean?' said Agnes, equally muddled. 'I wrote to tell you I would collect him this morning.'

'Yes,' said Mrs Sharp, 'I got the note. But an hour ago a young girl came, saying you had sent *her* to fetch Peter. You were going out for a drive, you had a carriage arranged, she was the driver's girl. She showed me the carriage – it was waiting at the corner of Cheapside. I saw a woman's face and a gloved hand wave. I assumed the woman must be you.'

Agnes regarded her incredulously, and for some moments was speechless. And then, as the dreadful realization sank in, her heart began thumping and her head pounded unbearably. Somewhere close by she heard the plaintive sound of a cat mewing for food. 'Tell me, she said faintly, 'what did the girl look like?'

'Like an urchin – ill-kempt, scrawny, hair unwashed, wearing dirty clothes, infested with vermin of all kind, I dare say. There was a red shawl wrapped round her head, as I recall.'

Agnes's spirits sank to further depths. Elsie. Why had she committed such an act of betrayal? But no sooner had she framed the question in her mind than the answer presented itself. Harry Drake was dead, and no doubt Elsie believed that Agnes had had a hand in his murder.

'Can you hazard who these people were?' said Mrs Sharp, as if she could read Agnes's thoughts.

'I fear I know who the child was, which leads me to suspect the person who lies behind the deed – even if he was not seated in the carriage at the time,' said Agnes. 'Marcus Pitt the thief-taker warned me of his influence.'

'Pitt! Would *he* take your child?'

'I wager he would enlist the aid of someone who would do worse besides take him.'

Mrs Sharp shook her head in disbelief. 'What do you mean?'

'Pitt desires vengeance for the part I played in his apprehension. The murderer who employed him is concerned that, even though the wine-cooler has been recovered, I intend to pursue him.'

'I can scarcely credit that Peter has become caught up in all that,' said Mrs Sharp, whey-faced as she comprehended the measure of Agnes's torment. 'What would you have me do? Shall I send for the constable?'

'No,' said Agnes, 'that would only waste precious time. There is only one thing to be done – I will have to go after them and get Peter back.'

'But where will you start?'

She thought for a moment. 'Pitt's premises in Melancholy Walk are as good a place as any.'

As she spoke, a shadow emerged suddenly from the stairwell. The stocky figure of Thomas Williams, dressed only in breeches and a half-buttoned shirt, his madly curling hair even more dishevelled than usual, appeared in the hall. 'And what will you do when you get there?' he said. 'Employ your feminine charms to persuade the murderer to give Peter back?'

She stared mutely at him for an instant. Her mind was unwavering: Peter's abduction was all she could think of. She answered brusquely, 'I will fathom some means when I get there. And now I must take my leave. Good day to you both.'

She picked up her skirts and hurried down the street in the direction of the river. A hackney carriage rumbled past, and she darted out into the road, waving feverishly. The driver turned and drew swiftly to a halt. 'Melancholy Walk – quick as you can!' she cried. Grabbing hold of the door, she opened it and clambered in. Startled at the sudden stop, the horses tossed their heads and jangled their harnesses. 'A shilling extra if you get me there within the quarter-hour,' said Agnes.

Just as the driver cracked his whip and began to move off, Thomas Williams came careering up, hair flying, boots untied, shirt and coat unbuttoned, sword clanking beneath, and took hold of the door handle. Agnes clung to the inside grimly to prevent it from opening and shook her head. Thomas released the door and leaped round to the rear, clambering on the step as the vehicle gathered pace. Agnes saw him stumble and fall back at the first attempt, but then he ran faster and leapt again, this time successfully. She caught sight of his head through the rear window, his cheek pressing against the mud-spattered glass as if clinging on for dear life. Agnes turned back to the relative comfort of her compartment and ignored him.

The vehicle, with Thomas clinging like a barnacle to the back, jostled through Watling Street and down towards the bridge. Agnes watched as the façades of glove-makers, hatters, stationers, booksellers, sellers of fishing tackle, breeches, leather aprons and ribbons, and the dilapidated Nonesuch House passed her window, and the great stone gateway came into view. The air was filled with the stench of urine from the tanneries, bones from the glue-makers, boiling fat from the makers of soap. But Agnes barely noticed the clamorous scene or the malodorous atmosphere. She tried to think of Elsie and what she had done and how she was going to trace her. It was better than thinking of where Peter was and what might be happening to him.

At the south side of the bridge, the carriage drew up at the gateway to wait for a wagon coming in the opposite direction. Agnes peered over the parapet and glimpsed a greyish-brown expanse, and on it the dark stooped forms of people searching for whatever flotsam they might find. It was while she gazed at these diminutive forms that something curious came into view on the south-eastern shore. At the top of some decrepit stairs leading down from the quayside that served a row of dark warehouses stood a carriage.

As a rule, the vehicles that frequented such places were wagons and carts, used for loading and unloading the barges. Today being Sunday, there was little activity or traffic, which made the sight of a carriage all the more remarkable. Thus drawn, her attention flitted over a blurred group of figures close by. There was a man, and two figures of short stature – children – one of whom wore something red. As she watched, the figure in red began running along the wharf and disappeared into the distance.

That brief sighting was enough to spur her into action. Agnes pushed down the window and shouted to the driver,

'Take the road leading to St Olave's, then turn left towards the quayside. I'm looking for a dark carriage.'

The driver pulled the reins in his left hand shorter, causing the horses to turn and the carriage to follow. But he had travelled no more than twenty yards before the road ahead narrowed to an alley, with another wider road leading off to the right. He pulled up the horses, jumped down from his platform and opened the carriage door. 'Can't go further, never turn round if I do.'

Agnes descended and looked about her. The river – a flash of silvery-brown light – was just visible through the black frame of buildings. A few figures, indistinctly silhouetted, were shuffling down the alley; a stray dog ambled along, sniffing the detritus in the gutter. There was no sign of the carriage. Reason told Agnes that if the hackney driver could not pass this way, and it had indeed been the carriage with Peter inside that she had seen, there must be another way down to the wharf. Nevertheless, the distance was not great, and it would be easier to find the carriage and its occupants on foot.

All this time she had ignored Thomas Williams, who had now descended from his platform and was standing some distance away, taking similar stock of his surroundings and looking up at a woman hanging laundry from an upstairs window.

'That's a shilling and sixpence, if you please,' said the driver.

Agnes fumbled in her pocket for the money. Conscious with every moment she wasted that Peter's fate might be sealed irreparably, she burned with only one desire – to do whatever was necessary to find him. She thrust a handful of coins – far more than the sum requested – into the driver's hand, then sidestepped Thomas and the hackney carriage and began running down the passage.

She was panting from exertion when, some minutes later, she emerged alone at the quayside, scouring the scene for any sign of the carriage. The warehouses and factories loomed over the river behind her, their chimneys spewing foul-smelling smoke. The wharf on the opposite bank was bathed in winter sun, but this side was shrouded in purplish shadow. She could discern no sign of the carriage, or Peter.

Moments later, Thomas emerged from another passage further up the river towards Pickle Herring Stairs, and ran out onto a landing. He pointed downriver, beckoning wildly that she should come in his direction. Agnes did not understand the reason for his gesture, but with Peter's life at stake she was prepared to take whatever assistance was available. Even Thomas Williams's. She hurried along the quayside, and when she was no more than ten yards distant called out, 'What is it? Did you see something?'

'No, but that laundress did – a carriage. She said she has an excellent view from her garret, and one passed beneath her not ten minutes earlier. She did not observe precisely how many were in it, but she did see a girl, a boy and a man descend and head in this direction.'

Agnes nodded. 'And do you see anything now?'

Thomas turned to survey the landscape. 'Nothing. But perhaps we should proceed further down.'

A keen wind ruffled the river and invaded the folds of Agnes's cloak, making her shiver. She had reached the steps leading down to the foreshore and now began to descend them. The tide was low, but whether it was ebbing or flowing Agnes did not pause to consider. When she reached the bottom, she could see the sagging underside of the wharf on her right. It was supported on massive wooden pillars, encrusted to the water line with barnacles and olive-green slime and ribbons of weed. Beneath lay an expanse of muddy foreshore invisible from above. To her left, the mud banked steeply down to the water's edge, its surface scarred with flotsam – wood, stones, rusting chains, lumps of coal, patches of slime and yellowish sludge. In some places the mud was no more than a yard or two wide, in others it extended like probing fingers into the choppy brown water. Here and there, the surface was traversed by rivulets of foul-smelling water, where the sewers and gutters of the city disgorged into the river.

The flatness of the scene was interrupted by the hulls of

various vessels – fishing smacks, barges, wherries, hay boats and schooners, some moored and afloat, others stranded by the tide, leaning sideways on the mud. There was no sign of life on any of the boats, but all along the shore an assortment of raggedly dressed people carrying baskets or bags were combing the mud for whatever they could find.

Agnes picked her way across the mud, her gaze drifting over the river-finders and among the darker shadows in search of Peter. Some moments later, a flash of unexpected movement distracted her. Something seemed to emerge from the dark shadows close to the wharf, then disappear. Had she imagined it? She halted, scouring for any sign of movement.

Thomas saw her stop and noted the sudden change in her expression. 'Did you see something?' he called down to her from the sagging wharf above.

She shook her head. Her anger with him had receded a little with Peter's abduction, but she hadn't forgotten or forgiven. She increased her pace, all the while peering intently into the shadows.

Thirty paces on, she saw the movement again – a spidery, hunched form, picking its way beneath the wharf. She ran further along the shore, faster than before.

'What is it?' shouted Thomas.

'There!' she cried back, forgetting her resentment in her excitement. Thomas dropped to his knees and stretched out over the mud, but found it impossible to see directly beneath the structure on which he stood. Agnes was already some distance from him, running away as he watched. He looked up and down the wharf and, finding no steps nearby, launched himself onto the mud.

He tumbled forwards, putting down his hands to save himself. A shower of black water splashed up as he landed, spraying his stockings and breeches. His boots sank in the soft mud, but he ignored this inconvenience. He wiped his palms hurriedly on his coat and ran to catch up with Agnes. 'What is it?' he demanded brusquely as he drew alongside. 'What did you see?'

'Under the wharf . . . fifty yards ahead . . . see them now, rounding that pier,' she gasped, pointing. 'Two figures, one of them Peter.'

She began to run away from him, oblivious to her feet sinking deeper into the mud with every step, and the water, whipped by a sharpening wind, now rippling towards her. She ran closer to the wharf, skirting areas of soft mud which were impossible to cross. She hurried over discarded wood and rocks and rubble, and foul-smelling rivulets, heart pounding with the effort. She knew that Thomas would be close behind her, but never once did she turn to look at him. Her eyes were fixed upon the figures ahead, her mind set on reaching Peter. And her efforts were succeeding; the distance between them was shortening.

But when they were still more than thirty yards apart, the shadowy form that was Peter turned and caught sight of her. He froze for an instant, then looked up at his captor and back again at Agnes, silently holding out his hands in her direction. She understood his meaning; he was beseeching her to come. But the captor had been alerted by something in Peter's tugging. He turned and, seeing Agnes and Thomas pursuing him, stepped out from under the wharf.

For some moments the man stood, legs braced on the mud flats, gripping Peter by the wrist, peering back towards them. This much Agnes could now see of him: he was a tall man; his bearing was upright; his head was covered with a tricorn, the front brim pulled low over his brow. He wore a muffler wrapped about his neck that covered the lower part of his jaw. He was youngish, she judged, from the speed of his movements. His dark cloak flapped about in the wind. His boots were long and brown and spattered in mud. Who is it? I must know him, she told herself. But what with the hat pulled low and the muffler and the distance, she squinted and peered in vain; she could not say who it was.

Agnes waited for him to speak. I will know him then, she thought. But the man remained silent, staring at them as though willing them to move and then see what he might do. Thus challenged, she began slowly to advance, taking small steps that she hoped would be hardly perceptible.

She had progressed no more than a dozen paces when Peter began to pull in her direction and cry out frantically. This was enough to cause the man to take fright. She watched in horrified silence as Peter, wrenching and twisting towards her, was yanked out across the mud flat, towards the river and deeper water.

The tide was coming in, creeping towards them over the dark mud, covering its surface with jagged peaks as it encroached. She saw Peter dragged ankle-deep, knee-deep, his panic-stricken face turning to view the water, then straining back at her. He kept calling out, shrill indecipherable pleas which only seemed to irk the man further. He tugged Peter by the arm and must have issued some threat, for after that Peter never once turned back.

'Hold firm, Peter! Hold firm, and all will be well!' cried Agnes, furious at her own impotence as her son was transported ever further away.

She pursued them, plunging and crashing her way through muddy water, oblivious to the piercing cold that reached up her skirts and to the curious stares of the river-finders, who had withdrawn with the incoming tide and were now standing on the wharf-side, bewildered at the spectacle of a foolhardy woman wading into deeper water. Several times she stumbled on some obstacle hidden beneath the water or stepped in a patch of quicksand and she felt herself sink, but each time she recovered her balance and continued. Thomas Williams kept pace, but said nothing and never once attempted to divert her from her course.

But the tide was a powerful opponent, and within a matter of minutes it was plain that the gap had once again widened. Where were they heading? As Agnes gazed ahead of her, their objective became plain. Some ten yards distant floated a wooden rowing boat moored to a post. The water was now up to Peter's chest and deepening steadily with each step they took towards the vessel. Peter began to wail loudly as muddy waves splashed in his face. The man halted and, taking swift stock of the situation, hoisted Peter onto his shoulders before continuing out towards the boat.

Minutes later, they had reached the boat and Peter had been bundled in. The man began to clamber over the bulwark after him. The sudden weight pulling down on one side unbalanced the small vessel and caused a quantity of water to spill in. But he was swift to roll himself in and a moment later was seated inside. For some time afterwards the boat rocked precariously, but, much to Agnes's relief, it did not capsize.

'Wait! Wait! Don't take him alone – let me come too. Whoever you are, whatever it is you want from me, you shall have it,' she called out wildly, knowing it was pointless yet feeling unable to remain silent.

The man's outline stiffened; he glared in her direction, but made no reply, concentrating his attentions on retrieving the oars from the hull and slotting them into their leather bindings.

'Wait! Please wait!' she implored again. This time he did not even look up at her.

At this juncture, Thomas surged past, waving his sword in the air. But while he was less hampered by his costume than Agnes, as the water deepened and the current quickened, he too found maintaining speedy progress impossible. He reached the boat just as the man, having successfully attached the oars, had loosened the mooring rope and let it fall into the water. Seeing what was happening, Thomas held fast to the stern of the boat and made lunges with his sword. When the man remained out of range, he wrapped his legs round the rudder and began rocking the vessel as though he meant to capsize it. 'Give back the boy or I'm not letting go,' he shouted between gritted teeth.

The man teetered, but maintained sufficient balance to return to the seat where the oars were fixed. He settled himself down and scowled at Thomas, who was doing all he could to upturn the boat. 'Ain't you now?' he mumbled, and with these words he lifted the right-hand oar, swivelled it backwards and dropped it down heavily on the crown of Thomas's head.

Thomas fell back into the water, clutching his head and his sword. Agnes, who was some distance behind, saw blood gushing from a gash on his temple. Thomas made a further attempt to clamber onto the boat. But the man hit him again, and when Thomas fell back once more he steered the boat clumsily away towards deeper water, where it caught the current and was wafted swiftly downstream.

Agnes stood with water swirling about her, watching as Peter, hunched in the stern of the boat, drifted away from her. Soon he was nothing more than a pale-grey shadow, his features lost, his shape almost indistinguishable from the dull sweep of the river.

Chapter Forty-one

'I'LL FIND ANOTHER BOAT AND PURSUE THEM,' SAID THOMAS, turning back to her in the muddy water, still clutching his sword in his fist.

'No,' Agnes said. 'He cannot row fast, it will be easier to follow them on land.'

She began moving downstream towards shallower water, regarding Thomas obliquely as she did so. Blood mixed with muddy water was trickling down his cheek; he looked pale and his lips were grey with cold. He sheathed his sword and began dabbing ineffectually at his wound with a damp handkerchief.

Agnes could not bring herself to look. She reminded herself that his efforts did not alter the fact that he had deceived her over Rose. Nor could she bear to think of what might be in Peter's mind. Instead she kept walking towards the bridge where the boat was headed, trying to fathom who the man was who had carried her son away, and what he intended.

'Who was it?' she said urgently. 'Didn't you see who it was when you were close?'

'I caught no more than a glimpse of him before he clouted me,' said Thomas, still rubbing his battered skull. 'I thought he seemed familiar, but the knock must have shaken my faculties. I don't recall now why.'

Agnes managed to rein in her exasperation, but made no sympathetic remark. Her mind was concentrated elsewhere. Peter's captor – the murderer – was someone she knew. Why else would he take the trouble to conceal his face? She thought back over what little she had seen of him – the tall, lean outline, the flapping coat, the hat and muffler. Nothing was distinctive or outwardly remarkable.

And what did he want? There had been ample opportunity for Peter's captor to kill him before now, if that was his intention. He must then have some other plan. Perhaps he had arranged a hiding place for Peter somewhere close to the river. The boat, Agnes guessed, was a fortuitous means of escape – not part of the original scheme. She had precipitated the flight by pursuing him when he did not expect it. But why snatch Peter in the first place? Agnes had known the answer to this all along. Peter was a lure. It was she he wanted to capture, not Peter at all.

But that being so, why flee, why not take her now, when she had chased him? She mulled on this and concluded that it might have been the presence of Thomas Williams that had deterred him, or the audience of river-finders. Peter's captor wanted the advantage, to be sure he would win. Pitt, Agnes thought suddenly, might adopt such a tactic. But Pitt was in the roundhouse awaiting committal.

'Where are they going?' said Thomas, intruding into these thoughts.

Agnes did not reply. She kept walking upriver, watching the man's dark figure rowing inexpertly, splashing water and spinning the boat. The vessel had veered back towards the shoreline, which made it easy to keep track of him.

'Where do you think they are headed?' repeated Thomas more urgently.

'I am not certain. Perhaps to Marcus Pitt's premises,' said Agnes, her eyes fixed on the boat.

Thomas rubbed his head as he walked. 'What makes you say so? Pitt has been apprehended.'

'Of course I cannot be sure,' said Agnes sharply, 'but have you a better place to start?'

'I should begin by calling on Justice Cordingly.'

'Then go, if you wish. But what will he care for the missing son of a cook? He has done precious little about the murders thus far. Besides, whether or not he wielded the knife, Pitt lies at the heart of the murders and the robbery. The murderer knows him and knows his house. He might regard it as a refuge.' She paused and regarded the bleak brown water ahead. 'In any case, why should I justify my reasons to you, Mr Williams? After the lies you have spun, you are hardly above suspicion yourself.'

Thomas gave her a calculating look. 'What? That's nonsensical,' he said. 'If I had been involved, would I be here offering you my assistance? Would I have saved you from Pitt yesterday?'

Agnes raised her eyes to the sky and regarded the mountainous pewter clouds that were now encroaching. She knew he spoke the truth, and did not seriously believe him culpable of murder, but she was still furious at his deception. And anger offered a useful distraction from her worry over Peter. 'Then if you are so innocent, as you claim, why conceal the fact that you were enamoured by Rose for years, and that you were engaged to marry her? Perhaps you killed her out of jealousy when she took up with Riley and Philip.'

Thomas stared at her. 'I kept the engagement from you because I knew it was irrelevant to recent events and would only mislead you – as indeed it has. Rose broke our engagement, and caused me much heartache at the time. Perhaps I was wrong not to have been more open. But my deception was mainly caused by my fondness for you. And I have never made that secret.'

Then, without further prompting, he proceeded to confirm the story Riley had told her. Rose and he had been engaged. She had followed him to London following the death of her father, and so detested her work at Lord Carew's she had wanted to marry him earlier than previously arranged. 'I would have agreed were it not for my situation with Blanchards'. The company's dwindling fortunes worried me; I did not want to wed and find myself unable to provide for her.

So I asked her to be patient and wait a while longer at Lord Carew's. But Rose was impatient; she broke our engagement in a fit of pique, saying she believed there were plenty of other eligible men who would happily provide for her if I would not. A month later, she changed her mind and tried to mend things between us. When I hesitated, she came to Blanchards'. Soon after, rumours reached me of her flirtations with Riley and Philip; I believe she took up with them to spur me to take her back. But her antics worried me. I saw I should never be able to trust her and I told her I could not. Had I acted differently, she might be alive today.'

Here Thomas halted, as if waiting for her response. But Agnes said nothing; she walked on, shivering as the wind whipped her wet skirts about her legs and chilled her to the core. The boat was now no larger than a walnut shell, a blurred shape against a swathe of oily water. As she watched, it disappeared through one of the cavernous openings between the piers of London Bridge, as if Peter had been consumed by some monstrous being.

Agnes tried to think dispassionately, but she was shuddering violently from cold and shock, and visions of Peter kept intruding. Thomas had marched ahead now. He was walking towards the steps leading up from the shore. She called after him, raising her voice to make herself heard above the wind, 'I have no appetite to argue the matter further now.'

With this, Thomas swivelled round, looking down at her from halfway up the steps. 'You talk of me deceiving you,' he declared, 'when it is *you* who deceives yourself.'

Agnes advanced slowly, climbing the steps until she had drawn nearly level with him. 'What do you mean by that?'

'If you really believed *I* was involved in Rose's murder, why would you have spoken yesterday of your errors of judgement, or permitted my assistance as you just did? You have fabricated doubts in order to barricade yourself from the truth.'

Agnes put out her hand to the wall to steady herself. 'On the contrary, I am perfectly open to the truth. Yesterday, thanks to your deception, I did not know it. And as for your assistance just now, much good that proved!' retorted Agnes unkindly. Then, infuriated as much by her own ingratitude as her weakness, she raised her hands and added more softly, 'For pity's sake, Mr Williams, leave me be.'

She continued to climb the steps, leaving Thomas behind. But he would not let the matter rest. He came after her, and when they were both at the top he gripped her by the elbow. 'And now you intend to go off alone, do you?'

Agnes wrenched her arm from his. Gathering the sodden folds of her cloak about her, she turned towards the towpath, squelching mud and dripping a trail of water with every step. Never before had she felt so cold. Her teeth were chattering and the wind felt like a dozen knives piercing her skin. Despite her fury and her worry over Peter, one particular phrase Thomas had said resounded in her mind. Had fondness for her been the reason for his deception?

The sky was overcast now and a thin grey mist had fallen over the water, turning the brown sails of the barges and sailing skiffs to black. Among the other vessels, Agnes fancied she could see the boat containing Peter draw in to the quayside. Squinting into the gloom, she could see that some yards ahead the path forked, the left-hand branch turning inland in a southerly direction. This, she reckoned, must lead towards Melancholy Walk. It seemed that her suspicion that the abductor would head to Pitt's house had been sound. Even as she watched, he was mooring the boat to a large metal ring on the quayside below.

Agnes instinctively shrank back, pressing herself into the opening of an adjacent doorway. She pulled Thomas with her, not wishing to accost Peter's captor yet. If he took fright and ran off, she might lose them again in the mist. It would be far better, she thought, to follow them to the house or wherever they were going and await her opportunity.

The two shadowy grey figures stepped from the boat and made their way up some creaking steps to the street above. They then plunged into an alley out of view. Thomas and she had not exchanged a word for the past ten minutes, but Agnes now turned and addressed him. 'Not a word, he must not see us,' she whispered. 'And when we arrive at the house, please stay back. Do not follow until I beckon you to come. It will be better all round if I approach alone.'

Thomas was unable to keep the incredulity from his voice. 'As a woman, you are hardly equipped to attempt such a rescue.'

Agnes grew agitated once more. 'Peter is my son. After all I have recently endured, I believe I am well able to manage my own affairs in a subtle manner.'

Thomas shrugged. 'Very well then, if that is your choice. Do you prefer me to leave?'

'Not now, or someone might see you.'

'Indeed,' said Thomas. 'Then would it not be in Peter's interest for us to formulate a plan on which we both agree?'

Vexed though she was, Agnes had to concede the logic of this suggestion. With Peter's well-being uppermost in her thoughts, her pride could be assuaged later. They spent some minutes arguing in whispers and eventually agreed that Agnes (she was unyielding on the point) would proceed ahead and find a means of entry without being observed. Having ascertained the abductor's whereabouts and identity, she would make herself known, thus allowing Peter's captor to believe she had fallen for his trap. On her signal, Thomas would arrive and apprehend the villain and she would rescue her son.

Thomas protested that the plan was too sketchy and it would be better if they both went in together. But she argued that two of them would be more likely to be noticed than one, and that once the element of surprise was lost, the abductor would have the advantage over them and might easily slip away without being identified. 'Once we are certain who he is, at least if he escapes we may inform the justice and have him apprehended. Without proof, we can do nothing.'

With Thomas still muttering objections, they walked carefully forward, taking the left-hand fork. The path now turned into a narrow alley, lined on both sides with a high wooden palisade. On the right reared the backs of a row of tall narrow buildings. 'Which house is it?' said Thomas.

'One of those over there,' whispered Agnes, waving at the houses. 'But the road is on the other side and from this vantage point I cannot tell exactly which it is.'

Treading carefully, they edged their way up an alley leading to Melancholy Walk. Presumably Peter and his captor must have travelled this way, but the mist had grown denser and there was no sign of them now. As she reached the corner, Agnes hung back and peered gingerly round into the street. Then through the veil of grey, she glimpsed a pair of silhouettes, one tall, one short, hurrying away. 'I see them,' she said. 'I will go alone from here.'

Thomas nodded. She sensed his misgivings, but when she walked off he made no attempt to follow. Clinging to the wall, Agnes followed Peter and his captor as closely as she dared. The cold was as piercing as ever and her clothes were still sodden, but so engrossed was she with thoughts of Peter she was scarcely conscious of the discomfort. A few yards on, the pair halted in front of a house, then mounted the stairs to the front door and banged upon it. Agnes shrank into the nearest doorway, in case they should turn while waiting for the door to be opened. She watched her son standing still, peering about, and the dark-cloaked figure looming over him like a colossus. After a while the door creaked open, and a short conversation ensued. Agnes could not hear what was said, but the occasional word drifted to her – 'boat . . . pursued . . . wait here . . .' Apparently this was sufficient to persuade whoever stood inside to let them in. A minute later they had disappeared and the door crashed closed.

Agnes crept up the street. She stood for a moment surveying the house. The sash windows were dark, the shutters closed, though it was not yet midday. It looked as if the house were entirely deserted. Only she knew it was not. She had seen the door open. There was someone inside – Peter, and his captor.

Agnes mounted the four steps leading to the front door and tried it. But as she expected, it was locked fast. She retreated to the street and looked up at the façade, searching for a means to enter without being noticed. To one side of the main entrance, a narrow stone staircase led down to the basement, the wall punctuated by a casement window. The window might have been large enough to squeeze through, but like all the others, it was tightly shuttered on the inside, and there were metal bars as a further precaution against intruders. Impossible. But then she saw that to one side of the basement, hidden beneath the stairs leading to the front door, was another smaller entrance. Perhaps this way would be unlocked, thought Agnes, or perhaps the door would be easier to force. Herein, she decided, lay her only chance.

Filled with trepidation, she descended the flagged stairs and tried the door handle, praying it would open. But the handle did not budge; here too the door was locked. She put her shoulder against the door and gave a sharp shove with all her weight, but the door was stout and there was no give in it at all. Disappointed, Agnes retreated. She would have to alter the plan and knock to gain entry after all, she decided. And then rely upon her wits to save Peter. There was no other way.

But as she turned, her boot caught upon something. Beneath the stairs leading down from the street, a wooden cover with a thick rope handle was set into the flagged basement floor. From the street, the cover was invisible. Perhaps, Agnes thought, hope rising once more, this was where coal was delivered to the house.

She stooped and tried to heave off the cover, but the wood was sodden and swollen and did not shift. Taking a firmer grip, she yanked again, harder this time. The rope bit into her palms, the cover creaked, she fancied she felt it give a little. But it remained firm. Undeterred, she heaved again with all her might, hands clawing the rope. This time her efforts were rewarded. She found herself teetering backwards, almost falling, the lid crashing to the ground to expose a square black opening.

Panting from her exertions, Agnes squatted down and peered in. Beneath her was darkness. Nothing but a glistening black mound some four feet beneath her: the coal cellar. She lowered herself onto the flagged ground, swung her legs into the opening, then inched herself down and let herself fall.

The drop was greater than she had calculated and she landed awkwardly, wrenching her ankle as she tumbled into the darkness. She cried out involuntarily. Coal dust filled her eyes and nostrils and made her want to cough and sneeze, but she stifled the desire. Scrambling to her feet, she peered about. At first she could see nothing but black, but after a while her eyes began to adjust to the light drifting down. She could make out the walls of the cellar, the beams supporting the ceiling, and a small arched doorway set into one wall.

Chapter Forty-two

AGNES LIMPED ACROSS THE CELLAR AND TRIED THE HANDLE; the door was unbolted and opened easily. She pushed it a few inches and looked gingerly through the gap. There was a corridor leading, she supposed, to the kitchen. Unlike the servants' corridor at Foster Lane, with its bustle and noise and heat from the range, all was silent, chill, deserted.

Telling herself that this suited her purpose very well, Agnes walked out into the corridor. Doors opened to the left – she glanced through into disused sculleries and pantries and a larder filled with nothing but cobwebs. The corridor opened into a kitchen with a staircase in one corner. Agnes glanced disapprovingly at the rusted, unlit range, and a heap of unwashed pots encrusted with residues of foul-smelling food. A rat scuttled beneath the skirting. Shuddering with cold and apprehension, she mounted the stairs.

Agnes found herself in the hallway. To the left was the front door and the room facing the street, where on her previous visit she had first met Pitt. To the right, the hallway opened into a wider space, where she had recognized Elsie sitting among the other children in Pitt's employ.

At first the place seemed deserted, but then she thought she heard a faint sound coming from the back – the muffled sound of footsteps, someone coughing. When the sound came again, more distinctly, she moved towards it. She saw then that there was another door to the rear of the hall. She sensed Peter's presence nearby and was half minded to call out to him, but managed to control herself. Steady, she reminded herself, I will stand no chance unless I surprise them. Scalp prickling with anticipation, the flesh on her cheeks taut, Agnes inched open the door and squinted in.

The room before her was sparsely furnished – a couple of deal chairs, an old splintered table, a desultory fire burning in the grate, a grimy window overlooking the river. But she scarcely noticed any of this, for standing in the centre of the room was Elsie.

The girl's face looked even more pinched than usual, her nose was redder than her shawl. She looked strained and worn, as if she hadn't slept for days. She was apparently suffering from an ague, for she was coughing quietly into a grimy handkerchief. Rose's boots were still on her feet.

It was seeing those boots that gave Agnes a jolt. Boots, she thought – that is what was troubling me. That is what I recognized. She recalled the lean dark form she had seen at the river, and nodded slowly. But a moment later, this thought was displaced by a surge of bitterness. Elsie had assisted in Peter's abduction. Elsie, with whom she had sympathized, whom she had tried to help.

'So, Elsie, I have found you at last,' she said, barging into the room, her determination to approach with caution temporarily forgotten.

Elsie span round. Seeing Agnes, she began to back away. But Agnes swept towards her and grabbed her arm. 'Where is Peter? How could you assist in such an evil scheme?' she demanded furiously.

Elsie jerked back, silent. She made no attempt to wrest her arm away. Rather she let it go limp, meeting Agnes's accusing look with one of equal rancour and indictment.

'Well,' Agnes said, 'why did you take my son?' In her heart of hearts, she knew the answer – Elsie must hold her responsible for her father's death. But she could not help herself from asking.

By way of reply, Elsie swivelled her eyes to direct Agnes's attention behind her, towards the door she had just entered through. Agnes became aware of a soft tread behind. Still clutching Elsie's arm, she turned.

A grimy figure loomed in the doorway. It was Grant, Pitt's henchman, looking even more unsavoury than on the previous occasions she had seen him. His gaze seemed blurred and unfocussed. His trousers were half unbuttoned, the belt undone. He was wearing the same filthy stained coat that he had worn yesterday, the soot marks still visible from where he had shoved Drake up the chimney. Behind him, Agnes noticed that the door to Pitt's front room now stood ajar. Grant gave a noisy yawn and belched unapologetically.

'Mrs Meadowes,' he said, stepping forward. 'What an unexpected surprise. Come to join us, have you?' As he approached, Elsie pushed away Agnes's hand and sidled close to Grant. The stench of stale clothes and sweat emanating from him was overpowering, but Elsie seemed not to mind. She looked up at Grant as though seeking reassurance, then fixed Agnes with a hostile glare.

'Join you?' said Agnes, taking a step back. 'All I want is to find my son. Some evil person has abducted him this morning and brought him here.' She was wary of Grant, but not unduly fearful. He was not the person who had taken Peter – she knew it was not his stocky outline she had seen. Perhaps, though, Grant might confirm her suspicion of who the culprit was.

Grant belched again. Agnes now caught fumes of stale beer, mingled with onions and other odours too noxious to contemplate. A leering grin was plastered across his face. 'Abducted your son?' he said, drawing uncomfortably close. 'That is a most tragic occurrence. Whoever would do such a thing? I trust you do not accuse little Elsie or I?'

Agnes glanced quickly through the window at the bleak grey landscape beyond. Somewhere out there, she thought, Thomas awaits my signal. She felt a sudden ridiculous urge to run and throw open the window and call him, but reminded herself that she had yet to fulfil the plan she had helped to devise – to locate and identify Peter's captor. 'No,' she said, leaning away from Grant, trying to disguise her revulsion and mounting unease. 'I do not accuse *you* in particular. But I saw my son and his captor enter here not fifteen minutes ago.'

Grant scratched his stubbly cheek. 'I never heard nothing, did you, Elsie?'

'No, sir. That's 'cos they ain't here,' said Elsie in an expressionless tone. 'You must've imagined it, Mrs Meadowes.'

Agnes could hardly contain her frustration. Ignoring Grant, she lowered her gaze to the girl. 'Elsie, I know it was you that took Peter away. Perhaps you did so because someone told you I was responsible for your father's death. I assure you, that is not the case.'

Grant glared. Elsie's eyes flickered to his angry face, then back to Agnes.

'Now tell me, do you know where Peter is?' Agnes said quietly.

Elsie's expression remained impassive. 'Why should I believe you? Why should I tell you anything?' she retorted.

'I do not know what you have been told, but I repeat I had nothing to do with your father's death. Nothing save finding his body after Mr Grant hid it. And since doing so, I have been much occupied in trying to ascertain who *was* responsible for murdering him, for it was the same person who killed Rose and the apprentice.'

'That ain't true, is it, Mr Grant?' said Elsie, looking quickly at him. 'It were her what got my pa killed, you said.'

Grant ignored the question. He came forwards, pressing his face menacingly towards Agnes's. 'And what of Mr Pitt? I suppose you had nothing to do with *his* apprehension, neither?'

'Since you ask, I was not responsible for the arrest of Mr Pitt, although I cannot pretend sorrow at his fate. But do not fret on his account; by his own testimony, his friendship with a certain judge will swiftly ensure his freedom. In any case, Mr Grant, now that you are left holding the reins of his enterprise, you cannot be entirely sorry he's out of the way. This house will be very comfortable without Mr Pitt to order you about. So if Elsie won't help, why don't you reveal what you know and keep Pitt where he deserves to be? Think of the fruits that would then be yours to enjoy.'

Grant's bloodshot eyes grew increasingly shifty. He scratched his groin and shuffled from side to side. Agnes observed Elsie watch him intently. Did she imagine it, or had a flicker of doubt now appeared in the girl's eye?

Grant cocked his head on one side, squeezing the fleshy folds of his neck into tight concentric rings. 'What d'you wish to know?' he growled.

'Where is my boy, and who in the Blanchard household lay behind the robbery of the wine-cooler?'

Grant snorted. 'Sorry, I can't help you on either count. I was just taking a nap and never heard a whisper. But if young Elsie says he ain't here, then he ain't. And as for your other query – I'm in the dark as much as you. Besides, I'd be for the noose if I said a word. Pitt'd find out somehow or other. He's too much hold on too many men of influence.' Then, giving Agnes a farewell nod, he added, 'I'll bid you good day now. I've urgent business to attend to,' and shuffled off along the corridor. Halfway along, he turned back, shooting a look at Elsie. 'And you, girl – how about making yourself useful and fetching us something for dinner? I'll be back in half an hour.'

'Yes, sir,' said Elsie meekly.

Grant opened the front door and disappeared. Elsie hesitated for a second and then, without looking at Agnes, made as if to follow. Agnes placed her hand on Elsie's shoulder. She would not let the girl leave before she found out what she knew. 'Wait a moment, Elsie. Listen to me. Whoever told you I killed your father only did so in order that you would help abduct Peter. None of it is true. I don't believe you want Peter harmed, or me killed either. That is why Peter has been taken – so that I would come after him and whoever murdered your pa would do the same to me. Is that what you want?'

Elsie regarded Agnes intently, then sniffed loudly and

wiped her nose with the back of her hand. Tears glistened on her lashes. 'I don't know his name. And even if I did, after what *you* done for my pa, I wouldn't let on,' she said stubbornly.

'Why would I kill your pa?' Agnes persisted. 'You only have Grant's word for it. And that is because he is afraid *he* might be murdered if he lets slip the real culprit. He knows who it is, though – you could see that as well as I. Did Grant tell you it was he that hid your pa's body in the chimney?'

'No.'

'Then take a look at how dirty his coat is. The stains on it are your father's blood and the soot from where he hid his body up the chimney. And if you still don't believe me, go and speak to Mr Pitt at the roundhouse. He knows the truth.'

Agnes knew that Elsie would never dare venture to the roundhouse to question Pitt, but she suspected that she would have noticed the dirt on Grant's coat. Agnes could see her waver as she absorbed the information. She waited, impatience mounting. Give her time, Agnes told herself. She is under no obligation to help. Do not press too hard.

Elsie sniffed again, then sighed miserably, 'It were Mr Grant what told me to take 'im to where pa's cellar were – he was going to take Peter there, down by Pickle Herring Quay,' she ventured.

'Take who?'

'I dunno who he was – a man, tall, dark haired, middling sort of dress.'

Agnes nodded, eyes gleaming. 'You are quite certain of that? You never saw him before?'

'Never said that, did I?' said Elsie, cross now at being doubted. 'He was all covered up in the carriage, but I fancy I did see him once before. Or if not, he were very like the man what chased after your friend by the river.'

'I see,' said Agnes, pondering. 'But it wasn't one of the menservants from Foster Lane?'

'No,' said Elsie without hesitation.

She hadn't expected so firm a rebuttal. 'I take it you know what Mr Theodore and Mr Nicholas Blanchard look like from watching the house. Was it one of them, or someone from the shop?'

Again Elsie firmly shook her head. 'Anyway, whoever he were, like I said, I went in the coach with him. When I spun Mrs Sharp the story he stayed in the coach; he put on a glove and waved from the window to masquerade as you. I was meant to keep an eye on Peter for a few hours, until someone came and took him away. He said getting a bit of a scare was no more than you deserved and the boy wouldn't be harmed.' She was looking at her feet as she spoke. At least she had considered Peter's well-being.

'It's all right, Elsie. I don't blame you. He duped me just the same,' Agnes assured her. She was puzzled by the girl's replies. Why had she not recognized the man in the carriage? There was surely something she had missed here. But she managed to smile and nod encouragingly, not wanting Elsie to halt. 'And once you had Peter, what happened?' she pressed.

'Him and me and the other fellow went in the carriage down to the river. I showed him where to come and ran ahead to make things ready. Only him and Peter never arrived, and when I came back up the steps to see where they'd gone I saw them both going off in a boat.'

Agnes nodded. 'What brought you here?'

Elsie blinked and her gaze slid away. 'I don't like being in that cellar much on my own, now pa's not there. Mr Grant told me I might stay here. He said pa's death and Mr Pitt's arrest needn't make a difference. I could help him just the same.'

'So Grant was never involved in the scheme to snatch Peter?'

'No. Only he told me to do what the man said.' Elsie looked nervously over her shoulder towards the door. 'I never told him nothing about all this, nor that they come 'ere. He was fast asleep just now, and never woke.'

Doubtless his slumbers were aided by a quantity of ale, thought Agnes grimly. 'Tell me, that night when you waited for the message and I asked you to come down to the kitchen, why did you run off?'

'I saw my pa standing there waiting in a doorway.'

There had been a figure sheltering opposite, she recalled. 'Waiting for you?'

'I thought so at the time, though it can't have been 'cos he never came after me. When I looked back he was waving his arms and making faces, but not at me.' She halted, looking towards the door. 'I'd better go fetch the dinner now or Grant'll be angry.'

'One more thing. Was it you that let Peter and his abductor in just now?'

'Yes. He said it would only be a short while afore you came looking. He wouldn't stay long after that.'

Agnes felt her heart pitch. So she had been correct in her assumption that Peter was taken as a lure. Her arrival was expected. 'And where did they go?'

'Upstairs,' said Elsie. 'Don't know where, though.'

Agnes nodded and smiled briefly. 'Very well. Hurry off now. And on your way up the road, you will pass an alley where a friend of mine, Mr Williams, a curly-haired man wearing a brown coat, is waiting. Tell him to come close to the front window of the house. I shall call him any moment now.'

Elsie nodded as she marched off. Agnes sensed the girl's regret at what she had done, but could see that she struggled to find the words to say so. She followed her down the corridor, waiting for half a minute, just in case Elsie should turn and say something more; but she disappeared out of the door in silence, and Agnes could wait no longer.

She was just about to climb the stairs when she observed that the previously open door to Pitt's front room was now closed. Grant had gone off for half an hour, she remembered. She had heard the front door close. Was someone else now inside?

Agnes turned the handle and pushed open the door. The room was shrouded in darkness, with just a thin line of light leeching between the closed shutters. She was uncomfortably reminded of the ride in the carriage when Marcus Pitt had insisted the curtains remained closed. She slipped into the room, heading for the window. She had opened the shutters no more than an inch or two when she heard shuffling on the stairs and a heavy tread in the hallway. She span round just as a head peered in. 'Mrs Meadowes,' said a familiar voice. 'Thank God I have found you.'

Chapter Forty-three

AGNES WENT PALE. 'PHILIP,' SHE REPLIED, SCREWING UP HER EYES with the sudden influx of light, 'whatever are you doing here?'

'Come to offer my heartfelt sympathy and, more important, practical assistance.' He strode into the room and closed the door behind him. He was wigless and hatless, dressed not in livery but in his ordinary clothes – a smart blue woollen cloak, black breeches and leather boots, all of which looked new but had been recently spattered with mud. 'I heard what happened from Mrs Sharp. She came to Foster Lane and told Mr Matthews that your son had been taken by Mr Pitt. Mr Matthews said we ought to offer you assistance. I knew this was where you would come since I'd accompanied you here before, so I said I'd come.'

'I see,' said Agnes quietly. 'You are most kind. But I already have Mr Williams to help.'

'I know – I saw him outside just now. But he alone is no match for all Pitt's cronies. Furthermore, he asked me to tell you he has gone for the constable and will arrive directly.'

Agnes nodded as she took this in. Why had she felt impelled to resolve matters in such a foolhardy manner, without giving Thomas so much as a hint of the person she believed might be guilty? Was this a last remnant of the reserved person she once had been? Philip, meanwhile, showed little sense of the urgency of his commission. He strode about the room, examining the book-lined walls, then picking up items from Pitt's desk one by one. A silver inkwell, a goose quill, a candlestick, a box containing sealing wafers. 'Nice things, ain't they, Mrs M.? Think he'd miss one or two, now he's in the roundhouse?'

She regarded him evenly, but made no reply for the moment. She was conscious of his hands, flecked with dark hairs, of his long strong fingers, picking up the objects one by one, turning them over. She had never noticed them before. What else had those fingers held? Despite being alone, she had never felt more certain or determined of the action she must take. 'Give me back my son, Philip. It will help your case. You will never escape now, but I will do what I can to assist if you release him unharmed.'

'What?' said Philip. 'Have you gone soft in the head? I told you, I'm here because Mr Matthews sent me to help you find him.'

'I doubt that,' said Agnes sternly. 'But Mr Williams is waiting for my signal even now. I have only to cry out and he will come.'

'No purpose in that,' said Philip patiently, as though addressing a wilful child. 'I told you he isn't there. Come, should we not begin our search for Peter at the top of the house?'

'Why?' said Agnes, not moving. 'Aren't *I* what you wanted? Or is it that you plan to dispose of me by shoving me off the roof?'

Philip's amiable expression altered. He began to look irritable. 'I told you, Mrs Meadowes, I don't mean you harm. I am here to help. Why won't you listen?'

'Why won't you see I know,' she retorted. She had waited for this moment, to confront him, but now it had come she hardly knew what to say. She thought of Rose as Elsie had described her, running for dear life across the mud flats. She thought of Noah Prout, whose life had been snatched, and Harry Drake's decapitated body. Turning suddenly back to the window, she unfastened it, threw up the sash and shouted into the deserted street, 'Thomas! Come now and help me search for Peter!'

But as she bellowed, a powerful arm suddenly wrapped about her neck and yanked her back from the window. Philip spoke slowly, directly in her ear. 'Whatever are you doing, making such a spectacle of yourself, Mrs Meadowes? Thomas isn't there. I told you, didn't I? And you have me to help you.'

'It's no good,' said Agnes, allowing herself to be drawn back. 'You may kill me, but you will not deceive me. Elsie saw you that night chasing Rose – she will identify you. Where is Peter?'

Philip laughed bitterly. 'Then if the girl betrayed me, I fancy some misadventure might soon befall her. Quiet, Mrs Meadowes. No more questions. Let's go and look for Peter together. And remember, you brought all this on yourself. I am only here to help.' He shifted his grip to her arm and began pushing her towards the door.

Agnes moved slowly, but with no overt resistance. 'My desire was only to uncover the truth. A woman who worked for me, and of whom I was fond, met an untimely death – is it so surprising I should want to discover what became of her?'

'Fond!' cried Philip, now pushing her up the narrow stairs. 'There's a joke. You was never fond of anything save duty.'

Agnes paused on the steps. Perhaps you were once right, but not any longer, she thought. Aloud she replied, 'Then I have become fond of Rose since her death. She was not perfect, I grant you, but she didn't deserve to be killed.'

Philip gave her a shove. They had reached the first landing, but another flight led up to the second storey. ''Course not – a veritable tragedy, it was.'

'I'm not entirely green,' retorted Agnes hotly, thinking of the pair of them in the larder. 'I know you killed Rose in a jealous rage, and Noah Prout and Harry Drake.'

Philip squeezed her arm tighter. 'Now you're going soft again. Why would I kill Rose when I loved her? Why would I kill any of them?'

'Because the poor girl wanted no more to do with you. You don't like being turned down, do you?'

Philip pushed Agnes more roughly up the stairs. 'I was demented, was I? That's rich. I would've married her. Is that a crime in your book? There's any number of women want me, only not you 'cos you're cold as granite, and not her. Even with money I wasn't good enough for her.'

'And so you followed her.'

'I went after her to tell her I loved her. What I'd done for her, how rich we'd be in a week or two's time. But instead she shamed me. Treated me like I was nothing. No other woman ever done that. And she had money all along – she offered it to me to leave her alone. It was that that done for her. Trying to pay me to go – like I was her lackey.'

They had reached the top landing, a long corridor with doors to attic rooms opening on each side, dimly lit by a garret window at the far end so darkened with grime that nothing was visible through it. Philip pushed her roughly to the window, yanked open the latch with his free hand and flung open the casement. 'Now look out there.'

Agnes raised her head and looked. Beyond the jagged black gables of the roof stretched a wide curve of dull grey river. Silhouetted against it, seated on a parapet like a frail bowsprit on a ship, sat Peter. His mouth was bound, a blindfold had been tied around his eyes, ropes about his ankles and wrists. But there was nothing to stop him falling. Agnes froze. She opened her mouth to call out to him, but found she could utter no sound. What if I startle him, she thought. If he moves an inch in the wrong direction, he will surely fall.

'Let me fetch him,' she whispered.

'All in good time. I have told him he will be quite safe so long as he behaves himself and doesn't move. Of course he can't see, so he doesn't know where he is . . .' Philip's eyes, Agnes noticed, had a curious dullness to them, as though he were in a dream. But there was nothing dreamlike about the menace in his voice. 'So, Mrs Meadowes,' he said, 'feeling less meddlesome now?'

'Ssh,' whispered Agnes. 'Don't let him hear or he might move and fall.'

He ignored her. 'All I desired was Rose and the means to support her,' he said. 'You, of all people, should comprehend. Yet with every turn you obstruct me. Your meddling spoiled my scheme. I lost Rose and the money I was due from Pitt.'

'My meddling had nothing to do with Rose spurning you,' whispered Agnes hotly. 'You might deceive yourself that you acted for love, but in truth you were propelled by other darker motives – jealousy, greed and fear.'

The effect of her remark upon Philip took her by surprise. Without warning, he lunged at Agnes and closed his hands about her neck. Agnes reared back her head, crashing against the window-frame. From the corner of her eye she saw Peter move, as if he were straining for the source of the sound. She gasped, stifling her impulse to cry out, trying to insert her own fingers beneath his to pull them away.

Philip grimly increased the pressure about her neck, so that, even had she wanted to, she could no longer speak. After a minute or two, sensing her waning strength, he removed one hand and fumbled in his pocket. He gave a sharp flick of his wrist and a blade sprang out from its handle, gleaming in the dim light. 'And now, since you are so very curious, I shall show you how I killed them so easily. Here is Mr Matthews's spare razor; he leaves it in his pantry drawer, and never remarks when I borrow it. The drawer is the same one where you left the wine label. It was seeing it there that made me see I would have to quieten you. But I presume that was your intention. To let me know you had found me out. Look how sharp it is.'

Still holding Agnes firmly by the neck, he wafted the blade in front of her face and sliced it down an inch from her cheek. A thick dark tress of hair fell onto Agnes's breast. She tried not to look at the blade, but it exerted a dreadful attraction and she could not help herself from watching it. Philip was speaking again, but his voice seemed to be fading and a mist was descending before her eyes. Somewhere below, she thought she heard the sound of voices, footsteps. She tried to turn away to loosen his hold, she tried to scratch his hands, she tried to say that of course she had not intended to threaten him by leaving the wine label where she did. But it was futile. At every sign of resistance, Philip shook her from side to side and back and forth, banging her skull viciously against the wall, bringing the blade closer, so that in the end it rested flat against her neck and even the slightest flicker of movement was perilous.

Agnes felt her eyeballs bulge, her tongue swell over her teeth, blood pounding in her neck and forehead. She could barely hear him now. She was aware only of echoing shouts, thundering footsteps growing louder, pain and fear, the blade still pressing against her.

He had brought his mouth close to Agnes's ear and was whispering again, asking her to choose which way she preferred to die. Which way? Blade across the throat or strangulation? Which way? She tried to whisper her response, but the mist had invaded her mouth and gagged her.

'Philip, what the devil are you doing?' a voice boomed suddenly through the fog.

'Shh,' murmured Agnes, so quietly she was all but inaudible.

The shout caused Philip to start and release his hold a little, as he turned to see who it was. 'Keep away,' he muttered. 'There's business here in which you are not involved.'

'Very well,' said the voice evenly. 'I prefer to avoid trouble where I can. But I am here to help Mrs Meadowes, and I don't like to leave her in this disorder.' With these words, brisk steps advanced along the corridor. Over Philip's shoulder, Agnes caught a glimpse of Thomas Williams at the moment he drew his sword and ran Philip through.

Agnes stood rooted to the spot, unable to speak or move, unsure for an instant what was real and what she had imagined. But as Philip's legs buckled under him and he fell to the ground, blood gushing from his mouth and seeping from his belly, she came to her senses. She turned wordlessly and looked out of the window. It was no dream. Peter was still sitting there, a statue set against the backdrop of the city.

Holding her finger to her mouth so that Thomas should not speak a word, she signalled to the window, then, without waiting for his response, opened it and tried to heave herself through. But the ordeal she had suffered had made her weak, and the sill was too high for her to gain a foothold. She attempted to lever herself up and failed.

She felt Thomas pull her gently to one side. 'Wait,' he mouthed soundlessly. In what seemed no more than an instant he had jumped up onto the ledge and squeezed his way through. In silence he inched his way on all fours towards the parapet where Peter was perched. All the while Peter remained as before – immobile, quiet, straining to hear. When Thomas was two feet away, Peter must have heard a faint rustle behind him. He half turned his head and went as if to move forward over the edge. Agnes resisted the instinct to call out only by closing her eyes. She opened them again immediately, just in time to witness Thomas's lunge. He caught Peter unceremoniously about the waist and dragged him back to safety. 'There now,' he said, without removing the blindfold. 'I've your mother waiting for you inside. Let's go and see her, shall we?'

Thomas lifted the shivering child through the window. Agnes lowered him down and carried him past Philip and down the two flights of stairs to Pitt's room, before she untied the blindfold and bindings, clutching his body against hers.

'I went in a carriage with Philip,' he said, his ribs heaving with emotion. 'After we went in the boat he said we would play a game and he would bring me to you, if I let myself be blindfold. But why did he leave me out there so long in the cold?'

'It's all right,' she said as lightly as she could, breathing in the scent of his damp hair. 'It's over now. He has gone. He won't trouble you again.'

Chapter Forty-four

'JEALOUSY,' SAID AGNES, THINKING OF THOMAS WILLIAMS AND the moment she had learned the truth about him and Rose, 'is as cruel as the grave. It leads men and women to desperate lengths, to take actions they would never under usual circumstances consider, to commit untold evil. Philip could not reconcile himself to the fact that Rose had cooled in her affections towards him. He was a handsome fellow, with an appetite for women of all shapes and sizes.' Here she glanced at Doris, and then at Nancy. 'And he was accustomed to having any girl he chose.'

She was holding forth during the servants' breakfast next day, having arrived back too late the previous night to apprise anyone that Philip had been apprehended and was now in Newgate Prison, awaiting trial for three capital offences of murder, not to mention abetting the robbery of the wine-cooler. She had decided she must let Mr Matthews know what had happened, but to avoid further rumour and misunderstandings, thought it best if everyone were present when she said what she had to say.

She was tired, her eyes were sore, her limbs ached. But she had woken at seven and had reminded herself that while she might have changed, the Blanchards and their expectations of her had not. They still had to be fed and the household was still a kitchen maid short. And now they were missing a footman too. She had risen as usual, but before beginning her duties had searched Philip's things. Secreted in a corner of his chest she had found a note from Marcus Pitt, arranging a meeting for the payment of his 'commission'. There was also a small leather purse containing fifteen gold sovereigns. The rest of Rose's money, Agnes presumed, had been spent on his new attire.

She paused to regard those seated around the table, hanging on to her every word. Mrs Tooley was pale-faced and astonished. In a minute or two, thought Agnes, she'll be reaching for her salts and wanting a lie down, but no doubt she'll hold her ailments at bay until she has heard what I have to say. Curiously, however, she no longer resented Mrs Tooley's weakness. Behind it, perhaps, lay not only the desire to manipulate without argument, but also a straightforward terror of change.

'If he had the pick of us all, why in heaven's name did he waste time on someone who didn't want him?' queried Nancy. She was brittle as ever in her demeanour, but there was a gleam of something indefinable in her eye. What was it, Agnes wondered. Anger that Agnes had not believed her story about the purse? Guilt at her involvement? Fear for herself and her unborn child?

'Because being spurned was new to him – and bothered him deeply. He convinced himself he loved her, and pestered her repeatedly to take him back. And Rose, as we all know, could be unkind on occasion.'

'Unkind – that's putting it mildly,' said Nancy. 'She was a hard jade and I don't care who knows it.'

Agnes sighed, comprehending Nancy's jealousy and bitterness. She had experienced similar sentiments not very long ago. 'Rose didn't care if she hurt Philip because she too had been hurt in love. She and Thomas Williams had become engaged when Thomas came to London to work for Blanchards'. When Rose's father died suddenly, she was obliged to seek work. She found a post as a maid to Lord Carew. But Rose detested life as a servant. She begged Thomas to marry her early so she could stop working, and when he refused, because he was worried about his own position, she broke off the engagement.'

'Then she'd no reason to feel sorry for herself, had she? She only had herself to blame,' declared Nancy.

'Quiet, Nancy,' said Doris, breaking in with unusual swiftness. 'Let us listen to what Mrs Meadowes has to say before we hear your thoughts on it.'

'She was a lively, headstrong girl,' said Agnes, proceeding hastily to smooth the antagonism between Nancy and Doris. 'After the quiet of Newcastle, London must have turned her head. Like Philip, she enjoyed the company of the opposite sex. She thought that with all the eligible men in London she would not find it hard to persuade someone else to marry her. But then a month or so later she realized it was not going to be so easy, and asked Thomas to take her back.'

'Then if she was after Thomas, why take up with Philip and Riley?' said Nancy disbelievingly.

'Because Thomas hesitated, he was still uncertain about his position. And being a determined, impatient character, Rose couldn't wait. She set about trying to make him jealous. She flirted with Riley, and then she turned her attentions to Philip. But her plan misfired. After a few months, Thomas Williams told her that he no longer trusted her and would never change his mind.

'Rose had tired of Philip by then and saw no reason to carry on with him. But Philip convinced himself he was smitten with her. So much so that he asked her to marry him. Rose laughed at him and told him he was an idiot even to think he could support a wife when he was only a footman, and he knew as well as she that servants were not allowed to marry.'

'And the man in the street?' said Mrs Tooley, dabbing her eyes with the effort of taking so much in. 'Was he another follower?'

'He was her brother,' said Agnes. 'He returned from abroad, and only then discovered what had become of his father and sister. He was aghast to find Rose living as a servant. She was, after all, an educated girl. He suggested that she come and help him in a school he intended to open in France. I think that was why she cooled towards Philip. She wanted to tell Mrs Blanchard – there was no other reason for her to have taken such an interest in her comings and goings. But in the end, possibly because she would never be listened to with sympathy, she decided against it.'

'I don't understand,' said Mrs Tooley, raising a bony fore-finger. 'Do you mean to say Rose had nothing to do with the robbery after all?'

'Oh no. Far from it. She was the reason it happened. Somehow, Philip got wind of her intention to leave. First, perhaps he overheard you, Mrs Tooley, ticking her off for talking to a strange man in the street. Then there was the letter Nancy found. In any case, he became desperate to change her mind. Remember, Rose had told him the reason they could not marry was because he couldn't provide for her.

'He turned his thoughts to how he might make money quickly. Being a friend of one of the apprentices, he visited the workshop frequently and knew what was happening there. He heard that a valuable wine-cooler was being crafted – the most precious item ever made by Blanchards'. It must have seemed a god-given opportunity, and so he devised a scheme to steal it.'

'But did he not feel disloyal for ruining the family that gave him employ?' said Patsy. 'I always thought him such a deferential fellow.'

Agnes nodded, remembering Philip dressed in livery, handsome, the perfect servant. 'He had a capacity for deference, I do not deny that, but underneath he resented the restrictions of his position much as Rose did.'

John exchanged an uneasy glance with Mr Matthews. Perhaps, thought Agnes, they are worried I might let slip their plans for the celebrations to mark John's coming of age, and the pilfering that has gone on to fuel it. 'But how did he set about orchestrating the scheme?' said John.

'Unlike you, John, Philip frequently passed his evenings in the ale houses of this part of the city. He claimed he was in the Blue Cockerel on the night of the robbery. In such places Pitt's reputation as a pre-eminent thief-taker is well known.' Here Agnes was unable to prevent an audible note of disapproval entering her voice. 'The business of thief-taking relies upon a vast retinue of informants. It would not have been hard for Philip to establish contact with one of them and then arrange a meeting with Pitt.'

Agnes paused and took a sip from her cup. Disturbing images crowded her thoughts, confusing her: of Pitt, holding her captive, pressing himself on her; of Philip's hands about her neck; of Peter sitting on the roof. She blinked, looked up again, took a breath.

'Pitt and Philip agreed that the reward for the wine-cooler's return would be split between the pair of them and a fee would also be paid to Harry Drake, who would carry out the robbery. But Harry Drake was a greedy man, and when he saw that Philip was employed in the house of a silversmith he had the foolish idea of extracting further money from him. On the night that Elsie came to take the message for Pitt, she saw her father waiting in the street, signalling to someone at the house. He was signalling to Philip, who was in the dining room at the time, threatening to reveal his identity unless he paid for his silence. Philip pretended to agree.

'Philip must have taken a wine label from the dining room – I later retrieved it from Drake's pocket and returned it to Mr Matthews's drawer. I fancy Drake must have protested that the wine label wasn't valuable enough to buy his silence. So Philip said he would find something more, and arranged a meeting later that night at the house where Drake was guarding the wine-cooler. Only instead of taking more valuables to Drake, Philip crept up and decapitated him.'

John glanced again at Mr Matthews, who then intervened. 'But why did Philip need to murder the apprentice? Why not simply incapacitate him?'

'I asked myself the same question.' Agnes glanced at Nancy. 'I believe it was because he had only just learned that time was short. Rose's plan to leave was more imminent than he had first realized. If the apprentice was not silenced, his scheme would be more perilous. The apprentice might overpower

Drake, in which case the scheme might fail and Rose would be gone before he had made himself rich. He was unwilling to take that chance.'

Nancy turned scarlet. 'It was him what egged me on to take the letter that was sent her. I only did so to make him notice me,' she said, growing suddenly tearful, one hand resting protectively on her belly. 'And then I meant to put it back, only she discovered it was missing and flew at me. I thought he'd lose interest in her once he knew she was going. How was I to know he'd kill her on account of it?'

'You have no need to blame yourself,' said Agnes gently. 'He was expert at using charm and flattery to get what he wanted. I too was misled by him in a way. Although the truth was there all along, it took me a while to see what it was.'

'How did you discover it was him?' said Mr Matthews, his gaunt old face seeming sterner than usual, making him resemble the statue of an Old Testament prophet more closely than ever. 'I never would have thought him capable of such devilry. You must have probed most carefully in places you were not entitled to go.'

'It was the boots that made me first suspect,' said Agnes, avoiding his pointed remark.

'What boots?' said Mr Matthews, frowning.

'The morning after the robbery and Rose's disappearance, there was a pair of boots standing on the kitchen table. Philip was in your pantry. Although he confessed to having been out that night, he pretended he did not know what had happened to Rose and said the boots weren't his.

'I thought no more of it, but when I found the gun in the cellar I decided that the culprit was most likely one of the menservants. Who else would have an opportunity to hide the gun in such a place? And then I began to reflect upon what Philip had told me of his relationship with Rose. He pretended there was nothing between them when she left, but when Nancy confessed she had taken the letter, I thought she would not have done so unless she had a purpose, and that purpose was most likely turning Philip against Rose. Philip said he had passed the night at the Blue Cockerel ale house, but while the landlord recalled seeing him, he had no notion when he left.

'When Elsie told me she didn't know who it was that had taken her in the carriage, and that it wasn't one of the men-servants, I confess I was baffled for a moment. But then on reflection it struck me that while she would have recognized Mr Matthews or John, she had never laid eyes on Philip.'

Mr Matthews ran his hand across his venerable head. 'But the time you went to Mr Pitt's house, Philip accompanied you. And I thought you met Elsie there.'

'That is true,' said Agnes, 'but Grant insisted that Philip wait outside. Had he not, perhaps Elsie would have observed him and identified him sooner as the man she had seen chasing Rose by the river.'

'I still do not believe that Rose was as innocent as you say,' protested Nancy. 'What of the salver I found her handling?'

'That was nothing to do with her. Theodore had established a duty-dodging scheme with Riley – cutting marks from one piece and putting them in another to try and save duty, in order to finance a move to the west of the city. I doubt it earned him much, but he yearns for a life free of his father's influence,' said Agnes. 'But none of it had anything to do with Philip and his evil scheme, or Rose's determination to leave.'

Mrs Tooley took a noisy sniff of her salts. Her hands were shaking. 'I have a replacement maid arriving this morning. I sincerely hope she's more manageable than Rose Francis.'

At this, Nancy and Doris bombarded Mrs Tooley as to the age, appearance and background of the new arrival. Then everyone fell silent for a moment, and Mr Matthews coughed and rose. The sternness in his eyes had now returned. 'I thank you for enlightening us, Mrs Meadowes,' he said. 'When you have finished your breakfast, I should like a further word in private in my pantry.'

Rose's purse and a folded paper lay on Mr Matthews's table. She knew as soon as she entered what he would say. She was gratified to note that he could not meet her eye. 'I am sorry,' he said. 'The decision of which I have to inform you is not mine. Sir Bartholomew Grey came to call yesterday. He told Mr Blanchard senior of your visit. Even without your having removed a letter that was not addressed to you from my office, there was nothing I could do. You will be paid a week's notice. To assist you with your child, I should like to add this to that sum.' And he handed her Rose's purse.

Chapter Forty-five

THE BELLS OF ST PAUL'S STRUCK TWO AS AGNES MEADOWES, laden with a basket of provisions, a cloth-bound recipe book and an assortment of cleaning utensils, unlocked the door to a small house in Watery Lane. Having deposited her possessions in a small dark passage, she made her way into a shabby front room, furnished with four tables and a counter, and covered with dust. Not for the first time, she remarked to herself that there was a great deal of painting and scrubbing to be done. Striding through to the kitchen, she slowly surveyed a range that was brown with rust and presently unlit, a floor shiny with unwashed grease, and a blackened dresser, the recesses of which she had not yet dared to explore. Upstairs, she knew, was a warren of sparsely furnished rooms in a state of similar filth and dilapidation.

Nevertheless, she felt not in the least despondent or downcast by this dingy scene. Rather the reverse; she was filled with anticipation at the uncertain fate ahead of her. Theodore's five pounds and Rose's fifteen sovereigns had gone to rent these premises, where she would begin a new enterprise as proprietor of an eating house and purveyor of pastries and pies. Agnes carried a bucket to the yard outside, where stood a pump and a recently delivered pile of coal. She filled her bucket with water, took it back to the range and began to scrub. A short while later, however, something caught on her finger and she was forced to stop – Rose's ring was no more comfortable to wear now than it had been when she had first struggled to put it on. It was rubbing, and causing a blister to appear on her finger.

Agnes pulled off the ring and turned it in her hand. She smiled as she remembered coming upon Rose in the larder, locked in an embrace with Philip. The past had forced both she and Rose along unwise paths. By some quirk of fate, she had been permitted time to set things straight. She slipped the ring into her pocket, where it chinked against the heart-shaped silver box, and returned to the task in hand.

Some time later, when the range was clean and the blacking of the iron well underway, Agnes heard a knock on the door. 'Elsie,' she said, seeing the thin-faced girl, still swathed in her rags and red shawl, and wearing Rose's over-large boots. Without knowing why, Agnes embraced her. 'You are here at last! There's a deal to be done before this house is habitable. Tomorrow, Sarah Sharp will bring Peter. This evening, Thomas Williams might call.' She smiled as she mentioned his name, and thought of his hair spread about his head like a mane, his arms flung out like the spokes of a wheel on his pillow. 'And suppose Mrs Tooley keeps her promise and comes to visit this weekend. You have never known anyone so particular as she is. The smallest cobweb is guaranteed to give her a turn.'

'Then why don't I make a start upstairs and you carry on down here,' said Elsie, her feline eyes surveying Agnes calmly.

'Yes,' said Agnes. But then she reminded herself that whatever Mrs Tooley thought or said no longer mattered one jot. 'But first let us take something to eat. I am half starved, and I am sure you must be too. There's nothing in the place save an oyster pie, a piece of gammon and an orange I brought with me.' Agnes fumbled in her pocket for Rose's ring. 'And since this is too small for my finger, I should like you to have it – for helping as you did, and joining me now.'

Wordlessly, Elsie slid it on her bony finger and rubbed it on her shawl to bring up its lustre. Then she looked up and cast her eye over the basket. Her hungry look reminded Agnes of the time she had snatched the orange, not so very long ago.

'Thank you, ma'am,' she said, 'Mr Pitt could never have fed me half so well. Did you hear, by the by, that his case has been dismissed for want of anyone willing to give testimony against him, and he's back in Melancholy Walk? I'll set a table, shall I?'

Acknowledgements

Agnes's cookery and the duties of other members of the house are based upon household guides such as *The British Housewife or the Cook, Housekeeper's and Gardiner's Companion*, Martha Bradley, 1756; *The English Housekeeper*, A. Cobbett, 1842; *The Servant's Practical Guide, A Handbook of Duties and Rules*, Frederick Warne (pub), 1880; *The Experienced English Housekeeper*, Elizabeth Raffald, 1997. Other helpful books included: *What the Butler Saw, Two Hundred and Fifty Years of the Servant Problem*, E. S. Turner, 1962; *Costume of Household Servants*, P. Cunnington, 1974; *Life Below Stairs*, Frank E. Huggett, 1977.

Descriptions of eighteenth-century silversmithing practices relied upon *Three Centuries of English Domestic Silver*, Bernard and Therle Hughes, 1952, and *Silver in England*, P. Glanville, 1987. Details of markings and duty-dodging were taken from *Hallmark: A History of the London Assay Office*, J. S. Forbes, 1999; I am also grateful for the assistance of the librarian at Goldsmith's Hall.

As ever, my thanks are due to Sally Gaminara and her editorial team at Transworld Publishers, and to my agent Christopher Little and his staff.

ROSEACRE